W9-DBS-902

HEART OF THE RONIN

THE RONIN TRILOGY: VOLUME I

HEART OF THE RONIN

TRAVIS HEERMANN

FIVE STAR
A part of Gale, Cengage Learning

GALE
CENGAGE Learning

Detroit • New York • San Francisco • New Haven, Conn • Waterville, Maine • London

GALE
CENGAGE Learning™

LIBRARY OF CONGRESS CATALOGING-IN-PUBLICATION DATA

Heermann, Travis.
    Heart of the Ronin : a novel / by Travis Heermann. — 1st ed.
        v. cm. — (The Ronin trilogy; v. 1)
    ISBN-13: 978-1-59414-779-1 (hardcover : alk. paper)
    ISBN-10: 1-59414-779-5 (hardcover : alk. paper)
    1. Samurai—Fiction. 2. Japan—Fiction. I. Title.
PS3608.E335H43 2009
813'.6—dc22   2008043360

First Edition. First Printing: February 2009.
Published in 2009 in conjunction with Tekno Books and Ed Gorman.

For Cheryl

ACKNOWLEDGMENTS
AND THANKS

Special thanks to Minori Iyonaga, Yuuko Shichiji, Yumiko Machino, and Michiko Sumi of the Chikugo English Speaking Society, for their kind advice on Japanese history and culture, and their tireless, painstaking efforts at correcting my English. Any mistakes they did not catch are purely my own.

I would also like to offer sincere thanks to Naoko Ikeda, hachi-dan master of Japanese calligraphy, for her generosity and friendship, and for her beautiful artwork that graces my humble story.

And lastly but not leastly, I want to say thanks to the numerous readers who offered their comments and advice, and helped me shepherd this story into its current form. You know who you are.

★ ★ ★ ★ ★

THE FIRST SCROLL: JOURNEY'S END

★ ★ ★ ★ ★

"Be true to the thought of the moment and avoid distraction. Other than continuing to exert yourself, enter into nothing else, but go to the extent of living single thought by single thought."

—*Hagakure*

Ken'ishi's extended blade cast a ribbon of morning sunlight onto the ground at his feet. He looked down the curved edge of his upturned blade at the man who wanted to kill him. Takenaga's eyes narrowed as he studied Ken'ishi's unusual stance and his unusual blade with its antique-style curvature. Silver Crane's hilt felt good in his hands, like a part of him. He braced his feet wide apart and dug his worn wooden sandals deeper into the dirt of the road, to ensure they would not slip. His body faced to the side, and he gripped the hilt near his chin, looking over his left shoulder toward his enemy.

The two men stood with their blades extended between them like lethal shards of ice glimmering in the noonday sun. Takenaga's hateful eyes blazed with cold ferocity, boring into him like awls.

Ken'ishi was accustomed to being shunned. He was a warrior

without a master, and thus a person outside normal society, someone to be feared and distrusted, but he still did not understand the vehemence of Takenaga's enmity toward him.

The older man's lips tightened. "Coward! You fear death!"

Ken'ishi's voice was calm, slow and even. "No, I merely wish to leave this village with its constable still alive."

Takenaga changed to the lower stance, dropping the point of his blade toward Ken'ishi's feet, testing, looking for a reaction.

Akao stood hunched, a few paces away, his rust-red mane standing on end, his tail down against his legs. A low, uneasy growl emanated from between his bared teeth, and his ears lay flat against his head.

But Ken'ishi was no longer aware of the dog, only his enemy. He did not move, standing still as a crane in a pool of water untouched by the wind. The flaring anger he had felt only moments ago was gone, subsumed by a strange wonder. Would he still live ten heartbeats from now? He had been in danger before, but never fought a real duel against a single, well-trained opponent. He had wiggled his way out of scrapes with clumsy town guards, faced down drunken bullies, and avoided angry innkeepers, but never a situation where someone's death was assured. He must kill this man. Merely wounding him would not be sufficient to protect his own life. He saw in Takenaga's eyes that he would not rest until Ken'ishi was dead. Did he have it within him to kill?

He reached for the nothingness, shifting his awareness to the Now, the instant, forgetting the before and the after. His blade hung motionless in the air before him. His eyes did not move; he was focused on a point several paces behind his opponent, but his awareness encompassed the smallest of Takenaga's movements; the shift of his weight in preparation to strike, his grip on the hilt of his katana, the flex of the muscles in his

12

forearms, and the inevitable explosion of movement.

Earlier that morning, before Ken'ishi even saw the village, the scent of smoke and onions wafting between the trees of the surrounding forest had sent his empty stomach into an uproar. His right hand absently massaged his empty coin pouch. Because he was ronin, he rarely found anyone willing to give him a job as even a common laborer. He was outside of society because he did not have a master, lower in some respects than even a geisha or a merchant. People did not trust ronin. There were no wars these days, not since the Minamoto clan had seized power away from the Emperor fifty years before. These days, lone warriors often resorted to robbery to support themselves. Ken'ishi could hardly conceive of such a vast gulf of time, of an era when all warriors had masters and respect. He had lived perhaps seventeen years—he did not know for certain—and fifty years was like a dozen lifetimes to him. Besides, he knew practically nothing of politics anyway. His teacher had taught him how to survive and how to use the sword at his hip, and little else about the world of men.

But there was something else his teacher had taught him, something he could do that other men could not.

Akao lifted his nose, taking in the scent, and spoke. "Smells like a village," the dog said. "Give us some food?" A whimper of hunger escaped the dog's throat.

Ken'ishi said, "Or maybe they'll beat us with sticks. Remember the last time?" From the first day they had met, Akao had always thought with this belly.

"Beat me with a stick and we ran away."

"Yes, we were lucky that time. The kami favored us."

"Always hate us."

"That's why we trust only each other."

"Yes, trust," Akao said, his tail wagging, his tongue lolling.

Until he had left his teacher and met his foster parents, Ken'ishi had thought everyone could speak to animals, and he remembered the sudden sensation of alienation when he found they could not, and the suspicion in their eyes when they found that he could.

The path led down the rocky slope straight into the village. Through small gaps in the thick canopy, Ken'ishi saw the terraced patchwork of fields in the valley, with farmers cultivating their spring vegetables. He could not remember the last time he had eaten a hot meal. The earthy taste of the wild roots he had dug up earlier this morning lingered on his tongue, but had done little except fan the fire of his hunger. Akao usually sustained himself with mice and other small creatures. But Ken'ishi could not share those meals. There was too little meat on them, and he could not bring himself to eat them whole. Once, the dog had been lucky enough to catch a rabbit, and they had shared it that night.

He hoped the peasants would still have some rice, since the winter stores of food were often depleted by this time of year. But this land was new to him, different, warmer than the northern island that raised him. Cherry trees here were already in bloom, earlier than in the north. The last of his coins had purchased his sea crossing a few days ago, and he walked this unfamiliar land with nothing. He had no idea what to expect here; but his feet had no wish to remain still. Hitching up the coarse rope supporting his worn, tattered trousers and adjusting his dusty traveling pack on his shoulders, Ken'ishi rested a hand on his father's sword, Silver Crane, as he resumed his trek down the mountainside.

Then he stopped as a strange tingling shot through his palm, lifting his hand from the silver pommel shaped like the head of a crane. He had never felt such a sensation before. Had he imagined it? He did not think so. The hairs on the back of his

14

neck prickled. Silver Crane rested quietly in its scabbard. Ken'ishi gripped the hilt lightly, feeling the cool silver fittings and the roughness of the ray-skin grip. A strange thought came to him, the sudden feeling that he would have to use the sword today. While he had never used it to kill, he did not doubt that Silver Crane had been used to kill in the past, many, many times.

He resumed walking again, going more slowly now, wary. As he walked, he listened to two sparrows hidden in the budding branches above. From the tone of the little birds' voices, he knew they were berating each other. Small birds were so ill tempered sometimes. The understanding of their speech danced around his awareness, in sight but out of grasp. The birds spoke a strange, unfamiliar dialect, just like the people of this land, and he found understanding any of them difficult at times.

The village came into view as he strode down the steep mountain path. It was larger than he expected, nestled between two forested mountainsides and straddling a narrow, rocky stream. He hoped he could find an inn or a teahouse that would offer a bowl of rice to an itinerant warrior. He had no money, but there were other ways a warrior could get a meal. He was loath to resort to intimidation or thievery, even though he was practically starving.

As he drew nearer, Ken'ishi noticed several peasants in the fields had stopped working to watch him. He saw little of their faces under their broad straw hats. The small hairs on the back of his neck rose again. Surely he had little to fear from untrained farmers. The feeling of uneasiness spread down his spine, dredging the words of his teacher from the depths of his memory: *"If your sense of danger alerts you, heed it. This is how the kami speak to us. If the kami favor you, they will help you in the face of harm."* Nevertheless, he thrust the hilt of the Silver Crane a bit further forward and added a bit of swagger to his step. Akao's senses were sharp as well, nearly always sharper than his, and he trusted the dog to warn him of any danger.

The villagers on the main thoroughfare did not appear threatening. They bowed politely, offering greetings as he passed, going about their own business. Everyone appeared to be well fed and adequately clothed. In all, this seemed a prosperous village. He was suddenly conscious of the shabbiness of his own rough-woven, hemp clothes, little more than sackcloth. Most of these villagers wore brightly dyed linen. He smiled to himself, realizing he must be a fearsome sight indeed, unshaven, hair tied into an unruly shock, bow and quiver within easy reach, and the long, curved sword with its well-worn hilt and scabbard hanging from his rope belt. Perhaps he could use that to his advantage.

As he strode into the center of the village, he stopped and looked around.

The nearby villagers slowed their activities to better observe the stranger. A man appeared from the large, central house, shuffling toward Ken'ishi. His face was round and plump, circled by wisps of graying hair. He moved with a peculiar limp, and one shoulder sagged lower than the other. His clothes were fine and crisp and brightly patterned, as if he had never worn them to do a day's labor.

The man bowed obsequiously. His lips were strangely soft and wet as he spoke. "I am Yohachi, sir, the headman of this village. A lovely morning, sir, isn't it?" His words were borne on a spray of distasteful, whuffling wetness, but at least he spoke in a dialect that the young warrior understood. The headman glanced uneasily at the dog, and the dog returned the stare, eyes narrowed with suspicion.

Ken'ishi bowed in return. "Yes, fine weather today." He drank in the morning air, turning his body so that his sword was clearly visible.

"We are honored to have a powerful man such as you paying a visit to our humble village. Where are you bound for?"

"Don't fear. I won't be staying long. Only long enough to find something to eat."

The man hesitated for only an instant. "Of course, of course! I was being rude! Please excuse me! Come along. Come to my house. My wife will make you something. And we have tea. Good tea!"

Ken'ishi glanced at Akao, and the dog grinned hopefully.

But as the headman turned and led him toward the large house, Ken'ishi thought he spied Yohachi making an almost imperceptible gesture at a boy watching them. The boy backed away between two houses and disappeared.

Uneasiness fluttered in his belly. That boy could be bringing a large village of angry farmers down upon him, but he had already executed his strike and now must follow it through.

Ken'ishi and Akao followed Yohachi through the front gate of his home, past the modest garden, and into the house. As was his custom, Akao sat down outside the door, where he would wait until his friend came out. Akao gave Ken'ishi a glance that said, "Bring me something this time."

Yohachi slid the door closed. "May I take your pack, sir?"

"I'll keep it with me. No need to trouble yourself."

The plump little man bowed again, perhaps a bit too low, then seated him in the main room and disappeared into the kitchen. Ken'ishi shrugged off his pack and untied his sword, placing it beside him on his left. All around him, he sensed small movements and voices throughout the house; hidden whispers and stealthy footsteps. Children? Servants?

Yohachi returned carrying a steaming bowl. Ken'ishi's nostrils flared at the scent. He took the bowl, but not too eagerly, and found it filled with hot, seasoned rice and green onions. His mouth burst with water as he readied the chopsticks and lifted the bowl to his lips. Barely taking the time to blow the steam off, he shoveled rice into his maw.

"If I am not being too rude, may I ask your name, sir?"

Past another huge mouthful of rice, the samurai answered, "Ken'ishi."

Yohachi shifted uncomfortably on the floor. "Where do you come from?"

Ken'ishi did not answer, taking another large mouthful instead. The savory taste of the seasonings and onions were more satisfying than any meal he could remember.

Yohachi nodded past the lack of response. "Where do you travel?"

"Wherever my expertise can be of use."

"Ah, a ronin, then. You have no one to serve."

Ken'ishi said nothing, and Yohachi fidgeted and squirmed even more.

"You have seen anything unusual on the road? We have heard tales of bandits in the area. Rumor says the bandits are led by an oni."

Ken'ishi raised an eyebrow. "An oni?"

"So they say."

"I haven't seen any bandits in these parts."

"Fortunate for you, then. Last month they raided a village in the next province. They stole almost all of the winter stores. The village has no seed rice for this year."

"That's unlucky. Has anyone given them food or seed rice?"

"I do not know. The story I heard only told of the demon." Yohachi licked his lips and looked away for a moment, then back. "An interesting sword you have there."

"What does a village headman know of swords?"

"Consider it a personal interest. It is of exceptional quality, is it not? And such a fine scabbard! It is very old, yes?"

Ken'ishi looked at the weapon he knew so well. The scabbard

was not fine at all. It was battered and stained. The once-beautiful cranes, inlaid in mother-of-pearl flying through silver moonlight, were worn and chipped, and the dark lacquer was cracked, revealing the wood beneath. Some of the silver fittings were tarnished. "It is. It was my father's."

"What is your family name?"

Instead of answering, Ken'ishi took another mouthful of rice.

The front door suddenly whisked open, and a large shadow fell over them. Yohachi bowed low, putting his forehead to the floor, and Ken'ishi put down the half-empty bowl. The man shed his sandals and strode into the room, towering over the two men seated on the floor. Ken'ishi sucked bits of rice from his teeth as he appraised the newcomer, noting how he carried his weight. Tall and built like a tree trunk, with thick, callused hands. The sleeves of his kimono were tied back to ensure freedom of movement. The hilt of his sword was well worn and stained with use. A vivid white scar ran across one cheek, over the bridge of his blunt nose, and into his eyebrow, perpetually twisting his features.

The man's voice was deep and accustomed to command. "I am Nishimuta no Takenaga. This is my village. What is your business here?"

Ken'ishi paused a moment before answering. "I am Ken'ishi," he said, bowing. "My business is just a bit of food, lord." He fixed his gaze in the distance, allowing his awareness to encompass all that lay within his peripheral vision, studying the towering constable without looking directly at him.

"Ronin are not welcome in my town," Takenaga said, rubbing the scar running across his nose. "I don't like them, and there are too many rough men around here."

"I mean to cause no trouble."

"So you say. But ronin *always* cause trouble."

Ken'ishi glanced purposefully at Yohachi. The moist smirk on the headman's lips melted away as he became aware that he sat well within reach of a sword-stroke.

"Get up!"

Ken'ishi kept his anger in check and glanced again at the headman, who trembled at the constable's words.

"I must bow to Takenaga-sama's wishes," Yohachi said, using "sama" in deference to the other man's superior status.

Ken'ishi clamped back his anger and scrutinized the samurai one more time. Takenaga moved with the surety and grace of a seasoned soldier. Even if Ken'ishi somehow managed to kill Takenaga, he would have to fight his way out of this village. He was still hungry, but its edge had been dulled. Losing his life was not worth half a bowl of rice. He regretted not having anything to give Akao.

He stood, and Takenaga stepped back, hand resting on the hilt of his sword. With deliberate slowness, Ken'ishi picked up his traveling pack with his left hand and his weapon with his right, a gesture meant to allow Takenaga the advantage, since now Ken'ishi could not draw his weapon without changing hands.

"Yohachi, my thanks for the rice. You are a generous man," he said as he bowed again. Then, he strode past Takenaga toward the door, slipping into his sandals as he stepped outside.

Ken'ishi did not look back as he walked into the street and headed for the edge of the village. Akao fell in beside him, his eyes scanning for threats. No doubt he had heard the entire exchange, but he did not understand human speech very well. Ken'ishi was aware of Takenaga escorting him ten paces behind, and his anger at the insult built within him like a thundercloud, roiling taller and thicker, like a towering black pillar of lightning. Then a small stone zipped past his shoulder from behind and bounced in the dirt, doubtless thrown by one of the young boys he had seen hiding between two houses. He did not turn, but held his jaw like an iron billet. Akao turned and barked a challenge.

Takenaga said, "You should keep your dog quiet, ronin scum. Or perhaps his skin will make a nice drum."

"He speaks as he chooses," Ken'ishi said, "and save your threats."

When they passed beyond the boundaries of the village and the road lay open before him, Ken'ishi suddenly dropped his pack and spun, switching his sheathed sword to his left hand, loosening the blade with his thumb. The arrogant smile on Takenaga's lips drew into a taut line, and he stopped, hand on his hilt poised to draw.

Takenaga said, "You would be wise to keep walking."

Ken'ishi's anger crackled inside. "You would have been wise to leave us alone. I am too young to be wise. And my honor would still be stained."

"Ronin scum like you know nothing of honor," Takenaga growled. The vivid white scar twisted his features even further into a sneer.

The young man's anger surged, filling his belly with fresh heat. "I am not ronin by choice. My family was slain by treacherous, hateful men, much like you."

The man stiffened, and his arrogant gaze shifted to cold calculation.

Ken'ishi continued, "I have dreamed of my father's murderers, and they look much like you. He would not stand for the treatment you have shown me. No better than a dog!"

"I would have fed a dog."

Ken'ishi whipped Silver Crane free of its scabbard, an action Takenaga followed a split heartbeat later. Ken'ishi tossed the scabbard aside and said, "If you choose, you can watch the sunset today. Your defeat will satisfy me, but your death is not necessary." Silver Crane was warm in his hands. He hardly felt its weight. It was an extension of his body, like a long, lethal limb.

"One fewer ronin will make the sunset brighter, after all. I've killed ten men twice your age, stripling! And three others have no hands, masterless scum wandering the countryside begging for scraps! All better men than you."

Ken'ishi raised his sword, assuming the stance taught him by his old teacher, legs braced apart, body turned sideways, sword blade upturned with the point aiming for his enemy's throat. His teacher had told him this was a master stance, unusable by anyone without the highest degree of skill. And it gave Takenaga pause.

Takenaga's sword was held straight out before him, the point aimed at Ken'ishi's throat.

Ken'ishi waited, allowing his anger to seep away, his jaw loosening, his shoulders relaxing, his muscles motionless. The immediate past melted away as well, leaving him in the present, the moment, the instants of one moment after another. The two men faced each other, and death was in the air.

Takenaga leaped forward, his blade flying up, then slashing downward in a stroke meant to sever at least one of his opponent's hands. Ken'ishi's small movements rippled like the water of a suddenly disturbed pool as the crane struck its prey, allowing the enemy's stroke to pass him by in the timeless instants between heartbeats. Only when Takenaga's missed stroke made a sufficient opening did Ken'ishi move, and Silver Crane flicked outward like the crescent of a crane's beak.

Takenaga grunted and stumbled backward, clutching at his throat. Bright, wet crimson pumped between his fingers. His eyes bulged with rage and surprise, and his scar blazed white across his blunt features. He struck at Ken'ishi again, but his swing was weak and off-target. Deflecting it with ease, Ken'ishi watched as the other man fell backwards on the dirt path, gasping through the blood gushing from his mouth and nose.

Ken'ishi stared at the bright blood as it spurted into the air, spreading across the dirt path, darkening the soil. Takenaga's body fought to breathe, to live, even as the realization dawned in the man's eyes that his life was finished. With a terrible sickness in his belly, Ken'ishi watched the light in the constable's eyes diminish like a starving candle.

Ken'ishi forced himself to look away from the moment of death. He noticed that dozens of villagers had watched the confrontation. They stared at him, their eyes wide in fear and amazement. Some ran for their homes. He wiped the blood from the tip of his weapon, then, with slow deliberation, sheathed it and tied the scabbard to his belt.

Yohachi thrust himself through the crowd. The headman's weak face contorted with rage, and he picked up a large stone and threw it at Ken'ishi. "Get out of here, criminal!" he shrieked.

The stone fell short, but other villagers followed his example, taking up more stones and the cry of, "Criminal! Criminal!"

A fist-sized stone struck Ken'ishi in the chest, shoving him back a step, driving the breath out of him. He gasped with pain and fresh anger. Ducking another hail of stones, he leaped to the fallen corpse, patted for the man's coin purse, snatched it, spun away, grabbed his pack, bow, and quiver, and fled down the road, stones bouncing around him and off his back.

As the ronin disappeared into the forest, Yohachi could only watch him go, feeling a mixture of fear, rage, relief, and wonder. Fear at having seen the cold, brutal face of death so closely. Rage at the loss of the village's protector, and Yohachi's carefully cultivated benefactor. Relief that the strange young ronin had fled. And wonder at how Takenaga had been such a formidable warrior, renowned for his swordsmanship, yet the young ronin had slain him almost effortlessly. Takenaga was known for his brutality and his hatred of ronin. Perhaps there was also some relief that Yohachi would never again live in fear of one Takenaga's drunken rages. But Takenaga's penchant for violence was only one of the reasons Yohachi had cultivated the samurai's friendship for so long. He was also an influential vassal of Lord Nishimuta no Jiro. Lord Nishimuta had given Takenaga this village to oversee because it was prosperous, to reward Takenaga for his faithful service, but also because it was several days' travel from Lord Nishimuta's estate, keeping Takenaga's rough demeanor at an acceptable distance.

That young bastard! The nerve of that scurrilous vagabond! The ronin must be dealt with! Yohachi knew that his voice was not one to inspire the villagers to righteous fervor, but he had to do something. He cried out, "Everyone, listen to me! We must capture this ronin and punish him!" He looked at the men standing around him and saw the same range of emotions in their faces that he felt. They were afraid, but also angry. "Find Takenaga-sama's deputies and bring them here. They must help us. Everyone, gather your weapons quickly. We must chase this ronin down!" Seeing the fear on their faces, he added, "Don't worry about having to fight him. When he sees all of us, he will turn coward and submit. He will not have the courage to face all of us. Now go! Gather your weapons. We must not lose him!"

The villagers dispersed to gather up whatever makeshift weapons they could find, clubs and pitchforks, even a few rusty spears left over from the wars of fifty years before. The three deputies arrived, Taro, Kei, and Shohei. They carried their jitte, the only weapons Takenaga would allow them to carry, unsharpened parrying weapons about half the size of a sword with a long straight "blade" and a shorter, parallel prong designed to catch and hold a sword or a spear. The deputies approached the lifeless body of their master, and their faces went slack with shock.

The eldest, Taro, stood over the body. He had always been a good boy, Yohachi thought, and now he looked so shocked and solemn that Yohachi could not imagine what he must be thinking. Takenaga had chosen his deputies from the strongest and most reliable of the village's young men, but he was not a kind man and had often treated them harshly. *What must they be feeling now,* Yohachi wondered. *Shock, anger, sadness, and . . . relief?*

While he waited for everyone to gather, Yohachi approached Takenaga's body, staring at the gleaming blade clenched in the dead man's fist. Swords had always fascinated him and had been a favorite topic of conversation between him and Takenaga. The constable had often boasted about the fine quality of his weapon. It was a gift from Lord Nishimuta, made in the new, heavier katana-style, rather than the antique tachi-style, and had seen more than a few battles against bandit gangs over the years. Takenaga had never let him touch it, and he had always wanted to feel its heft, to experience the power of a true warrior's weapon. Yohachi had never been a strong man. He had been gravely ill as a child, the long sickness leaving his body weak and twisted, unable to work as hard as others, unable to wield a weapon. His inability had fueled his fascination with the tools of the warrior. Now he knelt down, untied the scabbard from Takenaga's sash, and pulled it out. Then he pried the dead man's fingers from around the well-worn hilt of the katana and picked it up. It felt so heavy in his hand. He stared at it in wonder. Then he slid the blade into the scabbard and prepared to thrust the long sword into his sash.

A sudden voice stopped him. "Wait."

Yohachi turned to face the young man standing beside him.

"Are you able to use that, Yohachi?" Taro's voice was heavy with caution. "Takenaga always said that when you put on the swords, you become dead. Are you ready to die?"

Yohachi looked hard into the young man's face. In fact, he had heard Takenaga say those very words, but had never considered their meaning. But he liked the feel of the sleeping steel in his hands. "Takenaga-sama would want someone to use his weapons to avenge his death. This blade will taste that ronin's blood!"

The villagers standing nearby nodded, and a few voiced their agreement. Already Yohachi felt the power of the sword coursing through him. He stood a little straighter. His fingers caressed the silken cord wrappings, the roughness of the ray skin under the cords.

"Wait, Yohachi," Taro said, his voice hardening. "Do you truly know how to use those? Or do you claim them because you are selfish? I am Takenaga-sama's chief deputy. He has no heirs and no immediate family. I am strong and I know how to use them. Give the swords to me, and I will see that Takenaga's death is avenged."

Yohachi snorted. "But I am the headman here!"

"Yes and the village needs you. You must be alive to lead. I ask again, are you ready to die? Because that's what it means to wear those swords. If you are not, Takenaga's shade will know, and he will curse you for a coward."

Yohachi gasped and dropped the sword. It clattered on the ground. He had not thought of that. His greed for the swords had made him forget that Takenaga's spirit was still about, and doubtless angry.

Taro bent to pick it up. "You are a wise man." He thrust the sword into his own sash and tied the cords. The two other deputies stared at him as he bent to retrieve the short sword as well, placing it in his sash alongside the katana.

A mob had gathered around them, but Yohachi could only stare at the face of the heretofore quiet young man. What emotions were churning behind that solemn mask? The determination was evident in his bearing. Taro had meant what he said. He would do everything in his power to find the ronin.

When the crowd looked as if it had grown as large as it could—some forty-odd farmers and villagers and three deputies—Yohachi looked at the faces of his friends and neighbors, people he had known all his life. "That ronin must be punished for what he has done. We will find him and bring him back. Then we will decide what sort of death is best for him!"

Agreement murmured through the mob. "Let us go quickly! He has a head start!" Then Yohachi led them down the road in pursuit of the criminal.

Ken'ishi did not stop running until the village was long out of sight in the forest behind him. The sun-dappled road was deserted in both directions. A breeze brushed the upper branches, but did not reach the forest floor. He stopped beside a small roadside shrine, his breath huffing in and out like a smith's bellows. His ears burned with exertion, and sweat plastered a few loose wisps of hair to the side of his face. He let his pack, bow, and quiver hang loose in his grip, resting one hand on his knee as he tried to catch his breath, the other hand rubbing the painful bruise on his chest inflicted by the hurled stone.

Akao stopped beside him, his tongue lolling. He looked back down the road toward the village. "Coming." His deep brown eyes, slanted like a fox, searched the road behind them, his pointed red ears erect, his nose lifted into the wind.

Ken'ishi nodded. "How far?"

"Go soon."

"I am weak!" he growled. A swirling, leaden sickness in his belly drowned the remnants of his previous hunger. What would his dead father think of his actions just now? Would he be proud that his son had won the duel? Ashamed at the theft of the man's money? Neither? Both? "I am sorry for my weakness, Father!" he said, choking on his shame. He had fought the duel to defend the honor of his family, then he had soiled it himself just as quickly. For that matter, what would his teacher say? What about his foster parents? He could almost hear his foster mother clicking her tongue at him, as she used to do so often when he made some terrible blunder. Then her disapproval would be followed by some great kindness to show him that his errors were forgiven. Tears of shame trickled down his nose. He missed her kindness now. He missed a friendly face amidst a land full of strangers who did not care if he lived or died. He wanted to throw the money away, but he was so hungry and had been for so long.

His mind reeled as he tried to conceive of some way to atone for his misdeed. Would robbing the dead offend the kami?

"I'm sorry, my friend," he said to Akao. "I couldn't bring you any food."

The dog smiled, then padded closer and nudged Ken'ishi's knee with his nose. "Not hungry now."

Then a new voice piped up, small and high-pitched. "Who's talking down there?"

Ken'ishi looked around. Where had the voice come from? As his breath slowed, he wiped the sweat from his face with his sleeve, and his gaze stopped on the nearby shrine.

"Who's there?" he said.

No reply.

He looked at the shrine. Inside was a little statue of one the Seven Bodhisattvas. Had the small stone god spoken to him? He wondered what the shrine's significance might be, why people sometimes built these small structures filled with gods and offerings in the most unusual or out-of-the-way places. There was also a wooden placard inside with some writing on it, but he recognized only a few of the characters.

Then he noticed a sparrow sitting on the roof of the shrine, watching him with its small black eyes. Ken'ishi studied the bird for a moment.

"Did you speak to us?" Ken'ishi asked. Perhaps the bird could help him. Sparrows were good fortune.

"I did. You surprised me."

Ken'ishi said, straightening and bowing. "Good day, Mr. Sparrow. I am sorry to have startled you."

It smoothed its ruffled, pale breast feathers and said with some surprise, "Good day to you, big hairy man. How is it that you can speak my tongue?"

"I learned from my teacher."

"I have never heard of a man who could understand birds. Or dogs, for that matter. Do you have any seeds? I am hungry."

It was so difficult to speak to such small birds. Their minds flitted back and forth as if thoughts were branches. "I am sorry," Ken'ishi said. "I don't have any seeds."

"Do you have any stiff grass? I am building a nest for my wife."

"Again, my apologies. I have none." Then he thought for a moment. Perhaps he could offer the sparrow something, not only to atone for his earlier misdeed, but also because he could certainly use a bit of good fortune. His hair, tied into ponytail, symbolized his nature as a warrior. "Perhaps I could offer you some of my hair."

"What an excellent idea! An auspicious gift! You are very helpful."

Ken'ishi drew his knife, sliced away a generous lock of hair from his ponytail, and laid it at the sparrow's feet.

The sparrow bowed and said, "Thank you, strange big hairy man. I am in your debt. For your kindness, I think I will repay you with a bit of good fortune."

29

"Thank you, good bird, but there is no need to repay me. You have helped me to avoid my own despair."

"Too late. The good fortune has already been granted. You will meet it very soon. I hope you use it wisely. Why were you running? Is something chasing you?"

"No," Ken'ishi said, "I run from myself."

"What a silly thing to say! If you run from yourself, you are caught before you raise a wing! Have you any seeds?"

"No, kind bird. I'm sorry. What lies further down this road?"

"My nest is here! What lies down there does not matter to me!"

"Forgive me, I am being rude."

"If you have no seeds for me to eat, then be gone! You have wasted enough of my time, and I am hungry. I do not live as long as you!"

"Thank you, Mr. Sparrow. I'll move on." He had not remembered how fast the demeanor of the small birds could shift. They forgot kindnesses so quickly and remembered wrongs for so long. In that respect, they were much like people. Ken'ishi shrugged his belongings onto his back and prepared to continue down the road, then he paused. He pulled out Takenaga's coin pouch and plucked out the largest, shiniest gold coin. Then he placed it at the feet of the small stone god and clapped his hands twice, as he had seen others do to get the attention of the spirit of the shrine, bowed, and asked the shrine god for forgiveness for his deed. He received no response. With a heavy sigh, he moved on.

The smells of the forest, vibrant with life, helped to soothe the pain in his belly for a while, but as he walked, the constable's silken coin purse bumped into him with each step, driving him deeper and deeper into despair. His ears burned with the cries of "Criminal! Criminal!"

He did not feel like a criminal for killing the constable. That had been a duel of honor, and he had offered a chance to decide the duel without death. His teacher had prepared him for battle, but not for the reality—the finality—of it. In his mind, he saw Takenaga's pale face again, haloed by the expanding pool of blood, gasping, staring at him. Ken'ishi shuddered. He knew the memory of the duel would be burned into his mind until the moment he died, and perhaps carry into his next life. His anger at Takenaga's insults was gone, drawn away with the departure of the man's life. But he was thankful to the kami for his own life.

He looked at Takenaga's coin purse in his hand, with his belly a cauldron of emotions. He cocked his arm back to throw the purse into the forest, then stopped. Guilt churned in his belly. In his weakness, he had stooped to thievery, and that made him a criminal.

But now he could buy food for himself and Akao, for a little while, and in that time, perhaps he could find someone willing to employ him. Perhaps he could find a way to atone for his misdeed, but to do that, he had to live. Starving to death would serve no one. Samurai could also kill themselves to cleanse the stain of dishonor from their souls, but. . . . Suddenly he wanted to weep for shame, and a lump formed in his throat.

If another constable captured him, he would be tortured and executed. Would an honorable warrior steal from a dead man? Samurai aspired to be the epitome of strength and honor, but sometimes they were simply evil men who enjoyed bloodletting for its own sake. Like the incident in the capital a few weeks before, where he had seen both the best and the worst of what a samurai could be.

Standing on the road, with Akao beside him, he hefted Takenaga's coin purse. He guessed it contained enough money to feed him for a long time. It was easy to see why some ronin stooped to banditry to fill their bellies. Should he give the money to someone he might meet on the road, perhaps a priest or a peasant? But then the thought of eating grubs and roots again tightened his grip on the heavy silken pouch. He looked at it for a long time, until Akao nudged his leg.

"Go now. Whine later," Akao said.

Ken'ishi sighed, then put the purse inside his shirt and resumed his way down the path. Was this the weakness his sensei had told him all men possess? The darkness, the demons inside their spirits that make them greedy and cruel. Was this the weakness that his teacher had taught him how to conquer? Had he failed so quickly? Was this kind of evil the reason for his family's murder?

As he walked, Ken'ishi heard the sound of a stream gurgling over rocks. Perhaps what he needed now was to sit beside it for a while. As a boy, when his teacher had been harsh with him, he had often sat beside the stream that passed the foot of the mountain where he had been raised. The burbling sound had always calmed him, washing away whatever terrible feelings had filled him. Fear, anger, shame, all could be carried away by the smooth, serene sound of water sliding over the rocks.

He found the stream and climbed down the rocky bank to sit beside it. This was a pleasant spot. He noticed that Akao was gone, but he did not worry. The dog was stealthy when he chose to be, and had doubtless gone off in search of a meal. Bright green moss covered the moist rocks, and the abundance of bushes and bamboo along the banks gave him a feeling of seclusion. The stream was no more than ten paces across, and the water was clear. Suddenly a fierce thirst struck him, and he knelt to thrust his face into the cool, gentle torrent, sucking down a great draught. Wiping his face, he stood up. The smell of the moist earth, the gentle gurgle of the water, the whisper of the breeze through the bamboo leaves, the song of a bird singing to its mate, all worked together to dispel some of the shame he felt. The place where he sat was invisible from the road. He would be safe here for a while. When he was calm, his hunger would return. Languid fish slid through the stream, and his stomach rumbled at the sight. The day was far from over, but he no longer felt like traveling. He would camp here for the night.

Soon, however, the sounds of a group of people preceded them coming up the road. His relaxation evaporated in an instant. The sound came from the direction of the village; the angry mob searching for him. He crept up the bank of the stream toward the road, darting from brush to tree. The voices and footsteps grew louder. He stopped behind a thicket, where he was just able to see the nearby patch of road.

Before long, the mob came in sight. There was Yohachi, the distasteful village headman, three deputies, one of them carrying the dead constable's swords, and many more villagers with clubs and spears. Ken'ishi's chest clenched. He had angered them, like a nest of hornets struck with a stick. There were too many to fight, and he had no more stomach for killing today. Ducking behind his thicket, he waited until they passed, knowing he was fortunate that his presence had not been discovered. Were they following his tracks? Would they see where he had left the road? It was difficult for a group of people to remain vigilant for long periods, especially when traveling. After they had passed, he stole out to the road and studied the earth. The passage of the villagers had obscured any tracks he had left. He was safe, for now, but he could not stay here.

But now he had to be even more vigilant. These villagers would spread the word in the surrounding communities about what had happened. He would become a wanted man. It was no longer safe for him to travel. Everyone in the province would soon be on the lookout for him. What would he do? Avoiding every village would be difficult, especially when he needed food.

Perhaps after a while, the fervor would die down and the villagers would sink back into complacency, after they thought that the criminal had left the area. The only thing he was certain of was that he had to get far away from here as soon as possible.

"Warfare is the greatest affair of state, the basis of life and death, the Way to survival or extinction."

—Sun Tzu, *The Art of War*

The tall, waspish man dabbed at his sweating forehead with a soft cloth held in a thin hand, frowning at the hot, humid air. The tavern keeper kept his establishment far too warm for Yasutoki's liking. The hubbub of the common room was only slightly muffled by the rice-paper walls of the private room where Yasutoki sat, sipping his sake. Window shutters kept out the chill spring night. The sounds of gulls had subsided with the fall of darkness, but the ceaseless rumble of the surf remained. A little fresh air would do him good. And since the man he was waiting for was late, he opened his mouth to request that a servant open the small window.

The door slid open suddenly, and the smells of the sea wafted in with the man who entered. The stranger gazed down at Yasutoki with hard, slitted eyes. Then he spoke in his own barbarian tongue, without politeness or preamble. "You are the one called

'Green Tiger'?" His voice was rough and uncultured.

Yasutoki's nose wrinkled. This man was more uncouth than a common fisherman, and worse, he was a foreigner. Yasutoki answered him in the barbarian tongue, "I am Green Tiger. Come in and shut the door."

The man snorted with a wolfish smile of skepticism, but he slid the door shut behind him. "I was expecting someone a bit more . . . a bit bigger, perhaps."

Yasutoki studied the man's strange, blunt features, and his long, thin mustache. His clothes were rough and simple, but not ragged. At his belt, he wore a short, broad-bladed sword, or perhaps a long knife, in a leather scabbard. He stank of sweat and the sea, and somehow of horses. Even after a sea voyage, he still smelled of the horses for which the Mongol people were infamous.

The man's gaze scanned the room, flicking here and there. Finally, he settled himself on the other side of the table. Yasutoki allowed a measure of quivering into his hand as he poured warm sake into the bowl in front of the stranger, until he steadied himself with his other hand. A bit of weakness would put the barbarian at ease. He felt the stranger's taut power even across the table, like a drawn bowstring.

The man took the bowl of sake and downed it in one gulp. He grimaced. "I don't know if I'll ever get used to this stuff," he grunted. "Perhaps when the Great Khan is in charge, you people will learn to drink real liquor! Those Koryu dogs had better than this on the boat!"

Yasutoki ignored the man's uncouth words and sat back, smoothing his fine silk robes. "I trust your journey was a safe one."

"The most miserable experience of my life! I dread the day I have to return. I would rather stay in hell than ride a boat back to heaven!"

"This is a bad season for sea travel."

"Between bouts of vomiting I thought I would drown," the man grumbled.

Yasutoki frowned in sympathetic sorrow. "What a terrible experience."

The man grunted and held out his bowl.

Yasutoki poured again. "The Great Khan has sent messages to the Imperial court, has he not?"

The man's face grew sober. "Yes. The Golden Horde's lands extend so far to the west that our empire cannot easily be crossed. We have reached the lands where the sun sets. The Khan now looks toward the rising sun, to the sea. The Khan has ordered your Emperor to submit to his rule, or face invasion."

"Our lord is direct, as always," said Yasutoki. "I suspected that was his intention. Has the Great Khan sent me a message as well?"

The Mongol withdrew a bamboo tube from his tunic and placed it on the table between them.

Yasutoki took the tube, pulled the waxed stopper from one end and dumped a small scroll into his hand. He carefully unrolled the paper and read it. Allowing the Mongol to see no hint of his reaction to its contents, he rolled up the scroll again and placed it back in the tube, secreting the container within his robes. He rubbed his chin thoughtfully. "The Emperor and his courtiers are weak and soft. The mere thought of war with the Khan would fill them with fear. They might well consider his request. The Shogunate, on the other hand, is a different story. The Hojo clan will never agree to such a demand."

"But is not the Emperor in charge?"

Yasutoki shook his head. "My uncouth friend, you are ignorant of Japanese politics." The Mongol stiffened, as Yasutoki had intended. "The Emperor is our divine ruler, descended from the gods, but he has little real power. He and his court live in splendor and opulence, heedless of the lives and suffering of the people outside the palace. The Emperor relies on tradition and prestige to see his will done." He laughed harshly. "He is not even in charge of his own court! He is the impotent clown leading a parade of fools! Even the feeble power of the court lies in the hands of the Emperor's predecessor, the *retired* Emperor, who guides all decisions of importance in the capital from his sequestered chambers. But the *real* power does not lie in the capital. It resides in the Shogun."

"The Great General," said the Mongol. He had been listening intently, absorbing what he had heard with a sharp intelligence that Yasutoki had overlooked. He reminded himself not to underestimate this barbarian. His manners were rough, but his mind was as sharp as a katana.

"Yes! You understand military power, don't you, my horse-loving friend?"

"The only true power is military power. There can be no political power without it," said the Mongol. "When the Great Khan's grandsire, Genghis, united all the clans of the steppes, those soft Yuan emperors and their minions learned what real power was. The power of the horse and the bow and the steel thews of the men who use them!" His eyes flashed fiercely, and he clenched his fist.

"Yes, the power of the horse and the bow. The same is true here, but it wears a different face. We pay obeisance to the cloistered Emperor while the Shogun runs roughshod over our backs." A wry, contemptuous smile twisted Yasutoki's lips. "But even the Shogun is weak. It seems that every stronghold of power in my land is merely a façade. The true power of the Shogun does not lie in the hands of the Shogun anymore. It is in the hands of the Hojo clan, the Shogun's regents. The Shogun is a mere boy, a puppet, like the Emperor. The Hojo sometimes allow him to believe he is in control—and sometimes, perhaps, he truly is—but they make all the real decisions. And their spies are everywhere." Yasutoki realized that his voice had lost its careful neutrality, had grown fierce. He took a deep breath and composed himself, looking at the table. "A change is coming."

The Mongol laughed again. "Yes, a change is coming, and it rides on the backs of Mongol horses!"

Yasutoki nodded. "With regards to the Khan's demands, I am sure that nothing will happen quickly. The debate in the court and the Shogunate about how to reply could take months, perhaps even years. I would welcome the Khan's rule and be done with weak, corrupt officials. It would be better for the country."

The Mongol barked a laugh. "You're a fine one to call others 'corrupt!' I can hardly imagine someone more treacherous than one who betrays his own people."

Yasutoki pushed down a stab of anger. "Only the most corrupt can easily recognize corruption."

"I am certain the promise of riches beyond counting makes you all the more convinced of what is good for your country," said the Mongol. The contempt in his voice was plain.

Yasutoki tried to ignore the Mongol's jibe and kept his voice steady. "My reasons are my own. They do not concern a barbarian such as you, much less one who reeks of horseshit."

The Mongol laughed again, a deep, booming sound. "So the limp-wristed bureaucrat has a spine after all!" Then his voice grew grim, and his hand rested on the hilt of his sword. "You should not forget who your master is."

"I do not forget. I serve the great Khubilai Khan, *not* his unwashed, uncouth messenger boy."

The Mongol's eyes flashed with anger, and his grip tightened around the hilt of his sword.

Yasutoki kept his voice calm, slipping his hands into the sleeves of his robes. "Kill me, and you will displease the Great Khan. There are few men willing or able to provide the information I possess. I can provide the Great Khan with the knowledge of troop strength and movements, suitable landing sites, fortifications. I can give him Hakata Bay, and with Hakata Bay as a landing point and a foothold, conquering the rest will be easy."

The Mongol snarled, "The Great Khan could take this measly island and the entire country without your help!"

"Perhaps he could. But the capital is far from here, and you must take not only the Imperial palace, but the headquarters of the Shogun. It is a dangerous gamble, but with my help, the gamble will be less risky. Of course, a lowly horse-shagger like you would not understand such things."

"Why you sniveling—!" The Mongol's sword jumped halfway out of its scabbard.

Yasutoki's right hand flicked out of his sleeve, and something silver flashed through the air, quicker than sight. The Mongol flinched and stiffened. A small needle now protruded from his throat. His eyes bulged, and a great vein emerged on his reddening forehead. He froze in mid-movement. Yasutoki stood up, a calm smirk on his thin lips. With his toe, he pushed the paralyzed man onto his back, then leaned down and plucked the needle from his throat.

He leaned down and spoke into the Mongol's frozen face. "The Great Khan is powerful, and he does not remain so by being foolish. Fear not, barbarian dog, the poison is not fatal. You will be able to move again in a few hours. That is, after your bowels have emptied themselves into your trousers. Take this message back to Khubilai Khan. He should not underestimate me or my people. Not all of us are as weak as the Imperial court. I serve him by my own choosing. You may tell him that his offer is acceptable. He shall have what he desires from me. You understand, do you not, horse-shagger? I can see from your eyes that you do."

Then he straightened and smoothed his robes. "Well then, I have spent enough time in your distasteful company, and in this dismal place." He gathered his robes and turned toward the door, picking up his large basket-hat and dark coat. The hat was a fine thing for moving about discreetly; it concealed his face, and the dark coat would help him blend into the night.

After he had put on the hat and coat, he turned to the paralyzed man lying quivering in the middle of the floor. "My people feel that manners are important. Perhaps you should learn some. Good evening."

As Yasutoki faded into the darkness of the city of Hakata, plans were already forming in his mind. The half-moon gleamed on the bay, broken up by the dark shapes of ships and a tangle of masts around the docks. He would send out messages and put the first parts into motion. Tomorrow he would travel over the mountains to Dazaifu, ancient seat of this island's government, and meet an old kinsman and "friend."

"Not to borrow the strength of another, nor to rely on one's own strength; to cut off past and future thoughts, and not to live within the everyday mind . . . then the Great Way is right before one's eyes."

—*Hagakure*

Ken'ishi lay under a rock outcropping on the forested hillside, wrapped in his meager blanket. The spring night was cool and quiet, and he was well concealed. He felt Akao's warmth through the blanket as he lay beside him and smelled the warm, earthy scent of the dog's fur as the animal slept. He looked up through the bamboo leaves at the great black inverted bowl dusted with silver that was the night sky above him. He waited for sleep to come to him, and he thought back on the day's events.

How could some people be so cruel and others be so kind? He had done nothing to provoke the response he had received in that village. Never before had a village constable reacted with such hatred toward him. It had been a humiliating experience. That humiliation had angered him, led him to provoke the duel. As he thought about the duel itself, he realized that it had been easy. His training had taken over, and his actions had been effortless. He knew now that his victory had never been in question. At that, he felt a surge of pride. Takenaga had been a good swordsman, but not a great one. Ken'ishi's teacher had been great. His sensei had extolled his own prowess many times, saying that he was superior to nearly any swordsman walking the land, so Ken'ishi had learned from the best. The perfection of the movements and the finality of the act held a certain kind of beauty, almost like the majesty of nature. But he did not like the act of killing another man. It was ugly. His pride at winning now fought with remorse for taking the man's life. But the more he thought about it, the more he realized he could have done nothing else. Takenaga's arrogance and hatred had been his undoing. Martial prowess could lead one down the path of arrogance, and ultimately death, like the incident in the capital. There is always someone in the world that is stronger than you, and you must recognize that person when you meet him, his teacher had told him.

All roads in the province seemed to have led Ken'ishi to this thriving, ancient city called Kyoto. He had been in the capital for two days, trying to find his way through the endless warrens of streets, palaces, and tenements. The spectacle was more than he could fathom. The avenues and alleys swarmed with richly dressed courtiers and nobles riding in palanquins, gruff samurai bristling with weapons and pride, merchants and artisans in their shops, commoners hurrying about their work, and beggars sitting in doorways with thin hands raised in supplication. He had never seen anything like it. He had never imagined that so many people existed in the world. Akao had been the braver one, fascinated by the vast array of smells wafting on the breeze and in the wake of every passerby.

At first, it had been frightening, incomprehensible. He had seen scores of shops with placards outside that he could not read, because he had had no formal education. He had seen hundreds of people going about business he did not understand, because he had never encountered a city before. He was hungry, but he did not know how to get food, thirsty, but he did not know where to drink, weary, but he did not know where to sleep. He knew not a soul in the entire world. There was no one who could help them.

And the women. The women were so beautiful and delicate, with their dark, sparkling eyes, full lips, and lovely throats. Many of them smelled so wonderful, like goddesses. He could only stare after them in helpless amazement. They were so much more beautiful than Haru. But why, then, did he still think of her so often? Even after what she had done to him? And it had been so many months since he had seen her. When he saw her face in his memory, her pretty eyes glinting with deceit, he felt such a strange mixture of emotions. Desire, regret, longing, shame. Ken'ishi pushed thoughts of her aside as he passed a trio of lovely girls who had caught him staring at them. They giggled at him, covering their mouths with their hands as he moved away, blushing with embarrassment.

He had never seen so many women before. Something in him wanted to touch them, but he did not know what else to do. More than once, his loins stirred with an aching need he could not describe. So many women around him should make it easier for him to forget Haru, but somehow it did not.

One night, Ken'ishi walked the dark streets. Akao walked close to him, brushing against his legs to control his nervousness. The dog's hair stood straight across his neck, and his tail was tucked against his back leg. They passed windows and heard the musical sounds of women's laughter, and the deep laughter of men too. They sounded like they were having fun. He knew that he wanted to know women, to laugh with them, but he could not. He did not know how. Once he tried to enter a shop where he heard the sounds of merriment, but a huge man by the door grabbed him and threw him back out into the street. For a moment, anger flared in him, but the man slammed the door in his face before he could get up off the ground. He had been taught to recognize his own frustration and conquer it immediately. So he shrugged it off, picked himself up out of the dirt, and readjusted his ragged accoutrements.

He moved on down the street, passing darkened shops wherein through the thin walls he heard strange, gasping cries, or low, mumbled words. He found himself stopping to stare at the dark shapes silhouetted on paper screens, hidden from the eyes of the world. The streets here were dark and narrow, and some of the men he saw looked dangerous. They looked scruffy and unwashed with prominent scars and hungry, treacherous looks. He saw one man who looked as if his nose had been sliced off years ago. Some wore fine clothes and large basket hats to conceal their features. He gave them a wide berth, but he did not fear them. His teacher had made certain of that. But in an unfamiliar place, it was best to be cautious.

As he walked, he noticed a rough-looking man coming down the street toward him. He wore a fine silken kimono, trousers, and a wide-shouldered jacket emblazoned with some family crest. But he had only one sword, a short sword, at his hip. Ken'ishi thought this was strange, as many samurai he had seen—particularly ones who looked as wealthy as this one—wore two swords. He often wished that he had two swords like them, a mate for Silver Crane. The man's hair was immaculately styled in the traditional topknot, but his eyes were bloodshot, and his cheeks were flushed. He ignored Ken'ishi as he shouldered past him into a nearby shop.

A sign above the shop door read, *Souls of Samurai Polished Here.* In his limited education, Ken'ishi had most quickly learned the characters that applied to him, and he felt a moment of pride at being able to read the sign.

Standing in the invisible air of the man's passing breath, Ken'ishi caught the smell of sake. Peering around Ken'ishi's legs, Akao stood hunched and staring, emitting a low growl that only he could hear.

"Can you spare some coin, sir, for an old man?" came a voice from the shadows under the eave of a nearby house.

Ken'ishi looked over to see an old man squatting there, with a small wooden cup in one raised hand. His skin was wrinkled and leathery, stretched across his skull, with prominent brows and cheekbones protruding from starvation. Pale white whiskers dusted his spotted jaw, and his mouth had collapsed into itself with the absence of teeth. Ken'ishi kept his distance, but as he looked at him, he felt a mixture of revulsion at his ugliness and compassion for his plight.

"I was once a ronin like you, boy," the beggar said. "Until I lost my arm and my eye in battle." He raised the stump of his right arm, severed at the elbow, and lifted his face out of the shadows to reveal an empty, puckered eye socket. To make his appearance even more unpleasant, he had a large, purplish bulb in the center of his forehead that looked like a cluster of rotten plums stuck to his flesh and oozing down onto his brow.

"I am sorry," Ken'ishi said. "I have no money."

"Some food then?"

"I'm sorry. I'm hungry, too. I have no food and no money to offer you."

"That's too bad to see one as young and strong as you with such troubles. Good luck to you, young man." The old man bowed his head to him.

Ken'ishi bowed in return and moved on down the street.

After he had gone about ten steps, a door opened and a loud voice emerged behind him. "Ah, what fine craftsmanship! It looks better than the day it was first polished!"

Ken'ishi turned and saw the rough-looking samurai standing in the street outside the shop he had entered.

The samurai held aloft a katana that glimmered in the light of the street lanterns. "Outstanding!"

The sword polisher, a man of approaching late years, stood in the doorway of his shop, bowing deeply. "You are too kind to a man with skills as poor as mine."

"Nonsense, Masamoto! You do outstanding work!"

At that moment, the old beggar nearby said, "Can a fine, strong gentleman such as you spare some coin for an old warrior?"

The samurai turned toward the old man, noticing him for the first time. Ken'ishi saw a look of disgust appear on the samurai's face, then his expression furrowed with dark, cruel lines.

He stepped closer to the old man and, with a lightning quick motion, slashed sideways. The old man's head tumbled off his shoulders, bobbling across the dirt.

Ken'ishi stared in horrified fascination at the warrior's cold cruelty.

The samurai glared imperiously as the old man's body slipped and fell sideways, dribbling dark red blood from the stump of his neck. His voice was thick with derision as he said, "Thank you, old warrior, for allowing me to test my newly polished blade. You should have died on the battlefield like a true samurai and spared the world a helpless beggar." He turned to the sword polisher, who stood frozen with a look of queasy surprise and fear. "Again, Masamoto, I must say you do outstanding work. I hardly felt the resistance of the spine."

Trembling, the sword polisher offered him a cloth. "To remove the blood, sir."

The samurai took it and wiped away the little bit of wetness that clung to the gleaming steel. Then with movements like liquid, the samurai sheathed his blade and thrust the scabbard into his obi. Suddenly he turned toward Ken'ishi, his eyes glinting like red lanterns in the darkness. "What are you staring at, boy?"

Ken'ishi stiffened for a moment, then his master's training took over and he relaxed, prepared for battle.

"What, have you no tongue?" The samurai's voice grew angry. "You do not approve of me testing my freshly polished blade?"

Ken'ishi's chin rose in defiance, but he said nothing.

"You have a sword, I see. Where did a whelp like you find a sword like that? Whom did you steal it from?"

Ken'ishi stiffened, and Akao's growl grew louder.

A cruel leer split the man's face. "Do you know how to use that weapon, or do you just carry it around for show?"

Ken'ishi glanced down at the old man's head, lying on the dirt street, dribbling a thin trail of blood behind it, the body twitching as it lay crumpled on the ground. Such a senseless death. To have lived for so long and died so badly, so meaninglessly, at the hands of one so crass and cruel. The old man had deserved better.

"You have the look of a young cock ready for his first fight," said the samurai, squaring his body toward Ken'ishi with bloodlust in his eyes. "Perhaps you should be taught your place."

Ken'ishi thrust the hilt of his sword forward. He would not back down from a man such as this. Akao snarled and bared his teeth.

"Oho! A young cock you are then! A cock and a dog. But which is which? Perhaps you are both dogs." The samurai's words were jovial, but his tone was not. "Perhaps you're one head too tall as well."

Ken'ishi said nothing, but concentrated on the samurai's growing anger. The other man was accustomed to his harsh words causing others to back down from him. But Ken'ishi was not backing down. He planted his feet and tested his footing.

The samurai started forward and snarled, "Why you little turd, I'll—!"

Then another voice roared down the street, echoing between the shops and houses like the rumble of thunder. "Goemon! What the hell are you doing!"

The samurai stopped in mid-step. He turned.

Another figure approached. As the newcomer came into the light, Ken'ishi saw he was also a samurai. He was dressed in robes that were rich, but not opulent, and carried himself with the bearing of a man accustomed to command. He had strong, handsome features and sharp eyes. His gaze seemed to drill into Goemon, puncture him. The hostility bottled within Goemon began to seep away.

Goemon said, "Captain Mishima. I was just about to teach this rude young cock a lesson in manners."

Captain Mishima stopped about two paces away from Goemon. "You were doing no such thing. He neither said nor did anything to provoke you. I saw the whole thing."

Goemon stiffened as if struck.

Captain Mishima continued, his voice steady and controlled. "You are a disgrace. You're nothing but a drunken bully, and you bring shame to our master. We are retainers to a noble house, some of the highest ranked bushi in the capital! We live to a far higher standard than this! Your disgraceful behavior brings dishonor upon our master, and that I cannot allow!"

"But—!"

"Shut up. I have been looking for you since nightfall. You have gone too far. The owner of a certain sake house sent word of your . . . behavior tonight to my office. You debauch yourself with sake, opium, and whores, and then spend the rest of the night proving your superiority to boys and old men." He turned his penetrating gaze for an instant on the corpse sprawled in the dirt, and Ken'ishi saw a look of pity and sadness flicker through his eyes, quickly washed away by a controlled rush of anger. "Madame Matsuko has powerful friends, and you have angered her with your ill-mannered treatment of her girls. You are a disgrace. I swear on my oath to our master that you will answer for this."

Goemon's chin fell further and further toward his chest, his shoulders slumping at the verbal barrage.

Captain Mishima continued, "I would enjoy the chance to cut you down myself, but you are not mine to kill."

Goemon's head rose at those words, and his body tensed again as he placed a hand on the hilt of his sword.

Captain Mishima was unfazed, and his voice turned cold and deadly. "Do you think you can fight me? You are drunk and I can smell the opium on your clothes. Your death would be no better than his." He pointed toward the old man's corpse. "Come with me now and you may be allowed to regain your honor with seppuku. It is not my decision to make, however. If it were, I would cut you down like the dog you are. Disobey me and you will be hunted and executed like a criminal." He raised his arm and pointed back down the street in the direction he had come. "Now, go."

Goemon released his sword hilt, lowered his head, and trudged down the street.

Captain Mishima then turned to the sword polisher, who stood with his eyes downcast, embarrassed and frightened. "Please accept my apologies, Masamoto. You will have no more trouble from Goemon. My master is grateful for your skilled service."

The sword polisher bowed. "Your master is too kind to someone with such poor skill as I have."

Then Captain Mishima looked at Ken'ishi and gave him an appraising glance. Ken'ishi saw the calm intelligence in his eyes and a flash of respect. He blushed at the scrutiny. "You are a brave young man," Captain Mishima said. "Please accept my humble apologies for the behavior of my underling." Then he offered a quick bow.

Ken'ishi was nonplussed. No one of such rank had ever spoken to him before with such courtesy. Nevertheless, he had the presence of mind to return the honor with a low bow of his own.

Then Captain Mishima turned, thought for a moment, and said to the sword polisher, "Masamoto, please polish this young man's weapon. My master would consider it a favor."

The sword polisher almost hid his surprise, then he bowed deeply. "Of course, Mishima-sama. It would be my pleasure."

Then the samurai captain followed Goemon down the street.

After he had gone, the sword polisher turned to Ken'ishi and bowed with a feeble smile. "Please," he said, "allow me to polish your weapon."

Unsure of what else to say, Ken'ishi said, "Very well. Please do me this favor." He walked toward the sword polisher, untying his scabbard, then offered it up to the artisan with both hands. The sword polisher bowed low and received it with both hands.

"May I inspect it?" Masamoto asked.

"Of course."

The sword polisher drew the blade half out of its scabbard and inspected the steel in the lamplight. He gasped and let out a long slow breath. "Exquisite! What a fantastic blade!"

Ken'ishi's ears flushed with pride. "It is called Silver Crane."

"Did you say—? Ah, but it cannot be. It must be another

sword of the same name, but . . . look at the temper line along the cutting edge! It looks like feathers! What technique!"

Ken'ishi could not help smiling.

The sword polisher bowed again, deeper this time. "It is my privilege to polish such a weapon! I will have it finished for you in ten days. Please return then. Until then"—he stepped into his shop with Ken'ishi's weapon and returned with another weapon, a katana, in its scabbard—"please take this sword to carry until you return. It is hardly more than a piece of trash compared to yours, but a warrior should not be weaponless." He bowed and offered the weapon with both hands.

Ken'ishi bowed low and took it. "Thank you for your kindness. I will return in ten days' time." He tried to ignore the headless corpse lying a few paces away as he slipped the loaner katana into his sash.

He turned to go, but the sword polisher stopped him. "Please, wait a moment. Excuse me, but, are you ronin?"

"I have no master."

"When did you last eat?"

"Earlier today," Ken'ishi lied.

The sword polisher nodded. He pointed down the street. "Down that way is a small temple. The chief priest there . . . well, you should speak to him. He might give you a place to stay, for a time, until the sword is finished. Tell him I sent you."

Ken'ishi bowed again. "Thank you, again."

"It is nothing," the sword polisher said.

As Ken'ishi walked away, Akao followed some distance behind him, busily inspecting the corner of every building and small piles of garbage or litter on the dusty street. Ken'ishi thought about Captain Mishima again. He could not remember his father, but he wished that he were like the captain. Strong, confident, honorable, noble, with the skill and conviction to back up his words.

He had spent the next ten days waiting. Polishing a sword was a long and exacting process, just as important as the forging of the weapon. He felt both honored and honor-bound to have Silver Crane polished, therefore he could not have refused the offer. Besides, ronin could rarely afford to have their weapons polished by craftsmen as renowned as Masamoto, unless they were successful criminals.

Akao and he stayed at the temple, and the priest there gave each of them two rice balls every day. Ken'ishi accepted his with great discomfort, and Akao with great enthusiasm. He had done nothing to deserve this kindness, and the way the priest looked at him made him nervous. It would only be a matter of time before something bad happened and he would be turned out. People who were kind to him always turned him out, eventually. One of the few times the priest spoke to him, he said only, "I was a ronin once, until I entered the path of peace. You have a good heart. I can see that." But he did what he could to help the priest without being asked. He swept the walks clean of dust. He picked up fallen leaves and sticks and bits of detritus that drifted in with the wind. And he gave a portion of his rice ball every day to the jovial stone god of the central shrine. The priest told him that the god was Hotei, the Laughing Buddha. Ken'ishi thought the god looked like a kind, jolly old man.

When ten days had passed, he returned to the sword polisher's shop. Masamoto gave him back his sword, bowing deeply and offering it with both hands, an expression of profound solemnity on his face.

The sword polisher said, "It has been my great honor to polish this weapon for you, sir. May I ask, where did you get it?"

"It was my father's weapon."

"Truly? Who was your father?"

Ken'ishi did not answer. He looked away, took a deep breath, then said, "A great man."

Masamoto looked at him for a long time, his searching gaze so intent that a prickle of uneasiness crept up the back of Ken'ishi's neck. The sword polisher said, "Yes, a great man, indeed. Please, young man, hear me now. One such as I well knows that some swords are . . . special. Their smiths, their histories, their lineages, their masters, these things sometimes. . . . Well, I don't know all the secrets of Silver Crane, but I do know this. Wield it well, and it will honor you."

Ken'ishi could only stare at the sword polisher, puzzled, with a hundred questions on the tip of his tongue. But he did not dare to betray his own ignorance. Something in the man's eyes told him there was danger in the secrets he implied. Instead, he bowed and said, "I thank you. You have been good to me." Then he took the sword and hurried away.

Now that his sword was finished, Ken'ishi knew he could not stay with the kindly priest, so he left the temple. He was able to sell a few of his arrows for enough money to feed Akao and himself, but he could not keep that up for long. If he had been in the countryside, he could have fished or hunted or foraged, but here in the city there were no wild roots, no game, and no clean streams. The next day they moved on into the countryside, where he and Akao could find their own food.

Ken'ishi had thought about Captain Mishima often since then, wondering how much like his father he was. Seeing such nobility and quiet strength filled him with an admiration he could not describe. Ken'ishi aspired to become a man like him, one who lived with such integrity and power. Those like Goemon and Takenaga were to be reviled and destroyed. Someday, Ken'ishi would find a master, and he would prove himself worthy to that master with every fiber of his muscles, every drop of his blood, every bit of his strength. He wished his teacher had told him more about his father, so he would have more than his imagination and a few vague impressions.

While he had been lost in his memories, the stars had disappeared behind thick dark clouds, and silence had fallen like a blanket, as if in anticipation. The darkness would be a perfect time for him to move on without danger of being spotted.

Akao seemed to have sensed his wakefulness. "Move now?"

"Yes, let's go now. No one will see us in the dark." He sat up and began to roll up his blanket.

Akao stretched and yawned, then sniffed the air. "Rain."

Ken'ishi nodded. The clouds boded rain today, which would also help conceal them and obliterate their tracks. Those villagers would be less likely to be out searching in bad weather, more likely to be huddling indoors.

The road lay below them, about the distance of a long bowshot, and they threaded their way down through groves of bamboo and trees, then resumed their trek in the early morning darkness.

The day dawned gray and dismal, and the rain came with the daylight. It grew heavier and heavier, and before long, he was soaked, along with everything he carried. Akao looked like a bedraggled, rust-colored rat, with his bony ribs sticking out and water dripping from his drooping ears. Ken'ishi told him as much, the dog responded with an insult that only dogs used.

He had never seen such a rain. It poured out of the sky in bucketfuls, a thick, pelting gray mass that chilled him to the bone. As always, he was hungry too, and that did little to improve his foul mood. The cold mud of the road had almost numbed his feet, squishing between his toes in spite of the platform wooden sandals he was wearing. As he walked, they made sucking, slurping noises when they pulled from the muck. They passed by a lone farmhouse with a warm orange light glowing within, and he felt a pang of envy. The rain beat on his bare head, each drop like a tiny mallet, striking a rhythm that said, *You have no home! You have no roof to shed the rain!*

"Hate rain," Akao said. "Can't smell. Only water and mud."

A voice called out from somewhere nearby. "Hey!"

Ken'ishi stopped and listened. The voice had been faint, coming from off the road.

"Over here!"

He turned and looked. Several dozen paces off the path was a small, roofed shrine. Huddled under the roof, standing next to a stone statue of the shrine's god, was a soaked, disheveled woman. Her mud-spattered clothes clung to her like wet rice paper.

"Jizo will protect us!" she said. "You should get out of the rain!"

Ken'ishi saw no reason not to, so he joined her under the shrine's roof. He had to stoop, and there was hardly enough room for both of them, Akao, and the stone god, but the pattering against his skull had ceased. For that, he was grateful.

Akao slunk in between them, shouldering a space around Ken'ishi's feet. He looked up at the woman, his tongue lolling in a smile. "Thank you," he said, but she did not understand him. She edged away from him.

The shrine god was in the shape of a youthful monk carrying a pilgrim's staff with six metal rings on the end. The air under the low roof was redolent with the scent of incense from the bowl of ashes at the stone god's feet. Beside the bowl was a cup full of sake and a rice cake on a small earthen plate.

He said to the woman, "This god is Jizo?"

She nodded. "Yes." She looked as if she was a few years older than Ken'ishi. Her clothes were so sodden and soiled that he could not judge their quality. Her face had been powdered and her lips rouged, and the rain had caused her makeup to streak and run, giving her a strange, warped appearance. Strings of hair clung to her face and hung in disarray around her shoulders. She clutched her hands in front of her chest, shivering. He had no blanket to give her that was not soaked through.

He said, "My foster father told me about Jizo."

"He is everywhere. He sometimes watches over travelers."

"He helps those who are mired in unhappiness and despair, yes? He told me about other gods too, like Kannon, the Mother of Compassion."

As the rain pounded on the wooden roof, echoing strangely in the small, peaked cavity above his head, Ken'ishi remembered how his foster father had described Buddhas and Bodhisattvas. On a day like today, he began to understand why people called upon the gods and Buddhas for aid. His foster father had made them sound like wonderful, caring beings that helped the weak and the downtrodden. They sounded like the ideal that people should aspire to become. Precious little true kindness had come his way since he had left his foster parents in that little village far to the north. Since they had turned him out.

He said, "You're shivering. I have a blanket, but it is surely soaked through. I've been walking for a while."

She smiled and bowed. "No need to trouble yourself. Thank you for thinking of my welfare. The sun will come out soon enough."

They stood for a while in silence, listening to the slow, rhythmic surge of the rain's intensity.

Then she said, "Are you hungry?"

He looked at her, unsure how to answer. He was ravenous.

"Would you like a rice ball?" She pulled a large one from somewhere inside her clothes.

He looked at it. It was soggy from the rain, but his stomach roared. He could not take food from someone so poor. "No."

"Please, take it. I have two. See?" She pulled out another. "Please."

"Very well. Thank you." He took it, and he tried to resist

devouring it in a single bite, like Akao would. He broke the rice ball in half and handed one part to the dog, who, as expected, devoured it in a single bite. Together they ate their rice balls in silence. She smiled at him.

He said, "Are you traveling somewhere?"

"No. This village is my home."

He looked at her, puzzled. "Then why don't you go to your home? Why are you standing in the rain?"

"My house burned down not long ago. I have nowhere else to go."

"What about your husband?"

"I don't have a husband."

"Then how do you live?"

She looked away, and a look of sadness and shame welled out of her features, like blood from a puncture wound. Her lip began to quiver. She bit her finger, stifling a sob. "You are a boy. Are you so young you cannot see what I am? Otherwise I would think you cruel."

"I didn't want to be cruel!" he protested.

Some of her despair drained away, replaced by a weak smile. "Then perhaps I can tell you, and you will not think poorly of me. I lie down with men for money."

Ken'ishi did not understand, but he nodded sagely. "People do what they must to eat."

Her smile broadened, mixed with a look of relief.

He said, "Perhaps Jizo and Kannon look over you because you do not have a house."

"You are kind to say so. But I fear I am doomed to live a hundred lifetimes as an unclean woman, or worse."

"You are kind to give me your food. Perhaps the kami and the gods will reward you for your kindness."

"Are you a pious man?" she asked.

Ken'ishi blinked, then shrugged. "I don't know what that

means. I know that I trust the kami to guide me, to protect me. If they grow angry with me, they will forsake me. That I do know."

"I can see that you are poor, a ronin. And you have not starved either. I can see that you are not a bandit. You do not have the wolfish look of a bandit, and I have . . . seen many."

"I am glad you don't think I'm a bandit." It was all he could think of to say.

They stood in silence again, waiting for the rain to end. He watched her, as much as he could without being rude, to see how her face remained calm and warm, in spite of her shivering, and on a good day, she might have been pretty. He thought about the kindness and nobility in her manner and bearing. He could only conclude that such virtues could exist in every layer of the world, from the most powerful samurai to the lowliest whore. So strange. But what were those qualities that made them to be admired? He could not put words to them; he just knew he respected them. He knew them when he saw them, but that was all.

Finally, after about an hour, the rain diminished. Then he pulled out his heavy coin purse, and dumped half of the contents into his hand. The woman's eyes bulged with surprise, but he saw not a trace of avarice in them. He stuffed the handful of coins into his own pouch, then wrapped up the rest and held it out to her.

"Please," he said.

She shook her head and cringed away from him. "No, I couldn't."

"Please take it. You will be doing me an honor if you do. I have much to atone for. And you don't have to lie down with me."

She refused again, but when he insisted a third time, she relented and gingerly took the coin purse. She bowed low, thanking him profusely. He bowed in return, and then they went their separate ways. He never saw her again, and he never learned her name.

Leaf alone, fluttering
Alas, leaf alone, fluttering
Floating down the wind

—Anonymous

As he walked, the image of the spreading pool of blood around Takenaga's face crept back into his mind over and over, but he pushed it away. He did not dare to dwell upon it too long. The people who were searching for him knew his name. Every village in the province would be looking for a ronin called "Ken'ishi." He thought about what name he would choose, and many swirled through his thoughts, but he could settle on none.

Akao padded along beside him as they slogged through the mud of the road. He knew the dog was hungry. Akao's attention was repeatedly drawn toward the forest along the sides of the road.

"What is it?" Ken'ishi asked.

"Rain stopped. Rabbits are out now. Look for tender shoots. Going hunting."

"Very well." He knew the dog could find him easily when his hunt was successful.

The sun emerged, warm and strong, and tufts of cloud appeared among the dark crowns of the slender pine trees on the high hilltops above. The sun felt good, warming his flesh, drying his clothes. After another hour of walking, he noticed the puddles on the road dwindling and the soil firming under his feet.

The day had just passed noon when a distant scream snatched his attention. He cursed himself for not hearing the sounds of battle sooner, the clash of blades and cries of alarm. Akao would have warned him of danger long before. Perhaps he was growing too reliant on the dog's sharp senses. He needed to start using his own senses again, as he had been taught.

He ran down the road toward the sounds, holding his quiver steady to keep the arrows from rattling, slowing to a creep just before the source of the sounds came into view. He placed his pack out of sight behind a tree, marking the location in his memory. Then he slung his almost empty quiver onto his waist, pulled his bowstring out of its watertight wooden box, and strung his bow. Alas, he had only three arrows. He had sold most of them for food. No need to throw himself into someone else's fight, but a warrior should be prepared for anything. He slipped into the underbrush and made his way toward the fight, ducking from bush to bush and tree to tree. The ringing of steel and the cries of men grew sharper as he neared.

Kazuko eased back against the wooden wall of the carriage and sighed. The rhythmic movement of the palanquin lulled her. She was comfortable on the thick cushions inside, screened from the unpleasantness of the world by light cloth curtains covering the sides. And she felt fortunate today for the roof on her palanquin. The morning rain had been terrible, and she pitied her bearers having to slog through the mud. But thankfully, the rain had ceased, and the sky was beginning to brighten. The only sounds were the footsteps of her carriage bearers outside, the scuffle and splash of their feet on the road, the creak of the wood in time with the bearers' pace, the rustle of the breeze through the treetops high above, the chatter of the birds echoing in the lofty boughs, and the sound of Hatsumi's soft snoring as she napped on the seat opposite her in the palanquin. The smell of the moist, warm breeze wafting through the palanquin's flap helped to dispel Hatsumi's cloying perfume. As much as Kazuko loved her handmaid, the older woman always wore too much perfume.

Kazuko peered outside through the flap, widening the gap for a better view. The road was hemmed on both sides by towering forest, and the sun shining down through the leaves seemed to give everything a rich, greenish tinge. Spots of sunlight dappled the puddles in the road like scattered golden coins. Through her small gap, she saw one of her samurai bodyguards, walking just ahead of the carriage off to the side. He walked straight and tall, stoic and serious, alert. He was an imposing, handsome figure, and she admired the certainty of his stride, the confidence of his gait, even when he was soaked to the skin. His once proud topknot was now limp and disheveled. She watched him for a while, admiring the smooth movements of his body, the pleasant shape of his face, and his fierce dark eyes. He was so much more of a man than Yuta had been.

Yuta, a servant in the troop barracks, had been her first love, her dangerous little secret. Her father would have been furious if he knew she had let the boy touch her. He was lithe and beautiful, and his kisses had been so tender. She found herself comparing this strong-looking samurai to Yuta, and there was little for comparison. This man was warrior. Yuta was a poet in peasant's clothes. His cleverness had allowed him to slip surreptitious messages to her, in his clumsy, ill-educated, peasant's handwriting, into her father's house. Where Yuta had learned to write, she had no idea. His audacity had shocked her at first, but his sweet words had gained her attention, and then warmed her heart. His words had opened the box of her desires, ones she did not know she had. She found herself daydreaming about trying her secret knowledge with him, trying the schooling she had received about how to pleasure a husband. They had found a way to be together once, hidden in the stable one afternoon, but she was too nervous and frightened about being discovered to offer more than a few wonderfully fervent kisses. Part of her wanted to know the reality of what it was to be with a man, but part of her feared it terribly. Men were such coarse creatures, most of them.

One day, she ceased to hear from him. His messages came no more. She had looked for him around the grounds of her father's estate, but he could not be found. She could hardly inquire after him without raising suspicion. The first few weeks she spent fearing something terrible had happened to him, wondering, wondering, wondering. She tried to ask the servants what had happened to him, but discreetly. All of them claimed to know nothing, but how could that be? Eventually, she had given up, not knowing what else to do. She had missed him terribly for a while, but that had been six months ago. These days, she thought about him wistfully, with a pang of fear that something bad had happened to him, but the pain had passed. If something terrible had happened to him, she would have heard about it. Perhaps his family had been moved to a different part of her father's lands. Perhaps he had left his family to strike off on his own. Perhaps he had fallen in love with another girl, a peasant girl, and ran away to be married.

She found herself studying this samurai again, her bodyguard, and imagined for a moment that she had received some poems of love from him. Now, would not *that* be exciting!

Then Hatsumi's voice returned her attention to the cramped interior of the carriage. "Are we home yet? I must have been napping." Hatsumi yawned widely, exposing her prominent teeth without covering her mouth. Such an impolite gesture would have been unacceptable in public, but here in the confines of their small palanquin and the comfort of their long friendship, Kazuko did not begrudge her.

Kazuko smiled. "Of course we're not home yet. We have several more days of travel."

"Oh, I know that. But this traveling is so dreary and frightfully boring. We just walk and walk and walk and we never get anywhere. At least the rain has stopped, I suppose."

"I think it is exciting! The world is such a big place, and until we went on this journey, I had only ever seen my father's house."

Hatsumi sighed and folded her hands in her lap. "The world is so big that a person could get lost in it." She shuddered. "It's frightening! I miss home. I wish we were there."

"Everything is still too new and interesting for me to miss home. Perhaps if we were on a much longer journey I would begin to miss it. It's just so exciting! Haven't you enjoyed yourself at all?"

"Lord Tsunetomo's garden was quite nice. Very beautiful and quiet."

"And the cherry trees! They were wonderful! Everything was so wonderful! I could have wept for the beauty."

"Wet sleeves are always fashionable for young ladies. It helps to attract husbands, so they say in the court."

"But I'm not a weepy court maiden, Hatsumi," Kazuko said with a wry smile.

"No, you are a princess of bumpkins, and sometimes you think you are a man," Hatsumi said with an innocent expression.

Kazuko gasped and slapped Hatsumi's leg affectionately. "I cannot help if Father's estate is so far from anywhere important. I'm sure you would rather be the servant of some court concubine, someone with a more wealthy family, or higher standing?"

"Only if you were there, Kazuko. You know I could never leave you."

"And I also cannot help that Father had no other children."

"Sometimes *he* thought you were a boy. But one thing is certain. Lord Tsunetomo did not think you were a boy."

Kazuko's mouth fell open, and she feigned ignorance. "What do you mean?"

Hatsumi giggled. "I noticed him looking at you like a hungry tiger."

Kazuko felt herself blushing. "Yes, so did I. I . . . I didn't like it."

"Do you suppose your father is trying to find a husband for you?"

Kazuko shook her head vigorously. "Don't be foolish."

"*You* are the foolish one. You are old enough to be married now. You should start paying attention to such things. Why do you think Madame Hayako has been tutoring you in the ways of being a lady? Before you know it, you will be too old to find a husband, like me."

Kazuko protested, "But you're not too old! You'll find a husband someday!"

Hatsumi sighed wistfully. "I hope so, but I'm sure you'll be married long before me. No man ever notices me when you are nearby."

"I will talk to Father about matching you with one of his men."

Hatsumi smiled. "So you want to be my matchmaker, eh? Very well, you can be my matchmaker."

"Oh, it will be so much fun! And I'll be sure to find you a strong, handsome husband!"

Hatsumi patted Kazuko's hand. "I'm sure you will, Kazuko. And don't forget, he must be rich."

Kazuko giggled and looked back outside through her small opening in the flap at the bushi guarding the palanquin. "I do not know if any of these men are married."

"Captain Mitsubashi is quite handsome."

Kazuko leaned back out of view as the yojimbo she had been watching, a man named Harata, turned to glance at her as if he had heard part of the conversation. Her ears grew hot with a flush. Then she said, "Why do you think Lord Tsunetomo never married?"

"I heard that he was married once, long ago, but his wife died from a fever."

"Oh, that's terrible, but why did he not get married again? He is too old now. He is near retirement age. So unfortunate that a man of his status has no children."

"I do not—" Hatsumi was cut off by a sharp scream of pain from outside. The palanquin lurched. Hatsumi nearly fell out of it as the front corner fell to the ground.

Kazuko heard the shouts of her bodyguards and the other shouts from further away, along with a few vulgar taunts.

The palanquin lurched again and fell to the ground as if all eight bearers had dropped it together.

A chorus of more screams, in front and behind.

Another voice louder than all the others, as deep and penetrating as thunder, boomed in the air, laughing with malicious glee.

She peered out past the flap and saw three of her bodyguards, swords drawn, backing up from someone she could not see, looking upward, fear showing on their usually grim faces.

More of that terrible laughter.

Then the palanquin jumped into the air as if it had been kicked by a giant. Kazuko's head crashed into the ceiling. The palanquin came down on its side, and her breath was driven out of her in a whoosh as she slammed down onto the curtain with the ground beneath. Her vision hazed. Hatsumi moaned in pain. Kazuko closed her eyes and imagined that if she hoped hard enough, she would wake up and find this was all just a horrible dream.

Hatsumi yelped with surprise, then screamed, a scream that quickly receded. Kazuko opened her eyes again and gasped when she saw that Hatsumi was gone, and the side-flap of the carriage now hung open above her. The carriage heaved again, throwing her against the ceiling, and again her head struck a wall of the carriage, casting her into blackness.

When Ken'ishi reached the source of the noises, he saw an overturned palanquin lying in the middle of the road, surrounded by the bleeding corpses of its eight bearers. A brutal melee swirled around the fallen palanquin. Four samurai defended the palanquin against eight bandits. Their faces were grim and hard as they struggled to keep the bandits at bay. All of them bled from numerous small wounds, blood soaking the lips of the neat gashes in the fine, silken folds of their clothes. One of them clutched vainly at a slash in his abdomen; his strength was flagging.

The bandits laughed and taunted them as they fought, but their snarling faces held no true mirth, unshaven, twisted and ugly. Their clothes were rough and ragged, except for a few instances where one of them wore a fine obi or tunic they had doubtless stolen from unfortunate victims like these. Ken'ishi glanced down at his own clothes, and suddenly felt the weight of the coins.

The bandits attacked with swords and spears, one with a

sickle in each hand, and one with a strange weapon that Ken'ishi could only describe as a sword blade attached to the end of a one-ken-long pole. The blade was different from that of a katana or tachi, heavier and with more curvature near the point but straighter along the length.

Ken'ishi would feel no qualms about killing hardened criminals such as these.

A bandit with a katana charged into close quarters with one of the samurai, driving him back a step. The samurai stumbled, and the muscular bandit with the unusual sword-pole lunged into the opening with the long reach of his weapon, slashing with a powerful downward stroke with all the leverage of the pole and body. The curved sheen of steel split the hapless samurai in a diagonal cut from shoulder to hip. In a spray of crimson gore, the cleft body fell to the earth.

A wounded samurai summoned a surge of strength to batter one of the bandits' spears aside, then lunged in and slashed across the bandit's wrist. Half of the bandit's spear fell to the ground with a single hand and wrist still clutching the severed shaft. The bandit reeled back, howling in pain and fear, watching his blood spurting from the stump of his forearm, his scream fading as he passed out.

Another agonized shriek pierced the air, and Ken'ishi's gaze snapped toward the source. A woman's scream. Just off the path, the leaves of a bush shook with rhythmic violence, and a deep cruel laugh followed the scream like the rush of a bull. A scowl hardened Ken'ishi's brow, and he reached for an arrow. He stood to his full height, now only half hidden by the tree. With unhurried speed, he nocked the arrow, raised the bow to point skyward, lowered the point of the arrow and drew with a single motion. He released a heartbeat later, allowing the arrow to find its own way. The arrow hissed as it flew and sank deep between the shoulder blades of one of the bandit swordsmen.

The bandit lurched forward and fell on his face, clutching at the out-of-reach shaft. The remaining six bandits shuffled their position to put the samurai between them and Ken'ishi's position. The samurai followed, staying between the bandits and the carriage.

Ken'ishi nocked another arrow, drew, and fired. A spearman fell to the ground, convulsing around the feathered shaft protruding from his belly just above the groin. As one, the remaining bandits decided that they were finished playing with the three samurai. They rushed forward and impaled two of them on their spears. The one remaining samurai shouted a brave cry and slashed open the ribcage of one of the spearmen with a precise diagonal cut.

One samurai now faced four bandits. Two of the bandits charged Ken'ishi's position, the one with the sickles and the one with the strange sword-pole. He saw them coming for him in a strange slow motion, as if he watched them from the bottomless well of emptiness between instants. With what seemed to Ken'ishi no particular hurry, he readied another arrow and fired, sending the polearm wielder face down in the dust with an arrow through his heart. Then the sickle wielder reached him. The bandit growled and slashed with his wickedly curved blades. Ken'ishi dashed his bow into the man's face and leaped aside. The well of emptiness was gone like a dried-up pool, leaving him scrambling for his life. He dodged around the tree, and the sickle man hacked through the space he had just occupied, one of his weapons lodging in the bark of the tree.

Ken'ishi thrust himself closer before the man could jerk it free and smashed his left elbow into the bandit's teeth. As the bandit reeled backward in pain, Ken'ishi drew his sword and slashed with a single motion. The man gulped, and his eyes bulged as he staggered backward, his hands clawing at the neat slit in his belly that bared his entrails to the sun goddess.

Wasting no time, Ken'ishi spun to see how the last samurai fared. The last two bandits lay on the ground, their limbs jerking to the music of death. The samurai sank to his knees with the blood-smeared point of a spear protruding from his back just below the ribcage. His sword sagged to the earth, and his chin sank to his chest.

Ken'ishi ran toward the dying warrior and knelt before him. The samurai's half-lidded eyes opened, and his chin rose just enough to gaze up into Ken'ishi's face. "You are not one of them."

"No. Never!" Ken'ishi said.

"Then, I beg of you, save the lady. My strength . . . is gone. I fear I . . . cannot. . . ." The warrior's eyes closed. His torso sagged against the shaft of the spear and remained propped in its kneeling position as his final breath escaped.

Deep laughter rumbled like an avalanche out of the bushes beside the road, but no scream followed this time. Ken'ishi crept toward the bushes, but a soft sound from the overturned carriage turned him back around. He grasped the top of the carriage and set it upright. A young woman tumbled through the curtain and sprawled on the ground at his feet.

Her beauty struck him like a bolt from the thunder god. Even the ripening bump on her forehead could not mar the porcelain perfection of her features. A soft moan escaped her lips, and she stirred, like a fallen leaf caressed by the wind. Her eyelids fluttered.

"Are you a fox?" he said in amazement.

Her eyes opened and looked up at him, wide and glimmering. Her voice was breathless and weak. "A fox?"

A deep voice boomed behind him. "What the hell is going on here! Where are all my men?"

Ken'ishi spun, and a gasp escaped him. He stepped backward at the sight of what stood before him and almost stumbled over the young woman's body.

"Who the hell are you?" it roared.

The creature stood head, shoulders, and breast above him, its upper body looming above the roadside thicket. With skin the color of congealed blood, its rippling muscles stood out like ropes on its thick, gnarled limbs, barrel-like chest, and hunched shoulders. Its head had been carved from pure nightmare, glaring down at Ken'ishi with two beady yellow eyes set in deep, close-set sockets. Three yellowish-brown horns crowned its thick, low brow, each the length of a hand. A wild shock of coalblack hair was tied into an unruly caricature of a samurai's topknot. Broad, brutish features and thick, flabby lips twisted into a snarl that bared cracked, yellowed tusks. In one of its three-fingered hands, it gripped a tremendous, studded iron club caked with bits of bloody flesh and hair. It stalked out of the bushes. Standing out straight before the beast, thrusting aside its meager linen loincloth, was its monstrous member, the size of Ken'ishi's forearm.

"Jizo preserve me!" Ken'ishi whispered.

"Who the hell are you!" The creature's voice sent shivers down Ken'ishi's spine and raised the hairs on the nape of his neck, as if thunder itself were given voice.

He glanced toward the sound of a gasp. The young woman cringed away from the creature, backing against the palanquin.

The oni laughed again. "I've saved the sweetest for last, I see!" It leered down at her, its yellow eyes blazing with brutal lust.

"No!" Ken'ishi shouted, stepping between them to face the oni, raising his sword into the high stance. "You won't touch her! I'll kill her before you touch her!"

"It matters not to me whether she is alive or dead. Only that she is warm!" The oni laughed again. The oni reached down toward one of the dead samurai at its feet and wrenched an arm free of its socket, raised the dripping limb to his mouth, tore off a great chunk of raw flesh with its tusks and gulped it down. "Now, I must wash it down. Your blood will do, whelp!"

Ken'ishi clenched his teeth against his rising gorge. "Back to hell with you, demon!" Then he glanced down at the young woman. "Run!" he hissed.

She looked up at him.

"Run!" he shouted at her.

She scrambled to her feet and dashed up the road as quickly as her heavy garments would allow.

The oni watched her go with a look of irritated disappointment. "Now I must catch her again! Damn you, whelp! I'll peel your hide in strips and use your skull for a bowl!"

The creature crossed the distance between them in four great strides and swung its iron club with startling speed. Ken'ishi darted aside, and the iron club splintered the carriage like kindling. A three-toed foot lashed out and plowed into Ken'ishi's belly, sending him flying. Agony exploded in his guts, and stars flashed in his vision, but on the downward half of his arc, he spotted the upturned point of a broken spear in the path of his landing. He managed to twist in midair to extend his hands under him to avoid the spear point by a finger's breadth. He hit the dirt and rolled to his feet, gasping for breath, his belly a blazing ball of hot pain.

"Stupid monkey! I am the demon bandit Hakamadare! I am the Shogun of Robbers! When I was a man, I was the most powerful bandit chieftain in a hundred years! No one could stand against me then! How can you stand against me now that I am a demon?"

Ken'ishi tried to compose himself enough to seek the emptiness. He tried to steady his breathing, but the sight of the creature whipped his heart into a thunderous gallop. The oni was upon him again in two strides, and the tetsubo whooshed downward like a falling boulder. Ken'ishi threw himself backward, and the club thumped into the earth with a spray of wet earth. The impact of the blow pulsed through his hands and feet. The size of the club and length of the creature's arms gave it a great advantage of reach over Ken'ishi and his sword.

The oni swung the club again, this time through the space Ken'ishi's head had occupied the shaved moment before he dropped into a crouch. The oni spouted a torrent of vile curses as Ken'ishi dodged and darted out of reach. Then Ken'ishi noticed a slim, white figure dart behind the creature from the right. He purposefully glanced to the oni's left, away from the location of the approaching figure. The creature paused its attack long enough to follow his glance, and at that moment a shrill battle cry pierced the air. Ken'ishi saw the flash of steel and heard a sound like a blade chopping into wet wood. The oni grunted a puzzled curse, and its right leg collapsed. The slim white shape twirled away.

It was the young woman, wielding the strange sword-pole. The weapon spun in her grasp, and she assumed a stance that placed the blade of her weapon between herself and the creature, point down, razor-edge up, poised for a gutting upward swipe.

"My leg!" the creature roared. "You little bitch! I should have had you first!"

"Can you pierce me with your shaft hacked off?" Her words came out in a scream, shrill and half-crazed by fear and loathing. "Can you chase me with your legs hamstrung?"

"My flesh will heal quickly enough." The creature's sneer bared even more of its crimson-stained yellow teeth. "Come nearer. I want to taste yours!"

She had shed her heavy, quilted outer robes to allow more freedom of movement and now wore only the light silk undergarments. Her beauty was even more breathtaking as she gripped the sword-pole with well-trained ease. Her small breasts heaved against the silk.

Ken'ishi swallowed the lump forming in his throat and returned his attention to the oni. The creature rested on its knee, holding its tetsubo ready. Its head was now level with Ken'ishi's. He glanced at the young woman and began to circle the oni, remaining well out of reach of its weapon. Her fierce dark eyes fixed on him for an instant, and then she followed his example and circled the other direction. Then, almost as if they read each other's thoughts, they attacked as one from opposite directions. As it swatted at Ken'ishi with its club, the young woman's sword-pole, with its longer reach, swept up and sliced deep through the side of the creature's throat. The creature gurgled like a man struck a mortal wound, but Ken'ishi was astonished to see no blood flow from the gash. Instead, a thick black ichor like warm tar welled from a cut that would have been fatal to any human. A moment later, a nauseating stench struck Ken'ishi like a punch in the nose, as if its blood was the essence of death and decay. The oni covered the wound with his free hand to staunch the sluggish flow and swatted at the young woman. She danced back out of harm's way, and Ken'ishi seized his opportunity. He raised Silver Crane high and slashed with all his strength, focusing his spirit, sword, and body into the blow with a sharp battle cry. The oni's head tumbled from its shoulders into the dirt and bobbled away. Ken'ishi lowered his weapon.

A gasp escaped from the young woman. The oni's body did not fall. Its free hand groped for the fallen head. The head snarled and burbled and mouthed, tusks gnashing, yellow eyes bulging. Ken'ishi kicked the head away from the fumbling body. The tetsubo swung at him, missing widely. The young woman stepped behind the body and with a single slash severed the hand gripping the iron club, which fell to the earth with a heavy thump.

"What should we do?" she asked. "It won't die!"

"Burn it!" Ken'ishi said, his face taut with the effort of self-control.

"Use my palanquin for a fire!"

Out of reach of the oni's body, he speared the head with the point of his sword and dragged it about twenty paces from the body. He shook the head off his blade and ran back toward the body. His lips were pulled into a tight line, cinching down his revulsion. He began to hack limbs and portions from the body of the oni, and the monstrous shape thrashed in agony at every stroke, spewing black ichor in all directions.

"Hatsumi!" the young woman cried. "Where is Hatsumi?"

Ken'ishi paused in his gruesome work and pointed toward the underbrush. "I think there is a woman over there in the bushes."

Her large eyes widened to the size of rice bowls, glistening with fresh tears, and she dashed toward the bushes, forcing her way into the foliage.

A wail of grief erupted from the foliage, but he concentrated on the task at hand. Silver Crane's hilt was strangely warm in his grip. Was it tingling? But he dared not stop. Before long, the oni's huge form had been reduced to a quivering, twitching mass of a black-oozing demon-meat and entrails that writhed like a nest of angry eels. Then he turned to the ruined carriage and began breaking and chopping it apart, throwing the pieces of wood, bamboo, and cloth onto the unspeakable mass.

The young woman's voice rose from the foliage. "Please help me!"

With a glance at the demon's remains, Ken'ishi approached the dense bushes. A few paces within, he caught sight through the leaves of the young woman's white undergarments, and he stepped into the narrow area that had been mashed down by the oni's activities. Another woman lay on her back, her face a mask of blood. Her once-beautiful robes were ripped and stained with blood and dirt and grass.

The young woman had torn a large section from her own undergarments and folded it into a bandage that she had placed over the older woman's groin. "She's still alive! Carry her out there!"

Ken'ishi obeyed. He moved beside the other woman, slipped his arms under her and carried her onto the road. A plaintive moan escaped her as he eased her down.

"Will she live?" the young woman asked.

"I don't know," Ken'ishi said. "I didn't see what it did to her."

"She has been raped and defiled. We must find a priest to purify her! If she dies in this polluted state, she will return as a hungry ghost!"

"We've both touched the oni's blood." He looked at the black spatters on his arms, on his clothes. "It's all over us."

"Maybe we can find a priest who could help!"

He raised his hand abruptly and lowered his voice, cocking his head. "Wait here a moment." He stood, listening. He held his breath for several long moments. Then he began to walk down the middle of the road. Then, after perhaps forty paces, he lunged toward the underbrush. A surprised yelp burst from the bushes as his fingers closed around a handful of clothing, and he dragged the wearer into view. A woodsman tumbled onto the road, spilling his load of chopped wood from the rack tied to his back. The woodsman was old and thin, wisps of gray hair flying in all directions as he blubbered for mercy.

"Who are you?" Ken'ishi shouted.

"I am Dangai, from Uchida village! Please, do not hurt me! I meant no harm!" The old woodsman cringed away, protecting his face with his arms.

"Is Uchida village that way?" He thumbed over his shoulder, toward the village he had encountered the previous morning.

"Yes, brave sir."

"How long have you been watching?"

"I saw everything. I hid when I heard the bandits coming!"

"Your presence here is lucky, woodsman. Your wood might help us destroy the demon."

"Yes, brave sir, of course! I will help you!"

"Then let's take your wood up the road." He softened his manner to try to put the terrified woodsman at ease.

"Yes, brave sir!" The woodsman removed the rack on his back, set it upright, and Ken'ishi helped him gather his scattered cords of wood.

With the wood loaded into the rack, Ken'ishi and the woodsman walked back up the road. The young woman had fashioned a makeshift pillow for the older woman's head from scraps of cloth and cushion from the carriage. The older woman's robes were stained with blood, but none of her limbs appeared broken, and she had no outwardly grievous wounds.

The young woman stood and faced him, bowing. "Thank you very much, brave warrior, for saving us. Facing such a creature was most courageous."

He said nothing, merely looking at her. Her phrasing had been so polite and humble that he hardly understood what she said. She straightened, and their eyes met. She was the most beautiful woman he had ever seen, and he could not look away. Finally, she looked at the ground, and her cheeks flushed.

She said, "Umm, did you ask me before if I was a fox? It seemed like a dream."

"I did."

"Why?"

"Foxes sometimes disguise themselves as beautiful women so

they can play tricks on people. Sometimes they lead men to their doom."

"Why would you think I was a fox?"

He looked away and his ears burned. An image of Haru's devious smile flashed in his mind. "I must destroy the demon." He turned his back and took a step toward the demon's remains, then he stopped and looked at her again. His gaze lingered over the portions of petal-soft flesh revealed by her torn clothing, her lips, the curve of her neck, and the dark depths of her sparkling eyes.

Immediately she seemed small and vulnerable, embarrassed over her near-nakedness, and she tried to gather her thin clothing to cover herself.

He turned his back and heard her trotting up the road to retrieve her clothing.

"Dangai," Ken'ishi said, "stack your wood on that pile of meat there. And don't touch the stuff."

"Fear not, sir. I won't touch anything!" The woodsman shrugged his burden onto the ground. "Ah! It's still moving! And bits of it are growing back together!" The old man staggered backward, his eyes bulging, his face twisted into a mask of terror.

Several pieces of flesh had rejoined themselves, gathered together by the groping tentacles of the oni's black, ropy entrails. "Leave your wood and step back." The old man scrambled back, stopping several paces away.

Ken'ishi arranged the wood on the vile mass of black and red flesh, then he searched the area for any scattered bits of demon-flesh and flicked the morsels he found onto the mound with one of the spears.

Before long, Kazuko returned wearing her beautiful quilted robes of heavy silk, looking once again like a proper noble lady. The woodsman prostrated himself before her as she approached, and she thanked him for his help.

Ken'ishi gathered kindling and dry grass from the underbrush and lit it with his flint and steel. Soon the fire was crackling, growing, spreading through the cloth and dry bamboo. His lips drew into a taut line as he watched the fire, and his brow furrowed at the sizzle and pop of burning meat. A terrible stench rose from the fire with a column of oily yellow smoke. The flames changed from yellow-orange to a sickening green. If his stomach had not been empty, Ken'ishi may have lost his gorge at the stench, like death and decay but a thousand times worse, like a maggot-infested barrel of fish left to rot in the sun. The fire blazed with searing heat, and the demon's flesh crackled and blackened, curled and split. He approached the demon's living head. Its eyes blazed with feral yellow fire, spewing hatred at him as its teeth snapped in impotent rage. But Ken'ishi also sensed fear and pain there, too. He impaled it again on one of the broken spears, returned to the fire, and thrust the severed head deep into the flames. Even as the flesh charred and peeled away and the eyes sizzled and burst, the creature glared at him with utter hatred and mouthed breathless curses. The teeth blackened, the lolling black tongue curled into a strip of stiff leather, the blockish jaw clenching tighter with the crisping flesh.

When he was satisfied that the flames were doing their work, he asked the horror-stricken woodsman to cut two saplings, each two ken long and about as thick as his wrist. The woodsman hurried into the forest. Before long, the sound of chopping echoed among the trees. The young woman had wiped away the caked blood from the other's face. A large wad of blood-drenched bandages lay nearby. The injured woman's face was pale where not marred by swelling purple bruises.

The young woman said, "We must find a way to move her.

She is bleeding badly. We must find a healer. Can you carry her?"

"I could, but I know a better way. We must move quickly. This place is unclean. I'm afraid the spirits here have been angered by the oni, and its blood has defiled the earth. Has she awakened yet?"

"Not yet."

"Will she?"

"I don't know! Oh, this is horrible!"

"Who is she?"

"She is my servant, Hatsumi." Her eyes and cheeks glistened with tears, tiny green lights from the unclean fire flickering in the sliding droplets. "Her family has served mine for generations. She has been like my older sister since I was a child. I don't know how I would live without her."

"Let's move away from all this blood."

She nodded. He picked up Hatsumi's limp form and carried her about fifty paces down the road, with the young woman hovering close behind. After arranging Hatsumi on the ground, he retrieved his traveling pack and his bow.

He said, "You're good with that sword-pole."

"It is a naginata," she said. "You do my father a great compliment. He taught me. This one is for the battlefield, larger than what I am accustomed to using. The blade is heavier."

"I've never seen one before."

She looked surprised. "They're most often used in battle."

"I've never seen a battle. And I've never seen a girl who can fight like you."

"My father had no sons, so he taught me how to use the naginata. Where do you come from?"

"Far to the north of here."

"You're a ronin."

He stiffened. "Yes."

"That's an unfortunate thing. Masterless samurai aren't well regarded in this province. There has been much trouble with robbers."

He gestured toward the dead bandits back up the road. "I understand why."

"Having no master must be difficult."

He nodded once.

Her words caused him discomfort. "Forgive my rudeness. I'm certain a warrior as skilled as you can find service with a worthy lord."

He nodded again, once.

Then an idea darted behind her eyes. "In return for your aid, I will speak to my father. Perhaps he will offer you service."

The lump in his throat returned. "I would be in your debt, lady," he said, trying to keep his voice even and controlled.

"But I do not even know your name," she said.

Until this moment, he had been quite happy to dispense with names. "My name is. . . ." A suppressed bolt of panic shot through him. What should he say? Somehow, all of his desire to lie and give himself a new name disappeared when she looked at him. His mind was empty. "My name is Ken'ishi."

"I am Nishimuta no Kazuko. I am pleased to meet you."

Ken'ishi's breath seized up. She was a Nishimuta, the same clan as the constable he had killed. Should he have lied and given a false name? The entire area was doubtless looking for a ronin with his name.

"My father is lord of this province," Kazuko said.

"Your family is powerful."

"Not really. We are a small clan, but some of my father's cousins are close to the Shogunate." She spoke as if it were sometimes a great burden.

The bushes parted, and the woodsman reappeared, dragging two fresh-cut wooden poles. Ken'ishi took them and placed them side-by-side, sitting down beside them. As Kazuko and the woodsman watched him with curiosity, he took his bedroll, a large needle, and a ball of hemp string and began sewing his bedroll lengthwise to one of the poles.

Kazuko said, "You are very resourceful."

"A man learns many things to survive without a roof over his head."

Her lovely eyes widened. "You've never had a home? Is a ronin's life so harsh?"

He smiled grimly and shrugged. "I have survived this long."

"Didn't your parents give you an inheritance?"

"I don't remember my parents. They died when I was very small. My teacher told me my father had been a famous samurai, but would not tell me his name. He said I must make my own name."

"Who raised you?"

"My teacher." He finished with one side of the stretcher he was making and started on the other side.

"He must have been a kind and generous man."

Ken'ishi snorted with amusement. "Not really."

"Did I say something funny?"

He did not answer her. She stiffened. She was not accustomed to being ignored. He concentrated on his task.

Then, as if she could take the silence no longer, she blurted, "How did your parents die?"

"You ask a lot of questions."

"I'm sorry. Does it trouble you to talk about it?"

He said nothing, trying to concentrate on his sewing. An impatient shifting of weight by the woodsman reminded Ken'ishi of his presence. "Dangai, you may return to your village. Please tell the town grave diggers what happened here. These men need a proper funeral or they might come to haunt this road."

"Yes, sir. I'll go now and tell them. I hope they have returned. Yesterday, they went out looking for a ronin bandit."

Kazuko said, "Thank you, sir, for your help. We could not have destroyed the oni without you."

A bit of color returned to the old man's previously pale cheeks, and he smiled, a grin missing several teeth, and bowed deeply. "It has been my pleasure to serve. Good luck to you all." The woodsman again bowed to both of them and hurried up the road as quickly as his spindly old legs would carry him.

Kazuko watched the woodsman totter back up the road, and her gaze could not avoid the sickly green flames and the noxious yellow smoke of the oni's pyre. Her gaze drifted over the human wreckage covering the road, the dark pools of congealing blood soaking the dirt, mixing with the rain puddles. A tremendous heaviness suddenly fell upon her body, and her clothes were made of stones, weighing down her limbs. Tears burned her eyes, cooling as they trickled down her cheeks. She looked down at Hatsumi, lying unconscious in the dirt, wounded and defiled, soaked with blood, and sobs rose in her breast. Less than an hour ago, she could not have imagined that such horror and pain existed in all the world. And now it threatened to drag her down into an unimaginable hell of sadness and despair. "Poor Hatsumi," she whispered. The pressure of the sobs built, threatening to explode. Then she glanced at the ronin sitting on the ground, concentrating on his sewing.

She must not break down in front of this rude stranger. He observed no courtesies, and worst of all, he ignored her! She must be strong! As she spoke, she hoped he did not hear the quavering in her voice. "I must get the swords of my bodyguards. Their families deserve to have them. They fought with honor and courage."

He was hunched over his work, absorbed, but nodded his

head. "As you please."

She turned and walked back up the road toward the scene of the melee. The stench of the oni's pyre was almost overpowering, giving her something else to concentrate on so she could push aside her own weakness. She covered her mouth and nose with her thick sleeve, but even though the stench was screened out, the air felt oily and putrid against her skin. She felt unclean now, and she wanted a bath more than anything. The corpses of her carriage bearers lay sprawled in the dirt, riddled with arrows, twisted and fallen into unnatural positions, their glazed eyes staring into eternity. She looked at their faces, seeing some of them for the first time. So often, her servants were just faceless peasants, part of her life, yet invisible and taken for granted, like the wind. These poor men had not stood a chance in the ambush.

She picked her way among the puddles of blood. Her hands were shaking now, and her knees felt weak. The endless hours of practice and drill with the naginata had not prepared her for a fight against a live, deadly adversary. And she had never imagined she would meet a demon face to face. Was this what some warriors called the thrill of combat, and the naked, empty feeling that remained when the thrill was gone? Using the naginata had felt so natural; she understood now why the grueling hours of practice had been necessary. They had prepared her for the moment when all that practice had been vital, and she had not had to think. She had just acted. Thinking back about the moments of the fight, she marveled at how it had felt so effortless, so instinctive. Every moment was etched in clear detail in her memory, the horror of it, the sickening feeling in her belly, and the final elation at the oni's defeat. She clasped her hands to stop them from shaking, then lifted the hem of her robes to keep them out of the blood.

So much blood! It had gushed and poured from the savaged

bodies. She hesitated to touch the dead flesh for fear of becoming polluted by death. Then she realized that she was already polluted from her fight with the oni. She already needed purification, so she knelt beside the corpse and pried the sword from bloody, clenched fingers. Then she untied the scabbard from his obi, wiped the blade on his clothing, and returned the blade to the scabbard. She repeated this with the other three samurai, except for one whose scabbard had been slashed neatly into two pieces. This blade she wrapped in the soiled remnants of one of the curtains from her palanquin.

By the time she was finished with her grim task, she had gained control of her emotions. She carried the swords to where Ken'ishi still toiled, then went back to retrieve the naginata. The weapon's heft and deadly balance helped bolster her strength and resolve, as if the steel of the blade lent her some of its strength and made her feel less helpless and vulnerable. She wiped the tears from her face.

Then she jumped and nearly dropped the naginata as a bloodcurdling scream seemed to tear a hole in the air itself, echoing among the trees and up the sun-dappled road.

"Young men should discipline themselves rigorously in intention and courage. This will be accomplished only if courage is fixed in one's heart. If one's sword is broken, he will strike with his hands. If his hands are cut off, he will press the enemy down with his shoulders. If his shoulders are cut away, he will bite through ten or fifteen enemy necks with his teeth. Courage is such a thing."

—*Hagakure*

When the morning dawned, Taro awoke wondering why he was doing this. The rain had turned his small fire into sodden coals, and he was alone in the woods. The other villagers, even the other deputies, had returned to the village the previous evening. Why had he left his home to pursue this ronin? With Takenaga's swords nestled beside him in his blanket, the answer was easy. He had long dreamed of somehow being able to leave the village. True, it was the only place he had ever known, but he knew there was a wider world, and he yearned to explore it. In truth, life in Uchida village was frightfully boring and far too much work. That is why he was so happy to be chosen for one of Takenaga's deputies, to relieve himself of some of the relentless boredom and field toil that farmers endured.

But he found that he liked being a deputy. He liked the authority. Even though he was young, he became more powerful than many of the older village men. And pretty young girls admired him for it. He liked the training. The life of a farmer's son had made him strong and fit, but Takenaga's training regimen had made him stronger, more agile, more powerful. With his jitte, he was not afraid to face a man with a sword or spear. Once, he had even been able to disarm Takenaga during practice. Of course, this had angered his master, so he ultimately beat Taro bloody. Takenaga had hidden his frustration at being bested by one of his deputies as a "lesson in being prepared," but Taro was smart. He knew that it was just rage. Takenaga had been a man full of rage his whole life. Because of that rage, he had been placed far from Lord Nishimuta's estate. No one spoke of it, but everyone knew that was the true reason. Before Takenaga, Uchida village had had no constable at all.

When Takenaga was not watching, Taro had often stolen one of the constable's wooden training swords, practiced with it in the woods, out of sight of the village. The weight and balance of a steel katana was different, but he would learn that in time. Until he was more skilled with the katana, his jitte would serve him well.

From the moment he had taken up the swords, he sensed he had embarked on a path to something else, somewhere else. If he captured or killed the ronin, he might be able to become a real warrior. There were many tales of warrior-farmers who showed courage and strength of arms and became famous samurai. Some were said to have even founded their own clans.

And he owed it to his teacher to bring the murderer to justice. Even though Takenaga had been a harsh man, he had made Taro into something stronger, tougher than he had been before. It was Taro's obligation to see him avenged.

Taro had known, before the pursuit even began yesterday morning, that only he would continue. Yohachi was a weak man and had inherited his status as the village headman from his father, who had been a wise and strong leader. Yohachi was neither of those things. He was small-minded and greedy. Even the other deputies had tired of the pursuit when they had not found the ronin quickly. The other villagers had followed Yohachi's lead for a time, but their hearts were not in it. Too many of them secretly despised Takenaga and were happy he was dead. But Taro didn't care. It was enough that *he* cared. He owed his slain master a debt that he intended to repay. And carrying out the repayment of that obligation would serve him well as a stepping-stone to better things.

He resumed his way, hoping to find some evidence of the ronin's passing or some traveler or village who had seen him. He ate a rice ball from his satchel as he walked, chafing at the humid morning air, which made his coarse, hemp clothing smelly and soggy. But in truth, he could not remember feeling more alive. He rubbed the hard steel pommel of the jitte thrust in his sash. Excitement coursed like hot sake through his veins. The ronin could not be far away.

The day grew brighter and warmer and began to dry up the puddles. He met no one else on the road. What would he do when he caught the ronin? First, he did not expect the man to come willingly; he would have to fight him. The ronin had killed Takenaga, so he was a formidable fighter, but few swordsmen had ever faced a man with a jitte. The jitte was not meant for killing, even though it could; it was designed to catch the blade of a sword in its prong so the opponent could be disarmed.

Once the ronin was disarmed, Taro could then use fists, feet, or his weapon's pommel to knock his opponent senseless. He had brought a length of tough hemp rope to tie him up as well. Then he would take the ronin to Lord Nishimuta so that justice could be served.

Lord Nishimuta would be so impressed with Taro's skill that he would take him into service as a warrior. Perhaps he would learn to use the spear or the naginata. It would be a fine thing, indeed.

Then a strange sound caught his ear, from far in the distance, the most bizarre sound he had ever heard. Something akin to a human scream, a woman's, but. . . . It sounded like something from a nightmare. Goosebumps rippled down his arms and legs as he imagined the agony that caused such a scream. The scream echoed strangely under the forest canopy, as if the wind itself quailed at its touch.

Taro gripped his jitte with one hand, the hilt of the katana with the other, and ran toward the sound. He ran and ran, listening for another scream, but hearing nothing. Then he noticed that the air ahead was hazy, smoky, and a strange awful stench hung like the entrails of a corpse between the trees. It *was* smoke in the air, but like no smoke he had ever seen or smelled. It left a disgusting, oily taste in his mouth, and his pace slowed to a cautious trot.

A shape emerged from the yellowish-green haze ahead. An old man, a woodcutter. It was Dangai, from his village, trotting up the road, holding a cloth over his nose and mouth. His eyes were bloodshot and watery from the smoke. The old man was just as surprised to see Taro. And even more surprised to see him wearing two swords.

Taro saw the questions in Dangai's eyes, but he spoke first. "What happened down there?"

The old man rubbed his chin. "Well, there was a fight with

an oni and some bandits, and this young ronin saved Lord Nishimuta's daughter from the oni, and—"

"Ronin?"

"Yes, but—"

"And an oni?"

"Yes, and—"

"And what's this about Lord Nishimuta's daughter?"

"Well, you see this brave ronin saved her from the oni, killed it, you see—"

"Killed an *oni?*"

"Well, yes—"

"Tell me!"

The old man's eyes narrowed, and he took a deep breath. "I'm trying to tell you, you young fool! Just because you're wearing swords today doesn't mean you can speak to me that way, boy! I was selling wood to your parents before you were born!"

"I'm sorry, sir," Taro's face reddened, and he bowed. "Forgive me. Please continue."

"And what are you doing with swords anyway? Where did you get them? Fancy yourself a samurai? Going to become a ronin like *him?*"

"Of course not! Please tell me what happened."

The old man took another deep breath and told his tale. Taro listened impatiently. The old man actually admired the ronin he described. Could it be the same one? Who else could it be?

"Do you know his name?"

"He said his name was Ken'ishi."

Taro's teeth gritted. "This is the same ronin who murdered Takenaga yesterday."

Dangai's eyes bulged. "Murdered! How did that happen?"

"The ronin cut him down in a duel."

"Was it a fair fight?"

"I . . . I didn't see. I was in the fields."

"I would hardly call a duel 'murder.' Are you going after him?"

"Yes."

The old man sized him up for a moment. When he spoke, his voice was grave. "You would do well to go back home, Taro. That ronin is more than a match for you. He is not to be trifled with."

Taro stiffened.

"And he is not a bad man. A young cock, perhaps, but not a bad man. Killing the oni was a good deed."

"But still—"

"And I can see you are a young cock like him. Well, good luck. If you're lucky, he won't kill you. I have to go tell the grave diggers."

Taro's ears burned. "I'll find him, and he will pay for his crime."

Dangai nodded and walked away, shaking his head.

Taro watched him for a moment, angry at the disparagement of his abilities. Then he turned and ran on into the foul, smoky haze. The haze grew thicker, nauseating, choking him, until he could only walk quickly, covering his mouth and nose with a cloth, unable to breathe deeply without coughing and retching. But soon he found its source.

A fire burned in the middle of the road, and bloody bodies were scattered about like broken dolls. His stomach heaved at the overpowering stench, threatening to empty his meager breakfast into the dirt, but he clamped his mouth shut and looked around. The shock of seeing so much death made his knees wobbly as he stepped among the corpses, over dark patches of blood soaking the earth and sprays of what looked like tar.

And where was the ronin? He could not have gone far! Taro

looked ahead, down the road, but saw nothing.

The sizzle and pop of the fire drew his attention. A blackened skull leered at him from within the flames. His eyes watered fiercely from the heat and the smoke, and he covered his mouth and nose with a cloth again.

Then he yelped as pain lanced through his ankle. A sizzling, smoking, pulsing black rope wrapped around his leg like a tentacle, searing his flesh, squeezing with fearsome strength. It had snaked out of the fire, and the other end was still engulfed in flames. Something was biting, chewing into the flesh of his leg. He cried out in revulsion, drew Takenaga's sword, and slashed across the throbbing tentacle, severing it a handbreadth from his ankle. He scrambled away from the fire, with the thing still attached to his skin. Blood trickled along the sides of the tentacle, his blood. With the point of the sword, he tried to pry the thing off without hurting himself further, but after a few moments, he knew he would have to use his hands. Sitting down on the ground well away from the fire, he grasped the severed end and began to unwind it. It gripped him like a squid's tentacle or a snake. The thing came away from his flesh with a trail of slime and blood, but as it began to separate, part of it held onto him like a small sucking mouth. With a further cry of disgust, he ripped it free and held it away from him as it flopped and writhed. Small suppurating mouths lined its length, sur-rounded by multitudes of tiny teeth, stained red with his blood. Cold chills turned his shoulders into soft paste, and he cast it into the fire. Aghast at the terrible spiral wound, he knelt and gripped his leg. The searing pain did not diminish now that the thing was gone. Wisps of smoke still rose from the hot slime. His burned skin had peeled away with the tentacle. Rivulets of blood trickled from the holes where the tiny mouths had been torn away from his flesh.

Then, almost without him noticing, the last of his strength

drained away from his limbs, and the world fell black.

When Taro awoke, the pain had diminished, but his mind was still cloudy. He knew he should clean the ugly wound immediately, so he uncorked his water bottle and tried to wash it as best he could. He could hardly stand to touch it, but he tried to wipe the slime and blood away until the water was gone. When he attempted to stand, he found that he could put some weight on that leg. It was painful, but he would manage.

His mind began to clear, and he surveyed the scene. It was just as Dangai had described. Some blood-soaked bandages lay discarded in the grass by the roadside. Two sets of footprints and two parallel tracks left by the dragging poles. A bit of good fortune? He could follow them anywhere with a trail like that.

He started after them at a fast limp.

"Whether [one's] mind is correct or not is indiscernible by
other people. When any single thought arises, both good
and evil are there."

—*Takuan Soho*

Ken'ishi placed the makeshift stretcher beside Hatsumi and
eased her onto it. Then he tied a loop of twine under her arms
to prevent her from sliding off and fastened the rest of his gear
across the poles. The poles and bedroll creaked as he tested the
weight of the straps on his shoulders.

Suddenly Hatsumi's mouth fell open, and a horrible shriek
erupted. The sound was a barely human scream of rage, terror,
and anguish. Ken'ishi gasped, quickly lowered the straps, and
scrambled away from her. The scream lasted for several
heartbeats, then trailed off to a feeble rattle, and Hatsumi's
head slumped to the side.

Kazuko came running up to him. "What is it?" she gasped. "Is she dead?"

"I don't know. She just. . . ."

"Is she dead?" Kazuko's voice rose with terror. "All the gods and Buddhas, save her life!"

He moved closer on all fours, until he could put his ear close her nose and mouth. "She is still breathing."

Kazuko nearly melted with relief. "Why did she do that?"

"I don't know."

"That was . . . horrible." Her face was ashen, and her eyes were huge and glistening.

He nodded. "It sounded like . . . a ghost. Like something not from this world."

"We must help her. What can we do?"

"Find a priest. Someone who can heal her body and mend her spirit. She is in a terrible way. Worse than I thought."

"Then let's move quickly."

He stood up and pointed down the road. "Your home is this way?"

"Yes."

"You can sling the swords along the sides here so you don't have to carry them."

"Thank you," she said. "They won't make it too heavy?"

Ken'ishi sniffed. "Not at all." But he wondered what he would think around sunset, after he had dragged the stretcher all day long.

She placed the swords on either side of Hatsumi's unconscious body, and he set off down the road at such a swift gait that she had to struggle to keep up.

The feeling of unease from Hatsumi's scream left a pall of silence between them for a long time, and neither of them felt like speaking. A cold hand pressed against the base of his neck, like he had heard the depths of a hundred black hells calling out from Hatsumi's tortured throat.

He wished Akao were here. He hadn't seen the dog in so long, he was growing worried. He knew the dog would find him, if he were still alive. But what if Akao had encountered those same bandits earlier, somewhere else in his ranging? Perhaps Akao was lying dead in the forest, hacked to pieces. The thought made his heart heavy.

He was used to silence, but now he needed to talk. "How far is it?"

Kazuko started. Her face was still pale, and she was wringing her hands.

"How far to your home?" he asked again.

The sound of his voice seemed to calm her. "About four days' journey."

He did not relish the thought of dragging the stretcher behind him for four days. But he was happy that the sound of his voice seemed to help her. "Where were you traveling?"

"We were returning from Lord Tsunetomo's estate. About two days' travel from here."

"That is a long journey with only four bodyguards."

"My father is not a powerful lord. But those were some of his best men."

"They sold their lives dearly to save you. Even the strongest warriors can be overwhelmed by numbers and treachery."

"Father will be unhappy they are dead."

"They died like true warriors. Your father will be happy that you are alive."

"Yes, I am alive." She sighed deeply and looked at Hatsumi. "It could be me lying there, not Hatsumi. If not for you, we would all have died terrible, terrible deaths. I am happy to be alive, but I feel so badly for Hatsumi. How she must be suffering!"

He did not know what to say.

They walked in silence for a long time. Ken'ishi tried to think of things to say that would lighten her mood, but without success. Finally, he said, "Why did you go on this journey? Is Lord Tsunetomo a friend of your father?"

"He is a powerful lord from the Otomo clan. My father wants him for a friend, I suppose."

"What do you mean?"

"I wish I understood it myself."

"What did you see there? A powerful lord must have a great castle."

Her face brightened as recollections danced behind her eyes. "We attended a wonderful flower-viewing party." Her voice grew dreamy and distant.

"A flower-viewing party? I have never heard of such a thing."

Her surprise was evident on her face. "Truly? Everyone goes to see the cherry blossoms this time of year."

"Not everyone, it seems. I have seen the cherry blossoms, though. They are beautiful. But having a party to watch them seems a bit . . . useless."

"Oh, there are many reasons to have a party!" she said. "To be surrounded by nature's beauty makes life worth living."

"Perhaps, but sometimes nature is not so beautiful. I grew up in the mountains. Beauty won't keep you warm in the winter, or fill your belly."

"You have led a difficult life."

"Yes, but it made me strong. Many times, I wished for things like a warmer blanket or a bigger meal, but when I look back now, I know the lack of them has strengthened me. Have you ever passed a day without eating? Or seen anything truly horrible, before today?"

"Well, no," she said. Then she raised her nose and sniffed. "I have been blessed with a fortunate birth, a reward for past lives well spent."

"That is one way of looking at it."

"Tell me, then, O Wise One," she said with a smirk, "what 'horrors' have you seen?"

He thought for a moment. "I have seen how grave diggers live. And leatherworkers. I would rather live alone in a cave." He shuddered at the memory of the relentless stench and how they were reviled by everyone around them. "I have seen innocents slain by callous brutes. I have seen homeless whores, outcast and starving."

Her playfulness vanished, and she looked down. "You have seen a lot."

"I have walked a great distance."

"I have seen practically nothing." Her plump bottom lip protruded just a bit, and suddenly he wanted to know what it tasted like.

"You were raised in a different world from me. You have seen none of this because your family is powerful and rich. You have no need to see such places." His voice was not accusatory, but he sensed her stiffen.

Her voice was cautious. "You are right. You have lived your life, and I have lived mine. But that does not mean we should be unkind to one another."

He nodded and smiled at her. She smiled back.

The sun goddess, Lady Amaterasu, began her descent. As the road wound under Ken'ishi's feet, he contemplated his emotions. He wanted her to like him. She did not seem at all like Haru. His teacher had taught him to be aware of his own emotions, to control them. Master one's self, and the mastery of anything else was already nearly complete. But he did not understand how he was feeling. She was the most beautiful and fantastic creature he had ever seen.

They came to a small, clear stream gurgling across the road. Ken'ishi set the end of the stretcher down and tried to stretch the fatigue out of his shoulders and back. He was still spattered with dried blood and ichor, and his clothes were soaked with sweat. Moist strands of Kazuko's hair were plastered to her porcelain-smooth face. He waded into the shin-deep water and began to rub himself clean, watching the trails of rusty brown dispersing into the clear water. He splashed it over him, and the coolness invigorated him. His hunger flared again like a flash fire, but he had no food. So he took out his crude bowl and filled the snarling cave in his belly with cool, clear water. Kazuko dabbed away the crusted blood from Hatsumi's face, washed the bloody bandage and replaced it.

He filled the bowl with fresh water and offered it to Kazuko. She took the bowl and placed it at Hatsumi's lips, tipping a trickle of water into her mouth.

Hatsumi coughed once and swallowed. Her eyes moved behind the swollen masses of her eyelids. "Is that you, Kazuko?" Her voice was a hoarse croak.

"Yes, I am here."

"Are we dead?"

"No, Hatsumi, we are alive."

"So much pain . . . I thought I must be dead." Tears seeped from between her purpled eyelids, slid toward her ears.

"Here, drink some more water." Kazuko lifted Hatsumi's head and held the bowl to her battered lips. Hatsumi sipped at the water, and Kazuko let her take her time until the bowl was empty.

A mixture of a sigh and moan exhaled from the woman's mouth as Kazuko let her head back down. "Oh, Kazuko, what happened to that . . . thing? Where is it?"

"It is dead, and so are all the bandits. Our guards fought bravely, but all of them were killed."

"Then who is with you? I thought . . . I thought I heard you . . . speaking to someone."

"The brave warrior who helped us. He is escorting us home. His name is Ken'ishi."

"What clan is he?"

"Don't worry about that now."

"Oh, Kazuko, did . . . did the demon . . . when he was finished with me. . . ."

"No, Hatsumi. That was when Ken'ishi arrived."

"Oh, praise the Buddha! Lucky, lucky for you. . . ." Hatsumi's voice held a strange sadness and distress, despite her words, and fresh tears welled.

Kazuko stroked her hair.

"Oh, please do not touch me!" Hatsumi sobbed. "I am unclean."

"The blood of the oni touched us all. More water," she said to Ken'ishi, handing him the bowl without glancing at him.

Ken'ishi dipped from the stream and handed it back to her.

"Here, drink," Kazuko said. "We're safe now. We'll be home in a few days. You must rest and regain your strength."

"It hurts. . . ."

"You're strong. Soon you'll be your old self."

"I'm afraid I . . . will never be . . . the old Hatsumi ever again."

"Hush, now," she whispered. "You must sleep." Then she stood up and turned to Ken'ishi. "Pick her up now. We are moving again." She lifted the hem of her robes and crossed the stream.

"There is something to be learned from a rainstorm. When meeting with a sudden shower, you try not to get wet and run along the road. But doing such things as passing under the eaves of houses, you still get wet. When you are resolved from the beginning, you will not be perplexed, though you still get the same soaking. This understanding extends to everything."

—*Hagakure*

Ken'ishi and Kazuko walked in silence for hours. To Ken'ishi's tortured shoulders, it seemed that the stretcher's weight had increased ten-fold since they began. They met no one on the road throughout the day, which was not unusual during the spring planting season with all of the peasants working in their fields and gardens. The local lords were at peace, so there were no patrols on the road. Kazuko seemed certain of their route, so Ken'ishi followed her direction through several crossroads. They were heading west, and the mountaintops were not so high in that direction.

Ken'ishi wished more and more that she would speak. He enjoyed her voice. But where was Akao? It was unlike him to be gone so long.

He often caught himself looking back over his shoulder, hoping he would see his friend loping toward them, with his red tail high and eyes sparkling with pleasure, perhaps with a rabbit in his mouth.

When she finally spoke, her voice was hesitant. "Do you have anything to eat?"

Ken'ishi smiled inwardly at the irony of her words, but answered with an even voice. "I don't have any food. How far to the next village?"

"I don't think it is far."

"Someone there will certainly offer food to the daughter of a lord. And good food, too, not peasants' millet."

"Perhaps there is a constable there who can help us."

Ken'ishi stiffened and glanced to see if she had noticed his reaction, but her gaze remained demurely downcast.

Hearing her voice again brightened his mood. The weight on his shoulders seemed to diminish.

She glanced at him, and he sensed that she was mulling some questions. "How do you manage living with nothing?"

"There are many people with less. I have my father's sword. I have a good bow. I have a bedroll to sleep on. My teacher is a master of the blade. I fear no man in a fight."

"He must be a famous sword master."

"He is not famous. He prefers to remain unknown. He does not like people."

"A man like you must have had many adventures," she said.

"You might say."

"How old are you? How long since your rite of manhood?"

"My what?"

"Rite of manhood. Have you never undergone any ceremony to take your adult name? 'Ken'ishi' is strange. Did you choose it yourself? Who named you?"

Ken'ishi gave her a puzzled look. "My teacher thought people were full of silly customs. My name is my name. I took this name two years ago. Before that, I had no name at all. And I'm no child. I'm seventeen. How old are you?"

"I am seventeen, too." She smiled at him.

He liked that.

For a while, the only sounds between them were the dragging of the wooden poles and the soft swish of her clothing as she walked. Then she said, "I am sorry I cannot help you carry poor Hatsumi, Ken'ishi. My woman's frailty is a burden."

"You don't look frail carrying that naginata."

She looked at him with a faint smile, and he returned it with one of his own.

"I'm sure the cherry blossoms were beautiful," he said, "but I don't think they could compare to you." As soon as the words left his lips, he clamped his mouth shut, surprised that he had said such a thing. Panic surged through, and his flesh went cold. How would she react? Would she spurn him? Call him a fool?

A delicate pink spread through her flawless cheeks like the emergence of dawn. "Surely you jest."

A lump formed in his throat, preventing him from speaking. He shook his head in denial.

Her blush deepened. "That is kind of you, but it's not true." Her voice brightened with excitement. "Lord Tsunetomo's garden was breathtaking! A large family of ducks lives there in the pond. The drake's feathers were so beautiful. Did you know that mandarin ducks symbolize good marriage?"

He forced down the lump in his throat and his words tumbled out in a rush. "Ducks are wise," he said. "They know that their waddle on land makes us think they're stupid, but it's not so." He waggled his backside, mimicking a duck's gait.

She giggled into her hand. "How do you know what ducks think?"

He clamped his lips tight.

"You know about many things, but little about matters of custom and manners."

He thought about this for a moment, and his ears heated. "I . . . never learned about those things. I learned how to survive and how to fight. After my teacher sent me away, the couple who took care of me tried to teach me things, but I was not a very good student. They knew little of proper etiquette."

"Well, that explains many things. I suppose you cannot be blamed for your upbringing. You must have done something bad in a previous life to warrant such an unfortunate birth."

He stiffened. "Why do you say that? How can a man be punished for something he hasn't done?"

"That is the law of karma," she said. "If you live your life badly, you are reincarnated as a lower person, doomed to suffer, perhaps even to be born as an animal. Everyone knows that." Then she blushed. "Oh! I'm sorry. You haven't been taught the ways of the gods and Buddhas."

"My teacher taught me about the old gods, the spirits of the water and the earth. They were the gods of his people."

"Perhaps I could teach you! I have been tutored in many things!"

He spoke slowly. "Perhaps."

She sighed. "But I know little about the world outside my father's house and the gossip of the court." Then her voice brightened. "That is why traveling to Lord Tsunetomo's estate was so wonderful! I have never seen the countryside like this before. I have never traveled so far from home. My father's estate is beautiful, but being cooped up there for my whole life is so dreary sometimes! Sometimes I just want to fly like a bird and see the world from above!"

"My teacher once told me that seeing the world from high above is a wonderful thing, but it can also be a curse. When you are high, you can see far and wide. The higher you are, the further you can see. Once you get high enough, you cannot see the evils happening on the ground far below. It's a way of staying far above the suffering and plight of the poor, a way of remaining happily ignorant while believing that you can see everything. To see the truths of the world, he said, you should also look through the eyes of a tortoise."

Her voice sounded as if she were trying to decide whether to be offended. "I don't understand."

Ken'ishi smiled with relief. "I don't understand it either. He was a strange bird. He said a lot of things I didn't understand."

She smiled in return. "How did he know what it was like to look at the earth from high above? Could he fly?"

Ken'ishi shrugged. "He said that he could. But I never saw him do it."

Her eyes widened. "Was he a sorcerer? Or a monk? I have heard stories that some monks can make things fly through the power of their faith."

"He was neither of those things."

"How strange. . . ."

Ken'ishi listened to her voice for any hint of disbelief, but there was none. "He was strange, that's for certain."

Sometimes the coarse cloth chafed her and the crooked poles of the stretcher poked her ribs, moving with a jerky, rhythmic motion, the hot sun on her face, her cracked, dry lips, then all other sensations were drowned in a maelstrom of agony swirling around her groin. Fear and pain made her limbs into dead, useless sticks. Terrible images of blood and flesh and terror flashed and tore through her mind. Some of them were dreams; others, she was not sure. The pain throbbed and pulsed like a second heart, subsided to a black, tearing ache, then resurged. Strangely, the pain did not feel like a part of her, separate somehow, something that moved and acted on its own. Like a child in the womb? Her dreams flowed in and out of the real world. Little, clawed demons skittering into her and tearing out her womb piece by piece. Giving birth to a full-grown red-skinned demon that fell upon her like a beast, devouring her instead of suckling her. Drowning in a lake of blood, seeing Kazuko on the shore waving to her, with the ronin standing beside her, horns just visible growing on his forehead. Surrounded by dozens of snarling, laughing bandits, thrusting their spears into her body, their spears turning to flesh as they withdrew, smeared with her blood, calling out to Kazuko for help, but Kazuko changing into a fox and running away. Seeing the oni coming for her, reaching with its huge claws, then being unable to see because her eyes would not work, would not stay open, even though she tried to hold her eyelids open with her fingers. They felt pasted shut. She could not see. She could not run away because her legs would not work. She could not remember her name. She wondered if she had died and she was in one of the many hells now. The oni ravaged her, crushed her down, and she screamed in agony and terror, and she saw Kazuko sitting on the grass talking to a brilliantly plumaged mandarin drake, oblivious to her screams. The stretcher's movement jostled her, and she heard a moan of pain. What was her name? Something was pumping through her body, pulsing, like blood. Sometimes in the dead of the night, she could hear her own heartbeat, and the sensation she felt now compared to that one, but something was different. She could smell her own blood, and it smelled like hot copper. The black pain in her groin was dissipating, pulsing away with each spurt of her thundering heart, but it was still in her body, dispersing, not dissipating, like rats in a darkened room scurrying for hiding places when the door is opened.

She knew that she would not die. She was not in hell. She would live. The wound would heal, but the agony would never die.

Black, desolate moor . . .
I bow before the Buddha
Lighted in thunder

—*Kakei*

Yasutoki dozed in the shaded confines of his palanquin. The late afternoon sun warmed him and made him drowsy. Vague dreams of thundering hordes of barbarian horsemen tearing through fields and towns flitted through his mind. The barbarian hordes plowed through the lines of samurai, casting them aside like chaff. The visions of the dreams shifted to a scene of villagers marching in parade to the clang and rhythm of gongs and drums. The noise of the parade grew louder and louder, until Yasutoki realized that the noise did not come from a dream, and his awareness slid back into wakefulness. The noise was real. He rubbed his eyes and listened. It did indeed sound like a parade, and he could hear the happy chanting as well. Had his entourage encountered some sort of local festival?

He ordered his bearers to stop and called out to his chief

bodyguard. "Captain Yamada! What is going on?"

Captain Yamada, a broad, muscular warrior with a barrel chest and blockish head, approached the palanquin and bowed. "It is a parade, my lord. We have met them at a crossroads. It looks like over a hundred villagers. They are carrying something on a pole. And it looks like they have a prisoner."

"A prisoner? Why would a parade be leading a prisoner?"

The parade was growing nearer, with several villagers carrying gongs and drums, beating them with great enthusiasm. When they drew within a few dozen paces, Captain Yamada walked to the fore of Yasutoki's procession and stood in the middle of the road, fists on his hips.

"Halt!" Yamada called. He would brook no disrespect from peasants. "This is the procession of Otomo no Yasutoki, Chamberlain of Lord Otomo no Tsunetomo! What is going on here?"

The parade halted as well, milling about for a few moments. Yasutoki peered out of the palanquin and observed the procession. At the fore of the parade was a large man wearing the rough clothes of a farmer, carrying a long pole. Atop the pole was a strange object. Yasutoki's eyes narrowed as he studied the object. A skull. But unlike any skull he had ever seen. Twice the size of a human skull, bulbous and misshapen, blackened as if by fire, with huge cracked tusks and three scorched horns protruding from the forehead.

Its shape was somehow familiar to Yasutoki.

He listened as Captain Yamada spoke to the peasant who stepped out of the throng.

The peasant said, "Honored sir, please do not let our celebration detain you. I am Koji, headman of Maebara village."

"Why are you celebrating?" Yamada asked.

Koji pointed up at the skull on top of the pole. "For years, the bandit oni Hakamadare has terrorized this province."

As the sound of the oni's name, Yasutoki started. He knew that name well. He compared the charred, battered skull to his memory of the oni chieftain's dark, rough face. The three horns on the forehead were distinctive. It had been a fearsome creature, but also clever and resourceful, just as the human bandit known as Hakamadare had been so long ago. And it succumbed nicely to the allure of wealth, like most people. Yasutoki had a great deal of hidden wealth, thanks in part these days to the oni's occasional collaboration. Once, he had hired the oni to slaughter a recalcitrant merchant with too many political connections to be killed openly, one who stubbornly resisted Yasutoki's offer of an illicit "partnership." The oni and his gang had simply stormed into the town of Hakozaki during the night, set fire to the merchant's opulent house, and butchered everyone who came out. On another occasion, one of the governor's high-ranked retainers who had grievously insulted Yasutoki at a party disappeared without a trace on a journey to the capital. The oni had been a useful tool on many other occasions. Yasutoki and Hakamadare had forged a mutually beneficial relationship. The oni had provided Yasutoki with a ruthless club to enforce his will on the Hakata underworld, and Yasutoki had provided the oni with all the sake, gold, and tender young flesh he craved. Hakamadare had had his own strange sense of honor, and Yasutoki would miss his services. But how could such a creature have been laid low?

Koji continued, "Now, he is dead, and all of his henchmen with him! Except for this one." He thumbed over his shoulder at the bound, wounded man being dragged along near the rear of the procession. "He survived the battle that slew his master." The man's clothes were caked with dried blood, and his face was a shapeless mass of swollen bruises. His arms were lashed to a log tied across his shoulders, and one of the villagers tugged at the rope tied around the man's neck. A crude, blood-soaked bandage covered the truncated length of his right forearm.

"How was the oni slain?" Yamada asked.

"A woodsman from Uchida village says he saw the whole thing. He says he helped a wandering ronin kill the oni."

"A ronin?" Yamada said. "What was his name?"

"His name is unknown, but he is said to have saved the life of a noble maiden, even though her entire entourage was slaughtered in the attack."

"And wayward noble maidens just wander these woods? Who was she?" Yamada's voice grew more skeptical.

"The woodsman said she was the daughter of Lord Nishimuta no Jiro."

Yasutoki started. How . . . interesting!

This coincidence was not lost on Captain Yamada, either, who paused and glanced back at Yasutoki's palanquin.

The villager continued, "We villagers of Maebara heard what had happened, and we decided to help those from Uchida clean up the mess from the battle. The ronin had burned the oni's body to ashes and took off with the Nishimuta maiden. All that was left was the beast's skull. There is talk that the ronin was carrying the lady's wounded hand-servant, but not all the stories are the same. Even stranger still, the ronin matches the description of a man who murdered the constable of Uchida village the previous day."

"This ronin must be a dangerous man. Has anyone tried to find him? The murder of a constable is death sentence," Yamada said.

"A young deputy from Uchida village is trying to track the ronin down, but no one has seen him." Then the villager's voice grew dark and spiteful. "Five years ago, the oni and his gang came to my village and stole four women and fifty sacks of rice, burned five houses, and killed my brother. People from all over the land should be celebrating the oni's destruction, not hunting the ronin for some other offense! He is a hero!"

Yamada nodded. "Of course. The land has been freed from a great evil. What do you intend to do with the prisoner?"

Koji's voice grew contemptuous and menacing again. "We are taking him to Dazaifu to stand trial. A quick death is too good for the likes of him!"

Yasutoki called from the palanquin. "Captain Yamada."

The stocky samurai approached the palanquin.

Yasutoki kept his voice quiet so that only Yamada could hear. "I wish to speak to the prisoner."

Yamada bowed sharply, then turned back to Koji. "Bring forth the prisoner!"

Koji bowed and obeyed, motioning the other villagers to bring the prisoner forward. The prisoner stumbled and nearly fell as one of his guards jerked savagely on the rope around his neck. He gasped and choked, but kept his feet. He was hauled before Yasutoki's palanquin, and Yasutoki regarded him through a gap in the curtain. Yamada stood close, ready to protect his master.

The prisoner seemed to regain some of his senses and tried to peer into the palanquin's dim interior.

Yasutoki said to the prisoner, "Tell me of this ronin. Cooperating now may ease your death." Yasutoki did not recall this man, but from his wounds, he was all but unrecognizable.

The man licked his swollen lips with a bloody tongue, and his voice came out in a croak. "I did not see him. I fell before he came. When I woke up, the fire was burning and everyone had gone."

"What fire?"

The prisoner tried to peer deeper into the palanquin. "The fire that destroyed my master's body."

"Who was your target?"

"It was the procession of some noble, a Nishimuta."

"Why did you attack?"

"My master heard that the Nishimuta maiden was beautiful and wanted her for himself. We waited near the road in ambush for them to come."

"No one hired your master?" Could the oni have been working for one of Yasutoki's rivals?

"No. . . ." The prisoner stopped speaking and peered again into the shadows of the palanquin. Then recognition dawned in his eyes, and he whispered, "It's you!"

"Yamada! Kill him!" Yasutoki hissed.

Instantly Yamada drew his sword and slashed. The gleaming blade sliced into the log across the prisoner's shoulders, and the prisoner's head tumbled forward onto the road. As the body collapsed like a limp rag, Yamada jerked his blade out of the log.

Koji jumped forward, eyes wide. "What happened? Why did you kill him?"

"He attacked me," Yasutoki said smoothly. "He was a madman, and serving the oni made him evil beyond redemption. Unfortunate that his death was so swift, but it could not be avoided."

Koji stared at the twitching corpse pouring blood into the dirt and the severed head nearby. Yasutoki watched the tumult of emotions cascading through Koji's features. Shock, horror, dismay, disappointment, and perhaps disbelief.

"You could not see clearly what happened. The prisoner went mad and threatened my life," Yasutoki continued, attempting to reinforce his wishes with the astonished villager. "You may report these events to the magistrate in Dazaifu."

Koji swallowed hard and nodded. "I will see to it, honorable lord."

"Very good, Koji." Yasutoki paused for a moment to let the headman know that his name would be remembered. "After my procession has passed, you may continue your celebration."

Koji bowed deeply. "Thank you, my lord. It has been my privilege to speak to you. Thank you for dispatching our prisoner for us."

"It was nothing. Now, out of the way."

"Yes, honorable lord. Right away!" With that, Koji ran back to his place with the other villagers, and they all moved to the side of the road, prostrating themselves.

Yasutoki gestured to Yamada. "Let's get moving."

Yamada bowed. "Yes, my lord."

Leaving the corpse on the road, Yasutoki's procession resumed its travel. What was the fate of the ronin and the Nishimuta maiden? The only Nishimuta maiden likely to be traveling through this area would be little Kazuko. What a strange coincidence! Some strange shift in fortune was at work. But what had happened to her? And what about the ronin? A man who murdered a constable then saved a noble maiden from a horrible fate? Could they be the same person? If Kazuko was harmed, her father's wrath would a spectacle. Yasutoki's impression was that Nishimuta no Jiro worshipped his daughter and she him. When he had first met Lord Nishimuta, he had filed this bit of information away for future reference. He was always looking for such bits, so that he might use them later to twist situations to his advantage.

His thoughts returned to his own loss of advantage. He had been robbed of his most useful henchman. That vexed him. Then he had a flash of inspiration. Perhaps this ronin would make a suitable replacement! Ronin were well known for their flexible morals, and this one sounded like a fierce man indeed. And the murder of a Nishimuta clan samurai sounded like useful material for blackmail, if the man proved stubborn. He must be found, and quickly. Yasutoki must know more about him, another thing he must see to when he reached Dazaifu this evening. And he knew where to begin looking. The ronin might arrive at Lord Nishimuta's estate at any time, if his intentions were truly to see the girl to safety, and that was the perfect opportunity. Yasutoki was going there himself in a few days. If the ronin meant to spirit her away for himself, however, then Yasutoki would have to cast a wider net.

What a strange day.

Beautiful lady
Buffeted by rude spring winds . . .
What sweet storm you make

—Kito

Around mid-afternoon, the sun was too warm, and Kazuko was sweating inside layers of embroidered silk robes. Her light silk undergarments clung to her skin. She wished she could just remove her heavy outer robes, but that would not be proper. Ken'ishi had already seen too much of her, and the thought of how his gaze had been fixed on her, how his eyes had blazed so fiercely, moving up and down, filled her with embarrassment. Removing her heavy robes had been necessary at the time; she couldn't move freely while wearing them. Hatsumi would not approve if she knew how much of Kazuko's body Ken'ishi had seen. Kazuko guessed she must have looked like a simple peasant trollop, clad in only her undergarments. Hatsumi often corrected her when she skirted the edges of decorum and etiquette. Sometimes it was a game, with Kazuko trying to see what Hatsumi would let her get away with. Kazuko sometimes enjoyed throwing Hatsumi into a state by acting improper, but it was only a game. She would never do anything purposely to hurt Hatsumi's feelings.

She remembered how she had felt with the naginata in her hand, facing the oni, all but naked. She had felt . . . free. And alive. She remembered the thundering of her heart, the balanced weight of the naginata, and the determination to do whatever she could to live. Although she would never admit it to anyone, she had felt free from the restrictions of class and society, free of the weight of too many clothes and responsibilities and obligations. All those trappings of life had seemed so meaningless when her torturous death was standing over her with a tetsubo in its huge hand. She wondered if that was what it felt like to be a man, like Ken'ishi. Society placed so much emphasis on the willingness to die, especially samurai. This willingness to die was expected of samurai women as well. Before now, she had never truly considered what dying meant. Her spirit would go on and be reborn, she knew, but to die. . . . Was she a bad person, because she had wanted so badly to live?

She could sense that Ken'ishi wanted to be a part of society. He wanted to belong somewhere. She, on the other hand, wanted freedom. The wild, rebellious notion that she should leave home and become a ronin crossed her mind. She could become a famous warrior woman, giving strength to women everywhere, saving them from cruel husbands. It would be so exciting! But leaving home would hurt her father, who had no children but her, and her mother had died giving birth when Kazuko was ten years old. The infant, another daughter, was born weak and sickly and had died within a month. Kazuko sometimes wondered what her sister would have been like if she had survived. She missed her mother sometimes too, but she knew that her mother would have opposed her father in giving Kazuko any kind of martial training. Her mother would have wanted Kazuko to be a proper young woman, but not long after her mother's death, her father began teaching her the naginata. She was proud of how well she had learned. The fight with the oni had shown her that the endless, grueling hours of training had not been in vain.

She looked at Ken'ishi as he dragged Hatsumi's stretcher, his brow furrowed, placing one foot in front of the other with complete determination, the sheen of sweat on his arms and face, a single, crystalline droplet hanging from his chin, swelling until it let go, falling into the dust. Such a handsome face. A bit scruffy and unwashed perhaps, but handsome. He would make a fine lover, she thought devilishly. She imagined an affair with him, like the court ladies in the capital with their surreptitious lovers. She wondered if he could write love poetry, like her Yuta, like the famous courtiers in the capital who wooed with such eloquent abandon.

Then her gaze wandered down to Hatsumi's head lolling to the side with the rhythm of Ken'ishi's gait. A stab of pity went through Kazuko like an arrow, and her vision misted over with fresh tears. She dabbed at her eyes with her sleeve.

Then Hatsumi moved her head, not a weak, helpless bobbing, but more like someone rousing from a nightmare. Her purpled eyelids fluttered, trying to open. Her mouth opened and released a dry croak.

"Ken'ishi!" Kazuko said. "Please stop for a moment."

He stopped and looked over his shoulder at her quizzically.

"She's trying to speak."

Ken'ishi eased the stretcher poles down and stretched his shoulders and back.

Kazuko knelt beside Hatsumi. "Hatsumi! It's Kazuko. What

is it? Are you thirsty?"

Hatsumi's dry, swollen tongue touched her cracked, wounded lips. A whisper came out that Kazuko could not hear, so she leaned closer.

Hatsumi's voice was weak and hoarse. "So thirsty. Water."

"Ken'ishi, please give me your water bottle." He handed his gourd to her, and she held it to Hatsumi's lips, allowing a trickle to flow into her mouth.

Hatsumi gulped and swallowed and the relief on her face was plain. "More."

"Good, Hatsumi. You're going to be fine."

"Thank you." Hatsumi's voice was still hoarse but much improved. Then she reached up with a quivering hand and pulled Kazuko nearer. She whispered, "I'm very sorry, but I must make water. The pain is so terrible, but I fear I will wet my clothes. Can you help me?"

Kazuko felt the irony of Hatsumi's words. Her previously beautiful robes were caked with dried blood and covered with dust from the road. But she smiled and squeezed Hatsumi's hand. "Of course I will help you!" She untied the loop of twine that kept Hatsumi from sliding off the stretcher, eased the other woman's arm around her neck, and lifted her onto her feet.

A hoarse, whimpering moan escaped Hatsumi, and her face twisted with agony.

Kazuko nearly faltered and wept at Hatsumi's pain, but she took a deep breath and held firm. She took a slow, small step, and Hatsumi followed. Tears poured down her swollen cheeks. "You are strong, Hatsumi! You will be fine!"

Helping Hatsumi toward the bushes at the edge of the path seemed to take an eternity. All the while, she was conscious of Ken'ishi's eyes on her, his indecision between whether he should offer his assistance or remain apart from matters of such female privacy. Kazuko was glad he did not try to help. She could manage by herself, and in spite of Hatsumi's dire state, Kazuko still felt the pressure of ingrained propriety.

Out of sight of the road, Kazuko helped Hatsumi lift the skirts of her robes and steadied her. Again Hatsumi whimpered. "Oh, Jizo help me, it hurts! It burns!"

Fresh tears sprang forth in Kazuko's eyes, and she squeezed Hatsumi tighter. When Hatsumi was finished, Kazuko moved her back toward the road, but she shuddered when she noticed that the wet grass was sprinkled with large, dark blood clots. The relief on Hatsumi's face was plain, however, and that bolstered Kazuko's strength.

Hatsumi's voice was clearer but still weak. "Kazuko, is it really you? I have had so many nightmares. Am I dreaming? I can't wake up from them. . . . So horrible. . . ."

"No, it's me. Be strong! You must be strong!"

"So much blood!" Her voice quavered with mixed sobs. "So much pain! I can't stand it!" Then her voice began to rise in pitch with the sound of delirium. "I must be in hell! And you're not my dear Kazuko! You're a demon! Oh, demon, take me for good . . . I cannot stand it any longer. . . ." Her voice trailed off, and she sagged in Kazuko's grip.

Ken'ishi stood with his back turned, pretending to look at the trees.

"Ken'ishi, help me!" Kazuko gasped. Hatsumi was falling. In an instant, he was beside her, lifting Hatsumi's dead weight by the other shoulder.

Hatsumi's head lolled, and she screamed at the sky. "Don't touch me, demon!" She struggled as they lowered her back onto the stretcher, then she sank again into limpness.

As Hatsumi lay motionless between them, Kazuko and Ken'ishi looked at each other and their eyes locked. Suddenly she felt as if her heart would burst. Sobs exploded out of her, uncontrollable and violent as a spring flood. She did not know how long she knelt in the middle of the road with her face buried in her sleeves, but when the tears had exhausted themselves, her sleeves were dark with wetness. She glanced with embarrassment at Ken'ishi. He sat quietly, gaze respectfully downcast, hands placed on his thighs.

"I'm sorry," she said, trying to smile at him through her tears. "I must apologize for my weakness. I am too much trouble."

"Don't be foolish," he said.

"We should go."

As they continued on, Kazuko was annoyed with herself for breaking down. Ken'ishi must be annoyed with her as well. Most men were either annoyed or embarrassed when a woman showed emotion.

Then she heard something behind them and looked back. Standing on the road about twenty paces away was a rust-colored dog, with large pointed ears and a bushy tail tipped with a dark spot like a fox's tail. The dog watched them quizzically, warily, its brown eyes sparkling with cleverness.

Ken'ishi looked over his shoulder, and a wide grin split his face. He called back, "I thought you were lost!"

The dog padded closer, his nose in the air. His eyes flicked from Ken'ishi to Hatsumi to Kazuko and back again. A strange growling sound came from the dog's throat. Kazuko stepped back and gripped the naginata in both hands.

"Put up your weapon! Don't threaten him!" Ken'ishi snapped.

She realized that she had brandished the point of her naginata so she snapped it back upward.

"I'm sorry. Is this dog yours?" she said. Dogs had never been part of her life. She had seen them, but they were things that lived around peasant neighborhoods or were kept for blood sport by a few samurai lords. The raw intelligence in this animal's eyes made her uneasy, as if the dog were sizing her up.

It was only a few paces away now, moving toward Hatsumi. Its movements grew stiffer, and its shoulders hunched as it slunk closer to the ground, tail down, ears flattening. It growled again.

Then she jumped in surprise as similar sounds came from beside her. From Ken'ishi. She stared and her mouth fell open.

He glanced at her and said, "He is my friend." There was something quiet and powerful in his voice.

The dog and the man exchanged terse growling sounds as the dog padded closer to Hatsumi, nose extended, sniffing. The closer the dog moved to her, the more stiffly the reddish hackles on its neck rose.

Akao said, "Evil here. Terrible stench. Hurts my nose."

Ken'ishi said, "The oni attacked her. We killed it. Did you see?"

"Smelled the blood and came. Followed." The dog sniffed her clothes gingerly and drew back, snorting and spitting. *"Evil!"*

"We are trying to find a priest to be purified."

The dog glanced at him skeptically. "Bad spirit here. Dirty."

"Bad spirit?" Ken'ishi looked at his friend. Sometimes Akao's words were so terse that understanding him was difficult, and Akao rarely bothered to elaborate.

Akao moved stepped toward Kazuko, sniffing her legs. "Afraid."

"You are so frightening," Ken'ishi said with a wry smile.

The dog sniffed in derision. "Fierce! Rabbits fear!"

Ken'ishi smiled.

"Good smell, this one. Good spirit." He raised his nose higher. "Fertile. Receptive."

Akao eased closer to her and rubbed the top of his head against her robes.

Ken'ishi said, "You are shameless."

The dog stopped his nuzzling and looked at Ken'ishi. "Man breeds anytime. Dogs do not. Who is shameless?" Then he returned to his demand for attention.

Ken'ishi laughed. Sometimes he forgot how clever Akao was. He watched Kazuko as the dog nuzzled her leg. "He wants you to touch him," he told her.

"Really?"

He enjoyed the mix of wonder and trepidation on her face. Then she reached down and stroked the dog's ear. Akao nuzzled her harder.

"He's so soft!" She grinned.

"He calls himself Akao."

"You did not name him yourself?"

"No, he told me his name when we met."

She looked at Ken'ishi quizzically. "What do you mean? You're playing with me."

Ken'ishi said nothing.

Akao looked up at her and wagged his tail. He barked once, tongue lolling from his smile.

"Let's go," Ken'ishi said. Hatsumi grew heavier by the moment.

The drake and his wife
Paddling among green tufts of grass
Are playing house

—Issa

Late in the afternoon, they rounded a bend in the path, and the outlying houses of a village came into view. Ken'ishi stopped. The villagers would be looking for him.

Kazuko noticed his hesitation. "What is it?"

He said nothing. He might be recognized. Would Kazuko's status protect him? If she heard what he had done, would she be willing to protect him? Should he lie and say that it was not him?

Then he realized that his decision had already been made. He would protect Kazuko and Hatsumi with his life, a decision made the moment he decided to throw himself into battle on their behalf. He was their bodyguard and would remain so until they were safe at home. The actions of any villagers were irrelevant. He would deny nothing.

The village was larger than Uchida, and the appearance of Lord Nishimuta no Jiro's daughter raised a great commotion, with commoners coming out to prostrate themselves around them. His fears seemed to be unwarranted, because they paid only cursory attention to him.

Kazuko was gracious and courteous to the villagers. The village had no healer, but the priest had some skill. He could perform the rites of purification they required after their exposure to the blood of the oni and the bandits. The village headman offered them his entire house for their stay. He said his house and its rooms were the finest in the village, and he could not bear to have them stay anywhere else. The priest, however, said that they must stay with him to conduct the healing and purification rites. Ken'ishi noted that this seemed to annoy the headman. The jealousy in the headman's manner was obvious as the priest led them all back to his house.

The village constable was absent, having gone to Dazaifu on some business. The headman also offered them four other villagers to carry the stretcher the rest of the way to the lord's manor, but apologized that there was no carriage to save Kazuko the toil of the walk. She thanked the headman for his offer of stretcher-bearers, and Ken'ishi was grateful when she accepted. His back and shoulders ached from dragging the stretcher for so long.

With the villagers carrying Hatsumi's stretcher, they went to the priest's house near the local shrine. In their polluted state, they were careful to walk around the torii arch, not through it, to avoid offending the kami.

The priest's house was modest but well kept, with an outbuilding where he performed rites and ceremonies. Both buildings were nestled within a humble garden. The dwarfed bushes were manicured and arranged, and every stone on the footpath seemed to have its own place. The priest was a middle-aged man with a round, jovial face and kind, gentle eyes. Akao allowed him to pet his head. He called into the house to his wife, ordering her to heat water for tea, and to prepare a special bath. Meanwhile, he showed them into the special building. Akao lay down outside the door and rested his head on his front paws. Placards filled with writing covered the walls of the structure, and the air inside was thick with incense and smoke. Ken'ishi asked the priest what was written on the placards.

The priest answered, "Some of them are prayers to the gods to give strength and peace to those within these walls. Some of them are wards to keep out evil." Ken'ishi noted that the priest had a strange gait, with slow, almost languid movements. "Sit," he said, "please sit."

The villagers set down Hatsumi's stretcher. She moaned pitifully.

"Before we can begin the rites," the priest said, "you must be cleansed physically. After that, I will see that your spirits are cleansed. My wife will tell us when the special bath is ready."

At that moment, a woman opened the door and stepped inside, bowing, and carrying a tray laden with a steaming pot and three teacups. She looked at Hatsumi's bloodied clothes and battered body with a look of profound pity, but she said nothing. Setting the tray down beside her husband, she departed.

On one wall was a cabinet with numerous small drawers. The priest opened several of the drawers and picked out pinches of the contents, dropping them in a small stone bowl.

The priest said, "I am honored to have the daughter of Lord Nishimuta as a guest. I regret that the circumstances of your visit are not more favorable."

Kazuko bowed. "We are pleased that you are able to help us, gentle priest. You do us a great service. We fear for the sanctity of our spirits."

The priest said, "It must have been a terrible experience. Please tell me what happened." As he spoke, he took a wooden pestle and ground the contents in the bottom of the bowl. From where Ken'ishi sat, he could smell the strange pungency of the priest's concoction.

Kazuko told him the story, and he listened intently. After he finished grinding the ingredients in his bowl, he divided the fine powder into the teacups, then filled them with steaming hot water.

When Kazuko finished her story, the priest nodded sagely and rubbed his hand over his bald head. "Demons are terrible things. They bring great evil to the world. And you say his name was Hakamadare? I have heard old stories of the great bandit chieftain named Hakamadare, and I have heard stories of this oni bandit chieftain. In recent months, he has become infamous in these parts. But I had no idea they were the same person. They say Hakamadare died over a hundred years ago."

The priest handed each of them a cup of the greenish brown tea. Ken'ishi took a tentative sip. The tea was bitter and earthy tasting. He must have grimaced, because the priest said, "You must drink it all. It is an important part of your purification. It will help bring the yin and yang back into harmony."

Kazuko said, "We obey your wishes, gentle priest."

"How did Hakamadare become an oni?" Ken'ishi asked.

The priest rubbed his cheek. "They say that some people, evil people, turn into demons when they die. Sometimes the depth of their evil is such that they become demons even while still living."

"So all demons were once people?"

"No, sometimes demons simply are. Sometimes they simply exist like the wind and the earth. Perhaps some are simply evil spirits. It's hard to say for sure. You say you killed it, eh?"

Ken'ishi nodded. "Yes."

"Remarkable. I would have thought that only the gods could kill an oni. Remarkable, indeed."

"It was a vile creature," Ken'ishi said. "It's dead now."

"Not entirely. Some of its evil remains. It remains in you." He pointed at Ken'ishi, then at Kazuko. "And you, my dear." Then he gestured toward Hatsumi. "And especially her. All of you must be cleansed."

Kazuko sobbed and covered her face with her hands.

The priest continued, "All is not lost, however. Even demons can be redeemed, so there is no reason I cannot help all of you."

She wiped the tears from her cheeks. "Truly?"

The priest nodded. "There is a story about an ascetic monk, walking along a mountain trail. He met a terrible oni. It was taller than a house with flaming red hair and dark purple skin, and it had a long skinny neck and skinny legs. When the oni saw the monk, it began to weep. The monk asked the oni what was wrong, and the oni sobbed even louder.

"The oni answered him, 'I was a man once. Long, long ago. Three hundred years ago, I think. I had a terrible grudge against someone. These days, I do not even remember anymore who it was I hated. I woke up one morning, and I was like this. I was so consumed with hate that I murdered him and his sons, then his grandsons, then his great-grandsons, then his great-great-grandsons. There is no one left for me to kill anymore. If I knew where they had been reborn, I would kill them all over again. My rage and hatred still consume me, but my enemy's descendants are all gone! I have nothing left to vent my rage against! If only I had never felt this way! Oh, horrible! I might have been reborn someday, but hate has left me only this suffering. If you have a grudge against someone, it is like a grudge against yourself. I only wish I had known!'

"Flames leaped from the top of its head, and the tears poured like filthy rivers from its eyes. Then it fled up into the mountains. The monk felt so sorry for it, he prayed to the gods that the creature would suffer less. Even evil can feel regret and deserve compassion. Some say the oni eventually was allowed to die and be reborn into a normal life."

The priest smiled. "So, all is not lost for you."

At that moment, a bell rang outside the building.

The priest smiled wider. "Your bath is ready. Let us waste no more time."

The priest's wife ushered each of them, in turn, into the special bath at the rear of the house. Kazuko went first, being the person of the highest station. Night had since fallen. Inside the closed room, lit by the soft glow of a lantern, she shed her soiled clothing. She breathed deeply of the warm, steamy air. It was redolent with the smells of the healing, cleansing herbs that had been placed in the water. The priest's wife took all of her clothing and left her with a clean saffron robe to wear. Her clothing would be cleaned and purified, and she could have it back in the morning.

As she knelt naked on the slatted wooden floor, she washed her long, dark hair, scrubbed herself clean of road dust, and even found a few spots of blood that she had not noticed before. Her head ached from the bump on her forehead. The priest's bitter tea had settled in her stomach and seemed to churn there like a growing whirlpool and put down the hunger that had gnawed at her all day long.

Properly washed, she lowered herself into the large, wooden bathtub. It was large enough for her to stretch her legs and not touch the other side. The deliciously warm water came up to her neck, its heat seeping into her, and the strange scent of the herbs filling her nostrils. The headache diminished, and serenity suffused her limbs. She closed her eyes and tilted her head back, feeling as if she could simply float away.

As she basked in the steaming bath, thoughts of Ken'ishi drifted into her awareness like boats on a slow-moving river. The raw ferocity in his eyes did something to her, made her heart beat faster, but at the same time, he had been so kind to her. And to Hatsumi as well. His exterior was rough, but he had a good spirit. Strange how a man's hara, his center, could be both kind and fierce at the same time.

Then other images crept into her memory, like foxes in the darkness, and those images erupted into blood and death. She pushed them aside again. She could not count how many times her mind had revisited the horrible morning. Pushing them aside was easier now that she was clean and relaxed. Other thoughts came unbidden into her mind. What Ken'ishi had said about flying too high, how the noble class could not see the plight of the poor, carried the ring of truth. Until her experiences on this journey, she had never seen how peasants lived, and it was jarring. So many things she took for granted, like food and clothes and servants to obey her wishes. She had never gone hungry, not once, until today, and it disturbed her in ways she did not understand. She tried to imagine what Ken'ishi's life had been like, when hunger was the rule, rather than the exception, when privation was a daily burden.

"My lady?" came a cautious voice. The priest's wife.

"Yes?" Kazuko answered abruptly, tumbling out of her reverie.

"I just wanted to make certain you were well."

"Yes, thank you!"

"Very well, my lady."

Kazuko realized that she had lost track of how long she had been there and suddenly felt selfish that she had taken so long. Hatsumi must be cleansed too. And Ken'ishi.

She was out of the bath quickly and went outside to help the priest's wife with Hatsumi. Hatsumi allowed them to take her into the bathroom and to scrub and bathe her. Kazuko noted with great relief the bleeding had stopped. She had heard tales of women dying after childbirth with bleeding from the womb that could not be stopped, and she hated to think of that happening to Hatsumi. The priest's wife had to help Kazuko place Hatsumi in the bath. Hatsumi could not climb in by herself. Nevertheless, Kazuko noted with satisfaction that she appeared to relish the scented bath.

Hatsumi sighed, submerged up to her neck. Kazuko sat on the floor in her soft saffron robe that smelled faintly of herbs and incense. Hatsumi's eyes were nearly swollen shut, and her face was a mass of purple bruises. She almost looked like an oni herself now. Then Kazuko noticed that her hands, resting folded in her lap, were shaking. She gripped them tighter.

Before long, they took Hatsumi out of the bath, and Ken'ishi took his turn. The priest and his wife helped Hatsumi back to the outbuilding where he would perform the proper rites, and Kazuko followed them. She noticed a few well-chewed chicken bones lying next to Akao, who dozed fitfully. They waited in silence for Ken'ishi to finish, and the priest puttered around his room gathering sticks of incense, and chanting under his breath.

Hatsumi faded in and out of consciousness. She seemed aware but remained silent. The priest made a different batch of tea for Hatsumi, but it made her cough and retch.

Finally, Ken'ishi rejoined them from the bath, and Kazuko thought he seemed more handsome than ever, vigorous and vibrant. He wore a saffron robe much like hers, and his hair was clean and combed. He smelled as fresh and clean as a spring breeze, and the smell of the herbal bath clung to him pleasantly. He caught her looking at him, their eyes met, and her heart skipped a beat.

For the next several hours, the priest prayed and chanted over them and burned incense. He had Kazuko place fresh bandages, dipped in a mysterious poultice, over Hatsumi's groin. They sat quietly while he performed the rituals of purification.

Ken'ishi's mind wandered. Again and again, he found himself looking at Kazuko. The soft glow of the fire pit and the lanterns sparkled in her dark eyes. A few strands of coal-black hair fell across the glow on her flawless cheeks. She smelled like a field of wildflowers after a spring rain. He found himself imagining the touch of her small hands, the touch of her petal-soft lips. Her gaze caught his, and he was certain that she could read his thoughts, then she looked away, surprised at first, with a delicate flush in her cheeks. Then she kept glancing at him to see if he was still watching. When she found that he was, the flush deepened.

The priest remained oblivious to these silent exchanges, lost in his meditative chants and prayers. When he pronounced the rituals complete, it was nearly midnight. Ken'ishi's shoulders ached and his body was weary. His eyelids were heavy. The priest ushered all of them into the house and gave them a packet of herbal tea, instructing them to give doses of it to Hatsumi to strengthen her and ward off any vestiges of the oni's evil. Their clothes all hung drying on racks inside the house, near the fire.

They made ready for bed in the main room of the house. The priest's wife arranged futons for the women in near the fire brazier and one for Ken'ishi in a small, cold adjoining room. Ken'ishi noticed Hatsumi squinting toward him, trying to study him with her limited eyesight.

He listened to the frogs chirping in the darkness outside. The chill night air prompted the priest's wife to close the doors and windows before she went to join her husband in their room. The walls of the house only slightly muffled the music of the frogs, and the night breeze whispered in the rafters above.

Ken'ishi reached into his pack and withdrew his bamboo flute. Kazuko gave him a puzzled expression that gave way to surprise when he raised the flute to his lips and began to blow. The notes took form under his fingers, and the music rose into the air like the wings of a nightingale. After a few moments he stopped.

"That was lovely," Kazuko said. "Didn't you think so, Hatsumi?"

Hatsumi grunted.

Kazuko said, "Did you learn the flute from your teacher as well?"

Ken'ishi shook his head. "I taught myself. My teacher thought it was foolish, but I like the sounds."

"You are a strange man." Her face held a peculiar expression, one he could not identify.

"We all wear many faces, don't we? Even when we are alone."

"Do you know any songs?"

He shook his head. "I know a few, but mostly I just play, and the music comes out. It sometimes helps prepare me for sleep."

"It sounded like . . . like birdsong."

"I suppose it must. That's the song I know best."

"Why is that?"

He raised the flute to his lips again and played another long melody. He could sense the heat rising in her face, her cheeks flushing from more than the heat of the fire.

When he finished, she asked, "Who raised you?"

"My teacher."

She waited a few moments for him to continue, and when he did not, she prompted him. "What happened to him?"

"He set me free. He said it was time for me to join other people. He said I had learned all I needed from him."

"What happened to him? Would you tell me about him?"

"You ask a lot of questions."

"I'm sorry."

Ken'ishi smiled. "Ask me again tomorrow. I am too tired tonight, and the story is long."

She nodded. "Then would you play more? What songs do you know?"

"I learned a song when I was in the capital. I think it is called 'Cherry Blossom Moon.' "

Her eyes glittered. "Oh, could you play it?"

He nodded, then raised the flute again and began to play. This time the notes were thick and smooth and melancholy, filled with bittersweet longing. As he played, Kazuko arranged Hatsumi on her futon. All the while, her eyes were upon him, and the feelings this evoked took form in the music, altering the cadence and accents of the notes of the song. As he played, his mind drifted elsewhere, and the music flowed from the wellspring of his soul. He did not see her settle herself onto her futon, but even in his half-aware state, he felt her gaze fixed on him for a long time. When the song ended, he became aware of his surroundings again, and she was asleep.

He picked up his pack and equipment and turned to carry it into an adjoining room. Hatsumi peered at him with her single, open eye. The swelling and bruises on her face masked her expression.

Ken'ishi felt a pang of sympathy. She looked as if she must be in agony. He put his things down and knelt beside her. Not wishing to wake Kazuko, he spoke quietly, "Hatsumi, is there anything you need?"

Her open eye glared at him for a long moment, then she rolled painfully onto her side, turning her back to him.

Ken'ishi was taken aback. After an uncomfortable moment of silence, he stood up, gathered his belongings again, and retired to his room. As he prepared himself for sleep, he could not dispel from his mind the look in Hatsumi's gaze. The more he thought about it, the more he believed it looked like hatred.

"When one has made a decision to kill a person, even if it will be very difficult to succeed by advancing straight ahead, it will not to do to think about going at it in a long roundabout way. One's heart may slacken, he may miss his chance, and by and large, there will be no success. The Way of the Samurai is one of immediacy, and it is best to dash in headlong."

—*Hagakure*

Yasutoki crept up the shadowy path. The shadow of Ono Fortress threw the footpath into almost complete blackness. His bamboo basket hat concealed his identity but restricted his vision, making his travel up the rocky footpath more difficult. The fortress squatted liked a behemoth on the summit of Mount Ono, just north of the city of Dazaifu. Through the straight trunks of the bamboo along the path, the patchwork sparkle of the ancient city gleamed down the slope of the mountain to the south. The city had been founded six hundred years ago. For centuries, it had been one of the richest, most powerful cities in the land, a center of trade, learning, and government, fattened and buzzing with trade from lands across the sea. The ports of Hakata Bay, the cities of Hakata and Hakozaki to the north, funneled most of the trade through Dazaifu. To defend against possible attack from foreign lands, the massive fortress on Mount Ono had been built. A huge central keep, thick stone walls over seven ken tall, and a tremendous stone embankment that circled the entire construction, a distance of several ri. The silhouette of this magnificent fortress stood like a terraced black monolith on the mountaintop high against the starlit sky. The moon behind the huge structure made the whitewash on the upper tiers glow with a silvery light.

But in the darkness, the antiquity of the fortress was invisible. Like the rest of the city of Dazaifu, it had fallen into decline and disrepair. Its former glory and influence had fallen victim to the trudging centuries and the winds of political change. The rise of the Minamoto clan and the formation of the Bakufu, the Shogun's military government, had led to the decline of Dazaifu's importance both militarily and politically. After the Mongols had risen to power in China, trade had diminished. In the daylight, the fortress's cracked plaster and crumbling corners were readily visible. For Yasutoki, this was a symbol of Dazaifu's decline, and the result of how the Minamoto clan and the Hojo regents had betrayed their homeland. These days, this island was considered little more than a troublesome backwater, a land favored by ronin and samurai lords who wished to carve out a domain for themselves far away from the intrigues and pageantry of the capital, and far from the iron fist of the Shogunate. There were some advantages in *that*, however, Yasutoki supposed.

The governor here was still ostensibly in charge of the defense of southwestern regions of the country, but all of his power had been usurped by the Shogunate. In only a few short decades, even the Minamoto clan had fallen prey to the power-hungry, corrupt Hojo clan, who were now the true rulers. More than anything, Yasutoki wanted to see the fall of the Shogunate. His ancestors, the Taira clan, had been loyal servants to the Emperor, the divine ruler, the Son of Heaven, but the Taira clan had been cast down by the ambitious, ruthless samurai general, Minamoto no Yoritomo, a man who had killed his own brother to consolidate his power. Just over a hundred years ago, one of Yasutoki's ancestors, Taira no Kiyomori, had been given control of Dazaifu. Thirty years later, the Taira clan had been destroyed by Yoritomo, and the power of the Emperor was crippled, replaced by a new tyranny founded on lakes of blood. But scattered, splintered remnants of the Taira clan survived, and into one of those hidden, forgotten pockets Yasutoki had been born, and he had been raised to hate the Bakufu. Much like the man he was waiting to meet here on this dark, secluded path.

He paced back and forth on the path, rubbing his arms to dispel the night chill. The moon had come up not long ago, and in the dim light, he could see both directions down the path, in case anyone approached. The monks of Kanzeonji Temple chanted far down the mountainside below.

He thought about the mysterious ronin again. Earlier this evening, before sneaking out of his house, he had dispatched two of his spies to find the man. With luck, they might discover something by the time Yasutoki reached Lord Nishimuta's estate. He must see about recruiting this man as quickly as possible. The plans he had set in motion might require him to use a hired sword in the near future. It was always best to have contingency plans, and plans within plans. His network of spies and informants was extensive, and many years in the making.

139

He had people in Dazaifu, Hakata, Hakozaki, and Imazu, not to mention a few in Kyoto and even the Shogun's headquarters in Kamakura, who kept him apprised of events in the great seats of power. Of course, it would be troublesome if the ronin ran off with the beautiful young maiden, Kazuko. That would make him much harder to find. And Yasutoki already had plans for her.

Where was Kage? His irritation grew with each passing moment, increasing the chance that he would be discovered loitering in the darkness by some passerby. The path's seclusion reduced that chance, but. . . .

"No need for such nervousness, 'Green Tiger,' " purred a voice from the darkness within a couple of paces of him.

Yasutoki started, and his heartbeat leaped into a gallop. He clutched his chest and tried to control his breath. "Kage, I presume."

The leaves of the underbrush rustled faintly, and a black silhouette slid onto the path. The silhouette was clad in clothing so black that the edges seemed blurred and indistinct. A chill run up Yasutoki's spine. The figure's appearance seemed more like the flow of liquid shadow than the movements of a man. He wondered if this man had magic at his disposal that might enhance his abilities, then rubbed his eyes and tried to blink the shadows into solidification.

The man's voice was quiet and controlled, just loud enough for Yasutoki to hear. "I was pleased to hear from you, cousin."

"So you agree to my request then?"

"For a man who makes his way through politics, you have little patience."

"My apologies, Kage. It is simply that these are matters of importance and could not wait. Besides, you are late."

"On the contrary, I have been waiting here since before nightfall. But I could not show myself to you before now. A group of nuns was meditating at the shrine near one of the branching paths down the slope. I waited for them to leave, but then a drunken samurai came up the path to take a piss. Now, there is no one who might overhear our conversation."

Yasutoki nodded. "You have great skill. Do you have great loyalty as well?"

"Loyalty to whom? You? I think not. The Taira clan? The Taira clan is dead. My loyalty lies with me."

"But do we not share a . . . distaste for the same people?"

"Yes, but that does not mean I will put my own life in mortal danger without good reason."

"The destruction of the Bakufu is not reason enough?"

"Not quite. I require other payment as well."

Yasutoki scowled. He had hoped this man would help him on the strength of their ancestral bonds and a mutual hatred of the government. His voice was cold as ice. "How much?"

"We shall see. Before I agree to do as you ask, there are some things I must know."

Yasutoki sighed and tried to sound conciliatory. "If the answers to your questions are within my power to provide, I will."

"What do you ask me to do exactly?"

"I want you to provide me with information about all the lords on this island. I want to know how many samurai they keep as retainers, and I want to know their prowess. I want to know how many peasants or other troops they can levy. I want to know their general state of readiness. If their lands were attacked tomorrow, how well could they respond and how quickly."

"That is powerful information. And valuable. Who is it for?"

"That is none of your concern!" Yasutoki snapped.

"Then my price just doubled," the man said calmly. "How will you send me payment?"

141

"Through family channels. How will you accomplish your mission?"

"Through whatever means necessary. I will have expenses. They must first be determined." Yasutoki heard the smirk in the man's voice. "This is valuable information. Others might wish to pay for it."

Yasutoki hissed. He lunged at the shadowy figure and in an instant had encircled the man's neck with his arm. Yasutoki held him now with a needle glinting in the starlight, poised for the thrust into the man's right eye. His voice turned dark and deadly. "Enough banter! Listen to me, Kage. I have had enough of your vagaries. If you work for me, you work *only* for me! Do you understand? Betray me, and you will die."

Words fought their way through the man's clenched throat. "It is unfortunate that you resort to violence against a kinsman."

Before Yasutoki realized what was happening, a vise-like grip twisted his arm away from Kage's throat. The man writhed out of his grasp and buried a hammer-like foot in Yasutoki's belly, doubling him over.

The man's voice was cold and thick with menace, like an angry serpent with its fangs exposed. "You forget that we were taught the ways of secrecy and combat in the same training hall. And you have not kept up your training. You have been soft for too long. Nevertheless, your offer intrigues me, so I will not kill you. I will send word of my price before the new moon. If it is acceptable, then I will commence."

Yasutoki stood up, gasping, holding his burning belly, and took a deep painful breath. He adjusted the chinstrap and straightened his basket hat, which had been knocked askew in the scuffle. "Very well. You may have bested me here in the dark, but you would not be wise to underestimate my power if you betray me."

"As you say," said the shadow. Then it seemed to flow away down the path, until it merged with other shadows under the leaves and disappeared.

Yasutoki stifled the anger that had overwhelmed his self-control. His plans were too extensive to be betrayed by one of his own people. He could not allow such a thing. Perhaps he should hire a spy to watch his spy. In the meantime, the evening was growing colder. The warmth of his room at one of his lord's houses in Dazaifu sounded good now. He had a long trek still ahead of him. He trusted his personal servants to "forget" that he had been gone most of the evening, but pushing his luck was best avoided.

He made his way down the path, going over his plans for the immediate future. Tomorrow he would continue his journey to the estate of Lord Nishimuta no Jiro. He had a message from his lord to convey to Lord Nishimuta. Lord Nishimuta would be pleased to hear confirmation of the budding alliance between the Nishimuta and the house of Yasutoki's lord. Both estates were minor, but the two greater clans were powerful, and an alliance between them would strengthen both. Yasutoki toyed with the idea of sowing the seeds of destruction before the alliance was even complete, but he decided against it. Increasing the power of his lord would increase his own power, even though his ultimate goal was the destruction of all samurai lords loyal to the Shogunate.

The footpath before him was black and difficult. This made it the perfect choice for his illicit meeting, but it was difficult to traverse in the dark of night. More than once his slippered feet skidded on loose dirt, but he kept his balance. That is, until both his feet slid into a soft, heavy lump lying across the path. He suppressed a cry of surprise as he tumbled face-first over the obstruction onto the stony path beyond. Anger flared again, and he tasted dirt in his mouth. He rolled to his feet, casting his senses in all directions for evidence of anyone who may have perceived him. He heard only the songs of night creatures. At his feet was a dark, motionless mass, a human body. The head and feet lay obscured by the grass on either side of the narrow path so that he could not tell which end was which. After another quick check for witnesses, he knelt beside the body and peered as closely as he could in the darkness.

A pale, bearded face, with a samurai's hairstyle, stared with dead eyes at the starry night. Yasutoki could smell the sake. The man's mouth hung open, and Yasutoki looked closer to discover the cause of death. Was his throat cut? No. Had he been strangled? No, his throat appeared to be unharmed. No stab wounds on his body and no bludgeoning injuries on his skull. Wait. A shiny black trail of blood seeped from one ear, congealing like black jelly in the ridges of his ear, trickling toward the back of his skull. But his skull was not cracked.

Yasutoki grunted in appreciation of the assassin's skill. Surprising a samurai and delivering a needle thrust through the ear and into the brain required incredible skill. His new retainer was indeed worthy. He just had to make sure he could be controlled.

But Yasutoki had to get away from here as soon as possible. When this body was found, a citywide investigation would commence right away. He might not be allowed to leave Dazaifu. Or worse, he could have been seen leaving the house tonight, and he would then have to answer too many troublesome questions. His position and high rank would help him shed any substantive accusations, but his lord would not look favorably upon him if he were late reaching Lord Nishimuta's estate. He could not afford that.

Why had the assassin left the body here in plain sight? Such sloppiness was inexcusable, unless he had meant the body to be found. He had meant for Yasutoki to find the body, as a warning. He had known that Yasutoki would find and examine the body and make the proper deductions about the assassin's proficiency. He had also correctly predicted Yasutoki's initial reaction, to get away quickly, and even the secondary reaction, to stop and better conceal the body. A faint smile stretched Yasutoki's reptilian lips. With a wiry physical strength he usually kept hidden, he stepped over the body, lifted it by the hands, fighting against the growing stiffness in the limbs, and dragged it off the path into the blackness. He concealed the body under a bush as best he could, then returned to the path. Now, the body might not be found for perhaps a day, maybe two, giving him plenty of time to get away.

Now the swinging bridge
Is quieted with creepers . . .
Like our tendrilled life

—Basho

Ken'ishi sat beside a broad, placid lake. The far side of the lake was swathed in the red-orange conflagration of a sunset or perhaps a sunrise; he could not remember which it was. Flocks of birds filled the air like wind-driven clouds, adjusting their paths as if they were single entities. Behind him was the mountain where he had been raised. He did not need to see it to know it was there. It weighed down upon his shoulders like a past life, always following him wherever he went. He looked onto the flawless surface of the lake and saw its reflection.

146

Strangely, the lake did not give him his own reflection.

Ripples on the water drifted across his field of vision, distorting the image of the mountain. The ripples were formed from the wake of an oshidori, a mandarin duck, swimming calmly across the water. It was a brilliantly colored drake. With iridescent purple, green, white, and chestnut plumage and the feathered crest on the back of its arched neck in full array, it was a beautiful creature. Ken'ishi watched its course for a time. The drake seemed to be looking for something, and it grew more and more urgent, its bill turning this way and that way.

Heavy footsteps walked up beside him. He looked up over his shoulder and saw that it was the oni bandit chieftain, Hakamadare. He thought it curious that he felt so calm. Cradled in its huge, misshapen hands, the oni held another duck, a female. The oni sat beside Ken'ishi and placed the duck on the ground, releasing it. The duck waddled toward the lake. The drake saw her and began to paddle for shore. The two birds met at the water's edge. The drake shook the water from his fine, beautiful clothes, and the modestly garbed female stepped up to him and bowed. Her colors were plain, muted browns and grays, less ostentatious than the brightly colored drake, but the drake did not care. He preened himself with his bill, then laid his head against her delicately arched neck.

The oni's voice was rough, but unhurried, unthreatening, almost playful. "Go now, little ducks, before I eat you."

The ducks waddled together into the lake and began to paddle away.

Ken'ishi called after them, "Congratulations on your marriage, Oshidori!" His teacher had taught him that mandarin ducks formed long, loyal marriages. Even among humans, mandarin ducks symbolized fidelity and happy marriage.

He looked at the oni, and Hatsumi was there instead. Hatsumi looked out over the water with a blank expression on her face. "It's too bad they're gone now," she said. "I was hungry."

Ken'ishi watched the ducks move farther away until they were all but out of sight. The glow of the sunset had deepened to a blood red, reflecting off the surface of the water.

Hatsumi stood and walked down to the water's edge, knelt, and dipped her hands in the water. Ken'ishi could only see her back as she cupped her hands and raised the water to her lips, drinking deeply. She drank several handfuls, before she turned around. The lower half of her face was a mask of bright crimson blood, and she held out her blood-soaked hands to him entreatingly.

The entire lake had turned into a sea of frothy scarlet gore, and Hatsumi smiled at him, baring her bloody teeth.

Ken'ishi jerked awake. The horrid image faded into a view of the darkened ceiling of the priest's house. He sat up, the back of his neck cold with sweat, his robe damp. The dim, gray light filtering into the room through the slatted window told him that it was early morning. What a strange, terrible dream! He did not like the queasy fear lingering in his gut, so he stood and grabbed his sword. He would go outside and practice, hoping the physical exertion would help dispel these unwelcome emotions.

Stepping to the door to the main room, he reached out to slide it open. Suddenly a pale arm, tipped with blood-smeared black claws, tore through the rice-paper door. The claws snatched him by the chest, burying themselves in his flesh, and clenched. He gasped at the sudden agony. He was driven backward as his attacker tore through the door. Hatsumi's face, contorted into a clay mask of rage and hatred, eyes shot through with blood, with no whites, her yellowed teeth protruding like boar's tusks through blood-smeared lips. She snarled and laughed as her claws cut into his ribs. With incredible strength, she wrenched her talons back and ripped open his chest. His flesh tore apart as his ribs snapped and a hot deluge gushed down his belly.

He fell backward, every smallest part of strength draining like blood out of him. She loomed over him and laughed again. His head sagged back against the floor, and his vision began to blur.

Ken'ishi spasmed awake, gasping for breath. His heart beat against his ribs like a mill hammer. He clutched his chest, feeling the agony of the dream already fading away. For a long time, he sat hunched over on his futon, regaining control over his breath, his heartbeat slowing. Finally, with a shaky hand, he grabbed his sword. He needed the practice now more than before.

He stood up and stepped up to the door, almost expecting that horrible arm to seize him again. But nothing happened. Breathing a small sigh of relief, he slid the door open. Kazuko and Hatsumi both lay on their futons, fast asleep. He crept past them and went outside.

Hatsumi tossed and turned all night long. The priest's horrid concoction had left a terrible taste in her mouth. Mixed with the constant taste of blood, it left her feeling queasy. The pain in her nether region had diminished, but somehow she did not believe it was because of anything the priest had done. She only faintly remembered the terrible dreams of the day before, and she felt a perpetual unease, as if there were eyes on her, watching, boring into her soul. The day before felt like a deep, black fog of pain, and she felt as if she saw snatches of events through the shifting veil. Tonight, however, she was conscious, and she knew where she was.

She thought about how the ronin had played his flute. She had not known the tune he played, and the discordant squawking had grated on her already over-taxed nerves. She had been so relieved when he finally put the silly thing away. That such an uneducated peasant would presume to play an instrument irked her. Then she thought about his kindness toward her, his concern for her welfare, and she grew angry again. She did not need or want his concern! Should she not feel more grateful toward him for saving their lives? Why did she not? Perhaps because she would rather be dead than remember the horror of what had happened to her? Death would mean freedom from the pain. And she would not have to watch that unwashed ruffian pawing at Kazuko with his eyes! It was obvious what he wanted. But he had done nothing objectionable, yet, nothing that dozens of other men had not done ever since Kazuko had reached the flower of her womanhood. Those other men had not angered Hatsumi because they were men of proper station; they could do as they wished.

That was why Hatsumi had Kazuko's little plaything, Yuta, removed from the castle. Kazuko foolishly thought their little affair was a secret. Quite the contrary, as Hatsumi and most of the servants knew about the boy's secret love notes. He was a pretty boy, with good heart, but he was nevertheless only a servant. Hatsumi had him sent away and ordered the servants never to tell Kazuko what happened to him, on pain of the same fate. She allowed Kazuko to keep her little fantasies because they made her happy, and Hatsumi loved to see the way Kazuko's face glowed when she was happy. But they had been dangerously close to becoming intimate, and that Hatsumi could not allow. No man could be allowed to touch her except her husband. If Kazuko was not a virgin when she was married, her husband, whoever that might be, might consider himself slighted. And the ramifications of that could be tremendous. And now here was another man, again beneath Kazuko's station, with designs upon her chastity!

As she grew angrier at the ronin, she could more easily forget the kindness he had shown her and better remember the way he ogled Kazuko. Then she thought about how Kazuko behaved in his presence. She spoke to him as an equal! And worse, the girl was developing feelings for him. And he used none of the honorifics that were proper for addressing someone of higher station.

At some point during her ruminations, Hatsumi slid unnoticed into sleep. Before she realized it happened, she was again surrounded by tortured images, black fires and bloody lakes, suffering and weeping, ripping, tearing, gushing, suffocating, dying, healing, awakening, sliding back into darkness and despair. Throughout the night, the endless cycle of restless sleep, nightmares, violent wakefulness, and burning tears plagued her. She awoke once with her cheap saffron robe soaked with sweat. She pulled the blankets tighter around her. It was difficult to see with one eye still swollen nearly shut. The glow of the coals had faded to a dull orange. A voice cried out in the next room. The ronin, stirring in the deep silence, fighting against something in his slumber. Perhaps he had his own nightmares. As well he should! The gods should punish someone who tried to rise above their station.

But then, why was she being punished with nightmares? She had done nothing wrong! Maybe she should have fought harder against the oni. Perhaps she should have killed herself rather than be raped. But she had had no chance for that. Why had the oni chosen her instead of Kazuko? Why had Kazuko been spared this horror, but not Hatsumi? Why must Hatsumi be the one to suffer? And that foul little girl had the audacity to have feelings for that ruffian while loyal Hatsumi lay battered and beaten!

No.

Hatsumi took a deep breath, trying to clear her head. Such

feelings were wrong. They were evil. Hatsumi loved Kazuko with all her spirit. She could not imagine her life without the young woman. The oni chose Hatsumi first purely by chance. If the palanquin had fallen to the other side, if Kazuko had been sitting on the other side, if the ronin had arrived only a few moments sooner. . . . If . . . if . . . if. . . . And hating the ronin was wrong, too. Hate was one of the world's greatest evils, and it harmed one's soul. If she felt too much hate, she would be reborn in a lower station as punishment.

Why did she feel such hatred? She had never hated anyone before. She was a kind, patient person. It was strange. But then, she had endured a terrible experience, one that no one should have to live through, and she survived. She would survive.

Then the door of the ronin's room slid open, and she quickly closed her eyes. His soft footsteps passed within arm's reach, moving toward the door. A draft of cool air caressed her swollen face as the front door opened and closed. As she sank back into sleep, her dreams were less terrible, and she was grateful for the blessed numbness.

Ken'ishi went to the edge of the village, where he practiced his customary sword drills. He went through all of them twice. Then he sliced buds from the low-hanging branches of an old camphor tree. The morning was cool and moist, with patches of fog hanging low over the irrigation ditches. When he had worked up a good sweat, he thanked the tree for the use of its branches, wiped his blade clean, and returned to the priest's house, where he found Kazuko preparing to continue their journey.

He was surprised to see Hatsumi up and moving around. She moved gingerly, her back hunched over with pain and caution against any sudden moves. The bruises on her face had darkened, but the swelling around her eyes had diminished just enough for her to see. Kazuko was trying to be the mother hen, but the other woman would have none of it.

Ken'ishi watched their activity for a while, until Kazuko noticed him. "Ah! Ken'ishi, good morning." She bowed.

He returned her gesture. "Good morning, Kazuko, Hatsumi."

Hatsumi's bow was curt and did not distract her from folding up the futon she had slept on.

Ken'ishi tried to ignore the slight, but he could not forget the look in her eyes the night before. Nevertheless, the sight of Kazuko with her hair freshly arranged and her face powdered enchanted him. He took a deep breath of the crisp morning air, and said, "A beautiful day for travel, eh?"

"Yes. The bearers will be here shortly. The headman has given us food and water for our journey." She gestured toward a bundle of large pouches tied together in a clump and a string of stoppered flasks made of gourds.

The villagers were already about their own business. Some farmers were already hard at work carrying buckets of the village's waste out onto the empty rice fields, and others toiled with shovels and rakes to work the fertilizer into the soil. Later in the year, as summer approached, the fields would be flooded and the seedlings planted.

Within an hour, they resumed their journey. Ken'ishi walked some distance in front. Having Kazuko near was too distracting for him to remain properly vigilant. His ki, his spirit, was scattered. They were still vulnerable to another pack of determined bandits, and he had no wish to take chances. Unfortunately, Kazuko would be the only other reliable person in a fight. She carried the naginata like a walking stick, and he admired her ease with it. Four villagers carried Hatsumi on Ken'ishi's makeshift stretcher. When one of the bearers stumbled or missed a step, she would groan and admonish them to be careful. Kazuko walked beside the stretcher.

As they walked, Ken'ishi kept looking over his shoulder, his eyes searching for a familiar rusty-brown shape that was not there. Akao's absence continued to worry him, but he trusted his friend's cunning and resourcefulness. Ken'ishi told himself that perhaps his friend had discovered a bitch in heat and was courting her.

After they stopped to rest and eat near a stream, Kazuko came to walk beside him.

She said, "It's tomorrow. Will you tell me about your teacher?"

He hesitated.

"If you do not wish to. . . ."

"No, I'll tell you. But. . . . You'll think I'm deranged. Or a liar."

"I would not think those things of you. I trust you."

Warmth spread in his belly, and his heart skipped a beat. "I haven't seen him in almost two years. He saved me from a burning house when I was three. My parents had been killed. My father was a clan samurai who became a ronin. He retired from the warrior's life to marry my mother and work a small plot of land in the north."

"Did your teacher know your father?"

"Only by reputation. You see, my teacher spent no time among . . . people. He's not like us."

"What kind of man is he?"

"He's not a man at all." He watched her reaction, dreading what might come. "He's a tengu."

"A tengu?"

He nodded, glancing at her, looking for a reaction.

"I've never heard of a tengu raising a human child before. Stealing them sometimes. There are many tales of tengu, but I know of no one ever seeing one. But their skill with the sword is well known."

He breathed a sigh of relief, and his tone brightened. "Tengu don't like us. Men have moved into territories the tengu once had all to themselves. They are too few to fight us, and their magic is going away, so when the settlements of men come too near, they move away. Sometimes they play tricks on humans because they are angry."

"How wondrous to be raised by a tengu!" Her eyes flashed. "My own life has been so boring!"

"I knew nothing else, so it didn't seem very . . . wondrous. He was . . . difficult. I couldn't pronounce his true name, so he told me to call him Kaa."

"Again, monkey-face!" Kaa screeched.

The twelve-year-old boy flinched at the sound and attacked with his bokken. The wooden swords clacked together, and Kaa was a gray blur of spindly arms and legs as he leaped to the side, spinning behind the boy to swat him on the backside with the flat of the sword, adding another welt to the reddened, crisscross pattern already there.

The boy's eyes misted with tears of pain and anger as he spun and threw himself at his master with a flurry of wild blows. He was still clumsy with the sword. He had only been practicing with a wooden blade for a few weeks.

The sword master turned each slash aside with shameful ease. "Striking an enemy is not about the sword, boy! It is about the spirit! Seek the emptiness! You won't touch me until you do!"

The boy tried to do as Kaa taught him, to reach inside for the timeless void that existed between moments. He had been able to do it a few times, but only when given a chance to prepare. To release himself into that void in the midst of a fight was impossible. He knew that if he moved away from his master to try to settle himself for the release, his master would attack him and destroy the attempt before it began.

Sweat rolled into his eyes and slicked his palms, making the wooden sword slippery, in spite of the cool mountain wind that blew his hair around his face. He did all he could think of to do, throwing himself at Kaa with the strongest blow he could muster with his waning strength.

WHACK!

His hands went numb, and sharp tingling pains rippled up his arms. Kaa's sharp blow to the spine of the weapon had driven it out of his grip. Before the boy could blink, Kaa landed a sharp blow to his pate. Stars exploded in his vision, then blackness.

The next thing he saw was Kaa's face leaning over him as he stared up at the sky. Half-bird, half-man, with two forward-set black eyes, a head without ears, covered by a smooth coat of iridescent gray feathers, and a bright crimson beak that made up the lower half of the face. The round, black eyes blinked as they regarded him.

"Perhaps a bit too hard. . . . Good for once that you have a thick skull!" Kaa said.

The ground was rough under his back, the sky above him, bright, the throbbing knob forming on top of his head, painful.

"Enough lessons today!" Kaa stood up and offered Ken'ishi his hand with its long, three-jointed fingers and fine, gray feathers.

The boy took it, and the tengu's wiry arm jerked him to his feet. Kaa's laugh came out like a falcon's screech. "Improvement is good! There is hope for you, monkey-face!"

The boy bowed.

Kaa led the way down the narrow mountain path toward the cave that had been their home since the boy could remember. A rippling shiver traveled up the feathers on tengu's back. "Winter comes early this year. Tomorrow is wood-chopping day."

The boy's attention wandered to the evergreen forest below, undulating with the shape of the underlying mountains, the crystal-blue sky above, frothy with high clouds, and wondered about other people like himself. Kaa always said that other humans were out there, and for that reason had taught him the human tongue. The boy thought about the far-off day when he would rejoin his own people, after completing his education. It was a day he both longed for and feared.

They approached the mouth of the cave, an opening just large enough for the boy to walk upright. He paused, noticing a column of dark smoke in the distance, and pointed.

Kaa turned and followed the boy's gesture. The boy knew his sensei's vision was much sharper than his.

Kaa said, "A fire. Several of the houses in that village are burning."

"There is a village? A village of my own people?"

"Yes."

"So near. . . ."

"Do not get any ideas. The village is not that close. Perhaps two days of walking."

The boy's heart fluttered with excitement. "When can I see them?"

Kaa screeched a laugh again. "So eager! Do not be so quick. Men have too many strange ways. Too many rules. They either try to kill me or prostrate themselves before me. Men are dangerous. Quick to kill what they do not understand or what they dislike. Remember your own family. Their fate proves my wisdom. Before you go back to your own people, you must be able to talk to them, and you must be able to protect yourself from them."

The boy heard his master's words, but in his heart did not believe them. "But why? Am I not just like them?"

"Their customs are ridiculous!" Kaa snorted, making a strange whistling sound in his nostrils, shaking his scarlet beak. "I do not understand them, so I cannot teach them to you.

Sometimes they screech like monkeys over the silliest of things. They stole the art of swordsmithing from us!"

Ken'ishi had heard this tale before, but he kept silent. He liked Kaa's stories.

"Men of this land did not always have swords. I remember when the barbarians from across the sea first brought them. The tengu could fight against humans then, even with their sad weapons, because ours were so much better. Then some monkey-brained human smith stole a tengu blade and mimicked its creation. Fighting became much more difficult after that. Bah! We were masters of the blade centuries before men! Your people breed like rats. They look like monkeys and breed like rats! A bunch of monkeys with blades as fine as ours is still a dangerous thing! And bows! What a dishonorable way to fight!"

"Then why do you teach me the bow?"

"You'll be living among them! If they fight with bows, you must fight with a bow."

The boy thought about this for a few moments. His teacher always made his distrust and dislike for humans plain. At those times, the boy had felt guilty to be born one. Then something occurred to him for the first time. "If you so dislike humans—"

The tengu interrupted him, "Why did I raise you?" Kaa often finished the boy's statements for him, almost as if he could read the boy's mind.

"Well, yes."

"Because of who your father was. A great swordsman he was. A great samurai. So famous among your people that even I had heard of him. Most warriors these days concentrate on using bows, but your father was part of a new school among warriors. He was a master of the sword. I am a master of the blade, and the thought of a monkey calling himself a master of the sword made me angry. So I sought him out. I wanted to test his skill. Because he was a man, I expected little from him. I expected to humiliate him, to put him in his place. So I challenged him to a duel. It was a close match, but in the end, he defeated me. I lay on the ground at his feet, at his mercy, wounded. He could have killed me. He did not. Instead, he bowed to me, and thanked me for the chance to prove his skill against a true master.

"My opinion of your race was raised that day. To think that monkeys could come so far in only a few hundred years! But it seems if one monkey rises above the others, the others must drag him down. Your people have a saying, 'The nail that sticks up must be pounded down.' When his enemies came for him, I could not save him or your mother. I could only save you. Your father was a man of honor, and a man of true strength. And so will you be, if you listen to what I teach you."

"When will you give me his sword?"

"When you are ready. Not before. You will use the bokken until that day. Your father's sword is special." Kaa paused to smooth some feathers on his breast with his hard crimson beak.

The boy had asked this question before, but he tried again. "Please, will you tell me his name? What is the name of my family?"

"You have no family. Your family was wiped out when you were three. You were reborn into a new life."

"What is my name?"

"Names have power. You have no name, except Boy, and no power, except what you make for your own. On the day I give you your father's sword, you can choose your own name. And you must make of that name whatever you can."

"For a long time," Ken'ishi said, "I thought about what name I wanted. But I didn't know any human names. I only knew the names of birds and trees and fish. I thought I would choose the name of a fearsome animal, like 'Kuma' or 'Tora,' but I never decided on one.

"When Kaa told me the day had finally come, he gave me my father's sword and sent me to the village a couple of days' walk from my mountain home. He warned me that the people would think me strange, that they did not like strangers. He told me to be careful, but I was too excited to listen. I was venturing into the world for the first time! I was such a fool." He touched the small jagged scar on his forehead that traced up and merged with his hairline.

O moon,
Why must you inspire my neighbor to chirp
All night on a flute!

—*Koyo*

The young man's long trek through the mountains toward the village neared its end when he found a footpath winding through the pine forest. The path was too wide to be a game trail, and it pointed in the general direction he believed the village to be. Excitement surged in him, and his heart began to pound. He would see people again! It had been so long.

He walked faster through the thick forest. He heard and smelled the village before he saw it. So many strange scents he could not begin to identify, scents that did not exist in the wilderness. He heard voices calling out to one another, but too muffled by the forest to discern the words. He heard the river down the slope, the same river he had fished from and sought for comfort most of his life. He did not know if the river had a name, only that it passed near the mountain where he had lived until two days ago.

Silver Crane hung from his rope belt, banging against his left hip, and his bow and arrows hung from his back beside his traveling pack. With each step, feeling the weight of the steel weapon against his leg, he felt a beat of pride. He had waited for so long, dreamed of these days he was now living. He was free to see the world and to carry his father's blade. He sometimes feared he must be inside a dream, and that he would wake up to find himself sleeping in the cold, dark cave. The sword's weight still felt unfamiliar to him, but that would change.

He tried to think about what he would say to the people he found. How would they respond to him? His teacher had told him to be cautious, so he would be cautious, but friendly. He felt like a lost child, coming home.

The forest ended suddenly, and he emerged into the outskirts of the village. The path wended its way along the earthen embankments between rice fields toward the group of perhaps forty houses and buildings straddling the river. He saw a wooden bridge crossing the river among the houses. On the far side of the village, the mountains again heaved up out of the earth to create a deep green wall of pine forest, the trees with their long, naked trunks topped by bushes of green needles, a backdrop for the plain, wooden houses with their thatched roofs and weathered sides.

Then he noticed a man in one of the rice fields beside the path. The man squatted on his haunches, working, so that only his conical straw hat and his shoulders were visible in the sea of

162

green. The bright green rice plants rippled in the breeze, with the kernel heads just beginning to form on the grassy stalks.

The young man walked toward him and stopped on the path perhaps ten paces from him. He said nothing, but watched the farmer. He wanted to speak but did not know what to say. His teacher had little use for even simple greetings.

Then a voice cried out from the village. The farmer's straw hat jerked up and looked around. The farmer's eyes fixed upon him, and then almost bulged out of his head. The young man smiled at him. The farmer's face convulsed with fear, and he said something unintelligible. Two other men and a woman stood on the path, watching, frozen with expectation.

"What did you say?" asked the young man. "I did not understand you." His teacher had told him that men had many different tongues and often could not understand each other. Now he wondered if he would be able to communicate with these people at all.

The farmer jumped to his feet, turned and ran toward the village as fast as his spindly legs would carry him. The young man could only watch him go. He called out to the villagers, "I'm not going to harm you." He waved and walked toward them.

When the farmer reached the others, he stopped and turned to watch the young man's approach. The four villagers watched him, appearing to grow more fearful with each of the young man's steps.

He stopped. He did not know what to do. He tried smiling wider and showing them that he had no weapons in his hands. This appeared to change nothing in their demeanor.

Then, out of the corner of his eye, he caught a flicker of movement. He turned to look, just in time to spot another young man behind an embankment near a rice field, just in time to spot the fist-sized stone as it sailed toward him. The stone struck him squarely in the forehead. A blaze of searing pain, then nothing.

The young man awoke to a cock crowing and a splitting pain in his head. Opening his eyes was an act of sheer will. His eyelids felt as if he had been asleep for a year. His mouth was as dry as a bed of fallen pine needles, and his entire body felt as weak as a sparrow hatchling. His blurred vision took in the dark, thatched ceiling of a house. He heard sounds of incomprehensible activity around him. Voices outside the house, movement inside, the laughter of children, the rhythmic beat of a hammer somewhere. A hunched human shape sat near him with its back turned. He licked his lips, and a dry rattle escaped his throat.

The person sitting nearby turned toward him and became a shaven-headed man dressed in simple linen robes. His face was broad and weathered, and he had many wrinkles at the corners of his eyes. He looked strange to the boy. Then the man smiled, and a look of kind concern shaped his features into a smile. He said something that the young man did not understand.

He moved toward the young man, bringing a bowl with him. He lifted the bowl to the young man's lips and poured a trickle of cool water into his mouth. It was the sweetest thing he had ever tasted. He gulped at it.

The old man spoke again, and this time the young man thought he heard the words ". . . eyes . . . bright. . . ."

Another shape moved into view behind the man. A woman, her back hunched as if from a great weight, wearing simple clothes like the man, with her hair hidden by a scarf. Her face was lined and wrinkled like the man's, and her eyes sparkled with curiosity.

The young man wondered what they would do with him now. Was he a prisoner? Somehow, he did not think so. But why had the villagers been so afraid of him?

The woman spoke, and the young man heard the words ". . . look like . . . Ainu . . . dangerous. . . ."

The old man spoke: ". . . don't think so. His face . . . Ainu . . . wrong."

The young man said, "Please, more water." His voice was little more than a hoarse whisper.

The old man smiled. ". . . speaks!" Then he poured more water into the young man's mouth.

The young man said, "I cannot understand you. You speak strangely."

The old man listened, appearing to think about the young man's words. Then he nodded as if he understood. He spoke slowly. "My. Name. Is. Takao. I am a priest in this village. I am sorry . . . frightened of you . . . not dangerous . . . to me. This is my wife, Kayo. We have tried to heal you. You have . . . since yesterday." This time the young man understood.

He reached up to touch his head and felt it swathed in cloth. The cloth across his forehead was stiff and caked with dried blood.

"Be careful. Your skull was cracked. You must rest and heal a while longer."

"Thank you for not killing me."

Takao laughed, and his eyes sparkled. "No need to worry about that now. No one will harm you. . . ."

The young man allowed himself to slip into blackness again, where there was no pain in his head.

His periods of wakefulness grew longer each time. The priest and his wife fed him broth and rice porridge, and the next day he was able to stand without being toppled by dizziness. He was still afraid to go outside, however, for fear of another stone to the forehead.

The old priest tried to put him at ease, telling him that he was so heavily armed and looked so fierce that the villagers thought he was a robber or an Ainu raider. The young man understood. He might have done the same thing in their place.

"What is your name, boy?" the priest asked him one day.

"I don't have a name."

Takao's eyes widened in surprise. "No name? Have you no parents?"

"I have no parents."

"An orphan? Living in the wilderness? That is terrible!"

The young man did not know what to say.

"Would you like to have a name?"

He nodded.

"What kind of name would you like?"

"I don't know any names. Perhaps I could be called 'Bear,' or 'Wolf.'"

Takao laughed, and the lines around his eyes seemed to grow deeper. "Kuma? Okami? Do you *want* everyone to be terrified of you?"

"No."

"Then those names just will not do. They are too fierce. Your name should be strong but not fierce." The old man thought for a moment, rubbing his chin. "May I give you a name?"

"Yes, please do." The young man nodded earnestly.

"Then you will be called 'Ken'ishi.' You came to us with little more than a sword, and you have been trained to use it. 'Ken.' And a stone brought you to my house. 'Ishi.' You shall be called 'Ken'ishi.'"

The young man repeated it to himself a few times, trying to get the feel of it on his tongue. "Is it a good name?" Ken'ishi asked.

"Yes, it is a fine name!" The old man's smile widened, and his gaze seemed to look into the distance.

"Thank you, Takao. I am Ken'ishi."

"I am pleased to meet you for the first time, Ken'ishi!" Takao said, chuckling and bowing.

Ken'ishi smiled in return and bowed. "I am pleased to meet you, too."

"Come, let's go sit outside. There is a nice breeze." Ken'ishi followed him and they sat down in the shade of the house. A pleasant cool breeze wafted over them.

Takao picked up a stick. "Here, watch this. I'll show you how to write your name." In the dirt, the old man drew two complicated-looking characters. "There. This is your name. 'Ken.' " He pointed to the first one. "This character can also be read as 'Tsurugi,' but I think 'Ken' sounds better, yes? Simplicity."

Ken'ishi nodded.

Takao pointed to the second character. "And this one is 'Ishi.' Stone. Let me show you." He put the stick in Ken'ishi's hand, adjusted his grip. "Gently. Pretend it's a brush."

"What's a brush?"

Takao paused, then said, "Never mind. Just hold it this way." Then he took Ken'ishi's hand in his own and guided him through the first character's fifteen separate strokes, scratching the character into the dirt. They repeated this process a few times, and then Takao erased all the previous attempts with his hands. "Now, do it yourself." Ken'ishi's hand seemed to remember the order and direction of the strokes, and he repeated it flawlessly. Then they repeated the process with the much simpler second character.

This is my name, he thought. I am Ken'ishi.

"Good! Well done!" The old man chuckled.

Ken'ishi smiled, swelling with pride.

They sat in silence for a while. The young man thought about his new name, scratching it over and over into the earth. Ken'ishi. *Let the power begin here,* he thought. *Let my name draw its power from the symbols in the dirt.*

Then Takao said, "How long have you lived in the wilderness, Ken'ishi?"

"For as long as I can remember."

"Alone?"

Ken'ishi told him the story of how he had been raised by his teacher. The priest was surprised that a tengu had been so kind to raise a human child, and that one lived so close by. Tengu were uncommon, but not unheard of in these parts, and were given a wide berth to avoid any instances of unpleasantness. There were old stories of conflict between men and tengu. The tengu race's dislike for humans, along with their sometimes-foul temper, was well known. Takao said it explained the young man's lack of etiquette and manners, as well as his strange dialect. He told Ken'ishi that he could stay here as long as he liked. As soon as he was healed, Takao would teach him many things. Takao questioned him about his family, but he could provide no answers.

Takao explained that the villagers thought Ken'ishi to be one of the Ainu people, a strange race who had been driven out in ancient times. The Ainu now lived in lands far away, but they sometimes raided villages in the north in attempts to reclaim their ancestral territory. They were ancient enemies, and the hardy villagers were always on the lookout for them.

Before long, Ken'ishi felt hale and strong, and he began to work around Takao's house and the small shrine where the priest practiced his rites to the kami of the earth and sky and water, the guardian kami of the village, the spirits of the mountains and forest. It seemed like a lot of effort to please such capricious entities as the kami, but Ken'ishi understood it. He had learned well how to listen to the voices of the spirits. The priest had much responsibility to keep the village safe and prosperous, and if the kami were displeased, the village would suffer.

Every day, Takao made him sit down and learn new characters. Characters for numbers and things and gods. It was slow and difficult, and Ken'ishi often wondered about the purpose of writing, but he was glad that he could write his name. And something about it felt magical, as if the strokes of the characters gave order to unharnessed power.

He liked living in Takao and Kayo's house. It was warm and comfortable, and he had food to eat. He tried to allay the villagers' distrust and fear by behaving well, and it seemed that as the summer moved toward autumn, they began to accept him, and to become more at ease in his presence. But he could hear whisperings of the kami in the back of his mind, telling him that he could not stay here forever. The villagers might tolerate him, but they would never accept him.

He acquainted himself with the other young men in the village. He sensed the mutual distrust. They were afraid of him, because they had no weapons like his. And he remembered the face of the young man who had felled him with a stone. That young man's name was Ryoichi, and he was the leader of the young men. Ryoichi considered himself one of the protectors of the village, and to him Ken'ishi was a threat that must be contained. Some of the younger boys were friendly and tried to talk to him, but they eventually stopped coming to see him, and when Ken'ishi saw them in the presence of Ryoichi, they looked away sheepishly. This made Ken'ishi angry. He wanted to fight Ryoichi, to defeat the boy who had become his enemy, but he knew that he did not dare harm anyone. That would only make things worse.

He could not remember ever seeing a girl before he came to the village, but recognized them by the things that his teacher had said. He often watched them, trying to study how their bodies and faces were different from his. Sometimes their beauty entranced him. Like the young men, the young women were afraid of him too. He could sense their eyes on him when he was not looking, but when he smiled at them they ran away. Sometimes when they ran away from him, they giggled; sometimes their eyes were wide with fear. All except for one.

The first time he saw her, he was chopping wood beside Takao's house in the lingering light just after sunset. He happened to glance a slim, pale shape moving between some houses on the adjacent street higher up the mountain slope. He looked up and saw this same beautiful young woman, with lustrous hair and sharp eyes. She appraised him with an expression of curiosity and amusement before she slipped away out of sight. He saw her the second time a few days later, at sunset, when he was carrying water to the house. He spied her down the street ahead of him. She looked over her shoulder and flashed him a look that said, "Follow me if you think you can!" But he could not. He could not drop the water buckets, so he tried to trot after her without spilling the water. He thought he heard her laugh as she disappeared around a house at the end of the street. His curiosity was aroused, and he decided that the next day he would look for her.

He could not find her the next day, or the day after that, and it troubled him, because he wanted to see her face again. She was so beautiful. One day he decided that he would ask Takao about her that evening after supper. As he was returning from gathering wood in the forest, just before sunset, his arms cradling a large bundle of branches, he was astonished to see her on the path ahead of him, sitting on a rock as if she had been waiting for him.

Her voice was light and musical. "You are slow today, Ken'ishi." She smiled.

He stammered, "How do you know my name?"

"Oh, come now, don't be silly. Everyone knows who you are!"

He nodded, conceding that he was well known to everyone in the village, even though he knew almost no one. "But I don't know who you are."

"I am Haru. Can you come and talk to me for a while?"

"I'm sorry. I would like to," he said, "but I have to take this wood back."

Her lower lip popped out into a lovely pout. Ken'ishi blinked and stared. "That is too bad," she said. "I have been so looking forward to talking to you."

"I have been looking for you, too. 'Haru' is a nice name. 'Spring.' Can I talk to you tomorrow?"

"That would be quite nice."

"During the day?"

"No, I can't during the day. I keep my father's house during the day, and he would not allow me to leave. In the evening, I can sometimes get out for a while. We can meet here tomorrow?"

"Yes!"

"Good, but it must be a secret. Tell no one! My father would beat me if he found out."

"I will tell no one. Where do you live? Why can I never find you in the village?"

"I live in the forest, in my father's house. He is a woodsman. I am sorry, but I must go now, and so should you. You must not keep the good priest waiting."

He nodded. She stepped aside, and as he passed her, he caught her scent. He stopped, astonished. He had never smelled anything like it before. A heady mixture of spring flowers, pine needles, and a warm, earthy, musky scent he could not identify. Her smell was in his nostrils all the way home, even through dinner and into bed. He was hardly aware of the presence of his foster parents while he ate. Her smell was fresh in his mind when he awoke the next morning, and the image of her face in his mind was clear. He could hardly wait for dusk. All day long, he wanted to be with her, to touch her, to feel her, and he imagined what it would be like.

That afternoon, he told Takao that he was going into the woods to practice archery. He took his bow and arrows and practiced with them until the appointed time grew near. When he went to their meeting place and she saw him carrying his weapons, a look of terror crossed her face, and she recoiled away from him.

"No, wait!" he said. "Don't be afraid! I was just practicing!"

She seemed to relax a bit, but would not readily be put at ease. Her gaze kept darting toward the arrows. "I am glad you're here!" she said. "I have wanted to see you all day long!"

A huge grin split his face.

"I know a secret place where we can talk. We must keep our meeting a secret or my father will beat me!"

"As you wish," he said. He noticed a strange buzzing in his ears and wondered for a moment what it was.

He followed her up the path for almost two hundred paces, then she slipped off the path between the towering pine trunks, behind an outcropping of rock and earth. Behind the outcropping, a narrow game trail led up the slope of the mountain into the forest. He lost sight of the footpath behind him. He turned and watched her for a moment. Her gait and movements were so graceful and lithe. She looked over her shoulder at him, fixed him with a mischievous gaze, and smiled. The glint in her eye quickened his pace to catch up with her.

Soon she led him into a small clearing, nestled between two large boulders, surrounded by fallen logs.

"This is my secret place," she said.

He said nothing, but the sense of seclusion here was almost

palpable. The two boulders lay against one another, with a deep dark cavity hidden in their crook. The cavity looked cozy, like a small cave or a den.

"Let's sit down," she said. "Come sit beside me."

She sat down near the dark cavity between the boulders, and he sat beside her.

He reached out and touched her arm, then pulled back, unsure of himself. She did not flinch away from him. He looked into her deep dark eyes and saw the inner spark, joyous and free, laughing perhaps. Inviting. He touched her again, unsure what to do now. He had once seen Ryoichi kiss one of the village girls below the bridge. Ken'ishi decided to try it. He leaned forward and put his lips on her mouth.

He felt her smile at first, then her lips molded to his. Lightning shot through him, and the buzzing in his ears grew louder. Her teeth felt strange behind her lips. His body felt like a vibrating bowstring, and he grabbed her and pulled her close.

Laughter bubbled out of her, and she pulled away. "Are you hungry?"

His face was hot, and he clasped his knees. "Yes."

"I'll bring you some food. Wait here." She slipped away into the forest, leaving him alone. He had never felt such ecstasy as that kiss, and he wanted to do it again. An interminable time passed, and the world grew dark with night. He yawned uncontrollably. He felt indescribably weary, sleepy.

She was beside him again. "Don't worry," she said. "Don't worry about anything. You can sleep here for a while if you're tired. I have some food if you're hungry."

His stomach growled. "I am hungry. . . . After a nap though. . . ." He settled down and rested his head on a log. Why did he feel so sleepy?

Before he knew it, he had drifted off to sleep. And such pleasant sleep it was, dreamless, deep, without a care. He vaguely remembered Haru bringing him food, and he remembered waking up long enough to eat it, and he remembered eating it with relish, and he remembered drifting off to sleep again afterward. He remembered crawling deeper into the cavity between the boulders. It was such a comfortable, inviting place, so quiet, smelling of the moist earth and dry pine needles inside.

He did not know how long he slept, but he heard voices calling out. Takao's voice, calling his name. He had the strange urge to run away and hide and find a deep burrow where no one could find him. The voices grew louder, and he began to rouse from slumber.

"Ken'ishi!" Takao's voice. "Where are you?"

He sat up. "I am here! What is it?" His voice sounded strange to him for a moment.

"What? What's that?" A gaggle of confused voices. "Is that you, Ken'ishi? Where are you?"

"I am right here." He stood up and looked around. Haru was gone. She must have run away, not wanting them to be discovered together. Takao and a few of the other villagers stood staring at him a few dozen paces down the slope.

Then he noticed that the spot where he had been lying looked different than how he remembered. The massive boulders were not boulders at all, but only two stones that stood as tall as his waist, and what he remembered as fallen logs were only thick branches. Confusion threw his mind into chaos. He looked around. The cavity between the boulders was little more than a burrow. He was still standing there when the villagers reached him.

Relief was painted thick on Takao's features. "I am so happy we found you!"

Ken'ishi's confusion deepened. "Why? I have not been lost."

"What have you been doing in the woods all this time? Some of us thought perhaps you had run away, but I knew you would not leave your weapons behind."

"Why would you think I had run away? I have only been away from the village since this afternoon."

Takao and the villagers looked at one another. Takao asked cautiously, "What have you been doing up here?"

Ken'ishi blushed and hesitated.

"Please tell me. No one will be angry. We have been worried about you."

"I was with a girl from the village."

"For this long? None of the village girls have been missing. What was her name?"

"I don't want to cause trouble for her. She said her father would beat her if he found out."

Takao rubbed his chin. "Then you may tell me. I will tell no one." He turned to the other villagers standing behind him. "Please go down the slope a little ways, everyone. The boy wishes to protect someone's reputation."

The villagers grumbled a bit, but obeyed, and shuffled down the slope out of earshot.

"Now, Ken'ishi, you may tell me her name. I will disclose it to no one."

"Her name is Haru."

Takao looked at him and rubbed his shaven head. "Haru, you say."

"Yes."

"And she is from this village, you say?"

"She said her father is a woodsman, and she lives with him near the village, in the forest."

Takao rubbed his head again and fixed the young man with a searching gaze. "I'm not sure I understand, but. . . . There is no girl from the village named Haru. There are no woodsmen living near the village in the forest."

Ken'ishi frowned. She had lied to him. Why? "She was here

not long ago. She must be nearby. We must find her! She can tell us the truth!"

"Ken'ishi," the priest began, his voice slow and careful, "do you know how long you have been gone?"

"Since early this afternoon."

The priest shook his head sadly. "You have been missing for almost a week."

Ken'ishi felt the words like a blow to the head. A week?

"Yes, a week," Takao repeated.

His knees felt weak. He sat down against one of the stones. He looked down and saw the carcasses of three rabbits, now little more than tufts of hair, dried skin, and bones. Their flesh had been devoured.

"Something strange has happened to you, my boy. But you are safe now. We must entreat the kami to protect you tonight, or you may still fall prey to evil spirits."

"But what happened?" Ken'ishi asked.

Then one of the villagers cried out, "Look!" Ken'ishi and Takao turned and followed where the man was pointing.

There, atop another large rock, perhaps fifty paces distant, was a fox. Its rusty-brown fur seemed to glow with a healthy luster, its bushy tail hanging behind it, and its eyes were sharp and penetrating, sparkling with mischief.

Ken'ishi knew those eyes.

Takao glanced at the young man, and Ken'ishi looked at him for a moment. Understanding crept across the priest's features.

Takao called out to the fox. "Haru, you must trouble this boy no longer. He is meant for greater things than to go with you. Please do us this favor and trouble him no more."

Anger flashed in her sparkling yellow eyes, as if to say, "Do you think *I* would obey *you?*"

Takao turned to Ken'ishi. "Come, my boy, we must go. We do not wish to anger her any further. An angry fox can cause a lot of trouble." Then he turned back to the fox and bowed deeply. "We are sorry for troubling you, Haru! Please accept our apologies!"

But the fox was already gone.

And Ken'ishi was left with nothing but confusion and shame.

Takao and the other villagers led him back down the mountain toward the village.

Kayo was so pleased when Ken'ishi returned that she embraced him. She was normally so quiet and reserved that he was taken aback, but the warmth of her affection dispelled that quickly.

For days and weeks after his experience, Ken'ishi thought about what happened. How could he have been so easily duped? His master had warned him about foxes. He should have been more careful. Foxes hid in their dens during the day. The villagers left offerings of food and sake in the forest for weeks afterward, to appease the fox against any mischief she might cause.

One day, Takao walked up to Ken'ishi and said, "Don't worry about it too much, my boy. She was beautiful, wasn't she?"

Ken'ishi nodded.

The priest chuckled. "You're not the first man to fall victim to a lovely face. Nor will you be the last."

But he had fallen prey far too easily. What troubled him most was that it might happen again, because even as he wished to stay out of danger, he still wished to see Haru again. She was so beautiful, and she truly liked him, he thought, liked him enough to want to keep him with her. Perhaps he would have enjoyed being a fox for the rest of his days.

But no. Such thoughts were foolish and weak. Haru had lied to him, tricked him. His master had told him that he had no name except the one he made for himself. Well, he would make a name for himself, or die in the attempt.

He knew in his spirit that he would not stay here forever, but it seemed wrong for him simply to leave. But he did not have long to think about these things. Not long after Takao and the villagers saved him from Haru, a string of bad fortune swept through the village, in spite of their attempt to appease her. Two of the farmers were injured in a rockslide. Their legs were broken, and they would spend the entire harvest season unable to work. The livestock around the village began to disappear. Pigs, chickens, and ducks vanished overnight. The sake brewer's entire stock soured inexplicably. The potter's kiln cracked and fell apart. And worst of all, the entire rice crop developed strange black spots. The farmers feared for the harvest. The harsh winter would be devastating if the rice crop failed.

Ken'ishi noticed the unpleasant looks the villagers gave him. Some were so hostile that he found himself wishing he carried his sword. His weapons were hidden in Takao's house. This hostility increased as the weeks progressed and the village's bad fortunes multiplied. There were whispers that Ken'ishi was the cause of it all, that the strangeness of his presence had angered the kami, and the priest was powerless to placate them because the young man lived in his house. There were those who believed that all the bad fortune was the result of Ken'ishi's encounter with the fox. Haru was angry now and was taking her vengeance on the village. In any case, it was all Ken'ishi's fault.

He could sense that his foster parents were feeling the pressure. He saw it in their faces. They looked at him with such pity and kindness, but they would never ask him to leave. He wondered if they believed what the other villagers were saying, even a little. That was when he knew it was time to leave.

So one morning, at the break of dawn, he packed up his things, slung his pack and bow over his shoulder, tied on his sword, and prepared to depart. A heavy sadness weighed upon his shoulders and chest. He would never see anyone here again.

Takao was already sitting on a log outside the house as he stepped outside. The priest glanced at him, then looked down at the ground, his profound sadness evident on his face. He said nothing, only nodded.

Ken'ishi said nothing as he stopped before the priest, knelt, and bowed deeply, several times. Tears burned his eyes, and he wiped them away as he stood up. Then he turned his back and walked away, never to return.

Flowers in shadow . . .
A moon floating in the east,
In the west, the sun

—*Buson*

When Ken'ishi finished his tale, they walked in silence again for a while. For some reason, he had not told her about Haru, even though the shame and wonder of it were both still fresh in his memory. He told her only about the village and his foster parents, but the ripples of the memory's passing were still in the mind. He told her that they had a string of bad luck, and that the villagers blamed him for it, so he felt he should leave.

Akao trotted ahead of them, sometimes disappearing into the forest, in pursuit of what Ken'ishi did not know. Sometimes

Akao's carefree nature reminded him to worry less about people and simply to live.

After a while, Kazuko said, "A strange tale, Ken'ishi. But I don't think you're a liar, nor do I think you're deranged."

"Then what do you think?"

Another lovely flush spread across her cheeks. "That is a rude question."

Ken'ishi's ears warmed, and his heart flopped inside his breast like a fresh-landed fish. "I've told you two stories of my childhood. Now you must tell me of yours," he said.

"There's not much to tell really. I was my father's only child. He wished I were a boy. That is only natural, I suppose. Everyone wants to have sons. Wouldn't it be strange if everyone got their wish and no more girls were to be born? All the world would be sons! Anyway, that is why he taught me the naginata."

"A potent weapon."

She nodded. "In the hands of a strong person, I'm sure it is quite powerful."

"You're the only woman I have ever seen who can fight! Most women are either as submissive as kittens or as shrill and shrewish as a mother pig."

"That's an uncharitable thing to say. You just don't know about women. You thought I was a fox!" She giggled.

He clamped his mouth shut, and they walked for a while.

"What is it like to have wealth and privilege?" he asked.

She paused, as if trying to decide whether she should be offended.

He added, "It must be quite different from how I was raised."

His earnest tone must have convinced her that he meant no insult, so she thought before she answered. "I admit that it is difficult for me to imagine not having food to eat, or living in a hovel that does not even keep off the rain. All I have known is discipline and etiquette and boredom. Discipline from the endless hours of studying and lessons and naginata training."

"Discipline I know well. I know little else."

"There are so many rules of proper etiquette and behavior that my father commissioned a tutor for young ladies to teach me proper manners. Perhaps I could teach you some."

He smiled. "I would like that."

She blushed and looked away.

"And the boredom?"

"The boredom comes from all the endless hours in between, trapped in a manor house with no one to talk to except Hatsumi and nothing to see except the same walls day after day. I envy you your travels, Ken'ishi. You have seen so much. I have seen so little. Lord Tsunetomo's cherry trees were so beautiful. . . ."

"Doesn't your father have cherry trees?"

"Well, yes, but I see those every year! Lord Tsunetomo's estate was so much larger, and his gardens so much more beautiful! And he lives in a castle!"

"And I envy *you* the chance to do something as . . . well, as *useless* as looking at cherry trees. I have seen cherry trees in bloom, and they are beautiful, but only the wealthy have the time and money to take special journeys to view them. I spend my days wondering when I will be able to eat next. You do not have to worry about such things, so you are free to view cherry trees."

She thought about this, then sighed. "It is the nature of the poor to envy the rich, I suppose."

"But you envy the poor?" Ken'ishi said.

"Sometimes, perhaps, when the pressures and obligations of wealth become troublesome."

After a few paces of silence, he said, "So what are young ladies taught?"

"Oh, many things! Things like reading and writing, proper

manners, literature, poetry, dancing. And womanly things that you wouldn't understand. I tried to learn how to play the biwa, but I was a terrible musician. Hatsumi can play the biwa! She is quite skilled."

"It sounds like a lot of learning. It takes a long time?"

"Just like learning how to use a weapon, learning to use one's mind is a difficult thing. But it is a worthy one. I love to read books!"

"Have you read a lot of books?"

"A few."

"What is in them?" Even though he understood a few written characters, Ken'ishi imagined that books just held pages and pages of cryptic scribbling.

"Many things. Poetry, history, stories."

"What kinds of stories?"

"Stories about the gods, and demons, and animals, and lovers." She said the last word with an almost breathless excitement.

"Do you like that kind best? Stories about love?"

She smiled and her eyes sparkled. "Oh, yes! Those are the best!"

Then he looked ahead and pointed. "Look, there is the next village, Kazuko."

"Oh, good!"

When they reached the village, everyone was so obsequious that Ken'ishi was again surprised at the power wielded by those of high station. The villagers brought food and drink and even presented Kazuko with gifts of their local woodcrafts, small carved statues of Jizo and Kannon, beautifully lacquered and gilded.

That night, well fed and weary from the journey, they slept in the village inn. Ken'ishi tried not to think about Kazuko as he settled himself for sleep, but he could not help it. So beautiful she was, beautiful enough to drive caution from his mind, to make him forget what had happened the last time he was entranced by a beautiful face. Everything about her entranced him, and there, he sensed his potential downfall.

Now in sad autumn
As I take my darkening path . . .
A solitary bird

—*Basho*

When Taro reached the first village the following morning, he knew that he was the farthest he had ever been from home. Every step he took carried him farther away from everything he had ever known, and the thrill of the chase was intoxicating.

He spent the night sleeping in the crook of an oak tree. Before he had grown into a man, he loved climbing trees, and he often whiled away entire afternoons sleeping in the branches while his exasperated mother searched for him. But she was dead now. His father was still alive, but he loved his jars of sake more than his son. Was his father angry that he had gone away? Probably. Taro was the eldest, heir to the house and family plot of land. But he was sure that he would never be a farmer now. The thought of going back with his purpose unfulfilled was as loathsome as anything he could imagine.

He was happy that the wound in his leg did not pain him anymore. Yesterday had been agony. Today, his calf and ankle were suffused with a strange numbness. He did not remove the makeshift bandages. The wound must not be as bad as he first thought. In any case, he had other things to keep his attention, like following the ronin's trail.

When he reached the village, they told him that the ronin had indeed been there the night before, but he was protecting Nishimuta no Kazuko and her handmaiden. The village headman was alarmed to hear that the ronin had slain a Nishimuta clan constable. If he had known, he would have had the man arrested. The girl did not know of the ronin's crime. The three of them and their stretcher-bearers had departed early that morning. If Taro hurried, perhaps he could still catch them.

Taro thanked him for the information, and the headman then gave him several rice balls and some pickled plums to sustain him in his pursuit. Taro wasted no time. He mustn't let his quarry gain on him, so he moved faster now. His leg felt so much better! He could run for stretches, and he imagined how the ronin was slowed down by carrying the wounded woman. Today, he would have his quarry, and he could return home triumphant!

But at midmorning, he came to a fork in the road. Which way had the ronin gone? The ground was too rocky for tracks. And there were no drag marks in the dirt today, because some of the villagers were carrying the stretcher. But he could not waste valuable time with indecision. He simply chose a direction.

As he went, he looked for signs of passage on the road, but there were many sets of footprints. As the day approached noon, he saw a man and a woman seated in the grass in a small clearing, hunched over with their heads close together. A small shrine to Kannon stood nearby, and he smelled fresh incense from the offering.

As he drew nearer, his heart skipped a beat. The man was wearing a sword, and his back was turned. Was he a ronin? He tried to examine the man's clothes and appearance. He was young and shabbily dressed. The woman's robes were threadbare and worn, but her face was young and pretty. She pointed toward Taro with her head as he approached them. The man turned and looked at Taro. His eyes narrowed.

Taro stopped on the road and returned the man's gaze.

The man's voice was gruff and short of patience. "What are you staring at, boy?"

This man was too old to be the ronin he sought, and this woman was definitely not a noble maiden. Her skin was sun-darkened, and her eyes were hard with a cruel glint. Taro stood straighter and faced them. "I am looking for a ronin criminal. He has a woman with him. . . ."

The man exploded into movement. "Bastard!" he snarled, as he launched himself at Taro.

Taro scrambled backward, reflexively drawing his jitte with his right hand. With his other hand, he pulled Takenaga's short sword from its scabbard. Before he could think, the other man's blade was whistling toward his eyes. He brought up the short sword and deflected the blow high. If he had not, he would have lost the top of his head. He scrambled backwards under a rain of powerful blows, barely keeping the deadly edge at bay.

Then a strange sensation around his leg distracted him just

long enough to miss an opportunity to catch the man's sword with his jitte. For a moment, he thought that the pain in his wound had suddenly returned, until he tried to take another step backward and found his ankle ensnared in a chain. With a sneer on her lips, the woman hauled on the other end of the chain and jerked his leg out from under him. He fell hard backwards onto the earth. The man's blade hissed through the space occupied by his belly an instant before. The woman's fierce eyes and sly smile speared into his mind and awoke something lying hidden within. A strange roaring filled his ears, drowning all other sound.

She hauled on the chain again, spinning his body on the ground like a top and pulling him closer to her partner. Just close enough.

Taro slashed with the short sword at the man's legs and felt the blade grate against bone. The man grunted in pain and staggered backward. A thin red line crossing both of his shins began to drip crimson. The man fell backward, groaning. Taro dropped the short sword, grabbed the chain, and pulled with all his might. The woman gasped as he pulled her off balance. Her hard, dark eyes bulged and her mouth dropped open. He jerked again, and she flew toward him as if she was light as a feather. As her body tumbled toward him, he savagely thrust his jitte to meet her, and the blunt point speared deep into her belly. A gurgling scream tore from her lips, strangely muffled by the roaring sound in Taro's ears, and she fell to the earth. Taro scrambled to his feet and pulled his jitte from her body.

The man groaned, clutching his shins with bloody fingers. The roaring in Taro's ears all but drowned out the man's agonized curses. They came to him as if from a great distance. He stood over the man, and the man scrambled backwards, trying to get away.

"You fool!" Taro shouted, his voice rising. "I wasn't looking for you!"

The man just glared at him.

"Did a ronin and a noble woman pass this way? Carrying a wounded woman on a stretcher?"

The man shook his head.

"How long have you been on this road? Tell me and I will spare your life."

"All day. We have seen no one!"

The roaring in Taro's ears grew louder. He had chosen the wrong path!

His vision blackened for a moment, as if the sun had been snuffed, and all light disappeared. For a moment, he was overcome with dizziness. Then, just as suddenly, the light returned.

He looked down at the man again. The man's body now lay in two pieces, with a spreading pool of gore and entrails gushing from the cut across the man's abdomen. Taro shook his head in bewilderment. Had he done this? It was a powerful cut to cleave a man that way. He looked down at the short sword in his hand. The blade was smeared with dripping crimson almost to the guard. He blinked and tried to remember, his head swimming. He staggered back a step and sank to his knees. The stench of the man's entrails reached his nose, and he retched.

He did not remember how long he sat that way, trying to regain his composure, but when he did, he stood up and looked at the woman. Cold, lifeless eyes stared up at the bright blue sky. Strange how her eyes in death looked much like when she was alive. Then he noticed a cloth satchel lying in the grass where they had been sitting. It was lying untied and open. He approached it and looked inside. At first glance, the contents looked like only a bundle of bloody rags. He upended the satchel and out fell a clinking cascade of bronze and silver coins, and a few rags spattered with blood that was still fresh.

Well, it seemed that his fight was not useless. These two had been robbers, and some unlucky soul had died today to yield up this bit of coin. The bloodied cloth was fine pale silk, perhaps belonging to a merchant or a noble. Was this ronin bandit to be believed? The look in his eyes had told Taro that the man had not been lying. He had not seen Taro's quarry today. Taro had indeed taken the wrong path.

Time was too short to attend to these bodies. He had already lost half a day's pursuit in going the wrong direction. He discarded the bloody rags, took the coins and stuffed them in his pouch, and ran back the way he had come.

You ask me what I thought about
Before we were lovers.
The answer is easy.
Before I met you
I didn't have anything to think about.
                    —*The Love Poems of Marichiko*

Kazuko awoke with a start, heart thumping in her breast like a hare's warning. When she saw the ceiling of the inn and heard Hatsumi snoring softly nearby, she remembered the village where they had stopped for the night. Hatsumi's health had improved since yesterday, and she now slept more peacefully.

Just visible through the slats in the windows of her room was the dim gray light of early dawn. Something had awakened her from a wonderful dream, a dream she did not wish to leave. A dream where she was married to a powerful, handsome man, a wealthy man of high rank and great prestige, and they had many fine, healthy children playing in a wonderful garden, with cherry blossoms in the air and plums ready for the plucking. And a large pond filled with golden carp and snowy white cranes, and mandarin ducks and regal plum blossoms. And she and her husband. . . . A warm tingle formed in her belly and whispered up her back as she remembered her dream husband, tall and strong and handsome, playing his flute to the delight of their children.

Now as she awakened, a gossamer silence hung in the darkness, suspended like a mosquito net made of spider silk. It was that elusive time between morning and night when the crickets had fallen silent, and the birds had not yet awakened, and not a breath of breeze stirred the grass. But a quiet sound disturbed the silence, like the quick passage of breath through the teeth and the thump of a foot on the bare ground. The sound came from outside.

She rolled aside her blanket and sat up to listen. When it came again, she stood up and crossed to the window. Peering between the slats, she saw Ken'ishi in the garden behind the inn. His sword flashed in the dim, gray light as he moved from stance to stance. His clothes hung over a nearby fence, she thought for a moment he was naked, until she saw his meager loincloth. As one who had studied a weapon herself, she recognized the incredible precision and grace with which he wielded the steel in his hands. He moved with the fluidity of oil, and his sword was alive like an extension of his own body. With each blow at an imaginary opponent, his bare foot would strike the earth a hard thump, punctuating the hiss of his breath. The lean muscles of his arms and chest and back rippled like coils of sinew. His wild hair flew about his head, except for a few strands plastered to his face with sweat. He was like the heroes in stories. He was so beautiful, so wild, like an untamed stallion. Sitting a few paces away was the dog, Akao, watching his master with an amused expression, tongue lolling. Such loyalty between those two. She wondered what travails they had endured to form such a bond. And she wondered how it would feel if Ken'ishi could feel such loyalty to her. . . .

"What are you doing?" came a whisper from half a step behind her.

Kazuko gasped, her hand clutching her mouth. Her breath hissed out of her. "Hatsumi! You frightened me!"

"I'm sorry, dear," Hatsumi whispered. "What are you watching?"

"I heard a noise. . . ."

Hatsumi stepped nearer the window and looked out. Kazuko watched Hatsumi's expression change from curiosity to a frown. "It's not seemly to spy on people," Hatsumi said.

"I heard a noise! I just wanted to see what it was!" Kazuko whispered.

"You've been watching him for a long time." Hatsumi's voice was sharp with reproof, and she crossed her arms.

Kazuko sighed and looked back out the window. "Isn't he the most handsome man you've ever seen?"

Hatsumi snorted, and her face twisted into a sneer. "He's a ruffian! He has no more manners than a monkey! I would be surprised if he doesn't throw shit like a monkey."

Kazuko turned toward her. "Such talk! Where are *your* manners? He wasn't raised in a proper household. He hasn't learned proper manners. Not yet."

"Doesn't that make him a crude ruffian? I don't trust him."

"How can you be so unkind, Hatsumi? He saved our lives.

He carried you for a whole day."

Hatsumi's face softened abruptly. She sighed. "I suppose you're right, dear. I'm sorry. He is a strong man for one so young."

"We are the same age. And you aren't that much older! You are only twenty-four."

"I feel much older than that."

Kazuko's voice melted with pity. "I am sorry, Hatsumi. How do you feel today?"

"Better than yesterday. I can see with one eye. I can walk a little. By the time we reach home, I will be my old self."

Kazuko paused, thinking Hatsumi's voice was not as certain as her words. "Don't worry. Everything will be fine when we get home. When we get there, you can rest until you are healed. You are strong. I will talk to Father about taking Ken'ishi into his service. It is only fitting after all he has done for us." Kazuko thought she saw Hatsumi hesitate or nearly stumble at her last words. "This displeases you?"

"No, dear," Hatsumi said. "Of course not. He may learn some manners in a proper household."

Kazuko listened carefully to her tone. Hatsumi was seldom able to hide her feelings. But something was wrong.

When Kazuko looked back outside, she thought more time had passed than she realized, because the day had brightened, and the rest of the village was stirring. Ken'ishi had ceased his practice and was putting his clothes back on.

"Come away, dear," Hatsumi said. "It's not polite to spy."

Kazuko sighed and obeyed, thinking perhaps she had taken longer to turn away than Hatsumi would have liked.

Ken'ishi and Kazuko walked together at the head of the small procession. Akao ranged ahead as he often did, scampering from bush to bush, sniffing here and there, weaving in and out of the foliage in a never-ending cycle. Hatsumi was still in too much pain to walk any distance, so she rode on the stretcher. They sent the four original bearers back to their own village and borrowed four more from this one. Kazuko sent them off with generous rewards for their labor before the party continued its journey.

As they walked, Ken'ishi felt Hatsumi's gaze on his back, and for some reason it set him ill at ease. Now that the swelling in her face had diminished, he saw she was not a pretty woman. Her features were too broad and blunt, her eyes too small, and she had the teeth of a horse, even dyed black as they were. Kazuko's teeth were not dyed black, and he wondered why. That was customary among most women, especially those of means. Perhaps Kazuko was still too young. He could not fathom many customs, no matter how hard he tried. He liked Kazuko's fine, white teeth. Today it seemed that she walked a little closer to him than before. He could almost feel her warmth on the skin of his forearm. Perhaps this was why Hatsumi watched them so closely. But he sensed something else that he could not give a name. Perhaps this feeling was the voices of the kami, as Kaa had said. As the day progressed and the feeling persisted, Ken'ishi found himself growing ever more uncomfortable, a buzzing or tittering in his gut. He never glanced to see if she was watching. He did not have to.

Kazuko said, "You said that until you left Kaa's tutelage, you could remember seeing only one person, one human. Was that the person who gave you the flute?"

Ken'ishi nodded. "It was about two years before I left the mountain. He sent me down to fish from the river."

The boy sat quietly on the bank of the river, watching the waters of the river slide by, feeling the cool stiffness of the grass, the moist firmness of the earth under his backside. The long bamboo fishing pole rested between his knees. Its end bobbed faintly with the tug of the string as the water tugged on his hook and bait. The whispered ripple of the water soothed him, allowed him to feel a kind of calm that Kaa's incessant harping would not. The sounds of birds and insects echoed along the river valley, and there were no other sounds. That is, until he heard something strange yet vaguely familiar, but unlike anything he had ever heard in nature.

What was that sound? It grew louder. It whistled like bird-song, but the tones were strangely related, rhythmic, melodious. He looked upriver, toward the opposite bank. A head emerged above the tall rushes, the shaven head of a man. The man looked like he was blowing on one end of a bamboo stick, holding the stick in both hands as he walked.

The boy stared as the man grew nearer and the sounds grew louder. The man stopped opposite the boy, lowered the stick, and turned to look at him. The man spoke, but his words and inflection were strange and alien, and he spoke so quickly that the boy could only pick out a few words.

The boy said, "I cannot understand you. Who are you?"

The man spoke again, and his expression changed, his forehead growing all wrinkled. The boy could not remember the last time he had seen a human face, and this one with the shaven head fascinated him.

"You talk too fast," the boy said. "Who are you?"

The man listened intently, then nodded. He thrust himself through the rushes and down the riverbank to the water. Then he stepped down into the river and began to cross. The river was not deep or wide, but it was cold this time of year, chilled by fresh snowmelt. The water rose to his chest, but the cold did not appear to bother him as he sloshed across.

Soon he stepped up on the riverbank a few paces from the boy, dripping wet. The boy put down his fishing pole and stood up. The man bowed. The boy returned the gesture.

The man spoke, but the words were gibberish.

The boy said, "I cannot understand you. Who are you?"

The man listened intently, then nodded with a broad smile. When he spoke again, his words were slow and methodical. "My name is Doshin."

"My name is Boy."

The man smiled widely, and his eyes sparkled. "I did not expect to see anyone here. Do you live nearby?"

"Yes."

"How big is your village?"

"I don't have a village."

"Strange to see one so young all alone in the wilderness."

"I am not alone. I have my teacher."

"Oh? And where is he?"

The boy turned and pointed up the mountainside. "He is up there. I am fishing for us."

"He is your teacher, eh? What does he teach you?"

"The sword and the bow."

"Those are the tools of the warrior. You must be a fierce lad. My own tools are not so fierce." He raised the bamboo stick in his hand. It was almost as long as his arm, as thick as his wrist, and the boy saw that it was hollow, with a line of holes on the side.

"What is that thing?"

"It is a shakuhachi, a bamboo flute."

"It makes that pretty noise?"

Doshin nodded, then brought one end of the flute to his lips and began to play.

The boy was enraptured, motionless, listening with every fiber of his being. After a while, the sounds trailed off, and the boy blinked as if waking from a dream. "Are you a god?" he asked.

Doshin laughed, and his eyes sparkled with humor. "No, I am not a god. I merely serve them. I am just a simple monk."

"How do you serve them?"

"Through my faith, and by chanting sutras for others that they might reach paradise, and by playing music."

"What is paradise? It is a place?"

"There are many paradises, just as there are many hells."

"What is it like? Why do people want to go there?"

"It is a place of peace and plenty, without suffering and want. With music and—"

"Music? There is music there?"

"Certainly."

"Like yours?"

"Why, yes, only much better. The music of the heavens could make the gods themselves weep."

The boy's mind raced, trying to imagine such a thing.

The man continued, "Music is a gift from the gods. That is why I play this flute."

"Can you play some more?"

"Of course!" Doshin sat down on the ground and began to play. The boy sat down in front of him and listened.

The day wore on, and the monk played. The shadows of the mountains on the riverbanks grew longer. The boy's fishing pole sat forgotten next to him, and the lilting, melancholy emanations from the monk's flute washed over the boy, echoed down the riverbed. For a long time, the boy sat motionless, oblivious to everything else around him.

When at last the monk stopped playing, the boy sighed deeply. "How does it work?"

The monk answered, "You blow in this end and place your fingers over these holes. The holes change the note. Would you like to try?"

The boy's chin flapped up and down.

The monk smiled and handed him the flute. The boy took the flute, studied it, held it as he had seen the monk hold it, and began to blow. A shrill bleat burst out of the flute, and the boy jumped.

The monk chuckled. "Not so hard. Blow softly."

The boy blew again, softly, easing his breath into the bamboo tube until a tone formed itself in the air. A thrill of elation swept through him.

The shadows grew longer still as the sun sank to touch the mountains with incredible swiftness. The monk instructed the boy in how to play the instrument, to create tunes, to let the music flow. He pointed at his lower belly. "Remember that the belly, the hara, is the seat of all emotions. Breathe with your hara. Play the flute with your hara. Do not play the flute with your mind or your fingers. Play with your belly. Good, that is better! You learn quickly!"

Finally, the boy noticed that the day had almost fallen into night. His teacher would be furious with him! He had caught no fish!

The monk noticed his alarm. "I hope I haven't caused you any trouble."

"My teacher will be angry."

"I am sorry to hear that I have kept you from your duties. Please take the flute as recompense."

The boy's heart leaped. "Truly?"

The monk nodded. "I made that one. I can make another."

"I'm sorry. I must go now."

"Then go, by all means." His smile of farewell was warm and gentle.

The boy bowed to him, then snatched up his fishing pole. He turned to hurry up the riverbank, when he felt a tug on his line. He thrust the flute into his belt and took the fishing pole in both hands. Something was on the line!

The monk said, "Perhaps you need not go home empty-handed after all."

The boy pulled on the pole and drew in his line. In the clear water, the sleek dark shape of the fish writhed on his hook.

The monk said, "My! That's a big one!"

The boy backed up the riverbank, drawing the fish closer to the water's edge, then with a mighty pull, he dragged the fish up onto the ground, where it flopped and thrashed. The fish was as long as his arm. The boy pulled out his small knife, leaped down upon the fish, and stabbed it in the head before it could flop back into the water.

"What a fine catch!"

The boy grinned at him. "Do you want to eat with us?"

"No, I couldn't. I do not eat living creatures, but thank you for the invitation. I must be moving along. I have a long way to travel before I reach paradise." The monk bowed.

The boy bowed in return, then grasped the fish by the gills with one hand, his fishing pole with the other, and dashed up the riverbank, running for the trail leading up the mountain to the cave he called home.

He often pushed himself to run up the mountain faster and faster, and his lateness made this game seem more important. When he finally reached the cave, he was puffing with exertion, and the day had gone away to darkness. Kaa was waiting for him, and Ken'ishi saw by the puff of his feathers and the angle of his head that he was both worried and irritated.

"That is a fine fish, monkey-boy!" Kaa said, his harsh voice even more shrill than normal. "It took you all day to catch it?"

The boy said nothing as he offered it up.

"What is that you are carrying?" The tengu turned his sharp, dark eyes on the flute in the boy's rope belt.

The boy's ears reddened. "It's a flute."

"Where did you get it?"

The boy hesitated, unsure if he should speak of the monk. Finally, he said, "I found it."

"And I suppose you learned how to play it all by yourself. Don't look so surprised. How could I fail to hear all that terrible squawking? Next time that shaven-headed monkey calling himself Doshin helps you 'find' something, you better see your work done first!"

The boy froze. "Do you know him?"

Kaa's eyes blinked, and he preened the feathers on his shoulder with his beak before his spoke. "We have been acquainted. He may not remember me, though. When he saw me, I looked a bit different."

The boy looked at him for a moment, then he said, "You were playing a trick on him!"

The tengu's eyes closed in silent laughter. "It amuses us to play tricks on humans. Especially monks and priests. They think they are so wise."

"Why? Isn't it bad to play tricks on others?"

"Humans worship so many strange gods and things that sometimes it is amusing to act like one of them. The looks on their faces when we reveal the deception are priceless! It makes the losses my race has suffered over the centuries more bearable."

"So you do it for revenge?"

"Perhaps," Kaa admitted. "Trickery is less dangerous—and less painful—than war, isn't it?"

"Yes, teacher."

"You are lucky you caught that fish before you came back, or you would have been in for a beating."

"Yes, teacher." He looked at the ground, then said, "Were you watching?"

"My powers extend to more than mere 'watching.' You would do well to remember that."

"Yes, teacher."

"Very well. Let us eat!"

After Ken'ishi ended his tale, they walked in silence for a while. They occasionally passed tradesmen or itinerant merchants who prostrated themselves as the procession passed. They could tell from the richness of Kazuko's clothing that she was a noble lady.

The procession passed a filthy beggar who knelt out of their path, touching his forehead to the ground. Ken'ishi's nose wrinkled at his horrible stench. The man smelled as if he bathed in a cesspit and rinsed with urine. His cheeks were gaunt, and his ears were too big for his head. Sparse wisps of hair spotted his unwashed pate. His face was pressed against the dirt of the road.

The beggar's sobs wracked his spindly frame as he spoke. "Oh, noble gentleman and lady, please spare some money for a wretched beggar! My wife is ill unto death and I have no money to buy her medicine. Please, be merciful and kind to a poor creature such as myself."

Ken'ishi glanced at Kazuko. Her face had gone white, and she leaned unsteadily on her naginata. Her eyes held the look of one about to retch.

Ken'ishi felt the man's powerlessness at being too poor to help someone he loved. The man's stench was almost overpowering, however, and Ken'ishi had to clamp his teeth down upon his own revulsion.

The beggar cringed away from the silence hanging pregnant in the air, as if he now regretted opening his mouth at all, as if he feared that the silence was a precursor to being spurned. He tried to withdraw into himself, make himself smaller like a tortoise.

Kazuko had composed herself. She stepped forward, and her

voice was shaky but resolved. "I am sorry for your plight. Please accept this. Your wife should have the medicine she needs."

Hatsumi whispered from the stretcher, "Kazuko! Don't touch him! You'll be polluted again! Get away from him!"

Kazuko ignored her. She reached into her money pouch and tossed several copper coins onto the road near the beggar. The beggar began to weep and gathered the money in his hands. His tears dripped into the dust of road. "Thank you very much!" he repeated over and over, sobbing.

"Now," she said, "go and buy medicine for your wife."

The beggar scrambled to his feet and ran away up the road.

Kazuko smiled wanly at Ken'ishi. Then she looked at Hatsumi, and her tone grew serious. "The Buddha speaks of compassion for all things, Hatsumi, even filthy creatures like that beggar."

"Yes, lady," Hatsumi said. "I am sorry." Her bruised cheeks reddened. "My concern was only for your welfare."

Kazuko said, "I know, and thank you. But your concern should be for the beggar."

Hatsumi lay back on the stretcher, turning her face away.

Ken'ishi thought he heard her mutter something under her breath. He could not make out her words, but her tone set his teeth on edge.

Kazuko appeared not to have heard.

Ken'ishi said to her, "You are very kind."

"Perhaps I can do more to be kind to those below my station. Perhaps I *should* do more. Until I met you, I never thought of them at all. Thank you for opening my eyes."

"I did nothing," he said.

"You have a broad belly, a wide spirit, Ken'ishi. You would make a good retainer for any lord."

"I'm happy you think so."

"I will try to arrange a meeting for you with my father," she said and smiled at him again.

As they walked on, he thought about the beggar for a long time, and the strange mixture of repulsion and pity that had left Kazuko frozen.

As she lay upon her crude palanquin, Hatsumi thought about the beggar as well, but she burned with anger at Kazuko's rebuke. That filthy beggar had accosted her lady, and even worse, made Kazuko displeased with her. Hatsumi silently chastised herself for forgetting Kazuko's kind-spiritedness. She should have realized Kazuko would react as she did. How could she convince Kazuko that her feelings for the ronin were wrong, hopeless, useless, if the girl was angry with her? She would have to be more careful from now on.

Hatsumi wondered why she felt so ill tempered, almost as if it were in spite of herself. Her groin still throbbed and ached, but it was no longer a searing agony. She covered her eyes to protect them from the beating sun. The uncertain step of the peasants bearing her stretcher made her queasy, and her head hurt. She almost believed she would feel better now if she walked herself. She craned her neck to look at Kazuko and saw her walking closely beside the ronin. Too closely. Her fists clenched.

"Kazuko!" she called, keeping her voice carefully beseeching.

The girl turned and looked at her with that beautiful smile, as if nothing had happened. Could she have forgotten so soon? "Yes? What is it?"

"May we stop and rest for a bit?"

"Certainly, Hatsumi," Kazuko said.

Hatsumi noted the scowl of impatience on the ronin's face and quietly enjoyed it.

The bearers lowered Hatsumi's conveyance so that she could step off, and she sighed with relief. "My dear, could you help me?" She held out her hand to Kazuko, who moved to help her off the stretcher.

Hatsumi glanced at the bushes, and Kazuko nodded in understanding. Hatsumi no longer needed the help, but she was grateful for Kazuko's touch. When they were out of sight of the rest of the party, Hatsumi turned to her.

"Please forgive me. I shouldn't have been so rude to that beggar. You were right."

"There is no need for forgiveness. You were looking out for my welfare."

"As I always do. I am forever your humble servant."

Kazuko smiled. "You are more like my sister than a servant!"

Hatsumi smiled back, and for the first time in too long, she felt real warmth and love. The bitter darkness receded. She almost felt like she could chat with Kazuko just as she always had, but there was still something between them.

"Kazuko," Hatsumi began, then paused.

"What is it?"

"It is difficult to speak of such things."

"What is it? We can talk about anything, can't we?"

Hatsumi kept her voice carefully neutral, perhaps matronly. "I know you have feelings for him, Kazuko, and if it embarrasses you to talk about it, I'm sorry." Kazuko blushed deeply, just as Hatsumi expected. "But you must listen to me. You mustn't fall prey to those feelings. You must put them aside."

Kazuko looked away, her eyes glassy with tears.

"You are meant for a better man than him," Hatsumi said. "You must guard against those feelings, cast them out. I know it is painful. I only wish to spare you more pain. You and this man cannot be together."

Hatsumi paused, waiting for Kazuko to respond, but the girl lowered her gaze to a spot at her feet, unmoving.

"Your father would not approve."

Kazuko stiffened, but still said nothing.

"You must listen to me. You are too free with your love, my dear. It has already caused you trouble."

Kazuko's gaze snapped up to stare at her. "What do you mean?"

"I think you know what I mean." Hatsumi kept her voice kind, but firm.

Kazuko sniffed and looked away. "I know no such thing!"

"I'm sure you remember Yuta, who was so in love with you."

Kazuko's mouth fell open.

Hatsumi smiled and patted her cheek. "Yes, I knew about him. And I know you had feelings for him, too. You must guard the chambers of your heart and your body, my dear, because they do not belong to you. They belong to your family, to your father. Your feelings have consequences for those you favor with them. If your father had found out about Yuta, the boy's life might have been forfeit, and you would have been disgraced."

Kazuko's expression changed from surprise to shock and dismay. Tears burst into her glistening eyes, and Hatsumi felt a pang of remorse. "I am sorry, Kazuko, for opening up old wounds. I know you pined for him for a while. But rest assured that it was for the best."

"How could you!" Kazuko gasped. "How could you do that to me? For so long I wondered what happened to him, and no one would tell me! And that was your doing?"

"I'm sorry, my dear. It was for the best. He is alive and well, but far away. And you will never see him again." Hatsumi looked into her, and saw a storm of emotions, hurt, sadness, and more than a hint of anger. It would take some time for Kazuko to get over this, Hatsumi knew, but she would. She was a resilient girl. "Do not hate me."

Kazuko looked for a moment as if she would collapse.

"Please believe me when I say that it was for the best. It

could only have ended badly for everyone. Do you believe me?"

The girl looked toward the ground, her mouth agape, seeing nothing, tears trickling down her cheeks.

"Please tell me you will think about what I have said."

Kazuko wiped at the tears in her eyes, then she turned away.

When they returned to the rest of the party, Hatsumi tried to discern the girl's thoughts. She seemed solemn now, taciturn, with a faint wrinkle visible between her brows. Hatsumi sighed and resumed her place on the stretcher. That expression usually meant that the girl had resolved herself to disobey. Kazuko had a reasonable nature, but she also had a strong will that had never before had cause to be broken. The bitter darkness crept back into Hatsumi's mood as she contemplated what to do next.

Ken'ishi waited for them on the path, wondering why the kami were whispering to him so incessantly. He looked at Akao to see if the dog was feeling it as well, but he looked calm. Akao stayed close to Ken'ishi. The villagers carrying Hatsumi's litter made the dog nervous. Ken'ishi's uneasiness started this morning soon after they departed the last village.

The dog sensed Ken'ishi's uneasiness and looked up at him quizzically.

Ken'ishi said, "The kami are whispering to me. Something is wrong." For the hundredth time today, his eyes scanned the road, the forest, with the strange sensation of being hemmed in by the closeness of the trees. He sensed danger coming, but could not see from where. When it came, there would be no warning.

Akao said, "Foolish man. Nothing on the wind. Only *her.*"

"Kazuko?"

"No. Not right. Not good, that other one. Beware."

Perhaps that was why the kami were whispering to him so

incessantly. Something was wrong with Hatsumi? After that look in her eyes, he could believe that she wished him ill, but what harm could a poor wounded woman do to him?

When Kazuko and Hatsumi returned to the road, Kazuko was upset. She would not look at him, or at Hatsumi, and her eyes were red as if from weeping. He could only wonder what transpired between them while they were out of sight.

When Hatsumi was situated on her stretcher once again, Kazuko was terse. "Let us go."

They walked for a while in silence again, until he could bear it no longer. "How far?"

She thought for a moment, and the chilliness of her demeanor seemed to thaw slightly. "Perhaps by this evening."

"Are you weary?"

She nodded.

"I could carry you."

The last of her sadness melted away into a giggle. "Now *that* would be absurd! You? Carry me?"

He smiled back. "That is what I wanted."

Her smile became a blush, and she bit her lip.

"A smile," he said. "All I wanted was a smile."

She smiled again, and the conflict and tension he sensed in her was gone.

"Would you like me to tell you more about my master?"

She nodded. "Yes, please!"

"Very well."

Dewdrop, let me cleanse
In your brief sweet waters . . .
These dark hands of life

—*Basho*

The eight-year-old boy trudged up the steep mountain path with his bucketful of river water. He had nearly reached the cave, wending his way through the early morning shadows of the towering pine trees. The air was cool and still. The sun had only just appeared, and a still, ghostly mist clung to the ground. He was hungry. He had not eaten yet today. This water would be used to make the rice for his breakfast.

The blow came out of nowhere as something small and hard ricocheted off the crown of his head. The pain exploded like a burst of hot ashes, and the tears erupted from his eyes. The bucket of water tumbled out of his hand, dumping its contents and bobbling back down the narrow rocky path. He was powerless to stop it, almost paralyzed with pain, curled into a ball on the ground, clutching his pate with both hands. He could hear the bucket bouncing down the mountain. Through the haze of tears, he saw his teacher standing above him, with one gray-feathered hand holding a fresh, green bamboo tube as long as his arm.

"I'm sorry I dropped the water!" the boy said.

"Bah! Who cares about the water, monkey-boy! It only turns to piss!"

The boy stared up at the bird man, trying in vain to read his round, black eyes. The tengu did not move and just stared down at the boy as if expecting something.

The boy picked himself up and turned to go after the bucket. He heard a deep breath and a puff of air, and another searing pain on his left buttock tore a howl out of him. A smooth round stone the size of his palm landed a couple of paces away. He threw himself down the mountain path, glancing over his shoulder to see Kaa lowering the tube from his mouth. A few step later, he looked again. The path was deserted. The tengu and his tube were gone.

He stopped and listened. Was his master trying to sneak up on him? He backed down the path, his senses tuned. His pate and his buttock burned with pain, and he rubbed each with one hand.

He heard another hiss, and another impact tore between his shoulder blades. He squealed like a wounded rabbit and threw himself into the bushes, his back arched with pain, sobbing. "What have I done?" he cried. "Why are you doing this?"

Again, the tengu was gone. Had the boy not brought water fast enough? Had he displeased his teacher somehow? He stole out of the bushes, his eyes scanning the path above and below, then he hurried down the slope to where the water bucket had lodged in a thicket. He snatched it up and ran back down the slope toward the river. His teacher had never punished him like this before.

As he knelt in the shallows of the river with his bucket, he spared a moment for a concerted look around. No one was in sight. He lowered his gaze to fill the bucket. Then he felt a sudden urge to duck. Ducking saved him from the first stone, but not the second. The second glanced off his back, causing little pain. Anger flared in his belly and helped dull the pain of the purpling bruises. He spun and saw his master standing thirty paces away along the riverbank, smacking the tube against his palm, grinning. The old bird was fast.

Kaa said, "You are starting to listen to them. Listen harder." With that, he spun on his bird-like foot and ran up the trail.

The boy watched him go, puzzled and hurting. Listen to whom? To what? He was afraid to go back up the mountain. He wanted to crawl into a tiny cave with his back to the wall so that he could see anything that came at him. But if he did not complete his chores, his master might beat him even worse. After a while, the churning hunger in his belly roared anew. If he was to be pummeled with stones, he would prefer a full belly. He picked up his full bucket of water and started up the path, wary as a rabbit in the open. Twice on his way up the mountain, stones whizzed from bushes, so fast they were tiny gray blurs. The first time, he managed to spill only a little of the water. The second time, the water went flying, and the bucket went rolling back down the mountain again. With growing stubbornness, he refilled the bucket and stomped back up the mountain.

Somewhere nearby, the boy could sense the tengu laughing invisibly, hiding behind a bush or in a tree. His teacher was such a master of concealment that it was like magic.

It was mid-afternoon before he reached the stone shelf of the cave, and he was so jumpy that he did not want to eat anymore. As the cave came into view, Kaa was sitting in front of the opening with a small fire lit and a pot of rice hanging above it. The boy scowled and winced, trudging with weariness and limping from his many bruises. Kaa stood up. The boy stopped in front of him. The tengu reached out for the bucket. The bamboo tube was on the ground beside him.

The boy bowed and handed the bucket to him. His bow was curt with the heat of his anger.

Kaa took the bucket and threw the water in the boy's face.

The boy gasped in shock and choked back the mouth and nose full of water.

"You look hot, monkey-boy," Kaa said. "You should cool off."

The boy gaped before him, speechless and dripping.

"Now, sit and eat."

The boy obeyed and took up the bowl. He ate ravenously, and the tengu watched him.

When the boy was finished, he followed another sudden urge to duck. The blow that would have clubbed across his ear hissed over his head instead. The boy leaped to his feet and ran away, stopping several paces from his master.

"Why?" he cried.

"It is the only way to learn this lesson."

"What lesson?"

The tengu ruminated for a while, and the boy waited for him to speak. "You must listen to them."

"Listen? Who?"

The tengu continued as if he had not spoken. "You must train yourself to listen to the voices of the world around you, the voices of the kami, the spirits that inhabit every breath of air, every rock, every tree. When the kami speak to you, you must listen. They will tell you when danger is coming, if you know how to listen."

From that day forward, the boy never turned his back on his teacher. He went around corners and passed trees very carefully, always trying to hear the quiet voices of the spirits of the world. The attacks could come at any time, when he was carrying water, or wood, or sitting in the river bathing. That vicious tube was his nemesis, along with the master's seemingly endless supply of smooth round stones that all seemed to fit perfectly inside the tube. Until he was ten years old, his body wore cratered patterns of red, black, and yellow bruises.

As time passed, however, the number of marks became fewer. In the early months, whatever he was carrying often went flying as he scrambled for safety, but later he managed to keep a grip on his bucket of water or his bundle of wood.

His teacher became ever more ingenious at laying ambushes, sometimes waiting submerged under the water while the boy approached with a fishing spear. Wet stones were easier to hear coming, but they hurt worse. The tengu knew the boy's habits, where he went and when, attacking sometimes from above or below, so the boy changed his habits, taking different paths up and down the mountain at different times. This spared him some bruises. But as soon as the boy tried something new to outwit his master, the tengu found some new way to trick him. The stones flew so fast that the boy suspected him of using magical powers to propel them and to hide in the shape of a bush or a stone. The boy knew every stone, every tree trunk, and every bush on the face of the mountain, but sometimes those things looked different or out of place, and at those times he was the most wary.

As the marks on his body became fewer, his pride in his ability to avoid them grew. And as his teacher found new ways to inflict pain on him, so his pride in his teacher grew. Kaa was an ingenious old bird, cunning beyond compare. And in those instances of decreasing rarity, the boy was able to match wits with him and avoid the incoming sting. Without a word of instruction, the boy learned the difference between true alertness and mindless panic. He no longer passed by a bush or a tree while thinking of something else. He discovered the Now, and in that Now, he heard the quiet voices of the kami.

One day when he was ten years old, he was sneaking through the forest, his senses and awareness honed to sliver sharpness, and he came upon his teacher laying in ambush behind a tree, facing the direction from which the boy would have come, if not for his awareness of the kami. The boy felt a strange mixture of pity and jubilation. Pity for his teacher, who now would be dead if the boy had been an enemy, and jubilation that his skills had come to match his teacher's abilities.

The boy turned and stole away again, silent as a passing shadow.

That afternoon Kaa came to him with a strange scowl on his face and placed a wooden sword in his hands.

Ken'ishi was alerted by a sound like thunder on the road ahead.

Akao stood beside him, bristling, his shoulders hunched into a crouch, a low growl in his throat. "Beware!"

The forest had given way to fields, and dry rice paddies flanked the road on either side. Farmers worked the soil in the warmth of the late afternoon sun. A few moments after he noticed the sound, a column of mounted samurai rode out of the forest ahead, galloping toward them. One in the front carried a banner, lofted above his head. They bore down upon Ken'ishi and his small procession with startling speed. He stepped in front of Kazuko and gripped the hilt of his sword. Akao edged behind him, peering past his legs, growling softly.

Kazuko's voice was filled with relief and happiness. "No, Ken'ishi, those are my father's men!"

He took his hand from his sword, but he did not relax. The kami buzzed in his ears like a swarm of cicadas. He stepped away from her, knowing that they might perceive him as a threat to their master's daughter. These were Nishimuta clan samurai. A few days ago, he had slain one of their brethren. Would news of that deed have reached this far? He thought for a moment about the kind of death that lay in store for him if he was captured, but he did not have long to think before the riders were upon them.

The column reined up. Its leader was a middle-aged man with grim features, whose eyes flicked back and forth between Kazuko and Ken'ishi. "Lady Kazuko, is it you?"

Kazuko bowed. "Yes, Captain Sakamoto."

"Your return was overdue, so your father sent us to find you. Where is the rest of your entourage?"

"They are all dead. Bandits attacked us. My bodyguards and bearers were killed. Hatsumi and I were the only survivors." She gestured toward Ken'ishi. "This brave ronin saved our lives. Captain Sakamoto, this is Ken'ishi."

Ken'ishi bowed deeply.

Captain Sakamoto's voice dripped with cautious disdain, with an underlying thread of suspicion that put Ken'ishi on guard. "A ronin. Little more than a bandit himself."

Kazuko's voice was firm. "Captain Sakamoto, this man is a brave and capable warrior. After the bandits killed all of my bodyguards, he single-handedly defeated them and slew their leader, an oni. Hatsumi and I would have suffered a horrible fate if not for him. He has been our sole protector."

Captain Sakamoto grunted, and Ken'ishi felt the eyes of all the samurai upon him, sizing him up. Sakamoto said, "Forgive me, my lady. He does not look so fearsome as that."

215

Kazuko continued, "I intend to ask my father to take him into service."

"As you wish, my lady," Sakamoto said. "Please allow us to escort you home. I regret that we have no carriage for you. I will send one of my men for a carriage and bearers."

"I have walked this far. I will walk the rest of the way."

"Is Hatsumi injured?"

"She was badly hurt by the oni during the attack and cannot walk."

"An oni, eh? What did it look like? Was it Hakamadare?"

Kazuko described the creature.

Captain Sakamoto's voice gained a tone of respect. "I have heard tales of this monster and his pack of bandits. They have been attacking villages and travelers across several domains."

Kazuko said, "Yes, Captain. The body has been burned to ashes. Its death was neither quick nor easy."

For the first time, Sakamoto turned to Ken'ishi. "Then you have done this land a great service, sir. And you have done my lord a great service in the safe return of his only child."

Ken'ishi bowed deeply and tried to keep his voice from quavering. "Thank you." A wave of elation such as he had never felt rushed through him like a warm waterfall. His heart hammered in his breast like the clapping of a water mill. Gooseflesh rippled up and down his arms and legs. He turned to Kazuko and said, "Thank you, Kazuko."

She bowed in return. "It is a meager recompense for the gift you gave me."

The horsemen took up positions both before and behind the small procession, escorting them the last few ri to Nishimuta no Jiro's estate.

Ken'ishi could only revel silently in his good fortune. He thanked the sparrow. He thanked Jizo. He walked with as much silent dignity as he could muster, his back straighter, his shoulders square, his chin high, his step confident.

He had never seen horses so closely before, never been able to examine them. He marveled at the muscles rippling beneath the brown coats and wondered at how these strange beasts moved with such grace. Even more, how the samurai rode them with such masterful ease. He imagined himself on horseback galloping across open fields, the wind blowing through his fine flowing robes, Silver Crane freshly polished and gleaming in the sunlight.

The sight of Lord Nishimuta's estate shattered his daydream and stole the breath from his chest. The magnificent house seemed to hang on the side of a small mountain just off the valley floor, floating on a billowing avalanche of dense foliage, painted gold by the setting sun. A town nestled against the base of the mountain. As his gaze traveled over the gracefully sloping roofs and gables, Ken'ishi thought this must be the greatest day of his life. The moment he first held Silver Crane in his hands had been a profound moment, but the joy and pride he had felt then were quickly subsumed by the trepidation of facing the unknown for the first time. Today he felt his fortunes coming together, and he thanked the kami for their gifts. To find service with a lord such as this was his dream, to serve with courage and honor. Knowing this lord was the father of the beautiful maiden walking beside him made the dream even greater.

In the past few days, he had come to believe that Kazuko would be always at his side. Just like his only friend, Akao, he could no longer imagine his life without her in it. Her smile, her laugh, her scent. His mind slipped back to wondering if she felt the same way about him. The small inner voices of the kami told him that she did. But some part of him also wanted to hear it from her lips, some part of him that would never give itself over until he heard the words, some part of him that would always doubt he could receive such a gift until it was in his grasp. Love. Yes, this must be what love is. He had heard of it in songs and conversation, and had vainly tried to imagine what it must be like. But now he was sure, with a realization that came as simple and clear as the words themselves. He loved her. But part of him also knew that a wealthy lord like her father would never allow a poor, uncultured ronin to have his daughter. Girls were wed to make allies for their families; they rarely had any choice. But perhaps if he proved himself quickly, learned all the rules and manners as quickly as he could. . . . Daydreams filled his thoughts, making him practically giddy with excitement, masking the buzzing spark of the kami whispering to him, letting him forget that something was amiss.

I sit at my desk.
What can I write to you?
Sick with love,
I long to see you in the flesh.
I can write only,
"I love you. I love you. I love you."
Love cuts through my heart
And tears my vitals.
Spasms of longing suffocate me
And will not stop.

—*The Love Poems of Marichiko*

Ken'ishi sat alone in a small room, a single lamp casting huge shadows on the latticed, rice-paper walls. The people of the household muttered and shuffled around him with fleeting shadows on the walls. Captain Sakamoto had ushered him in here and told him to wait. Someone would come for him soon enough. Akao had disappeared into the village to search for food; all the armed men and throngs of people around the manor house made him uneasy. When they parted, Akao gave him a long, mournful look. "Beware, Ken'ishi. Danger. Waiting here." Ken'ishi's belly swirled with unexpected misgivings. He did not like leaving his friend alone in a town full of strangers.

A great commotion erupted at the return of the lord's daughter. The house servants rushed out and gathered up Kazuko and Hatsumi and bundled them into the house almost before he could blink, and the uproar receded like a storm into the depths of the house.

The manor house was a beautiful structure, tall and stately, its white plaster walls reaching up three stories to grasp the rays of the dying sunlight, the flaring, tiled roofs bathed in a deep crimson, built into the slope of the small mountain above the valley floor. A single, narrow road led up the mountainside. There was no palisade or other fortification to protect against attack. The manor was a complex of buildings, with stables and barracks and servants' quarters that were camouflaged by the rocky, forested slope. From this vantage point, the entire valley spread out below him, disappearing in the hazy, blue distance, the patchwork of green darkening with the coming of night, the falling sun raising the shadows on the mountainsides.

Captain Sakamoto had led Ken'ishi into the house and placed him in an empty room near the entrance where guests customarily waited. With a twinge of discomfort at leaving Silver Crane, he allowed the servant to take it from him and place it reverently in the rack for guests' weapons near the entrance. The servant also took his bow and pack, leaving him feeling naked and vulnerable.

As he sat in the empty silence, he wished for his flute, but it was in his pack. Music fluttered in his chest like a nightingale, yearning for release upon the spirits of the air.

He imagined Kazuko speaking with her father. Ken'ishi knew that she would speak well of him, and he hoped with all his being that Lord Nishimuta would heed her words.

"Father, I am home," Kazuko said as she shuffled into his chamber.

Lord Nishimuta no Jiro looked up from the scrolls on his desk, and his dark eyes widened with pleasure. Her father was a large man, whose once-powerful thews had softened with the luxury of his life. His graying hair was perfectly cut and styled, as always, his robes glimmering with the opulence of fine red silk and gold embroidery. He was dressed finer than was his custom, and she wondered why for a moment. He preferred simple samurai kusode and trousers, perhaps imagining himself still the young warrior who had once seized these lands from his older brothers. A smile twitched at the corner of his lips, so she knew that he was indeed pleased to see her. The relief was evident in his voice. "Ah, my dear, it is good that you are home. I was . . . worried."

"I am sorry to worry you so, Father. But I have such an exciting tale to tell!" She knelt politely across the desk from him, folding her hands in her lap.

"Exciting, eh?" His voice took on the tone that it always did when he was humoring her.

Her tale of the bandit attack, and the oni, and Ken'ishi, and the long walk home tumbled out of her in a breathless rush. She could hardly speak fast enough. As she did, she saw glimpses of emotion flickering across her father's almost immobile features. Surprise, disbelief, anger, sorrow, relief, amusement. He listened to her quietly, with no need to spur her on. The more she spoke, the more penetrating his scrutiny became. She felt it boring into her.

When she finished, he asked her, "And where is this ronin now?"

"I'm sure he is waiting to meet you. He is ever so strong. He is an . . . interesting man. He wishes for a worthy master, Father. There are none more worthy than you."

Her father laughed. "There is no need to flatter me, my dear. If he can kill an oni, he is certainly a man worth some consideration."

"Thank you, Father. I am so sure he will serve you well. But tell me, why are you so dressed up today?"

Her father leaned back on his heels and rested his palms on his thighs. "We have a guest coming today. A man from Lord Tsunetomo's court."

"Really? Why? Who is it? I met many people there . . . before."

"And how was the cherry blossom viewing, my dear?"

"Oh, it was wonderful!"

"And how did you find Lord Tsunetomo? Was he a gracious host?"

"Oh, yes, Father! He is a very kind man, a very strong man."

"I am glad to hear you say it. Now, be a good girl and send Hatsumi to my meeting hall. I need to speak with her."

"Of course, Father." Kazuko smiled, but she still felt a twinge of distress at being so quickly dismissed after her long ordeal.

Lord Nishimuta sat on the dais in his meeting hall. His deep-set dark eyes gazed down on Hatsumi with an inscrutable glitter. She swallowed hard, feeling a sick blackness swirling in her belly like tar. She clenched her hands in her lap to keep them from shaking and shifted uncomfortably at the sharp ache in her nether region.

"So, Hatsumi, what do you wish to speak to me about?" His broad mouth bore a concerned expression. "What was so important that could not wait?"

Hatsumi prostrated herself. "Thank you for allowing me to speak, my lord." As she straightened into a sitting position, she allowed a bit of worry to slip into her voice. "It is about Kazuko."

Lord Nishimuta's face lit up at the mention of his daughter, then darkened again as he said, "What is it? She is fine, is she not?"

"She has spoken to you about the ronin, yes?"

"Yes, she has. I am going to speak to him later this evening."

Hatsumi took a deep breath. "My lord, I wish to give you another view of this man before you speak to him yourself."

"Go on, then."

"My lord, the ronin is a strong man, tough, and a skilled warrior."

"That must be true for him to have defeated the oni."

A chill skittered down Hatsumi's spine. Dim flashes of memory sent all other thoughts spinning into oblivion. The blunt explosions of pain as the creature's fists pummeled her into the bushes. Something tearing at her clothing, either branches or claws. The creature's obscene laughter. The tremendous weight upon her, crushing her into the carpet of dead leaves like the weight of a downed bullock. The splitting, stabbing agony as its huge, blunt organ tore into her womb. The hideous, horned face and feral, yellow eyes, only inches from hers. Foul spittle dripping into her mouth. Vile breath in her face, suffocating her. The final merciful blackness. . . .

Lord Nishimuta's voice jerked her awareness back to the moment. "Isn't that true, Hatsumi?"

The tone of his words made her wonder how long she had

drifted away. He was not a man who allowed underlings to waste his time. She said, "Yes, that's true, my lord. But, my lord, he is a ronin. He has no family."

"A ronin by unfortunate circumstance of birth, not by choice or failure. I don't believe that to be an unfavorable mark against a man. There are many great warriors who came from humble beginnings."

"My lord, he is not merely a penniless ronin, but an uncouth ruffian. Have you seen him?"

"No."

"My lord, I cannot imagine anyone with worse manners and bearing. His manners are worse than most peasants'."

Lord Nishimuta grunted. "Another unfortunate circumstance of his upbringing. No fault of his own. Besides, with time he could learn what manners he needs."

"My lord, he is a mean, cruel man. He almost killed a diseased beggar. He didn't like the beggar's smell."

"What of that? Killing one of the unclean is no crime. Doubtless, this beggar frightened my daughter. She mentioned this beggar. His actions must have been in her defense. This shows great loyalty and proper vigilance, unusual in a man with no proper education."

"My lord, we do not know the truth about his upbringing. Did Kazuko speak of that?"

"No, she didn't."

"He told us a tale of how he was raised. I don't believe it, because it makes him either a liar or a madman."

Lord Nishimuta's eyes narrowed.

"My lord, he claims to have been raised by a tengu."

His eyes widened. "A tengu!" His words tumbled into a brief chuckle. "That would be quite a tale indeed!"

"My lord, no one that I know has ever seen a tengu, nor have

I ever heard of anyone seeing one. They are creatures from stories!"

Lord Nishimuta laughed again. "Ah, Hatsumi, I have never seen my ancestors either, but that doesn't mean they don't exist! I have never seen a kappa, or an oni, or the Buddha himself but that doesn't mean they don't exist. Evidence of their presence is all around us, but we cannot see them. Perhaps his tale is true. Perhaps it is just a tale. Telling a tale doesn't make him a madman. I will size him up when I speak to him." His tone indicated this conversation was nearly over.

Hatsumi took another deep breath. "My lord, there is one other thing you must know." She paused for a moment, gathering her courage. If Kazuko ever found out she had spoken of this, the girl would never forgive her. She lowered her voice almost to a whisper. "He is in love with your daughter."

She glanced at Lord Nishimuta's face. His left eyelid began to twitch, and the pleasant mood disappeared from his face like the blue sky behind a gathering typhoon. But somehow, surprise was not present.

His voice hardened along with his face. "Have they been alone together?"

"No, my lord, never. Nevertheless, my lord, if I may be so bold, she reads too many pillow books. She is not as worldly as you and I. I would never question her honor or loyalty, but her sense of duty is stronger toward her own desires, not toward the family. May I be forgiven for saying so, but Kazuko is in love with the ronin, too. My lord, from her own lips she confided in me her feelings for him."

"Enough!"

Hatsumi prostrated herself again, quivering. She feared death, but if her death meant that the filthy ronin would not sully the body of her precious Kazuko, then her death would be welcome.

He appeared to relax just a bit, like a stone block in a castle

225

wall settling into place. "I have already made my plans for him, and this changes nothing."

Hatsumi's mouth fell open in shock.

Lord Nishimuta ignored her reaction. She studied his face, trying to glean some indication of his thoughts, but it was like trying to read the face of a stone block. His piercing gaze speared her to the planks of the floor, and his voice was slow and cold. "Hatsumi, listen well. You will never speak of this again. Never. Do you understand?"

She gulped and bowed. "Understood."

Someone softly approached in the hallway outside his room. A woman's silhouette appeared on the rice paper, knelt outside the door, and said, "Excuse me, sir. I have a gift for you from Lord Nishimuta. Please accept his gratitude. May I come in?"

"Yes."

The door slid open, and the servant woman bowed to him, lifting forward a bundle wrapped in bright blue cloth, tied with a yellow string. He turned on his knees and took the bundle in both hands, bowing as he did so. He said, "Please send your master my sincere thanks."

"You are invited to dinner this evening in honor of his daughter's safe return. Dinner is in one hour. Do you desire a bath?"

"A bath would be good."

"Then may I take you there?"

"Please."

She took him to the bathhouse, a small building separated from the manor house. The water was warm and comfortable, and the wooden bathtub was huge, wide enough for him to stretch his legs, and deep enough that the water came up to his neck. Bathing in warm water was still a novelty. Until the priest's house, he had only cleaned himself in cold rivers and icy streams. As he soaked in the warm water, images of Kazuko filled his mind. After he climbed out of the bath, he slipped into a clean robe left for him inside the door and found the servant woman waiting outside to escort him back to his room.

Upon returning to his room, he unwrapped the package the servant had brought him. Inside he found crisp black trousers, a long black sash, and a deep-blue robe made of fine, soft silk. He gasped at the richness of this garment. He would look like a proper gentleman wearing these clothes! Another shiver of excitement rippled through him.

When the hour came for him to be summoned to dinner, he was well dressed, a fine, handsome figure. He stood straighter, his step surer than if he had been dressed in his old rags. His breast filled with pride. But even so, when he entered the hall where the meal was served, the sight of so many noble eyes upon him left a queer fluttering in his belly, like a fresh-killed game fowl spitted on an arrow.

Lord Nishimuta sat on the raised dais at the far end of the room, with a vision of pure loveliness seated beside him. Kazuko's garments were fresh and beautiful. Her hair was combed and styled, her face lightly powdered, her lovely lips rouged. About a dozen other people sat in two facing rows stretching away from the platform. Captain Sakamoto sat on the floor nearest to the lord's right hand. His gaze was hard but curious as he regarded Ken'ishi, as if he was waiting for something momentous to happen. Hatsumi was absent. He wondered if that was because she was only a servant. So many subtleties, so many unknowns in the society of people. He felt even more unarmed and helpless than ever, like a fish trying to walk on land. He tripped over the doorjamb as he stepped into the room, causing a polite stir of amusement among those gathered. Nevertheless he knelt and prostrated himself before the lord's household, introducing himself as he did so.

227

Lord Nishimuta's voice was deep and commanding. "Ken'ishi, I am Nishimuta no Jiro. I am pleased to have you as a guest in my house." He gestured toward an empty place at the end of one of the lines, farthest away from the platform.

"I am honored to be your guest, Nishimuta-sama." Ken'ishi bowed again, lower, and then took his place. His place was located next to a plump, stuffy-looking man with ink-stained fingers, who kept glancing at Ken'ishi surreptitiously. His bearing suggested varying degrees of curiosity and distrust.

"Honored guests," Lord Nishimuta said, "this is the man who saved my daughter's life, rescuing her from the clutches of a terrible oni and his criminal cohorts. Let us all drink to his honor and prowess!" He raised his sake bowl, the others did the same, and they all drank together. Ken'ishi's ears burned again, and he squirmed. He did not like being on display.

Lord Nishimuta continued, "We have another most honorable guest tonight." He gestured toward the waspish man, thin, bookish, and sour looking who sat opposite Captain Sakamoto. The thin man bowed in return. Ken'ishi could hardly see this other visitor from where he sat because of several people interposing. "This is Otomo no Yasutoki, chamberlain to Lord Otomo no Tsunetomo."

Yasutoki said, "It is the greatest honor to be a guest in the house of Lord Nishimuta. May this be the first of many cordial meetings between our two houses."

The servants brought trays of food to the guests. Before Ken'ishi moved a muscle, he watched the people near him, observed how they behaved, how they ate, how they held their bowls, how they moved. The effort at controlling his perpetual hunger in the face of so much food was difficult. No one laughed at him, or looked at him with scorn or derision, so he considered that he must have succeeded in his efforts to appear respectable.

Throughout dinner, Ken'ishi stole surreptitious glances at Kazuko. Once, he caught her eye, and he smiled at her. She quickly suppressed her own smile in return, but could not hide the faint blush in her cheeks. The warmth of affection in his belly stirred, the promise of a shared secret.

When the meal was over, he was certain that he had never eaten so well in his entire life. His belly was full, and his head was swimming from the potent sake.

"Ken'ishi!" Lord Nishimuta called. "You have been remarkably silent for an honored guest. Please regale us all with the tale of how you slew the oni."

Ken'ishi nearly wilted. "My lord, I'm not a storyteller. There's not much to tell."

"Come now! I won't have 'no' for an answer. To hear my daughter speak of it, one would believe it to be the stuff of legends."

Ken'ishi blushed and proceeded hesitantly. "Very well. I don't have the words of a poet. I can only speak plainly." He took a deep breath and squared his shoulders.

"Then plainly it is. Let us not put a robe on a pig!"

The guests tittered.

Ken'ishi swallowed hard, trying to decide whether the lord's statement was meant as an insult. Then he began his tale, slow and halting at first from his care not to use words the listeners might consider vulgar or unseemly, but as he drew further into the tale, he found that it took on a life of its own. He tried to note the reaction of Lord Nishimuta and his guests, but their faces were inscrutable. Even as he spoke, he thought the whole story sounded unbelievable; however, he had been there, and he remembered it with perfect clarity.

As he spoke, he noticed that the feeling of unease had returned stronger than ever. Danger was near. But how could that be, in a place like this? Then he noticed the man named Yasutoki watching him. His gaze was as sharp and penetrating as the point of a spear. The man had a lithe grace about him that he tried to conceal, but Ken'ishi noted it well. Ken'ishi also noted the glint of something else in the man's eyes. It was as if Yasutoki knew him, but Ken'ishi was certain he had never met Yasutoki before. Yasutoki noticed that Ken'ishi had observed him, and all expression and interest left his eyes like an extinguished flame. The hairs rose on the back of Ken'ishi's neck. He must beware of that man.

He ended his tale with a recount of the journey to Lord Nishimuta's estate.

"Well told, Ken'ishi! Well told! You do not have the words of a poet, but you have the heart of a tiger!"

"I could not have defeated the demon without Kazuko's help. Lord Nishimuta must be a great warrior to have taught her so well."

Lord Nishimuta laughed. "And you do have the tongue of a courtier! Yes, my daughter is quite skilled with the naginata. It is a traditional weapon in my family, and alas, I lack the sons to teach it to. Thank you for the tale, Ken'ishi. I now have a tale of my own. An announcement, to be precise."

The dinner guests' attention now focused on Lord Nishimuta.

Lord Nishimuta continued, "The visit of the honored Yasutoki is not merely one of pleasure, but of auspicious news. He brings us welcome news indeed."

Yasutoki said, "Nishimuta-sama is a gracious host and a worthy friend to my lord, Otomo no Tsunetomo." His voice was smooth as oil, and he spoke with deep, measured tones.

Lord Nishimuta said, "It is my honor and pleasure to announce a new alliance between the houses of Nishimuta and Otomo. Our two houses are like stones in the same castle wall, side-by-side, as firm as the earth itself, an alliance that will form an anchor of power in this land. And my beautiful daughter will form the mortar between those two stones. I have offered her in marriage to Lord Tsunetomo, and he has accepted!" Lord Nishimuta's smile was broad and beaming.

The dinner guests clapped in pleasure and nodded their appreciation at the good news.

The rest of the evening's conversation dissolved into a muffled buzzing in Ken'ishi's ears, like a hornets' nest covered with a blanket, and his belly felt as if someone had just kicked him. He could not help staring at Lord Nishimuta. The older man's dark eyes flicked toward Ken'ishi just for an instant, and in that instant, Ken'ishi read the full knowledge of Lord Nishimuta's words. The lord's eyes were not spiteful or vicious, but they were resolved. A poor, masterless warrior would never have *his* daughter, not even for an instant. The idea was ludicrous.

Ken'ishi noticed that his hands quivered in his lap like windblown grass. The dinner guests expressed their congratulations to Lord Nishimuta while Kazuko sat as silent as a stone beside him. Her gaze was fixed and unmoving on the floor in front of her, and she looked pale. Sake bowls were raised and drained to celebrate Lord Nishimuta's good fortune. Ken'ishi's mind raced, and his heart thundered. Why did she not say anything? Why did she not protest? But he already knew the answer. She did not dare. The quivering in his belly began to congeal into anger like a gobbet of molten lead. He wanted to leap to his feet and run, to flee this castle, this betrayal, and never look back. But he could not. Insulting Lord Nishimuta with unseemly behavior might cost Ken'ishi his life. So he just sat quietly, trying to breathe, struggling not to explode like a toad hit with a hammer.

Mercifully, dinner was over soon after that, and Ken'ishi retired to his room. He felt numb, as if he had just been beaten by a hundred clubs. He wondered if he would be angry in the future, because he had a vague feeling that he should be. The logic of it all was clear, even in the fog of his shock and dismay. Kazuko would never be his. Never. She belonged to another. How could she let him fall in love with her when she was already promised to another? But at the same time, he knew that their love had been impossible from the beginning, and perhaps he was angry with himself for ever allowing such feelings for her. Part of him raged with anger and hurt, and part of him spoke with a calm inner voice saying that it could never have been any other way.

He shoved these flashes, these stabs of emotion aside and settled himself again into the cold, logical numbness. Lord Nishimuta's gifts and compliments had been nothing more than a show, a way to thank publicly the poor, penniless, masterless beggar, while doing nothing of substance, and making certain any complications to Kazuko's betrothal were removed.

Then with crystal clarity, he realized that his life was in danger. Lord Nishimuta, or one of his retainers, might well decide to remove him more permanently. He had to get away. He began gathering his things for departure. He looked up as one of the sliding doors whished aside, revealing Captain Sakamoto standing above him.

"Come with me." Captain Sakamoto's tone was carefully neutral. A sliver of ice pierced Ken'ishi's breast. Death was near, and he welcomed it.

Ken'ishi stood, picking up his things, saying nothing, and instinctively began to measure Sakamoto's stance and carriage. Sakamoto led him back to the foyer of the manor house. Ken'ishi's heart beat like a smith's hammer against his breastbone, seeming to choke off his air. Sakamoto picked up Ken'ishi's traveling pack and thrust it toward him. Ken'ishi took it. The sliver of ice in his breast became a chunk of iceberg, crushing his ribs from within. Sakamoto then took Silver Crane from the rack, but did not hand it over.

More than anything now, he wanted Silver Crane in his hand. He needed its strength. In the course of an hour, his life had become nothing more than a hollow shell. Ken'ishi's spirit reached out for his weapon, yearned for it in his hand, and he felt something strange, unexpected, yet familiar.

The blade returned his call. Like a distant voice across a chasm.

Sakamoto gestured toward the open door. Ken'ishi's jaw locked shut, and his clenched fists could have ground a sapling to splinters. He stepped outside, and Sakamoto followed two steps behind.

With each step down into the lamp-lit courtyard, Ken'ishi's stomach grew colder and heavier.

Sakamoto stopped, and Ken'ishi turned, bathed in the lamp-light from the house. Sakamoto held out Ken'ishi's sword. With the light behind Sakamoto, Ken'ishi could hardly see his face, but the man's voice was dead. "Regrettably, your services will not be required."

Ken'ishi reached out, took his weapon, and slid it through his fine new sash. His clenched teeth would barely let him speak. "I saved his daughter's life! That is worth nothing?"

"What sort of reward were you hoping for? Her hand in marriage?" He threw his head back and laughed.

Ken'ishi said nothing, feeling his ears burning with anger.

Sakamoto's voice grew as cold as steel. "Today, before you arrived, we received news that a Nishimuta clan vassal named Takenaga was slain in a duel in Uchida village. He was slain by a ronin matching your description. If you wanted to remain undiscovered, you should have had the sense at least to change your name."

Ken'ishi's back stiffened. "It was a duel of honor! And I offered Takenaga two chances to make it a non-lethal bout, but he refused."

A flicker of surprise flashed in Sakamoto's eyes. "So you do not deny it!"

"I deny nothing."

Sakamoto snorted with disdain, then his voice rose with anger. "Takenaga was my friend and comrade. We fought many battles against men just like you. He was a great swordsman! He was preparing to open his own training hall."

"I was better, and that is why he lost."

"Why you arrogant little cock!" Sakamoto laughed again harshly. "Be that as it may, you saved the life of my lord's daughter and brought her safely home. Saving her life purchased yours. For now. If you are present in the village at sunrise, you will be arrested and executed. Go now. Leave this province and never return."

Three other samurai took places behind their captain.

Ken'ishi turned without another word. He could not breathe. He could not speak. But his dignity would remain intact. The wood of his scabbard creaked with the ferocity of his grip. He walked into the darkness, the rubble of his dreams strewn behind him.

A silent shadow shifted imperceptibly in the blackness between a storehouse and a stable. The shadow watched Sakamoto hand over the sword to the ronin. Yasutoki was amused to see that the ronin was close to exploding. Ah, the furious emotions of youth and their obsessions with love. So predictable, so easy to manipulate. The sword glinted with silver in the lamplight as the ronin clasped it. Then Yasutoki's eyes fixed on the weapon.

Something familiar about that sword. . . .

Silver cranes on the hilt, mother-of-pearl cranes on the scabbard. He stifled a gasp of surprise. Could it be? How was it possible?

Yasutoki watched the ronin go, and silently cursed that he

could not follow. Even though he had retired to his room for the evening, an extended absence might be missed. He had to get back inside soon.

How had a weapon like Silver Crane fallen into the hands of a young ronin like this one? How had it ventured so far? Did the ronin have any idea how many men would kill to have that sword in their possession? Did he know of the powers it was said to possess? How could he? For all of the ronin's formidable prowess, he was little more than an ignorant bumpkin.

Now he had even more reason to seek this ronin. Recovering a weapon like Silver Crane, one that had been lost to the world for so long. . . . A swirl of fresh greed and ambition formed in his belly, and he smiled. No, a ronin like this could not be allowed to despoil such a weapon. It must be returned to the hands of a true noble, a noble of the proper clan.

He cursed again as the ronin disappeared into the darkness. He would find him. There was no question; it was only a matter of time.

Making love with you
Is like drinking seawater.
The more I drink
The thirstier I become,
Until nothing can slake my thirst
But to drink the entire sea.

—*The Love Poems of Marichiko*

Kazuko sat on the floor in a limp, inconsolable pile, weeping into her sleeves. The soft cloth was soaked with tears. She did not know how long she had been weeping. She remembered little after her father's announcement of her betrothal. She wanted nothing more than to leap to her feet and scream in protest, but the slightest hint of public protest would have dishonored him. He might have hated her forever, perhaps disowned her. Then in the midst of her shock and grief, she remembered Ken'ishi and thought that she would not care what her father did, as long as she and Ken'ishi could be together. She remembered stealing glances at Ken'ishi afterwards, seeing the utter devastation in his face, the sick agony, the desperate fear, all barely concealed. She had grown to know him well in the short time they had been together, and she could read him well.

She prayed that he did not hate her. She could not bear that. He must think that she had betrayed him. What he must think of her brought a fresh torrent of tears and shuddering sobs.

Hatsumi's voice intruded on her misery. "Now, now, dear. It's not as bad as all that. Lord Tsunetomo is a good man. He will make a fine husband."

"I don't care about that!" Kazuko snapped.

"You need not weep so for that ronin, Kazuko. He will be fine."

"No, he won't! I won't!" It was all too painful. She could hardly gather her thoughts to speak.

Hatsumi sighed and sat down gingerly beside her. "He is just a ruffian." She touched Kazuko's shoulder, and her tone was kind and concerned. "It is better that he's gone. Remember what I told you about. . . ."

Kazuko turned on her, feeling a flash of rage. "Never speak of him again!"

Now Hatsumi bristled back at her. "I did what was best for you! I always do what is best for you! The ronin is better off gone from here!"

"How can you say such things! He saved your life! He carried you!"

"Yes, he did all those things. But I am wise enough to know the danger of a caged animal. Inside the cage, the wolf paces back and forth, yearning to be free, until it attacks its keeper in its desperation to return to the wilderness. The ronin is just such a creature. He is dangerous, wild. This house would be a cage to him."

Kazuko deflated again, and another sigh shuddered out of her breast. "He must hate me. I cannot stand it."

"Oh, now, I'm sure he doesn't hate you. He's not a stupid man. He understands the necessity of what your father did, and why it cannot be changed. It is the way of the world. Your father has given you to Lord Tsunetomo, and that is that."

"But I want Ken'ishi!" Kazuko knew she sounded like a petulant, spoiled child, but she could not help it. It was the truth.

"Out of the question, I'm afraid. Your father's wishes have been expressed publicly. He cannot change them now without severe consequences. He would lose face and insult Lord Tsunetomo. Your father would then have him as an enemy, not an ally. It might even mean open war between them. You cannot refuse."

A fresh burst of sobs consumed all of Kazuko's thoughts and words.

Hatsumi continued, "Kazuko, you must let the ronin go. You must forget him. Put him out of your mind."

Kazuko's mind screamed *NEVER!* But she said nothing, and just wept. Her heart hurt so badly she feared she would die. She had to do something.

Hatsumi kept talking, her voice matronly and soothing. "Try to calm yourself. I'll prepare your bed for you. You will feel better in the morning. Put the ronin from your mind. If you have any further contact with him, it would mean his death."

As Hatsumi unfolded Kazuko's bed and prepared it for her,

puttering about with blankets, Kazuko's sobs slowed, then began to diminish as a plan formed in her mind. The plan congealed from the formless, black mass of her emotions, taking the wild chaos and giving it shape, taking away its power to rule her and giving her purpose and resolve. The more real the plan became, the more her grief faded away. Doubtless Hatsumi felt that Kazuko's change in mood was because of her comforting words, but Hatsumi was wrong. Every word Hatsumi spoke about Ken'ishi made Kazuko even more resolved.

Kazuko lay down in her bed and pretended to go to sleep, but every heartbeat she was alert. The patience required for her to wait until Hatsumi was asleep was almost more than Kazuko could bear. In the darkness, Kazuko waited for Hatsumi's breathing to slow, waited for her telltale snoring. It seemed like a thousand lifetimes. Then finally, Hatsumi began to snore, and Kazuko slid from under the covers.

As Ken'ishi neared the village, the numbness in his mind suffused his body and soul. Akao emerged from the darkness to meet him, looking at him expectantly, but Ken'ishi could not speak. The two of them stopped and faced each other.

Akao regarded him for a moment, but in the end said nothing. He walked forward and placed his forehead against Ken'ishi's knee.

Ken'ishi reached down to touch the soft fur of his ears, but his hands felt like wood.

The village innkeeper was reluctant to admit anyone at such a late hour, but the jingle of Ken'ishi's purse and the fierce look in his eyes helped make the decision in his favor. As Ken'ishi sat in his small room, bathed in the feeble light of the oil lamp, his vision fuzzed with tears. He contemplated death as a release from the swelling pain, a pain that he feared would grow to unbearable proportions. His mind became the emptiness he usually sought only in battle. No thought. No emotion.

He gazed at his shadow on the rice-paper wall. His dark silhouette quivered in the light of the lamp. The next single moment he noticed was the moment the lamp went out. Some interminable time had passed. The only light now came from the flickering orange fire pit in the common room reaching through the thin rice paper, lighting Ken'ishi's room with a lattice of orange squares. He felt a twinge of alarm at having been so oblivious for so long.

He heard a sound from the common room, that of the front door of the inn sliding open. Who would be moving about at this late hour? He picked up his scabbard and approached the door to the common room. He slid the door open a crack and peered out. A small, cloaked figure in plain clothing, carrying a bundle under one arm crept across the room. A dark scarf concealed the figure's head. The figure looked uncertainly around the empty common room, taking a few steps further. Ken'ishi then recognized the gait of the figure, and all the numbness mercifully protecting him exploded like a lightning strike.

A small sound must have escaped him, because the figure's gaze snapped toward him, and the glistening brown eyes behind the scarf confirmed his fears.

Kazuko moved toward him, the only sound the swishing of her robes. Her voice was a breathless whisper. "Ken'ishi! Is that you?"

"Yes," he whispered through the cracked door.

"Please, I must speak to you!"

He stepped aside and opened the door. She all but ran into the small room. Before he could speak, she threw herself against his chest. Her fingers twisted into his new robe, and he felt the heat of her face on his breast. Her shoulders shuddered. He closed the door, leaving them in almost total darkness.

"Oh, Ken'ishi, it's horrible!" Her voice became a hoarse whisper, and the warm wetness of her tears seeped through the fine silk across his chest. "How could he be so cruel?"

He said nothing. His arms were rising to embrace her, but he fought the urge, forcing them back down to remain immobile.

Her words were muffled by his clothing and wracked by sobs. "Please believe me, I tried! When I first spoke to him, he was impressed. I was sure he would. . . . But I don't know what happened! Oh, Ken'ishi, I'm sorry! Please forgive me! I couldn't stand it if you thought badly of me!"

His mouth worked but no sound came forth. The pain and shock of the evening's events were once again fresh in his mind.

She pulled back from him and looked up into his face. Her face seemed to glow in the faint light, eyes and tear-tracks glistening. He looked down into her face, falling into her searching dark eyes.

Then she looked away. "I shouldn't have come. You're angry with me!"

No, wait! he wanted to say, but somehow his anger took hold of his mouth. He said, "You were betrothed, and you didn't tell me." *And you were a wanted man, and you did not tell her.*

"I didn't know! I didn't know until the moment my father made his announcement!" The helplessness in her voice convinced him she was telling the truth. Then bitterness crept into her tone. "The flower-viewing party was more than that. It was never for me."

"It was a 'wife-viewing,' " Ken'ishi said.

"Oh, Ken'ishi, you must forgive me. I didn't know. I was a fool." She began to weep, her soft sobs pricking at Ken'ishi's defenses. She took another small step back. "I'm sorry. I'll go. Your feelings aren't—"

His weapon clattered to the floor. His arms flew out and grabbed her, crushing her to his chest.

Her soft, lithe body melted against his, and fresh sobs poured out of her. A warm burst of bittersweet tears cooled against his chest, and they stood locked as one. The prickly pain of his loss began to disappear into the spreading warmth of her embrace.

She whispered, "We could run away together. I can't stand the thought of never seeing you again! I can't stand the thought of marrying another man, when I will be thinking only of you!"

He spoke slowly, the truth taking shape in his mind as he spoke. "We could run away, but we would be hunted. I would be hunted. If we were caught, you might be allowed to live, since I would be blamed for your abduction. But you know as well as I that I would be tortured and executed like a criminal. If we are discovered here, like this, the result will be the same."

Another sobbing sigh shuddered out of her.

"You know I speak the truth."

"We could go farther than anyone could look for us! We could go to your homeland. We could go across the sea!"

"I doubt we would reach the border of this province. And if we could, messengers would be sent to all the surrounding provinces. Someone would see us."

"We could disguise ourselves."

"I will not hide in the bushes like an animal for the rest of my life. I'm trying to live like a man now! We would be prisoners of our own flight."

Her fist released his clothing long enough to strike his shoulder in frustration, and her shoulders quaked with sobs.

"Please, don't cry," he said. He lifted her face to look up into his and smiled.

"How can I go on and not see you? How can I lie down with my husband and not wish that it were you! Ah, a spear has pierced my belly!" she said, but the despair in her face diminished as she looked into his eyes. "You asked me once what I knew of suffering. I know it well now."

"You must remember me with joy."

"Don't say such things. You speak as if you are already gone."

"By morning I must be gone."

"Where will you go?"

"I don't know. Far enough that I'll never see you again." He could not bear to see her and not be able to touch her.

For a long moment, they gazed into each other's eyes. Then her lips parted, and she pulled his head down to kiss her. Her voice was husky and moist. "Then this night must be one to remember always. We must make a lifetime's worth of love in one night."

Then her lips rose to his, warm and petal-soft. A moment of panic swept over him. He had never been with a woman before. In moments, his manhood stirred with powerful, throbbing heat, a yearning to . . . he did not know.

"Don't worry," she said breathlessly, as if reading his thoughts. "I'll show you. I have been educated in the ways of pleasing a man." Then she smiled like a vixen. "But it was all theory and no practice."

He was not sure what she meant, but again she covered his mouth with her own. The softness of her lips, the moist warmth of her breath, the silky smoothness of her skin, the delicate softness of her breasts pressed against him. All sense of caution and reserve disappeared. He crushed her to him, his manhood pressing into her soft belly. She pulled him down to the tatami mats, tugging at first at his clothing then her own. He was free of his trousers, thrusting himself between her soft thighs, his hips grinding of their own volition, with an instinct as old as mankind. Her questing fingers parted the folds of her under robes as his mouth devoured her lips, moved to her throat. The soft flesh of her throat thrust up against his lips, and a soft moan escaped her. Her cool fingers clasped him. Her legs parted, and he magically settled between them, still blindly thrusting against her. She guided him into her, and he plunged deep. A single gasp burst out of them. The look of pain on her face made him pause.

"No, don't stop," she said.

Within a few moments, Ken'ishi felt a series of sensations such as he could never have imagined as his entire body convulsed with an explosive climax. But still his body would not stop. His movements slowed for a few heartbeats as he recovered from the shock, feeling the waves of ecstasy diminishing. The look of pain on her face was gone, replaced by something else. Her eyes were a profound cauldron of emotion; he could identify no individual element, except one. Desire. Raw, fervent, desperate desire.

Her small cries of mounting pleasure drove him on. He tasted her sweat on his lips, heard the desire in her breath, saw the longing in her eyes. She thrust herself up against him, clamping his legs with hers. Then a hot shudder seized her. A whimpering cry of ecstasy breathed into his ear. The muscles of her body gripped him even tighter, bringing him to another climax. He continued to move against her for a few moments, until he realized that he was sated for the time being.

Then he tumbled off her, still almost fully clothed, gasping for breath, their shared perspiration cool in the darkness. For a long time, neither of them said anything. They lay side by side, looking at each other.

She spoke first. "You know, I was taught that this is best done without clothing."

With amazement and awe, he watched her shed layer after layer of clothing, until the deepest mysteries of female beauty were revealed to him. He could only stare at her, a dry lump in his throat. He stared at her until she blushed, in spite of their intimacy.

"I never knew. . . ." His voice trailed off.

"What is it?" she whispered.

"I never knew that such beauty existed in the world," he breathed. After a long, silent moment, he said, "You're crying again. Have I offended you?"

She shook her head, and her voice was barely audible. "No." She knelt beside him, and began to undress him. He opened his mouth to ask her why she wept, but she pressed her fingers to his lips. "The night is already half done," she said.

Because I dream
Of you every night,
My lonely days
Are only dreams

—The Love Poems of Marichiko

Kazuko was gone two hours before dawn. She left him with a fleeting kiss and a cloth bundle. As she disappeared into the dying night, he wanted to call after her, *Yes, let's run away together.* But something stopped him. Something inside him knew that their love was not meant to be. They had loved each other like a lightning bolt. Bright and thunderous and painfully brief. He worried that she might be discovered sneaking back into the estate. If that happened, Ken'ishi's time in this world would be short. In moments, he gathered up his meager belongings, put on his old, ragged clothes, and stole out of the inn. He left a few copper coins on the floor of his room and crept out into the night, wishing to leave the village behind as quickly as possible.

Akao was awake and waiting for him outside when he stepped out of the inn. "Today is new."

Ken'ishi said nothing.

"She had a good smell."

Ken'ishi gave the dog's ears a stroke and strode past. The thought of her amazing scent was as fresh and bright in his mind as the rays of the sun. Intoxicating. In truth, he felt drunk now. His voice was thick, his lips raw from the heat of their kisses. "We must hurry."

He broke into a run, and Akao loped alongside him. He hardly noticed the road, caught up in the warmth of bittersweet joy in his breast. His nether region ached with the longevity and ferocity of last night's use, but he paid it no mind. By their third coupling, she was showing him secrets of how to prolong their ecstasy. He had never known such pleasure was possible. Images of her were seared into his mind's eye. He would cherish the memory of this night every day of his life, and he hoped he would never see her again. Strangely, he could not remember the name of the man she would marry. He vaguely remembered that announcement being made during the banquet. Why did his mind fail to remember such a simple fact? He tried to remember the later parts of the banquet, but all of them seemed like a useless fog.

Only when he stopped to rest and drink from a nearby stream did he open the bundle she had given him. A fresh draught of emotion blew through him, as many colored as the wind. Inside was a folded bundle of new clothing, redolent with her luscious scent. Another crisp black hakama and a fine silken robe, similar to the clothes Lord Nishimuta had given him, this one a deep rich maroon, with finely woven patterns of white thread. He laughed bitterly.

He had traded love for a set of fine clothes.

As he unfolded the clothes, several small items tumbled to the ground. A fine, lacquered wooden comb. A small, razor-sharp knife. A clinking coin pouch.

The anger swelled in him again as he gathered everything up, carefully repackaged it, and hid it inside his pack.

Suddenly the kami began to whisper fiercely in his ears. He stood up and looked around. A man stood on the road about thirty paces from him, facing him. The man was measuring him with his gaze, as if he knew him. Ken'ishi had never seen him before. He was young, perhaps about Ken'ishi's age, and carried a jitte thrust into his sash with two swords.

Akao was so startled that he barked once, something he rarely did; he considered barking vulgar.

Ken'ishi faced the man. Silver Crane hung from his old rope belt. He felt no fear, only the dead despair left by the emptiness in his breast. He waited for the man to speak.

"You are the ronin called Ken'ishi."

"What do you want?"

"I want you to pay for your crime."

Ken'ishi's lips tightened and his fists clenched. Sakamoto had lied. This man had been sent to kill him. "I have paid for too many things today. I'll not stand any more payment for Takenaga's death."

"I'm here to take you back."

"I'm not going back."

"Then I'll take your head to Lord Nishimuta."

"You can try." Ken'ishi laughed once, harshly. "If you succeed, my head will try to bite him. Come and try. I must be moving on, and I'm in no mood for games today."

He drew his sword and held it relaxed at his side.

Akao began to whine. He spared a glance at the dog. The dog was quivering with fear. Why? This man was no older than Ken'ishi.

He studied the man. His clothes did not look like those of a samurai. They looked like peasant's clothes. Another ronin? Why would Lord Nishimuta send a ronin to kill him?

"My name is Taro," the man said as he drew the jitte from his sash with his right hand, and his short sword with his left.

"I don't care what your name is. You're a fool. And you're wasting time."

Ken'ishi tried to settle his spirit, to prepare himself for battle, but the emptiness in his breast was so vast that he could not. His spirit rattled around inside him like a pebble in a bucket. He tried to breathe deeply, as he had been taught, but he could not. His chest felt crushed under great weight.

Suddenly his opponent flew at him, short sword slashing. Only Ken'ishi's reflexes saved his life.

His opponent had closed the distance between them, over thirty paces, in a single leap.

Ken'ishi leaped to the side, spun, and raised his weapon.

Taro lunged toward him with the short sword, and Ken'ishi deflected it easily, but he was wary of the jitte in the other hand. He had never seen a weapon like that before. It did not look sharp, but it could be used for thrusting, and that strange prong. . . . Taro came at him with a flurry of clumsy blows. His opponent was ill trained, Ken'ishi realized, but the strength behind those blows sent shocks quivering up his arms. What kind of man could leap thirty paces? Had he imagined it? Ken'ishi looked in his eyes and saw . . . nothing. Only blackness. He recoiled slightly.

"Who are you?"

Taro drove him back a step with a powerful stroke. "I am Taro. Why do you ask now? Are you afraid?"

Ken'ishi's hands stung from the raw power of Taro's blows. He must release himself into the Void, let go of everything but the Now, but his spirit was too scattered.

Taro came forward again, this time with the jitte, but Ken'ishi noticed immediately that his intent was not to attack the body, but the *blade*. He realized then the weapon's purpose. Ken'ishi pulled his blade away and retreated again.

Now.

Reach for the Now.

Find it.

Forget all.

Release.

Taro lunged, a wild look burning in his eyes, closing the distance in an instant. But all the time Ken'ishi needed existed between instants.

Ken'ishi adjusted his stance half a step to the side and slashed.

Taro grunted in surprise. Ken'ishi heard the splatter of blood on the road, and something fell.

Taro screamed in rage and slashed with the short sword, but the strength in the blow was gone. Ken'ishi batted the weapon away and slashed again. Taro's body fell to the earth with a soft thud, and blood seeped from a terrible cut across his left thigh. His right arm was now a stump severed just below the elbow, pumping crimson onto the road. The short sword fell from his fingers, and Ken'ishi kicked it far away. Taro's face was dazed, almost unconscious. Ken'ishi snatched the long sword from the scabbard in Taro's sash, and cocked his arm to throw it away.

Takenaga's blade.

This young man was from the village. Ken'ishi said, "You are a fool!"

Taro's eyes focused on him weakly, but he was losing consciousness. Ken'ishi saw the filthy bandage wrapped around the young man's lower leg. It was crusted with blood and something else, something dark and unwholesome.

Ken'ishi sighed. "I'm in no mood for killing today, Taro." He knelt, grabbed Taro's limp torso by the collar and lifted him closer. "Listen to me. Go home. Don't come after me again. I will never come this way again. Let it go."

Taro's eyes rolled back, and his head sagged backward. Ken'ishi snorted, let go of him, and stood up.

Akao stood about ten paces away. His teeth were bared into a snarl, and his whole body quivered. His tail was tucked between his legs.

"It's finished," Ken'ishi said, wiping the blood from his blade and sheathing it.

Akao said, "No. Not finished."

"What do you mean?"

But the dog said nothing else. He launched into a dead run.

Ken'ishi sighed again, picked up his things, and followed after Akao at a trot, leaving the bleeding body behind him on the road. Now, if he could escape this province alive, he might be able to forget the pain gnawing at his spirit.

> Fires
> Burn in my heart.
> No smoke rises.
> No one knows.
>
> —*The Love Poems of Marichiko*

So ends the First Scroll

★ ★ ★ ★ ★

THE SECOND SCROLL:
A NEW LIFE

★ ★ ★ ★ ★

A camellia
Dropped down into still waters
Of a deep dark well

—Buson

Kazuko climbed out of her palanquin and looked up at the imposing central keep, the toride, of Lord Tsunetomo's castle. Somehow, it did not look as impressive now as the first time she visited it so many months ago. Now it was home. She found herself remembering the wonder of that day. But now in the winter it seemed only grim and gray and heartless, in spite of all the festive New Year decorations. Her clothes still smelled of incense from the temple. She had gone to the temple to pray for fertility, and for happiness in the coming year, and entreated all the gods and Buddhas to ease her suffering.

She walked through the front gates of the castle and began the labyrinthine climb to her chambers at the summit of the central tower. The castle and its environs buzzed with preparations for the New Year celebration. All of the land was awash in festivals. She had always looked forward to the festivals of the New Year, but now she found herself looking forward to nothing at all. She moved through her life like a mindless ghost. She sometimes felt lost in a gray netherworld of endless despair. Hatsumi often chided her for never smiling, but she never felt any smile inside herself waiting to be given life.

She felt one small measure of relief at being home again, because now she could seclude herself. She had once enjoyed the company of other people, but no longer. Now the only people she saw regularly were her husband and Hatsumi. But she also felt something was improper about this, and that only served to make her more displeased with herself. Why could she not be happy? Why must she suffer so? Every moment of life, both waking and sleeping, was like a dull ache. On the days before her marriage, she had considered killing herself, but she had not gone through with it, because she could not bear the thought of dishonoring her father.

As she moved through the house, servants cleared a path, bowing deeply. She passed by the great hall, where she spotted one of her husband's advisors, Yasutoki. Yasutoki was in the midst of an earnest conversation with Tsunemori, her husband's younger brother.

Tsunemori had the same well-built frame as her husband, with handsome features and sharp eyes, only with less gray in his hair and fewer lines around his eyes. Tsunemori's face wore an expression now similar to so many other times when he was speaking to Yasutoki, a look of reflexive skepticism, as if the veracity of Yasutoki's every word was suspect.

Yasutoki was an ambitious man, ruthless with his opponents and heartless toward servants. Hatsumi told her that all the servants hated him. She sometimes wished her husband would get rid of him, but it was not her place to speak of such things. Yasutoki often had a strange glint in his eyes when he gazed at her, like a cat watching an oblivious mouse. It made her uncomfortable. Perhaps that was why she did not trust him.

Even before she married Tsunetomo, he looked at her that way, with a bemused smugness, as if he *knew* something.

She tried to hurry past the door of the great hall before Yasutoki noticed her, wondering what Tsunemori was discussing with him. It was an open secret in the household that Tsunemori and Yasutoki were bitter rivals. She overheard Tsunetomo and Tsunemori speaking one night over a jar of sake. She recalled the conversation clearly, because it was soon after she arrived, and she had still been unfamiliar with things in Lord Tsunetomo's household. She should not have been eavesdropping, but she could not help it. Yasutoki had gone to Hakozaki to see to a shipment of trade goods from across the sea.

Tsunemori asked, "Why do you keep such a man in your service?"

Tsunetomo answered with his usual good humor. "You've been quarreling with him again, have you? It is unfortunate that you cannot get along with him."

"But why, brother? I can hardly imagine a more unpleasant, spiteful man."

Tsunetomo laughed. "Because he is my friend. And he is a brilliant. And he has friends at court. I rely on you, brother, for martial affairs. I rely on him for political affairs. And he has not always been so sour. His family's lack of rank weighs upon him."

"He is too ambitious."

"Because of his birth, he cannot hold a high office. It has made him bitter. I do not blame him. It is just the way of things. But he serves me well." Kazuko heard the smile in Tsunetomo's voice. "He arranged my lovely new bride, did he not?" Her ears burned, and she tried to slip away without them hearing the swish of her robes. She would be even more embarrassed if they discovered her, and her husband might be displeased. She slipped away without being noticed, and her eavesdropping gave her much to ponder. Even within one house, politics were rampant.

She continued her way through the house, up the stairs, passing through invisible clouds of different scents. The sweaty, oily, metallic smell of a group of guards. Numerous dishes of food, each with its own aroma and special significance to bring luck and prosperity in the coming year. The smell of incense from a small house altar. She observed these things without paying them any attention. Her mind was focused on her own inner darkness. She often wished she could forget the things that made her feel this way. Hatsumi still tried to comfort her sometimes, but Hatsumi was long-since frustrated and impatient with her. Kazuko was frustrated and impatient with herself. This should be a joyous time, and all she felt like doing was sulking.

She finally reached the uppermost chambers of the castle, her chambers. When she entered, she found her husband sitting at his writing desk, brush in hand.

He turned to look at her. "Good morning, my lady." His voice was warm and deep.

He was a man in his late forties, thirty years her senior. His eyes still burned with the energy and verve of a young man, but were tempered by the wisdom and wit of age. His hair was shot with gray, but somehow it did not make him look old. His alert, good-tempered eyes were surrounded by fine lines, but even those did not make him look old. The vitality and strength of his spirit masked the physical indications of the years and made him seem like a man half his age. Indeed, he possessed the virility of a young man.

He lay with her nearly every night since they had been married, and she did her duty to please him. He told her she was beautiful, and that he honored her, but she knew there was an underlying need that went beyond her. On their wedding night, she had concealed her loss of virginity by pricking herself with a pin, hoping the flow of blood would be enough to deceive him. He had been pleased to see the blood on their bed clothes. When he did not challenge her about it, a tremendous weight of anxiousness lifted from her heart.

Today she tried not to let her husband see the pervasiveness and persistence of her despair, so she bowed and smiled at him. "Good morning, husband. I trust you slept well."

"Yes, I slept well. The morning was not too cold for you? You went to the temple this morning?"

"Yes, but the weather was not too cold. Shall I make you some tea?"

"Certainly. Tea would be good."

She bowed again and began to warm some water for tea over the brazier of coals. As they waited, he said, "Did you speak to the nuns?"

And there it was. The underlying need that drove his physical lust for her. In spite of all their nights together, Kazuko was not yet with child. There was, as yet, no heir. Every morning he tried to find out if she was pregnant, asking politely, in a roundabout way. She asked the nuns at the temple to pray for her fertility every time she visited. She sometimes felt that once she produced an heir, her husband would have no further use for her, and then she would be even lonelier. But perhaps she was being unreasonable. Tsunetomo was kind to her, and he was a gentle, if insistent lover. He had gone to great lengths to make her happy when she first arrived, showering her with gifts. He attributed her despair and sadness to missing her home. He had no idea of the truth of her pain. He had thrown parties and banquets for her, hiring entertainers to provide her with spectacle, all at great expense, and she had been incapable of enjoying any of them, even though she tried to put on a pleasing face.

These days, Kazuko wished that her womb would bear fruit. She wanted a baby. Perhaps a baby would fill the void of loneliness in her belly. She worried that she was barren, and she prayed that it not be so. Some days, she feared that her indiscretion before her marriage had displeased the gods, who then left her barren. Her indiscretion. It was the single most spectacular night of her life. Must she now be punished for one night of true happiness?

"Yes," she said, "I spoke to the nuns. As always, they are praying on my behalf."

"Good. I'm glad to hear it. I spoke to a healer yesterday and asked him for a remedy, something to increase fertility."

"Thank you, husband. You are always thinking of me. I am sorry you have to go to so much trouble."

"It was nothing. And you're no trouble at all. You brighten my life, Kazuko. I look forward to seeing you every day."

She blushed, and a small, fleeting warmth stirred in her belly. It lasted for only a few heartbeats before being quenched by the cold heaviness in her spirit. Was that what it was like to feel good? She tried to remember; it seemed so long since she had.

"For years I have missed the wisdom and kindness of a woman in my house. You are like a breath of spring air, like a freshet bubbling from the earth. You make me happy." He reached over and laid his hand on hers. She felt the thick calluses, rough on her skin, as he squeezed gently.

Tears welled in her eyes.

"I'm sorry," he said, "I did not wish you to cry. I only want you to be happy with me."

She dabbed at her eyes and said, "I am sorry, husband. You make me happy. You are a kind man."

He said, "You are a good wife to say so, but I can see the unhappiness in you. Sometimes I see you from afar, when you forget that anyone might be watching. Do you miss your home?

Your father?"

She saw the opportunity to lie and took it. She nodded and looked at him apologetically. "I am sorry, husband."

"It's quite all right," he said. "It is only natural for a young woman to miss her home. But you are a good wife to me."

"Thank you, husband." Tears burned in her eyes, because she knew what was troubling her, knew the source of her longing, her aching need that all the kindness in the world could only diminish, never erase.

A look of true concern and compassion creased his brow. He moved around the table next to her and took her in his arms. She allowed her head to rest against his firm chest and let the tears come. His body was stiff against her, unaccustomed to the display of softer emotions. She could sense his discomfiture, his uneasiness, but she also sensed that he knew what she needed and was doing his best to give it to her.

After a time, the blackness in her spirit began to fade, like the coming of a cloudy dawn. She looked up into his face, and he looked down into hers. She kissed him. His eyes widened with surprise, then he responded to her kiss.

After a moment, she pulled away. "Am I too bold? Too unladylike?" Only one thing could make her aching loneliness go away, if only for a little while.

"No." Then his arms squeezed her close to him.

Hatsumi sat in her chambers, a couple of walls removed from her mistress's rooms. Kazuko and her husband were having breakfast, and Hatsumi did not like to intrude. She sat waiting for one of the servants to come with her breakfast. She had called them once already, but they had brought nothing yet. She gathered her robes to cover her feet better. The air in the room was chilled with winter, in spite of the brazier of glowing coals on one side of the room.

"Where is that Moé? Silly girl," she muttered.

Hatsumi did not like to be kept waiting. She enjoyed her superior position as the lady's chief maidservant. And Lord Tsunetomo was much wealthier than Lord Nishimuta. He had more land in his fief, and the cultivation was better. And the tea produced in his area, newly cultivated with plants from China, was considered superior to tea produced anywhere else in the land. The tea was Hatsumi's favorite thing about living on Lord Tsunetomo's estate. If only Moé was not so slow about bringing it.

She opened her mouth to call again when she heard someone coming down the hallway. A vague silhouette appeared on the shoji screen and knelt outside. A breathless voice called softly, "I am sorry, mistress. I am too slow."

Hatsumi let the surliness emerge in her voice. "Well, come then. I'm waiting."

The shoji slid aside and the young servant girl entered the room carrying a tray with Hatsumi's breakfast, a bowl of rice and some pickled plums. Moé was perhaps thirteen or fourteen years old. Her face would have been pretty, Hatsumi thought, except that her eyes were crossed and she had a large mole on her nose. She set the tray down in front of the older woman and bowed deeply.

"Haven't you forgotten something?"

The girl's eyes widened as she cast about almost frantically.

"The tea." Hatsumi's voice dripped with derision.

Moé gasped. "I am sorry, mistress! I will return immediately!" She leaped to her feet and ran from the room.

"Stupid girl," Hatsumi muttered, just loud enough for Moé to hear before she was gone. Part of her pitied the poor girl, but that part was overpowered by annoyance at the girl's ineptitude. Hatsumi would not touch her breakfast until the tea came, so she waited impatiently, fidgeting, looking about the small chamber.

Her gaze meandered across the room, resting upon a beautiful bundle of neatly folded cloth resting on a shelf. The bundle was a new robe of lovely forest-green silk, brightly embroidered. It was a gift from Yasutoki. The day before, a servant had brought her the robe, and bundled inside was a slip of paper with only Yasutoki's name, and no explanation. She had not yet worn it; she was saving it for a special occasion, because it was beautiful, and expensive, and she could not determine why he had given her such a gift. She had never received a gift from a man. Was he making advances toward her? What were his intentions? The thought that a man might be interested in her filled her with a distasteful mixture of exhilaration and revulsion. Being the object of someone's desire was an exciting thought, but the ultimate goal of that desire involved an act that filled her with a horror she could not contemplate. Forever burned into her memory were the smell of Hakamadare's foul breath, the taste of his spittle, and the tearing agony of his demonic organ. She had once longed for the touch of a man, imagined what love must be like, but no longer. It seemed that love, the act of love, would be forever lost to her. Besides, Yasutoki must know what had happened to her. He had been at Lord Nishimuta's castle when they returned. How could he be interested in her after she had been so fouled? Still, why else would he send her such a luxurious gift?

The tug-of-war in her belly was interrupted by the sound of footsteps approaching quickly. The door slid open quickly, revealing Moé carrying another tray, this one laden with a teapot and cup. She was breathing heavily as she entered and prepared to pour the tea. Hatsumi noticed that the girl's hands were shaking as she turned over the teacup and placed some dark emerald leaves in the pot.

Hatsumi said nothing, just watched her impatiently.

The girl sensed Hatsumi's impatience and worked with speed and efficiency. She poured hot water into the teapot over the shredded tea leaves, then placed the lid on the teapot, gently swirled the water in the pot, then poured the bright green tea into the waiting cup.

Then some noises came from the direction of her mistress's chambers, heavy breathing and small rhythmic cries, building. "You may go, Moé," Hatsumi said. "That will be all."

Moé bowed and stood up quickly. In the act of standing however, her knee bumped the small table. The teacup jumped into the air and overturned, spilling hot tea into Hatsumi's lap. Moé froze, staring in horror.

Hatsumi jumped to her feet with a cry of anger, staring at the wet stain on her robe. "Stupid twit!" she snarled. She picked up the teapot and dashed the steaming hot water into the girl's face.

Moé squealed in pain and covered her eyes with her hands. Hot water dripped from her chin. Soggy tea leaves clung to her face and hair. Her eyes were squeezed shut in pain. She spun and ran blindly from the room, her squeal receding. Hatsumi felt a pang of remorse. She hoped the girl was not blinded. She would be useless now if that was the case. Lord Tsunetomo might be displeased with her harming one of his servants. But the girl deserved punishment. Clumsy girls were worse than useless. She must learn to be more careful. Hatsumi felt obliged to teach her properly. Would the other servants hate her now? If they did, it would not matter. They must still obey her.

She sat down at her breakfast table again, but as she considered eating, she noticed that her stomach felt like a swirling pit of blackness, like a strange void. And her hunger was gone. Strange. The noises coming from her mistress's chamber had subsided, leaving a heavy, encumbered silence in the air.

Why did the air seem so oppressive now?

Yasutoki kept his manner cordial, even though the man sitting across the writing desk from him was his enemy. Tsunemori, Lord Tsunetomo's younger brother, had been a thorn in his side for longer than he cared to consider. No matter how Yasutoki tried to put Tsunemori at ease, all the better to wheedle information from him, the more impregnable the wall Tsunemori built between them. Tsunemori, it seemed, would not fall victim to Yasutoki's manipulations, and that made him dangerous to Yasutoki's plans. Such powers of perception made Tsunemori a dangerous man indeed.

"I'm sure you can understand, Tsunemori," Yasutoki continued, "my need for comprehensiveness in this year-end report. I thought that I would better serve my lord, your brother, by presenting all the pertinent information together. It would also allow me to better plan for the consumption of food and other supplies so that his troops would be supplied with the greatest efficiency."

Tsunemori's perpetual look of skepticism deepened. "You know full well that your sphere of responsibility is political and official matters, not military ones. The food and weapons stores for my brother's warrior retainers are none of your concern. There is no need for you to include them in your report."

"But the horses—"

Tsunemori cut him off. "The horses fall under my domain as well, Yasutoki. The horses are to be used only by samurai. The draft ponies fall under your domain. I appreciate your . . . concern, but it is unnecessary. I am preparing my own report to my brother. He is an intelligent man, able to draw his own conclusions from separate bits of information."

Yasutoki burned with frustration, but he took care not to show it. "As you say. Lord Tsunetomo is a man of high intelligence. I am merely trying to serve him in the best way I know."

"I know he appreciates your efforts." Tsunemori leaned back on his heels with an air that this conversation was finished.

"Thank you for your time, Tsunemori," Yasutoki said.

Tsunemori bowed, stood up, turned, and strode from the room with the swagger of a trained, seasoned warrior. He was not a man to be trifled with, Yasutoki reminded himself. Therefore, he must be circumvented. So Tsunemori was preparing a report on the military stores and strength of Lord Tsunetomo's castle. It seemed obvious, therefore, that the information in the report must exist somewhere, and Yasutoki thought he knew the most likely location. Tsunemori spent far more time in the training hall and on the field than he did in his office. So much the better for Yasutoki's intentions.

Spying Lady Kazuko out of the corner of his eye, passing by in the corridor, Yasutoki indulged in a moment of considering his plans for her. He was always looking for ways to gain advantage or leverage. He may have need of her someday. For that reason, he would tell no one of her tryst with the hapless ronin, Ken'ishi. Something happened between those two in the forest. Yasutoki had noted the ronin's reaction when Lord Nishimuta announced Kazuko's betrothal. The ronin had done an admirable job of concealing it, but Yasutoki knew well the look of a young man in love. And Kazuko had been no better. Nevertheless, she had done her duty and married Lord Tsunetomo. Yasutoki admired her for that. In such young men and women, love could become everything, the emperor of their spirits and actions. That Kazuko had the strength to put it aside for the good of her family told him that she would not be easily manipulated. Nevertheless, her weakness was the ronin, and weaknesses could be exploited. The mere thought that her love for the ronin could be exposed might be enough to make her more malleable. She and the ronin had ample opportunity to consummate their love. He suspected that they had, but he could not be sure. Lord Tsunetomo would have been incensed if Lord Nishimuta had given him a wife who was not a virgin.

The ronin himself had been unexpected. Yasutoki had expected someone larger, stronger, older, rougher looking. But this young man with such a peculiar innocence in his face, could he have killed Hakamadare? A young man like this one could easily be underestimated. But his naiveté could also be exploited. If only he could be found again. He had been escorted from Lord Nishimuta's house hurriedly, and he disappeared into the night. After that, Yasutoki's spy lost him. The spy was still looking, however.

Perhaps Hatsumi also knew the whole truth about what happened between Kazuko and the ronin. Poor, plain, wounded, unloved Hatsumi. Here was a woman ripe for the plucking. He sensed her desperate loneliness, the longing for any sort of romantic liaison. She was like a wounded bird, fluttering, fearful, vulnerable. A woman like that had many uses. She could be a means to reaching the deepest secrets of the Lady Kazuko, or perhaps Hatsumi had some secrets of her own worth delving. He would have to approach her carefully for fear of frightening her off, however, after what happened at the hands of the oni bandit. He had already set that plan into motion with the gift of the robes. They had been expensive, but the means to the best information sometimes came at a high price. He had a good instinct for such things, and he was seldom disappointed. Besides, beautiful clothes and trappings were a tried and true ruse to draw women into his bed. He occasionally coupled with several of the prettier servant girls in the castle. They were a lovely diversion, a release of the energy of his sometimes-precarious existence.

Tsunemori was another matter entirely. Yasutoki's attempts to gain information from him were always fruitless. Someday

Yasutoki would find the key to unlocking Tsunemori's secrets. Someday.

"There was a man who said, '[That] person has a violent disposition, but this is what I said right to his face. . . .' This is an unbecoming thing to say, and it was said simply because he wanted to be known as a rough fellow. It was rather low, and it can be seen that he was still rather immature. It is because a samurai has correct manners that he is admired. Speaking of other people in this way is no different from an exchange between low-class spearmen. It is vulgar."

—*Hagakure*

The air was damp and chilly on Ken'ishi's face as he walked along the rocky coastline. The cold gray of the waves merged in the distance with the colorless sky, making it difficult to discern where the sea ended and sky began. The neighboring mountains rose into the shrouds, losing their heads in the mist, their forested slopes soaking up the mist like a sponge. A few small fishing boats bobbing on the frothy crests of waves were the only features in the endless gloom. The thunderous crash of the surf drowned out the cries of the sea birds dipping and hovering on the wintry air. But even so, the weather was more hospitable than he remembered the winters in the north, winters he spent huddled in a cold, cheerless cave hoarding the warmth of a tiny fire.

His quilted undergarment now kept the worst of the cold at bay, and he kept his hands inside his robes. Back in the port town of Hakozaki, he purchased a less expensive set of clothes than those he had received as gifts. He did not wish to ruin those with the dust and unpredictability of the road. At least, that was what he told himself.

There was no road here, only endless stretches of rocky shoreline trailing around the skirts of towering mountains and hills, interspersed with a few modest beaches. And he saw no one, except for Akao, who picked his away among the rocks ahead, mindful of the ever-oncoming surf. Back in Hakozaki, Ken'ishi had overheard two merchants discussing a public notice and description of a criminal who murdered a Nishimuta constable. Apparently, his pardon had lasted only until he was out of Lord Nishimuta's sight. Wanted criminals were harder to spot because of all the people visiting the city for the New Year celebration. Even though he had thrown away his old tattered garments and now wore his hair properly cut in the traditional warrior's style, he thought it best to leave quickly. Hakozaki was now lost in the hazy distance behind him, somewhere around the curve of the great bay's shoreline.

The grayness of the sky started to darken with the coming of evening when he spotted a small fishing boat coming toward shore, tossing on the waves. The fisherman was oaring heartily to keep the bow of his craft across the waves. Ken'ishi's gaze followed the boat's course to a sheltered inlet, where the shoreline hooked sharply out into the sea. Nestled in the inlet were several low docks, with other boats tied alongside. Among the trees, houses with roofs made of closely packed sticks and walls of gray, weathered timber stood like hunched tortoises, lights shining through paper screens.

Akao stopped to wait for him. The dog was feeling the same trepidation that always came with entering a new village, but he was hungry, too, as always. "No meat on crabs. Want fish!"

"Are you going to steal some?" Ken'ishi asked, teasing.

Akao smiled back, tongue lolling. "Perhaps."

They approached the village by the stretch of beach near the docks. Even from a distance, the smells of fish and smoke were heavy in the air. A few fishermen worked at the docks, putting up their boats for the night or trussing up their catch. They noticed the man and the dog approaching, but upon seeing he was a warrior, pointedly ignored them. A few townsfolk walked the streets, and the sight of a stranger among them bearing weapons caused some suspicious second looks. But Ken'ishi no longer looked like a bandit or ruffian; he looked like a respectable samurai, and he had some money left to buy a room at the inn. He no longer needed to beg, at least for a while yet.

Flamboyant streamers covered with painted characters hung from poles all around the village. They were a New Year custom, covered with prayers and wishes for the coming year. The sounds of music and revelry drifted from the center of town.

Akao stopped. "Smell good! Eat now!" The dog took off at a trot.

Ken'ishi took one step after him. Akao was an accomplished thief. He wouldn't go hungry tonight.

Ken'ishi discovered that the music was coming from inside what looked to be the inn. As he stood outside, the warm smells of fish soup, rice, pickled radish, and the sharp pungency of sake struck him in the face. He stepped inside and placed his shoes among all the others near the door. The revelers hardly noticed him. The music was coming from two men playing the drum and biwa, and the celebrants were tipping jars of sake, heads bobbing to the music. Most of them appeared to be townsfolk, fishermen, and farmers, but Ken'ishi noticed a samurai sitting alone in one corner of the room. The samurai noticed him as well. They nodded to each other, then the innkeeper stepped in front of Ken'ishi, bowing.

He was a tall, thin man with an abundance of merry wrinkles at the corner of his eyes and a bulbous, sparsely haired pate. "Welcome, sir. Have you just come to town?"

Ken'ishi nodded. "Have you any rooms?"

"Yes, sir. You're in luck. I have one room left."

"Very well."

The innkeeper showed him to a room at the rear of the inn. It was small but clean, just large enough to spread a futon. The thin paper walls hardly diminished the sounds of the music and conversation. "One of my best rooms, lord. The bathhouse is across the street. Shall I bring you some food? We have many special treats tonight because of New Year!"

Ken'ishi nodded. "Yes, food would be good."

The older man departed. Ken'ishi left his pack and weapons in his room, taking only his sword with him when he returned to the common room.

He noted that the lone samurai watched him but did not appear to be suspicious, merely watchful. The way the man sipped his sake indicated that he was not drunk.

The innkeeper brought Ken'ishi's food promptly, tasty fish soup, a bowl of rice, some pickled plums and a handful of sweet, sticky rice cakes. He enjoyed his repast in silence, allowing the revelry to ebb and flow around him. The music's strange rhythms and tones danced in his mind, and he wondered if he could reproduce it on his flute.

When Ken'ishi was nearly finished with his meal, a man came

into the common room from one of the rooms in back and took a place among the other patrons. Ever alert, Ken'ishi wondered where he had been. His question was answered when he saw a woman dressed in brightly colored but threadbare robes. Her face was freshly powdered, and she seated herself near the hallway.

After a moment, Ken'ishi realized that she was not a woman at all, but a girl, probably younger than him. She might have been pretty had there been any spark of life in her eyes. He recognized her bearing and posture as like that of other whores he had seen, weary, beaten down by a harsh existence.

The girl had not been sitting long when a man stood up from among the patrons and staggered toward her. He reeked of fish, his eyes were dull, red-rimmed, and watery, and he walked as if the floor was a heaving boat under his feet. The man was old enough to be her father, perhaps grandfather. After the man passed her, the girl stood up and followed him out of sight. No one else paid any mind, and Ken'ishi wondered why he had. He had seen whores and their patrons in inns and sake houses before, and none of them had gained his attention for more than an instant. Why was this time different? The longer the girl was gone, the more attuned to his surroundings his senses became. With a sudden insight, he realized his instincts were preparing him for a fight. The kami were speaking to him.

Moments later a terrific slap and a squeal of pain ripped through the air from the back rooms, halting the music and dropping silence over the revelry like a blanket. The musicians recovered from their surprise and tried to resume playing, until the girl came running out of the hallway and stumbled through the crowd, one hand covering the large red welt on her cheek, the other hand clutching her robes together. The innkeeper came out of the kitchen, and she ran toward him, throwing herself at his knees.

A few seconds later, the drunken fisherman followed her out of the hallway, using the walls to support himself. "She tried to rob me! That thieving little whore!" His words were so slurred they were barely intelligible.

The girl looked up desperately into the man's face, shaking her head in denial, tears streaming down her cheeks.

The drunken fisherman's voice rose. "Give her to me! I'll show her what it means to steal a man's money!"

Ken'ishi heard her breathing whispered pleas to the inn-keeper. The innkeeper's eyes said that he did not believe the fisherman's accusation, but the fisherman was a big, rough man.

The samurai stood up, holding his scabbard in his left hand, and interposed himself between the innkeeper and the fisher-man. His voice was measured and terse as he spoke to the fisher-man. "Yoba, do you still have your money?"

"Well, yes, but. . . ."

"Then I will see to it she is punished for trying to steal from you. Tomorrow."

"No! Give that bitch to me! I'll beat her!"

The samurai's voice remained steady, but hardened. "Let it be. This is the New Year, a celebration."

But Yoba staggered forward with drunken persistence. "No! I'm going to punish her!"

The samurai assumed a ready stance, prepared to draw his weapon if necessary.

A young man jumped up from the floor and stepped in front of the fisherman. "Father, stop this! She is not worth it!"

The fisherman shoved the young man aside, sending him sprawling across two other patrons. "Stupid boy! You don't understand. She needs to be beaten! Stay out of my way or I'll see to you too!" He took three more steps into the room.

The girl was quivering with fear, huddled against the innkeeper's knees.

The samurai said, "Leave now. I will not warn you again."

The fisherman stopped, took a deep breath, and his head sagged against his chest. The young man extricated himself from the patrons he had fallen on and stepped behind him. "Let's go home, Father." The fisherman nodded, allowing his son to support him as they made their way toward the door. As the samurai stepped aside to let them pass, Ken'ishi noticed the glint of cunning in the drunken fisherman's eyes, and his body tensed with the warning of danger.

The fisherman used his son's body as a pivot and lunged at the samurai, colliding with him. The samurai grunted and staggered backwards, driven by the fisherman's weight. A dreadful hush fell over the room. Ken'ishi saw the crimson-smeared boning knife in the fisherman's fist. The samurai staggered back a step, clutching his side with his right hand, wearing an expression of speechless surprise on his blanched face, falling over a stunned patron onto his back. The young man, aghast, his mouth working but no sound coming out. The fisherman, his face beaming with triumph, his bloodshot eyes turning toward the girl, burning with fresh anticipation, taking a step toward her.

"Now, girl!" the fisherman rasped, his breathing husky and drenched with sake. The horrified girl jumped up and hid behind the innkeeper, whimpering in terror. The older man's gaze was glued to the crimson blade, his eyes wide, frozen.

"Stop!" Ken'ishi said.

"Eh?" The fisherman turned and squinted through watery, bloodshot eyes at Ken'ishi. His eyes widened for a moment, then narrowed, and he flipped the knife in his hand to grip it by the blade. He cocked his arm to throw.

Silver Crane's blade caught him just below the ribcage, neatly parting his shirt and creating a pair of wet red lips stretching across his torso. A choked sound burst from the fisherman's throat as he clutched at the spreading wound with his empty hand. After a long moment, he fell forward onto his face, blood and entrails spilling from the great gash in his belly.

"Father!" The young man's face twisted with shock and horror.

Throughout the inn, dead silence.

The young man glared at Ken'ishi. "You killed him!"

Ken'ishi said nothing.

"He didn't have a chance!" The young man's gaze fell to the corpse on the floor and watched the slow spread of the scarlet pool at his feet.

The innkeeper said, "Your father didn't give *him* a chance." He pointed at the wounded samurai, who lay on the floor, gasping, his lips stained with blood. The samurai stared at the ceiling as if trying to concentrate on breathing, but the awareness in his eyes was diminishing. Then his chest ceased to rise, and his gasping ceased with a wet rattle.

The young man's voice shrilled as he turned to the quivering, terrified girl. "He wouldn't have hurt her! Slut! This is all your fault! Unclean whore!" He took a step toward her.

"Don't." Ken'ishi's voice was cold as he raised his weapon.

Another young man jumped up and grabbed the first by the arm. "Chiba, don't be a fool."

Ken'ishi said, "Listen to your friend. According to the law, the penalty for murder is death."

"What do you know of law? Are you a constable? Or are you just a murderer!" Chiba said, challenging.

"I have this authority," Ken'ishi said, raising his gleaming blade, "and the knowledge of what is right. The samurai was killed by a drunken, treacherous fool. There is no honor in that. Justice has been done."

Chiba's companion whispered, "Let it go, Chiba. Let it go for now. He'll kill you, too."

275

Helpless, Chiba looked from his companion, to Ken'ishi, to the cowering girl, to his father's body. He knelt and rolled the corpse onto its back, then he and his companion picked up by the body by the hands and feet and carried it outside, dribbling a trail of dark blood behind them.

Within moments, the musicians and other patrons scurried out of the inn like a stampede of frightened rats. Ken'ishi was left alone with the innkeeper, the girl, and the dead samurai. He cleaned and sheathed his blade. The girl ran from behind the innkeeper and threw herself against Ken'ishi, weeping and sobbing words of thanks.

The innkeeper approached him. "Thank you, sir, for your help. Yoba has always been a drunken fool, always causing problems. Tonight he went too far. Only his family will miss him."

"Family?"

"He has three sons, Chiba, Koba, and Utsuba. His wife ran away years ago."

Ken'ishi pointed at the samurai's body. "This man's family will want his body, and his sword."

The innkeeper said to the girl, "Kiosé, go and bring Norikage-sama. Tell him what happened."

She bowed, then turned away and moved toward the door.

The innkeeper said, "Kiosé."

She stopped and turned expectantly.

"Did you try to steal his money?"

She shook her head vehemently.

"Then why did he attack you?" Ken'ishi asked.

The welt on her cheek darkened with the redness of her face. She hesitated, her gaze falling inward. "He . . . couldn't. And it made him angry."

The innkeeper nodded, then gave her permission to go. She trotted off into the night.

Ken'ishi nodded toward the dead samurai. "Who was he?"

The innkeeper sighed. "Regrettably, he was our constable. His name was Hojo no Masahige."

"Who is Norikage?"

"Masahige's assistant."

The innkeeper moved to straighten a table that had been knocked askew, stepping around the large pool of thickening blood on the floor. "In ten years I have never had a brawl such as this." He was speaking half to himself. "Why would Yoba do something as stupid as kill the constable? That fool! And poor Kiosé! I have not had her long. I hope he didn't hurt her badly."

"Where did she come from?"

"I bought her from a geisha house in Hakozaki. She cannot sing or dance, so she was useless to them. But she is pretty enough, and the men in the village seem to like her. It is fortunate you were here, sir. He might have killed her. And perhaps me, too. What is your name, sir?"

"Ken'ishi."

"Ken'ishi-sama, thank you very much for your help tonight. My name is Tetta." He bowed low.

Ken'ishi bowed.

"If I may ask, how long do you plan to stay?"

Before Ken'ishi could answer the question, a new voice came from the doorway. "What happened here? Where is Masahige?"

Ken'ishi turned to look at the newcomer. Trotting into the inn came a small, thin man, with a narrow face, his age about thirty. He stopped and squinted up at Ken'ishi with his beady eyes. "Who are you?" Before Ken'ishi could answer, the man's gaze began to flick about the room, fixing on the corpse on the floor. "Ah, my lord! What has happened to you? You are dead!" The man's voice was rich and sonorous, despite his size.

Kiosé followed him a few paces behind, her eyes downcast, hands properly folded.

"Who did this?"

Tetta said, "Norikage-sama, Yoba the fisherman killed him in a drunken frenzy."

Norikage's beady eyes narrowed even further. "Masahige was a capable warrior! How could he be killed by a simple fisherman?"

Ken'ishi said, "Treachery, sir. The fisherman had a hidden knife and struck without warning."

Norikage rubbed his thin, pointed beard. His hands were soft and thin. His gaze flicked toward Ken'ishi. "And who are you?"

"My name is Ken'ishi. I have just come to this village tonight."

Norikage said, "And where is Yoba now?"

"Dead," Ken'ishi said. "I killed him."

Norikage said gravely. "Yoba was a base, vulgar peasant. The world is a better place without him. You should beware of his sons, however. They are as stupid as he was. They might seek vengeance."

Norikage's eyes shifted about, glancing from Ken'ishi to the corpse, from Tetta to the floor, his lips pursed, brow furrowed. Then he said, "Ken'ishi, come with me. There is something we must discuss."

Something in the rat-like little man's demeanor made him uneasy. "Where?"

"To my office. We can speak privately there. This will not take long."

Ken'ishi bowed. "Very well."

"Excuse me, Norikage-sama, but what about the body?" Tetta asked tentatively. "My inn will be polluted!"

"We'll see to it in good time. Ken'ishi, follow me please."

Norikage's office was a dark, cramped place, with a small desk stacked deep with dozens of documents. Ken'ishi seated himself opposite the desk from Norikage, and he noticed the little man wince with pain when he sat down himself, as if he were nursing an old injury. The room smelled of ink and dust. Norikage sifted through a stack of documents, pulled out one and gathered his inkpot and brush. Ken'ishi waited as Norikage brushed several lines of characters onto the paper.

"Ken'ishi," Norikage said, "please tell me again what happened in the inn. Leave out no detail."

Ken'ishi told the story.

When Ken'ishi was finished, Norikage said, "Aoka village is now without a constable. You seem like a man who hears the call of justice, and a man capable with a blade." His brush fluttered over the paper, leaving a black trace of swirls and lines.

Ken'ishi nodded.

"Masahige was my superior, and now he is dead. I cannot become constable myself because I have no skill with weapons. I am not a samurai, but I am an able administrator. Masahige and I worked well together. We had . . . an arrangement, an understanding."

"Are you Nishimuta clan?"

Norikage stopped speaking for a moment, an emotion Ken'ishi could not identify flicking across his face. "No. I . . . have no family name. Is that funny? You are smiling." His smooth voice rose slightly.

"I also have no family name."

Norikage's eyes narrowed. "A ronin? That explains your presence in these parts and answers many of my questions."

"What are you writing?"

"A deputization order. The constable assigned to this village is dead. I believe you are a man who can be trusted, and you can handle yourself in a fight. I also sense that you are a man looking for an opportunity. I am offering you an opportunity. What do you say?"

Blood rushed in Ken'ishi's ears. He tried to keep his voice even. "You're offering me a place as constable of this village?"

"Of course, you would take orders from me, rather than the other way around."

"Why would you do this? You do not know me."

"I have many reasons. After tonight, this offer will not be open. What do you say?"

"Very well," Ken'ishi said. "I accept."

Norikage grinned like an eel. "Excellent! We will work well together, I think. Now, sign your name to this document." He handed Ken'ishi the document he had been writing.

Ken'ishi took the document and the brush and signed his name in ink for the first time. "What does it say?"

"You cannot read?"

"Only a few characters."

Norikage blinked once and paused. "Well, that's more than anyone else in this village except for me," he said briskly. "This document is mostly formalities, but states that you are now the village's protector, and that you are subordinate to my orders."

Ken'ishi nodded, but said nothing. He handed the document back to Norikage.

Norikage hid the traces of his smile. "No matter. Your name is 'Ken'ishi.' That is a strange name. What character is that? Your calligraphy is atrocious. Is it 'Sword?' "

"Yes."

He placed the document in front of him and brushed some more characters. "A proper constable must be able to read and write."

Ken'ishi said nothing.

"Teaching is not a task I like, but it is necessary, I suppose. I will teach you."

"Thank you, Norikage-sama."

Norikage grimaced. "Not 'sama.' Save that for the provincial governor."

"Very well, Norikage. Thank you for the . . . opportunity."

As Ken'ishi walked back to the inn, feeling the cold moistness of the night air on his face, he wondered about his reactions to what had just happened. Finding service as a constable was not what he had envisioned. A constable. Him. Nevertheless, he was thrilled at the opportunity to have a place to sleep and food to eat. And he would not be an outlaw. How strange it would be not to be a criminal any longer. He had worn that face for far too long. But he would watch Norikage. That man was too slippery to be trustworthy. Ken'ishi had seen others of Norikage's kind when passing through the capital, a great city of fabulous wealth and beauty, but also one rife with corruption and poverty.

Yes, he would wait and see. In the morning when Akao returned, he would share in the dog's insights. The dog would be happy to have enough food as well.

When he entered the inn, Kiosé was on her hands and knees, scrubbing the bloodstains from the wooden floor. The water in her bucket was as red as fresh blood. Masahige's body still lay where it had fallen. She turned toward Ken'ishi and pressed her forehead to the floor. She said, "Thank you for all you have done, Ken'ishi-sama." Her voice was soft and quavering.

Ken'ishi bowed. "I only wish to be of service." He stepped around her and glanced at the samurai's face on the way to his room. The eyes stared at the ceiling, and the skin had taken on a grayish cast.

In his room, he spread out the futon and prepared himself for sleep. The room was chilly and had no means of heat, but the blanket was heavy. He blew out the candle. Moments later a silhouette appeared on the rice-paper door of his room, kneeling outside the threshold.

Kiosé's voice was soft and quavering. "Sir, may I come in?"

"Yes."

The door slid open, and she entered, tentatively, closing the door behind her. She bowed and slid toward him on her knees. "I'm sorry I'm so forward. Please forgive my rudeness."

"What is it?"

She sniffled and dabbed at her eyes with her sleeve. "He would have killed me. I have but one thing to offer you in return for my life."

He turned the blanket aside and beckoned her.

She lay down beside him, and he covered her with the blanket. He encircled her with one arm and held her against his chest. Her hand delved lower, seeking his manhood, but he stopped her with a gentle touch.

"There will be time for that later," he said.

"Later?"

"I will be staying here for a while, in the village."

She nodded and rested her cheek upon his breast. For a long time, they lay together, embraced, drifting toward sleep like unmoored boats. He felt the weight of her body against his, the softness of her flesh and the sharp impressions of bones beneath, perhaps too close to the surface. He breathed in the scent of her hair, but there was another face in his mind.

Neither of them spoke again, but soon her tears were cooling on his chest.

"It is a good viewpoint to see the world as a dream. When you have something like a nightmare, you will wake up and tell yourself it was only a dream. It is said that the world we live in is not a bit different from this."

—*Hagakure*

The priest approached the small house, his tread growing slower at every step. Uneasiness whispered along his backbone, a nameless dread, and the tray of rice and tea in his hands began to rattle. When he reached the door, he slid it open, allowing morning sunlight to spill into the darkness within. The square of golden sunlight revealed a rumpled sleeping mat and blankets in careless disarray, and that strange smell that always lingered around the man inside wafted out, as if drawn into the fresh air. The smell was almost metallic, akin to hot iron left in a forge, but with something of the smell of blood as well. That the smell of blood still lingered was strange, because the man's injuries had healed. But something was still amiss. The man's body had healed, but his spirit had not. The man came outside into the day only rarely these days.

Outside the walls of the temple could be heard the lively hustle of the port city of Hakata. The cacophony of voices, the rumble and creak of cart wheels, the bleat and squawk of livestock, the fresh breeze billowing from the sea, the clatter of carpenters mending a roof, all were audible but muffled within the quiet confines of the temple walls and garden.

In the sunlit patch, the man's outstretched legs joined a shadowy form sitting in the corner of the room. A hoarse voice croaked from the dark shape, "Good morning, priest."

"Good morning, young man. I have your breakfast, as always. And a message arrived for you from Master Koga. Would you like me to read it to you?"

"Of course!"

The priest sensed the man edging forward, expectation rising in his voice. As he placed the tray on the floor, he said, "Very well." He then pulled a letter from his robes, untied the silken cord, unrolled the paper, and began to read. " 'Sir, I hope the New Year finds you well and happy, with a year full of promise. To that end, I would like to offer you a place in my training hall for instruction. Please come at your earliest convenience. Sincerely, Koga no Masaharu.' Ah, this is good news isn't it? You have waited so long!"

"Yes, this *is* good news!" The man's voice betrayed his jubilation. "Now, I can return to the path I set myself upon. I have unfinished business."

"Ah, yes, the man who injured you."

The man said nothing.

"That was a terrible wound on your leg. You are lucky it healed so well."

The man reached out of the darkness with his right hand, the hand that was always swathed in bandages. As he moved into the light, the priest saw that his flesh had grown pale, and his hard eyes were rimmed in red. He pulled the tray back into the darkness.

"Revenge and hatred are not The Way, Taro. They lead only to death and suffering."

"Again with that, priest? I thank you for your kindness and hospitality, and I will never forget how you helped me, but I grow tired of hearing those things. The man who did this to me will die. Only then will I rest. I'll be leaving today for Master Koga's training hall."

The priest did not relent. "All this hatred for an old leg wound? It is bad for your soul."

"It is more than that. It was his contempt. He did not respect me enough to kill me. So every day I suffer. I was foolish before. I was not ready. But next time we meet, I *will* be ready." The longer the man spoke, the deeper his voice became, until it had become an almost animal growl, like that of a hungry tiger.

A pang of fear drove the priest backward a step, and he swallowed. "Your soul will suffer in future lives if you pursue this path." His shaven pate beaded with sweat.

"I don't care! There is time for atonement later. Now I must have revenge. Now, please, leave me alone."

The priest bowed and retreated, almost gratefully. Something deep within him was shaking with fear, a quiet, insistent dread. He was happy to return to the temple and resume copying sutras. Today, he needed to concentrate on the power of the sutras, to think about only the words and the meaning behind the words, and he applied himself with unusual enthusiasm.

He never saw his guest leave. That night, when the priest checked the guesthouse and found it empty, a wave of relief so intense almost collapsed him.

Out of one wintry
Twig, one bud, one blossom's worth
Of warmth at long last!

—*Ransetsu*

The morning came, quiet and gradual, masked by the cold grayness of clouds and mist. There was no fire in Ken'ishi's room, so he was grateful for the warm, sleeping body lying next to his. Kiosé slept the sleep of the exhausted, nestled against his shoulder. Even in sleep, her hand clutched the front of his robes.

He looked down at her face. While she was sleeping, she was pretty. Her face had none of the weariness and despair that weighed upon her when she was awake, diminishing her beauty. He studied the shape of her face, and found himself comparing her to another face that was burned into his mind. Her ears stuck out a bit more. Her teeth were a bit crooked, but not unpleasantly so. Her throat was smooth and soft, and she had a small mole below one ear and another on the opposite cheek.

Then he gritted his teeth and purged thoughts of comparison from his mind. Enough! *She* was gone! Even so, the sound of her name floated around the periphery of his mind. Enough!

Kiosé's eyes opened, blinked, and looked into his. He looked into them, and there, deep in their dark depths, was a spark that last night he had thought extinguished. Here, in the quiet, vulnerable morning, he saw it was still there, hiding, hidden. Then she looked away and sat up, rubbing her eyes.

"Good morning," he said.

"Good morning, sir," she said.

He sat up beside her, took her arm, and pulled her to him. She came to him willingly, without resistance. He kissed her, and she kissed him back. His desire rose to a boil, and he clutched her to him. Part of him was surprised at the fervor of his need, but she accepted it, welcomed it, and clutched him onto her, into her. As he entered her soft, moist heat, the flash of another face intruded in his mind, and closing his eyes would not drive the image away. *Enough!* The ghostly countenance, beautiful beyond compare, faded into the mists of his memory.

The mounting cries of their passion filtered through the rice-paper walls, but they did not care. The shuddering convulsions of their ecstasy drove away all thoughts of modesty or decorum. When it was over and their frenzied breathing began to slow, she looked into his eyes, smiling, biting her lip. She plaintively touched his face, and said, "Again?" So he obliged her with fresh fervor.

Outside the inn, Ken'ishi sat down on the veranda, dangling his feet over the ground. He held a small wooden box filled with rice and pickled plums, a small bowl of fish soup, and three rice cakes sweetened with red bean paste and wrapped in moist leaves. Tetta had given him all this food free of charge, leftover from the New Year celebration that had been cut short. Before long, a familiar rusty-brown shape poked between his legs from under the veranda, and looked up at him with bright brown eyes.

Ken'ishi scratched his ears. "Have you eaten today? You smell of fish."

"Fishing village. So, smell of fish. Yes, found some fish to eat. Rice ball?"

Ken'ishi scooped up half of his rice with his hands, squeezed it into a ball, and handed it to Akao. The dog gobbled it down in one bite, then licked the sticky kernels from Ken'ishi's hands.

Ken'ishi opened the leaf around one of the sticky rice cakes and thrust the whole thing into his mouth. He was hungry.

Akao sat down beside him. "Leaving today?"

"No," Ken'ishi said. "Staying today."

"Leaving tomorrow."

"I don't know. We'll see."

"You smell of female. You are shameless." The dog grinned, tongue lolling, laughing silently.

At that moment, Kiosé stepped out of the inn with a pot of hot tea. Wordlessly, she poured him a cup, set the teapot down, and went back inside.

The dog laughed again. "Smell like her!"

Ken'ishi smiled and said nothing. Norikage walked toward him. The small man's face was cheery, but somehow the mirth did not reach his eyes. "Ken'ishi, good morning."

"Good morning."

"I am happy to find you awake." He eyed Akao for a moment. "Is this your dog?"

"You can call him Akao."

Norikage nodded slowly, appraising Ken'ishi's words. "Shall I show you to your house?"

"My house?" His eyebrows rose.

"Yes. The village constable's house."

Ken'ishi let the pleasure of this revelation sink in. "Very well. We will go as soon as I finish." Ken'ishi scooped the last lump of rice into his mouth.

"As you wish." Norikage waited while Ken'ishi continued his meal.

Kiosé came out and brought Norikage a cup and poured him tea from the pot. He drank the tea while Ken'ishi finished the soup and rice cakes.

Norikage said, "You already have an admirer, I see."

Ken'ishi looked up from his bowl. "What? Admirer?"

"Kiosé. I saw it by the way she looked at you. And she came by the door twice since she brought the tea, just to look at you."

Ken'ishi said nothing, sipping his tea.

Norikage smiled wryly and sipped his own tea.

Ken'ishi's house was a small but comfortable one near the constable's office. Norikage showed Ken'ishi around. "I already had Masahige's belongings moved out, with arrangements made to send them back to his family. Yes, I know the place feels empty, but you can buy a futon and such with your salary."

"I receive a salary?" Ken'ishi said, hardly able to contain his surprise.

"Yes, of course! I receive both of our salaries from the village taxes, and we each get a monthly sum. Obviously you have never had such an arrangement before."

"I have not. But I am grateful." He tried to keep the excitement out of his voice.

"You are a good man, Ken'ishi. And you will serve this village well, I think."

"I will try."

Then was a soft knock on the front door, and a woman's voice. "Ken'ishi-sama. Norikage-sama. Are you home?"

Norikage gave Ken'ishi a devilish smile. "Your admirer."

Ken'ishi's face betrayed no emotion, but he was pleased that she had come. He called out, "Enter!"

The door slid open, and Kiosé bowed. "I am being rude. Master Tetta sent me to give you this." In her hands, she held a covered basket.

"Very well," Ken'ishi said. "Bring it in."

She stepped inside tentatively, taking off her zori, and handed the basket up to Ken'ishi. "Thank you," he said.

"It was no trouble, sir. If ever you need anything, please call me." She bowed deeply, and there was a strange tone in her voice that he could not identify.

He bowed in return.

"Please excuse me," she said, "I have much work to do." With that, she turned, put her sandals back on, and departed.

"Indeed!" Norikage said, grinning at Ken'ishi. " 'If you need anything,' she said."

"Do not make fun of me," Ken'ishi said. "Or of her."

"Ah, Ken'ishi, don't be so serious! There is nothing wrong with amusing banter among men! In truth, she looks better today than she has of late. I have never seen her smile before. I wonder why she smiles today."

"I can't hazard a guess."

"Very well. But I should warn you. Keeping a secret in a village such as this is impossible."

"I will keep that in mind."

"One other thing I should tell you. Cavorting with a whore is one thing. Everybody does it. It is expected. But do not make the mistake of believing she will ever be anything else to the people of this village."

Ken'ishi's brow furrowed and his fists clenched.

"My apologies. I am merely trying to help you."

"Thank you for your concern. Now, if you will forgive me, I must practice."

"Very well. Afterwards, please come to my office. I have much to teach you."

After Norikage departed, Ken'ishi spent an hour practicing sword drills, the formulaic practice movements that Kaa had taught him. He would soon have to arrange for himself a proper practice ground. Perhaps, with enough money, someday he could even have his own training hall. After he was finished with his practice, he looked in the basket Kiosé brought him. Inside were several small packages, rice balls, pickled fish, a bundle of dried seaweed leaves, a jar of sake, and a bag of uncooked rice. A fine gift. He would thank Tetta later.

When he stepped outside and walked toward the constabulary, the passing villagers looked at him with a mixture of wonder, curiosity, and apprehension. Doubtless, all of them had heard accounts of last night's events. In fact, many of the village men had been there to witness the whole thing.

Norikage stepped outside to greet him as he approached the constabulary. The thin, rodent-like man ushered Ken'ishi into his office and offered him some tea. Then he said, "So, Ken'ishi, are you ready to begin your education?"

Ken'ishi's teacup halted a finger's breadth from his lips. "Education?"

"Yes. You want to learn how to read and write, do you not?"

"Yes."

"Then it is a simple matter of beginning, is it not? 'The journey of a thousand miles begins with a single step,' as they say."

Ken'ishi nodded. "I suppose so."

"Good! Henceforth, we will have lessons every day at this time."

"Every day?"

"Yes. A proper education takes time!"

Ken'ishi sighed. "Very well. I'll come every day after weapon practice. Perhaps *you* require some lessons."

"Me? Whatever for?"

"Learn to use the sword and the bow!"

Norikage laughed. "Me? Use the sword and bow? That's a good jest! I am a weakling! I can hardly lift a sword, much less draw a bow."

Ken'ishi scowled. "Practice makes you stronger."

"Nonsense! My young friend, strength is why I have *you* to fight for me." He laughed again.

Ken'ishi's scowl softened. "Perhaps some people aren't born to use a warrior's weapons."

"Indeed." Norikage then pulled out several sheets of paper, an inkpot, and two brushes. "These are the tools of a scholar and a gentleman, Ken'ishi. With diligent study, you will learn to use them. Now, let's begin."

That night, after a long, full day, Ken'ishi lay back on his futon, staring up into the dark rafters. He could not remember ever living in a house before this. The shadows cast into the underbelly of the roof by the brazier of coals beside him danced and shifted, creating dream-like, half-formed shapes and voids. He contemplated the events that led him to this turn of fortune, the path his life had taken since leaving the north.

The day had been a full one, a succession of new and wondrous experiences, meeting some of the people around the village, familiarizing himself with the village and its environs, and the most mind-boggling experience, the new journey to literacy. He returned from his lessons with Norikage to find his house freshly cleaned and tidied. He suspected only one person.

He thought about Kiosé. Kiosé was so different from . . . her. She was so weak and vulnerable, soft, but with the same sort of kind spirit. And he sensed her fervent desire for something better in life than the lot she had been given. What crimes had she committed in previous lives to sentence her to the life of a common prostitute? He should protect her, help her, even though there was little he could do to improve her place in life. Tetta owned her, and Ken'ishi did not have enough money to buy her contract. He could not deliver her from the life of servitude in which she was trapped. He had known so few women that he could make no comparisons. Why would a man sell his own daughter to a geisha house? Were daughters such a burden? Then he thought about the many courtesans he had seen in the capital, so beautiful, so graceful, with their beautiful clothes and immaculate appearance, like painted, porcelain goddesses. Did all of those women come from such unpleasant origins? Were all of them slaves?

The wind rose and began to caress the roof, to whisper through the eaves and cracks in the walls. He shivered and scooted closer to the coals. Then something heavy struck the wall of the house, thudding against his leg with a blunt sting against his leg. A fist-sized stone bounced onto the tatami mats.

Outside his house, a man's voice cried out above the wind. "Get out of here, you base coward! Get out or we'll finish you!"

Ken'ishi leaped to his feet and ran to the door, whipping it open. He heard running footsteps quickly receding, swallowed by the wind. He looked over at the ragged hole torn in the rice-paper wall by the stone. The paper fluttered as the wind whispered through the hole.

His eyes searched the darkness, and his shoulders tensed with the urge to chase his cowardly assailant through the night and punish him. But he resisted. Another death so soon would only make more enemies for him. He had to befriend the people of this village. The thought of enemies waiting to stab him in the back or spread poisonous words in closed rooms only stoked his anger, but he pushed it back down. He would just have to be more vigilant and act when the time was right.

"You cannot tell whether a person is good or evil by his vicissitudes in life. Good and bad fortune are matters of fate. Good and bad actions are Man's Way."

—*Hagakure*

A knock at the door of his office drew Yasutoki from his reverie. He had been thinking about Silver Crane again, the famous blade that had been gone from the world for over thirty years. Gone from the world, but not from memory. A weapon prized by the Taira clan during the long war with the Minamoto clan. The rediscovery of such a weapon might be enough to galvanize the scattered remnants of his kinsmen, reunite them, bring them back to power, once the Minamoto clan and their allies had been cast down by the Mongol invaders. The door slid open, revealing one of the house servants. "I am sorry, Yasutoki-sama. I am being rude. There is someone to see you. He says you are expecting him. His name is Akihiro."

Yasutoki had not been expecting this man so soon. "See him to my office. And bring some hot sake as well."

"As you wish, Yasutoki-sama. Excuse me." The servant shut the door again.

Yasutoki suppressed a surge of excitement. His months of preparation might begin to pay off. He hoped that this man had been worth his effort. He did not suffer disappointment with a pleasant nature. In the meantime, he made sure several of his poison-tipped shuriken were prepared. A servant brought warm sake and two cups. When the door opened, he was waiting behind his desk.

"Greetings, Akihiro," Yasutoki said cordially.

The man stepped into the room, and the servant slid the door shut behind him. He was dressed in the dusty robes of an itinerant merchant. The man bowed and seated himself across the desk from Yasutoki. "Greetings, Yasutoki-sama."

"How is the sake trade?" Yasutoki asked, loud enough to be heard in the hallway. "Would you care to sample some of our own local brew?"

"Business is terrible," the man replied. "Let us sample your sake."

Yasutoki studied his face. Was this the same man he had met on Mount Ono? He had not seen the man's face in decades. His face was remarkable in that it was completely unremarkable. He was so nondescript that Yasutoki wondered if he would remember the man's appearance a few days from now. It was the perfect face for someone of his profession, a porcelain mask, betraying no emotion. Yasutoki wondered if some sort of shadow charm or magic was at work here, manipulating his perception of the man's features. There were tales of such abilities, and Yasutoki wouldn't have put it past Kage to have discovered them.

Yasutoki offered him a cup, which he took, and poured some sake for him. "So, Kage," he said, his voice little more than an imperceptible mutter. "I have been looking forward to your visit for some time."

"I'm sure you have," Kage said, in a similar voice. "I have accomplished much."

"I hope it is worth the price."

"First," Kage said, "payment."

Yasutoki stiffened, but kept his composure at the man's abrupt manner. "Very well." He pulled a silk purse from his sleeve, heavy with the weight of coins and precious stones, and placed it in front of him on the desk. Kage unslung a satchel from his shoulder and placed it upon the table, then he reached for the purse. "Wait," Yasutoki said, laying his left hand on the purse.

Kage's hand froze, but his mask-like countenance betrayed no emotion.

Yasutoki said, "First, you must tell me what I can expect to find in here."

Kage's voice was dispassionate, and his hand remained poised above the table. "Detailed observations of the fighting strength of every Nishimuta and Otomo lord in the north. Information on the lesser families and clans of the central provinces will be coming soon."

"What about the Shimazu clan in the south?"

"Soon enough. I thought it best to concentrate on the most important forces first."

Yasutoki nodded. "Very good. Excellent." He took his hand off the purse.

Kage's hand resumed its forward motion, picked up the pouch, and withdrew with it.

Yasutoki said, "I trust the amount is sufficient to our bargain."

The purse disappeared into Kage's robes. "If it is not, I will return for the rest."

Yasutoki ignored the comment. "The rest of your payment

will come when I receive the information about the remaining fiefs. Our business here is concluded then."

"So it is." The man known as Kage bowed to Yasutoki, stood up and left the room with the sound of a shadow.

Yasutoki picked up the satchel, untied the flap, and looked inside. There were dozens of small, tightly wrapped scrolls. He picked one at random and opened it. With a grin, he found it concerned the fief of Lord Nishimuta no Jiro, Lord Tsuneto-mo's father-in-law. Two hundred able-bodied samurai, potential conscripts numbering over a thousand, four hundred horses, two master swordsmiths, four apprentice swordsmiths, four armorers, four bowyers. . . . He put a lid on the bubbling pot of his inner glee. Kage had indeed been thorough.

He put the scroll back into the satchel and stuffed the satchel inside a secret compartment in the rear of his writing desk. If this were found, it would cost Yasutoki his head. Already his mind was swirling about how best to compile the information and relay it to the Khan. He would have to travel to Hakozaki on some imaginary errand and send word to the Khan's spies there. This information was the key to the Great Khan's conquest, and he knew the Golden Horde would put it to the best possible use.

All that remained for him was to uncover the same informa-tion from Lord Tsunetomo's fief. Tsunemori was secretive, as if he could sense the danger in allowing it to Yasutoki. If Yasutoki made any direct inquiries and observations around the castle, Tsunemori's suspicions would be even more aroused. No, only in Tsunemori's complacency could Yasutoki operate at will. Ya-sutoki would have to undertake this task personally.

While his mind was on the subject of spies, he wondered again what happened to the spies he dispatched so long ago to find the ronin, Ken'ishi. Yasutoki had many other things oc-cupying his attention lately, but the ronin and his stolen treasure were never far from his mind. He was a curiosity, an unusual tool. Of course, there was no question that Silver Crane would be wrested from him eventually. The ronin could not be allowed to keep it, but he seemed to have been swallowed by the earth. Nevertheless, the men Yasutoki had hired to find him were skilled and resourceful. They would succeed, of that he had no doubt.

Look at the candle!
What a hungry wind it is . . .
Hunting in the snow!

—*Seira*

Ken'ishi sat in Tetta's main room, sipping his hot tea, listening to the sound of the winter wind outside the inn. The cold wind swept off the ocean and washed over the village, but it was not bitter cold. Ken'ishi remembered well the bitter cold gales that swept across the snow-blanketed mountainsides in his boyhood home, so for him this winter here seemed mild. But the village was so close to the ocean that he sometimes thought he felt the frigid salt spray even when he was dry.

Tetta sat down across the table from him, carrying a jar of sake. He grunted as he sank down as if he were exhausted. "Cold today, eh?"

Ken'ishi nodded. "But it is warm enough in here."

"So it is, isn't it? How was the soup?"

"It was delicious. Just what I needed on a night like tonight."

"You are too kind. Sometimes my wife's cooking tastes like piss." Tetta smiled good-naturedly.

Ken'ishi smiled back. "I'm sure she would disagree."

"I tell her that all the time. She ignores me. Hah! She ignores me most of the time! Someday when you have a wife you will know what I mean!" Tetta chuckled, then grew more serious. "Ken'ishi, there is something I've been meaning to discuss with you."

Ken'ishi put down his teacup. He suspected that Tetta wanted to talk to him about Kiosé. Before Tetta started speaking, Ken'ishi had a feeling that Kiosé was listening from somewhere nearby.

Tetta said, "This is difficult to discuss. I am indebted to you. You saved my life, and you saved Kiosé's life. Without her, my family would be poorer this winter. Ah, this is difficult. I know that she cares for you."

Ken'ishi said nothing. He could not deny it.

"I think she looks at you as her protector. She is very sly about it, but she often asks if there is anything I would like her to do for you. Sometimes I indulge her. It isn't good for me to let her get too attached, do you understand? She may think that you will help her if she decides to disobey me."

Ken'ishi said, "You have been good to me, Tetta. I have no wish to interfere with your affairs."

Tetta rubbed his oddly shaped pate with a gnarled hand. "Ah, that's good, isn't it? It does me good to hear you say it. Please don't misunderstand me. Kiosé has given me no trouble at all. She does as she is told, and she's a hard worker. She serves me well, and I think my guests like her. But there's something else I need to talk to you about. Since . . . that night, Yoba's family has been spreading lies about me, about you, about Kiosé. They say that you work for a yakuza gang in Ha-kozaki. They say that Kiosé is riddled with disease. They say that my food is poisonous."

Ken'ishi scowled. "They are an evil brood. I think most people are smart enough to recognize their lies."

"So it seems, but . . . they have yelled threats at Kiosé. She's terrified of them. Perhaps they're just trying to scare her. Or perhaps they're working themselves up to do something terrible. I don't know. But I don't want anything to happen to her. And not just for my own sake, you understand. I care for her almost as my own daughter."

"I don't believe that you mistreat her, Tetta."

"My son, Gonta, is sometimes short with her, but my family looks out for her. I am already indebted to you, Ken'ishi, so I hate to ask anything of you, but you are the only man in the village capable of defending her from Yoba's family. They hate you, but they fear you as well."

"It's already my duty to ensure there is no trouble, Tetta."

"I understand. Kiosé has been cleaning your house and cooking for you sometimes, hasn't she? It's because of my debt to you. And I know she wants to do it. Do you understand?"

Ken'ishi nodded.

"I just wanted you to know that anything she does for you is with my blessing."

"You are too kind, Tetta."

The innkeeper protested. "No, no, not at all. I think you have been a gift to this village. Hojo-sama was a good man, but he was unhappy here. His unhappiness sometimes got in the way of his duties. He could have done something about Yoba long ago. It is unfortunate that you had to kill Yoba, but I am glad that he is gone. I hope you don't have to do any harm to his sons, but most people would understand if you did."

"I will do whatever is necessary to make sure that they harm no one."

Tetta nodded with appreciation.

"There is something I would like to ask you now, Tetta," Ken'ishi said. "I know that Kiosé is worth a lot of money to you. I'm sure you had to pay handsomely for her."

"She is valuable to me."

"But she could be replaced, could she not? You could go to Hakozaki to buy another girl's contract?"

Tetta rubbed his chin. "I suppose if I had the money, I could do that. I would be taking a big risk that the new girl would be lazy, or inept, or disobedient. Kiosé is worth more to me than I paid for her. And it's a long walk to Hakozaki for these old bones."

Their eyes met for a moment. Tetta knew what he was asking. Ken'ishi said, "What if you had the money?"

"But where would I get that amount of money?"

Ken'ishi emptied his teacup and put it down firmly. "Perhaps you could think about how much money that would be."

"Perhaps I could," Tetta said, nodding amiably. "It is always good to plan for the future, isn't it?"

"As you say, Tetta." Ken'ishi said. "Now, please excuse me. The hour is growing late. Thank you for the fine meal."

As he walked the short distance back to his house, Ken'ishi sidestepped patches of snow from a storm two days before that still remained in the areas shadowed from the daylight sun. The dirt of the village street was soft with melted snow, but stiffened by the night chill. Ken'ishi trusted the innkeeper, but he had no idea how much it might cost to set Kiosé free. And the money he received from Norikage each month was more than he needed to buy food and supplies. He did not know how long he would have to save his coins to cover the sum Tetta might ask.

Thoughts bounced around in his mind like a flock of chattering sparrows.

Then he stopped in the middle of the street, his senses sharp. His hand was on his sword hilt. Something was wrong. A chill breeze whispered through the darkness under trees surrounding the village, between the weathered wooden houses, under the dark eaves. His eyes scanned the darkness. Someone was watching him. Yoba's sons, prepared for an ambush? His house was only fifty paces away. Where was Akao? Was someone hiding inside his house? No, the danger was . . . more distant. But someone was watching him, he was sure of it.

He resumed his purposeful stride and headed again toward his house. After listening at the door and hearing nothing, he went inside and shut the door behind him. He did not remove his hand from the hilt of his sword. The inside of his house was cold, so he moved to the hearth in the center of the room, removed the lid over the coals, and began to fan them, throwing bits of kindling on them to build the fire. All with one hand ready to draw steel.

The feeling of uneasiness subsided. Before long, the fire warmed the interior of his house. A soft scratching came at the door. He opened the door, and Akao slid inside. The dog wiped his feet on the reed mat before stepping up onto the tatami and sidling up to the fire.

Akao said, "Strange smell tonight."

Ken'ishi asked, "Have you seen anything strange?"

"See nothing. Smell strange."

"A stranger?"

"Not like a man smell."

A soft knock came at the door, and he turned to face the door. "Who's there?"

Kiosé's voice. "It's me."

"Please come in."

The door slid open, admitting a fresh, chilly draught of night air, and he saw Kiosé revealed in the glow of his firelight. "Excuse me. Am I intruding?"

Ken'ishi put his alertness aside, but did not let it go. "Not at all." He gestured her inside.

She smiled back shyly. Ken'ishi long ago noted that she always resisted smiling, except when she was with him alone.

"I am sorry. Tetta did not send me. He does not know I am here. They think I am sleeping." She removed her sandals and slipped up onto the floor, sliding across the floor on her knees to sit near him.

"Tetta will be unhappy with you."

"Perhaps. But I had to see you," she said. She looked so pretty in the firelight. The darkness and shadows of night masked so much of the weight upon her spirit, the small imperfections in her appearance, the worn, threadbare clothes. In the firelight, she looked more innocent, childlike. She brushed aside a few wisps of hair from her cheek. He was glad for her company.

"Did you mean what you . . . the things you said to Tetta?"

"What things?" he asked with false innocence.

"You are teasing me." She blushed.

Ken'ishi chuckled. "You were listening."

"I could not help but hear. I was cleaning the hallway. I just wanted to say thank you for your concern, but you shouldn't go to so much trouble for me. I am already in your debt for saving my life."

"You're not in my debt."

"You are too good to me. If you bought my contract, then I would be even more indebted to you. You should not put yourself out for me. I am just. . . ." Her voice trailed off as if she could not bear to finish the words.

He looked at her for a long moment, then leaned over and

touched her face.

A look of surprise flickered across her face, then she allowed herself to lean her cheek into his caress.

In the protection of the firelight, they embraced, sharing their warmth against the moan of the frigid winter wind. As they lay together, Ken'ishi could not help but wonder what other dangers lurked in the darkness outside.

April's air stirs in
Willow leaves . . . A butterfly
Floats and balances

—Basho

Norikage saw Ken'ishi's brow furrow in frustration sitting across the desk. The desk was littered with pages covered with scrawled calligraphy. The paper maker in Hakozaki had been happily producing more of the coarse, fibrous wood pulp paper at Norikage's request. Even the cheap wood paper was expensive, but he loathed Ken'ishi's idea of scratching characters in the dirt. It was just too . . . rustic. Proper writing must be taught with paper, brush, and ink.

Morning sunlight spilled through the open window like liquid, golden warmth. The air was rich and moist with the coming of spring, smelling of vegetation and the sea. Then one of the village farmers walked by carrying a filthy bucket, and the stench hit Norikage in the nose almost immediately. He made a disgusted noise. "Can't those peasants find a different route to carry fertilizer through?" The farmers in the rice fields were working the village waste into the soil in preparation for the spring planting. Some children were playing a game of tag with Ken'ishi's dog in the street, punctuated by the gleeful laughter of the children and playful yips from the dog.

He glanced at Ken'ishi, who was concentrating on brushing a character onto his paper. He said, "No, this character is written *this* way. Do it again." Ken'ishi had difficulty in writing characters with more than ten strokes. Until Norikage began teaching him how to write, the young warrior had not known how to count past ten. Norikage showed him again how to write the character for "garden," counting out the final strokes as he did so. "Eleven . . . twelve . . . thirteen."

Aoka village had been quiet over the winter. There were a few minor disputes between townspeople, but Norikage handled those. Norikage had seen little of Chiba and his brothers since Ken'ishi killed their father. The rest of the townspeople seemed to tolerate Ken'ishi. He spoke to them with none of the haughtiness Masahige had shown, almost as if he were one of them. Of course, he could never be one of them, because he was not born here. If he lived out the rest of his days in his village, Ken'ishi would always be an outsider, just as Norikage was. But Norikage accepted that. He knew that this village was just a stepping-stone on a longer journey.

"Why must I learn characters that have no use?" Ken'ishi protested. "When will I ever write the word for 'garden'?"

Norikage's normally well-controlled voice shrilled with his own frustration. "Do you wish to be nothing more than an ignorant bumpkin? An uneducated peasant like the rest of the people in this village who cannot read and write?"

"I've made my way just fine."

"Fool! You are lucky to have survived!" Norikage snapped.

"Perhaps I can explain in terms you will understand. Warriors are taught to seek the advantage in every situation, yes?"

Ken'ishi's eyes turned wary. "Yes."

"Imagine two men, both physically equal, both strong, capable men. What if one of them is educated and the other is not? Who has the advantage?"

Ken'ishi said nothing, but Norikage saw the calculation behind his gaze.

"What if these two men sat before their lord, and their lord said that he could choose only one of them for an important promotion? Who would be the most suitable choice?"

"The stronger of the two."

"But they are both equal in strength and prowess. What if one of them can read and write important documents? What if one of them knows about history and religion, better to advise his lord? Who should be chosen?"

The young man finally sighed. "Very well. The educated man."

"And well he should. Unless, of course, the lord is seeking nothing more than a mindless brute. This sometimes happens, to be sure, but not in positions of great delicacy or responsibility. The same is true of the Imperial court, except the weapons used are words, not blades."

"What do you know of the Imperial court? You have been in the capital?"

Norikage looked at the papers on the desk without seeing them. Perhaps he had said too much.

Ken'ishi said, "You have too many secrets."

"Eh?"

"You are hiding something from me."

"As you are hiding something from me." Norikage put the proper air of indignance in his voice. He had learned in the Imperial court that the best way to defend oneself was to steer attention to someone else. "Come now, you have been here nearly five months, and I have been waiting for you to tell me. There is something in your past that haunts you. I assure you, I have no interest in exposing your secrets to anyone else."

"I don't trust you."

"What a rude thing to say! But of course, I do not trust you either. I trust no one in this world. Very well, as a show of good faith, I will tell you something." Norikage took a deep breath. To divulge such a secret of his own went against his nature; divulging the secrets of others had always been easy, however. But now his curiosity was too strong; to get something, he had to give something. "My father was a minister in the Imperial court, so I was raised among wealth and power. He was always in the midst of court politics. A more backstabbing, vicious lot of people never existed. They sheath their weapons in poetry and fine arts, but they are sharks! A mere word from one of the powerful courtiers behind the throne can end a man's life. Alas, I did not realize what this meant."

Norikage glanced at Ken'ishi, but the young warrior sat stoic and silent. Then he continued, "One of the Emperor's concubines was a rare beauty. Since I was a boy, I had watched all these court nobles, men and women alike, trading lovers among themselves as if they were sets of fine clothes. So I saw nothing wrong with arranging a liaison with this exquisite creature. Besides, she was not even favored by the Emperor at the time. He did not have time for her. So beautiful she was! In the prime of her womanhood at fourteen! And she favored me as well, or she would have never accepted my advances. Court nobles sometimes use love to form their political alliances, but those alliances change with the passing breeze, and this lovely girl was artless as a babe. Only when she grew large with child did I discover that the Emperor had been saving the flower of her virginity for himself, for a special occasion. Why do you smile?"

The faint smile Norikage had seen developing on Ken'ishi's face disappeared like a wisp of smoke on the wind.

Norikage continued warily, "In any case, the child died of a fever before it reached a year, or so I was told. To preserve our family's status and wealth, I was banished from the capital and stripped of my family name. If I was a warrior, you might call me a ronin."

"So how did you come be the assistant of a Hojo constable?"

"The flow of money from the Shogun's headquarters to a place as far away as this becomes a mere trickle. Masahige was originally from Kamakura, near the Shogun's headquarters, but his family is not one of the thickest branches on the Hojo tree; they could be pruned."

"You talk like a courtier. Speak plainly."

Norikage sighed and rolled his eyes. "His family barely survived the great war between the Taira and Minamoto clans that led to the Shogun's government. After the Hojo clan became the Shogun's regents, Masahige's grandfather attached the family through marriage to the Hojo, and took on the Hojo name. So when Masahige reached his majority, his family sought a government post for him. Constable of Aoka village is the post he was given, and not a very lucrative one, as you well know."

"I consider myself wealthy. I have food to eat and a house to live in."

"You have little more than a hovel!" Norikage laughed. "Ah, Ken'ishi, you are a man of simple tastes and pleasures. Masahige was not. He had fallen into debt, and he could not pay his creditors. Before I left the capital, my mother told me she did not want me to live as a pauper, even though I was banished from the family, so she gave me some money. Quite a lot of money, actually. I met Masahige in a geisha house in Hakozaki, the place where he had accumulated most of his debt. I saw an opportunity, and I took it. And so I am here. If the government were to discover my position here, however. . . ."

"I understand."

"So now you must tell me your secret."

Ken'ishi hesitated, just as Norikage had. Norikage wondered in the silence what kind of dark deeds might lie in the past of a warrior as young as this one. Then the young man began his tale. The more Ken'ishi spoke, the more Norikage realized that the youth was telling more than he intended, but somehow could not stop himself, as if his life was so filled with events, so crammed into such a short time that he had to release them somehow. He had to *tell* someone, and so Norikage listened to the young man's tale of poverty and want and endless wandering, and to the tale of the beautiful noble maiden, and of the oni bandit chieftain. Norikage often spurred the tale onward, enthralled by the young man's simple words.

Norikage said, "I have heard the story about this ronin oni-slayer. It has made the rounds through every sake house in the province! That was you?"

"I have not heard any such story. Ka— the young maiden and I killed the oni."

"I heard tales of the oni that lived in those parts. He was a bad one, they say. Sometimes he and his gang would make forays into Hakata in the dead of night to rob someone's house or steal the wares of a wealthy merchant. A horrible creature."

"It was."

"In the capital there were rumors of courtiers who were really oni in disguise. Foul creatures they were, but powerful, with webs of intrigue that reached into every corner of the Imperial court," Norikage mused. Then he grew serious again. "The girl's father is a fool, whoever he is! But you are better off!" He laughed. "You are here!"

Ken'ishi smiled wanly. "Yes, I am here."

"And you have Kiosé now. You can forget your noble maiden. Come now, tell me who she was!"

Ken'ishi looked out the window, a trace of wistfulness in his gaze that Norikage knew he would never admit to. "I cannot tell you her name. And as for Kiosé, I do not have her. She still belongs to Tetta. But he allows her to cook for me, and to clean my house."

Norikage nodded. Of course, he would not mention in Ken'ishi's presence that he had partaken of Kiosé's womanly charms a few times before the night Ken'ishi arrived in Aoka. The young man did not interfere with Tetta's business, but Norikage knew he did not like that Kiosé had been bedded by most of the men in the village. Kiosé made a great deal of money for Tetta. Nevertheless, Norikage recognized the young man's protectiveness of her and had not visited her since. He did not wish to instigate any unpleasant feelings between them.

Ken'ishi said nothing.

"It is no secret. If you show too much favor for her, your reputation might suffer. You could buy her freedom."

"Someday." Then he looked at Norikage. "But I don't plan to go into debt."

Norikage smiled. "I would suggest no such thing! It's too bad. She is a pretty girl. But you do not love her."

Again, Ken'ishi said nothing.

"Forgive me. A man like you does not speak of such things. And yet you protect her."

Ken'ishi nodded. "Chiba knows better than to harm her. Cowardly wretch."

"It is only natural for him to wish to avenge his father."

"Then he should seek his vengeance on me. A few weeks ago, he cornered her behind the inn when she was washing laundry. He beat her with a switch."

"I am surprised that you did nothing about it."

"She didn't tell me about it. I overheard Tetta and his son talking about it afterwards."

"Well, she is an easier target than you. He cannot hope to face that blade of yours."

"That makes him a coward." The venom in Ken'ishi's tone and the cold, stony glare in his eyes gave Norikage pause. Until that moment, he had not realized how deep Ken'ishi's convictions and determination ran. In the Imperial court, everyone had a price, a limit that could be reached without too much difficulty, a point of compromise, thus Norikage assumed that everyone in the world was much the same. It seemed that Ken'ishi had no such point of weakness or compromise.

"Forgive me for taking a contrary position. It's my argumentative nature. Chiba and his brothers are scum of the worst sort. Perhaps we should see them punished."

"They know I'm waiting for the chance."

"Yes, unfortunately it's not a crime to beat a whore. I think Chiba and his lot will continue to push. We will have to deal with them soon." He rubbed his chin. "I am sorry to change the subject, but there is something else I've been wondering about you. You have told me nothing of your family. How did you become ronin? You sound as if it is the only life you have ever known."

"It is."

"What of your parents?"

"Dead. I was little more than an infant. I was raised by my teacher."

"You have no idea who your parents were?"

Ken'ishi shook his head.

Norikage could not help laughing again. "You might not even be from a samurai family! You might be nothing more than a peasant with a pretty sword!"

Ken'ishi's eyes flashed with anger, and Norikage choked off

his laughter.

Ken'ishi's words were quiet, fierce, and steady. "This is my father's sword. My father was samurai."

"Again, Ken'ishi, forgive my rudeness. A sensitive topic of conversation, I see. Perhaps we should continue the writing lesson."

"Tomorrow. My mind is weary. I must train the body for a while."

"Very well."

"And please order three more bokken from Gorobei the carpenter."

"You wear out the wooden swords so quickly!"

"Few things in the world are as strong as steel."

"Very well. I will contract Gorobei for three more bokken."

Then Norikage heard a timid step outside his office. "Who's there?" he called.

"It is Kiosé," came a soft voice. "May I enter, sirs?"

"Yes, come in," Norikage said, trying to observe any reaction from Ken'ishi or Kiosé when she entered the room. Ken'ishi may as well have been carved of basalt. Kiosé kept her eyes properly downcast as she shuffled into the room with a woman's soft step. "What is it?"

"Please pardon me. I am looking for Tetta-sama."

"I haven't seen him since yesterday morning," Ken'ishi said.

Norikage shook his head. "Nor I. Not since breakfast yesterday."

"That is why I am worried. He left yesterday afternoon to go fishing, and he has not come back."

Norikage rubbed his chin. She was not the kind of girl to make wild claims. "That is unusual for him. Perhaps his boat was swamped. The seas were high yesterday."

Ken'ishi shook his head. "He does not have a boat. He prefers to fish in a pond about one ri inland."

"Do you know where the pond is?"

"He told me once where it is."

"Then perhaps I will make a few inquiries around the village to see if anyone has seen him," Norikage said. "Perhaps he went to Hakozaki."

Kiosé said, "Excuse me, sirs, but if he planned to go to Hakozaki, he would have told me, or taken me with him, I think. He does not like leaving me alone for long after . . . what Chiba did."

Norikage nodded. Her words seemed reasonable. "What do you think, Ken'ishi?"

"I think I should go to the pond. Perhaps something happened to him along the way."

Kiosé said, "Ken'ishi, would you . . . allow me to come with you. With both you and Tetta away from the village, someone might . . . something might happen."

Norikage said, "It may be more dangerous to go with Ken'ishi."

"Ken'ishi is a strong man, and I will be no trouble! Please, sirs."

Ken'ishi nodded. "You may come. But you must be alert."

"Single-mindedness is all-powerful."

—*Samurai Proverb*

"I have never seen someone fight with such ferocity in a mere contest," said Master Imamura. "The other students are afraid of him!" He spoke quietly, behind his fan. It was a warm day for spring, and the training ground rang with the cacophony of wooden swords smashing together and cries of exertion, pain, and concentration. Birds sang in the meticulously pruned pine trees surrounding the periphery of the practice yard, just inside the stone wall that screened the sword academy from the rest of the world. Puffs of dust rose and hung limply in the air from the scuff of feet trampling back and forth.

A melee swirled in the practice yard, twenty-four students with wooden swords in a dangerous free-for-all. Blows from the wooden swords were usually not lethal, but sometimes accidents did happen, and limbs could be broken or skulls cracked. The students' means of protection were padded gauntlets, lacquered breastplates, and stiff leather skullcaps.

Koga no Masaharu, master of the Koga Sword Academy, leaned toward his guest and replied, "Many of my students *are* afraid of him. His technique is mediocre, but he makes up for his deficiency with raw strength. In less than half a year of training, he has injured three other students so badly that they were forced to quit."

Together the two teachers watched the surging melee. They were both in their late fifties, having devoted their entire lives to the study of the sword, fighting battles and skirmishes, and finally having gathered enough money and prestige to open their own training academies. Their schools were rivals, but the two men were old friends and had known each other since they served the Otomo clan together as young men. They wore the clothes of accomplished warriors, functional and simple but made of fine, richly colored silk. They sat together in the shade of the training ground observation platform. Their gray hair was identically styled with shaven pate and warrior's topknot. The easiest way to distinguish one from the other was the long pointed gray beard that dangled from Master Koga's chin. Master Imamura wore no such hair on his face, and his eyes were set deeper and further apart.

Taro had already felled two of Master Imamura's best students by splintering their wooden swords with his own and driving the wind out of them with powerful blows to the belly.

Master Imamura said, "How did he come to be so strong? He is no bigger than anyone else."

"I'm not certain, but it might be the desire for revenge. He told me of a ronin he fought who defeated him and left him for dead. He is training so that he can find that ronin and kill him."

"Ah, he's just taken down Sato! That's three now! Poor devil, he's unconscious! That man of yours is quick! Sato didn't even see it coming." Master Imamura's heavy brow thickened into a frown.

Every two years, the old sword masters met for a tournament of their top students. It was usually a good-natured affair, but sometimes the masters' friendship was strained by the rivalry of their students. Injuries were to be expected, but serious injuries only caused bad blood.

"Even your own students are staying away from him! See, look! They should be fighting together. Now my boys have taken the advantage by fighting as a team!" His frown changed to a smirk of satisfaction.

Master Koga saw that he was correct. Six of the Imamura students remained, facing four of the Koga students, including Taro. The Imamura students had just taken out three Koga students in quick succession by working together and fighting as a team. It was Master Koga's turn to frown. The tournament was going badly for him. Over the years, he held a significant advantage in victories over Master Imamura, and he had been confident of another victory this year. But now his pride was at stake. Master Koga's students stayed away from Taro, because he fought with such ferocity and wild abandon that he was just as likely to injure one of his fellows as the enemy. Master Koga had not told Master Imamura that Taro killed one of his students during a training bout a few weeks before. The death had not been intentional, but Taro lost control and struck with such force that both swords had been shattered, along with the other student's skull. The unfortunate student had taken three days to die.

Master Koga said, "I have warned him repeatedly that good technique will beat him every time, but he doesn't listen. And I have no student with the technique to match his strength."

Master Imamura grinned wolfishly. "Perhaps I have such a student! Michizaemon is my best. The leader. He comes from a strong family, and his control is superb."

"I think we will soon see."

Three of the Koga students clustered themselves and faced the Imamura students, while Taro stood alone, edging toward the outside of the practice yard, facing the Imamura student, Michizaemon. The larger melee was five versus three, but Master Koga could not peel his gaze away from the impending confrontation between Taro and Michizaemon.

Taro's eyes were hard and calm, like those of a warrior who had seen a hundred battles. That alone was rare for one so young, but his flesh looked so sickly as well, pale and gaunt, belying the fearsome strength in his lithe limbs. His jaw was hard-set, and his hands gripped the wooden sword too strongly. Master Koga had often warned him against gripping the hilt too fiercely with his right hand. The true power of the cut was in the left hand, and focusing on the right hand made all Taro's other techniques too stiff and wooden to be skillful.

With a sharp cry, Taro charged, lashing out with a powerful cut to his opponent's belly. Michizaemon easily deflected the blow, but the power of the strike drove him sideways a step, and Master Koga saw the surprise in the young man's eyes, and the flash of restrained fear. For several thundering heartbeats, the two young men traded blows and counterblows. Michizaemon's skill was superior, but Taro had strength. Master Koga found himself wanting to see Michizaemon victorious. He wanted Taro to be taught, once and for all, that power was not everything. The superiority lay with finesse and technique, not savage strength. Their feet scuffled back and forth across the dirt, and he heard their grunts of exertion, smelled the dust and the sweat and scent of pine needles from the trees.

A surge of satisfaction rippled through him as Michizaemon sent Taro's wooden sword spinning away out of his grasp. Taro was now weaponless. Michizaemon prepared to strike him, which, by the rules of the melee, would mean that he was "dead." Then Taro's eyes blazed with rage, and he lunged forward. His left hand caught his opponent by the throat, and his right hand drew back and lashed out again. He punched Michizaemon squarely in the chest. The force of the blow cracked through the practice yard like the sound of a splintered tree trunk, and Michizaemon flew backward, skidding to a halt on the ground several paces away.

Michizaemon coughed once, little more than a wet, feeble gurgle, and blood gushed from his mouth and nose. The rest of the melee ceased, and the other fighters stopped and stared at Taro, then Michizaemon. Taro stood stock still, his fists clenched at his sides, his breathing ragged, his eyes brimming with red fury. Michizaemon spasmed once and then lay still, his bulging eyes staring at the heedless blue sky, blood bubbling from his mouth and nose. Dead silence settled over the practice yard.

A feeling of sick dread settled into Master Koga's belly. And resolve.

Master Imamura leaped to his feet. "He's dead! You bastard!"

The rage began to drain from Taro's eyes. He unclenched his fists and bowed deeply. "I'm sorry," he said.

"You're sorry!" Master Imamura roared. "You are a disgrace!"

Master Koga said quietly, "Calm yourself, my friend. He is my student. I will deal with him. And as you can see, you have already won the battle. I declare this tournament finished. The victory is yours."

Master Imamura stopped and looked around. Master Koga was correct. Only Taro remained, versus four of Master Imamura's students. Nevertheless, Master Koga was certain that Taro could have defeated them all, even without a sword.

Master Koga continued, raising his voice to the students, "Thank you all for your display of skill and courage. I concede the victory of this year's tournament to the Imamura School." As he spoke, he watched Taro's reaction and saw the young man's face harden with fresh anger. "Michizaemon fought bravely. Let us all honor him." He bowed to the corpse, and everyone followed his example. "Now, everyone go to the training hall to see to your wounds." The students relaxed and turned to go inside. "Except you, Taro." He kept his voice even. "Wait for me in my room."

Taro bowed. "Yes, Master Koga." Then he took up his fallen wooden sword and went into the school by a back entrance.

Master Koga turned to his old friend and said, "Master Imamura, I must express my most profound regrets. Warriors must always be ready to die, but this death was wasteful and unnecessary. I'm sure you will agree."

Master Imamura grunted something that sounded like agreement, but his face was pale. What he had seen had shaken him, the way Michizaemon had been killed. A single blow to the heart, *through* a lacquered metal breastplate. . . .

"Please excuse me for a moment," Master Koga said, "I must go and see to my student."

Master Koga entered his room. Taro was waiting for him, as instructed. He had doffed his gauntlets and cap, but still wore the breastplate. Sweat plastered his hair to his face and neck. With the gauntlets removed, Master Koga could see Taro's discolored right hand. Up to a point just below his right elbow, the entire hand and forearm was a mottled deep red and purple, like a puddle of congealed blood. The nails on that hand were cracked and thick and yellowed. Seeing that hand always made Master Koga feel a little unsettled, because it was so grotesque. Taro said his hand had always been that way, but Master Koga had never heard of or seen a birthmark or deformity like it.

He crossed the room and sat down opposite Taro. The coldness he felt came out in his voice. "You have gone too far. Have you anything to say for yourself?"

Taro bowed deeply, pressing his forehead to the floor. When

he sat upright again, he said, "Only that I am sorry, Master. I did not mean to kill him. It was an accident."

"I do not believe you. I saw your eyes. You would have killed every man on that training ground!" He took a deep breath and regained control of his voice.

Taro's face turned red, and Master Koga saw the barely restrained tension in his hands. For a moment, he sensed Taro's desire to attack him and knew that his decision was the correct one.

"As such," he continued, "there is nothing further I can teach you."

He waited for his words to sink in, and he met Taro's angry gaze with a cold, steely one.

Taro's voice deepened. "But warriors are trained to kill! I am a warrior!"

"I train warriors here, Taro. Today you were not a warrior. You were an animal! You fought like an animal, without control or regard for the rules of this contest. And as a result, you have dishonored yourself and this school. I cannot countenance such behavior. You are finished here. Master Imamura would be within his bounds to demand blood for blood. But we are friends, so I think he will not."

"But, Master, I'm learning so much and—"

"Enough. My decision is made. Pack your things and leave now. Cause any trouble in this, and I will have you hunted down like an animal."

Taro's terrible right hand opened and closed, flexing repeatedly, and his dark gaze burned into the floor.

"Go, now."

Taro stood up and left the room without another word.

Master Koga sat in silence for a while, deep in thought. Taro had shown such promise in the beginning. His skills with the jitte were impressive. Even then, with the jitte he could disarm most of Master Koga's students. But something had happened since then. He had become ever more bloodthirsty, often bragging to the other students the terrible tortures he would exact upon the ronin he sought when he found him. His descriptions were terrible to hear, even for a seasoned warrior, and unseemly. What had gone wrong with his student?

Then the first scream tore through the air.

A second followed close behind, a gurgling cry of agony.

Then a third.

Now would be the true test. Calmly, he stood up and approached the rack where he kept his sword. He thrust the scabbard into his sash and tied the cords.

A cacophony of anger and fear filled the halls of the school, echoing down the rice-paper passageways. His sword slid easily from the scabbard, well oiled and polished to perfection. The muffled splatter of spewing gore, the tear of sliced flesh and bone reached his ears as he readied himself.

He slid open the door to his chamber. The sounds of battle grew louder. He strode down the hallway toward the training hall. When he reached the training hall, the fight was over.

Bodies and pieces of bodies lay like hacked and ravaged dolls, dismembered and strewn about. The air reeked with the stench of fresh-spilled blood and bowels. The polished wooden floor glistened with pools of spreading scarlet. Only two figures remained standing, and one of them had no head. Master Imamura's head was tumbling to the floor, where it splashed and rolled across the floor through the blood, and his body fell backwards to land with a wet plop, legs and arms twitching. Now only Taro remained standing, holding his ensanguined blade one-handed at his side. His face was split with a wide, gleeful grin, horribly free of any mirth.

His eyes burned from within like red coals. He was spattered and splashed with gore from face to foot.

For the first time in decades, the shiver of ice swept up Master Koga's back and turned his insides to cold gravel. But he would face it like the warrior he was. There was no more cause or room for words. Now, only battle and death. He raised his sword. He would teach this creature the meaning of skill and technique.

He squared his body to face the bloody figure and waited.

Fifteen paces separated them.

Taro's face twisted for a moment into something that might have been regret, but it quickly disappeared, like a seashell on the beach engulfed in relentless surf.

In a single leap, he closed the distance between them and brought his scarlet sword down, down, down, crashing into Master Koga's blade with the force of an avalanche.

The last thing Master Koga saw was the snarling, grinning mouth, with its yellowing teeth and dark red tongue, filling his vision, and the words of the funeral sutras echoing in his mind.

"I take refuge in the Buddha, I take refuge in the Dharma, I take refuge in the Sangha. . . ."

"A warrior should not say something fainthearted even casually. He should set his mind to this beforehand. Even in trifling matters the depths of one's heart can be seen."

—*Hagakure*

Ken'ishi and Kiosé walked the path leading to the fishing pond. Akao loped ahead of them with his nose to the ground. The path wound inland, through rocky outcroppings, bamboo groves, and thickly gnarled trees. As they walked, Ken'ishi kept his attention on the path, trying to observe any signs that Tetta might have gone this way, or anything else that looked unusual. Kiosé followed along, doing her best to stay quiet and out of the way, as she did so often.

She did so much work for him, even though she spent long days working for Tetta. How she found time to do things for Ken'ishi he did not know. He enjoyed her company and her warmth in his bed. He sometimes wondered why his pleasure was never as intense as it had been . . . once before. He pondered this, and then he did his best to put those memories away, to lock them in a box of iron within his belly. Sometimes Kiosé's timidity was too much for him to take, but he could hardly chastise her for it. Everyone else expected her to behave that way, and she had been trained harshly in the geisha house. Only in their most private moments did he see the inquisitive, passionate spirit that she kept hidden from Tetta and all her patrons. Only with Ken'ishi did she reveal it, like removing the lid from a pot containing a single, beautiful spark. He did not like to think about all the other men, but he felt privileged, because they did not get to see what he saw.

But he had been worried about her lately. She had been acting strangely, and sometimes she was pale and weary looking, as if she was ill.

"Um, excuse me," she said. "There is something I must tell you."

He stopped and turned. "What is it?"

She stopped and looked down at the dirt path. "There is something. . . ."

"What's the matter? Are you crying?"

She flinched.

Had his voice been too sharp? Sometimes he had to be insistent to make her speak her mind. "What is it?"

Her voice was shaky with emotion, and he sensed that sobs were bubbling just below the surface. "I thought you should know. . . ."

"What *is* it?" He grew more insistent.

"I . . . I. . . ."

He crossed his arms and waited impatiently.

"I . . . I am with child."

His mouth fell open, and he stood motionless, thunderstruck. He had no idea what to say. An avalanche of unpleasant images tumbled through his mind. Images of starvation, and want, and sickness, and suffering. All he could imagine now was how much more difficult her life would become now that she would have to care for an infant. Tetta gave her enough food, but how would he react when one of his best sources of income was put out of service? When she began to grow large, no man would touch her, and not for a while after she had given birth. She would be polluted by the blood for a time afterwards. He hoped that Tetta would not throw her out, or sell her to someone else when he discovered what had happened. Ken'ishi could not yet afford to buy her contract.

She stood motionless, as if waiting for him to say something, but he could think of nothing. He did not wish to hurt her feelings by being harsh, nor did he want to fill her with the false hope that he could rescue her from her plight. Perhaps in few more months, he could. And he felt pity for the child as well. It would be born the bastard child of a common whore. Its existence was already doomed. Did she mean to tell him that the child belonged to him? How could she know that? It could be the progeny of almost any man in the village.

So he said nothing. He turned and continued up the path, stopping when she did not follow him. Her soft weeping brought him around to see her standing in the same place, her shoulders quaking, her cheeks dripping with tears of pain and despair.

He sighed and walked back to her. "Come, Kiosé, brace up!"

She looked up at him tentatively. "You are not angry with me?"

"Angry! Of course not! Have courage, and the gods will smile on you."

"I have never had courage."

"Of course you have! You had the courage to tell me of your situation. You could have hidden it."

"Not for much longer, I'm afraid. The child will be born in

the autumn."

He did not know how she knew. It was one of the great mysteries known only to women. But he nodded sagely. Then he reached out and stroked her head. She almost collapsed against him, seized by a fit of sobbing. He held her for a while until the weeping stopped, then he said, "Come, let's go."

She nodded and wiped her eyes, giving him a feeble smile. As she glanced up at him, he saw the mixed fear and thanks in her eyes.

Ken'ishi called ahead, "Akao! Did he come this way?"

The dog's voice called back from ahead. "Don't know! Only smell wild pigs." Moments later, his face appeared from the bushes beside the path, and he stopped to look at them. Kiosé sniffled and wiped at her tears. Akao stepped forward and licked her hand.

A giggle fought with her sobs, and came out victorious for a moment. "He is so smart," she said.

Akao said, "Of course!"

Ken'ishi chuckled.

She said, "Can you really talk to him when you make those sounds? Can you understand him?"

Ken'ishi nodded. "Perhaps I could teach you."

She laughed. "No, I am too stupid for that. I can't read or write."

"Neither could I, not so long ago. But I am learning." He laughed and pointed at the dog. "He can't read or write either!"

Akao barked at him. "Not necessary."

She laughed again and rubbed the dog's ears. "It is no wonder that everyone in the village loves him. He is so kind and smart."

Akao asked Ken'ishi, "What did she say?"

"She said everyone in the village thinks you are smart and kind."

"They should! True!" His eyes sparkled with laughter for a

moment, then darkened. "But some of them hate."

"Hate? You?"

"Us."

But Kiosé was oblivious to this dark turn in the conversation. "Where did you find him? Have you been together long?"

"About two years now. And he found me."

The world just went on and on, without end. Ken'ishi had no idea it was such a big place. He had walked for weeks, up and down trackless mountains, through valleys and along rivers. He was tired. He rubbed his soiled, bare feet, caked with dirt and bits of fallen leaves. The day was hot, the sun beating down through the treetops onto the leaf bed soaked from last night's rain, turning the still air into a sticky, oppressive soup. Sweat dripped down his nose. He took out his water gourd, but as soon as he lifted it, he remembered that it was empty. He had already drained it after filling it with rain the night before. He took out the rice cakes wrapped in leaves from his pouch. Two days before, he passed through a village holding a summer festival, and the villagers' drunken merriment worked to his benefit. They had given him a handful of sticky, delicious rice cakes. These were the last two; he had eaten the rest. He ate one and put the other back in the pouch. He might be hungrier later. But the sticky cake almost stuck in his throat, and he had no water to wash it down. With great effort, he choked it down and felt cheated for a moment at being robbed of enjoying what little food he had.

A flash of unreasoning anger and frustration shot through him, and he kicked the ground. Always he was starving, or nearly so! Always searching for his next meal. He walked the land unprotected from the rain. All of his things were still wet from the day before. He was a warrior, not a beggar! He kicked the ground again, harder this time, and struck a stone. A sharp pain lanced up his leg, and blood flowed from the sole of his foot.

He collapsed on the road, flopping down in a disconsolate pile. His eyes burned with tears and sobs rose in his throat with such strength he could not hold them back. His tears made streaks down his dirty cheeks. He missed Takao and Kayo. He missed Kayo's kind smile and Takao's lessons. He missed having food in his belly, and someone he could trust. Someone he *thought* he could trust. But the people he trusted had turned him out. He understood why they had done it, but it still hurt. And he still missed them. They were the only human beings he had ever known, and they turned him away. And the only girl he had ever known wasn't a girl at all, and she betrayed him, tricked him. Haru was so beautiful. Even now, he remembered the warmth of her cozy den, the smell of her skin, the touch of her nose. Perhaps life would have been easier as a fox, with food to eat and someone to share it with him.

He had been so eager to leave his mountain home, to leave his teacher, to meet other human beings, but he had been foolish. People were so often cruel, heartless, unfriendly. Everywhere he went, he was an outsider to be feared or distrusted. Now, seeing his harsh, abrasive old teacher again would make him so happy. Even the comfort of the drafty old cave on the mountaintop would have been preferable to yesterday's relentless downpour.

He set his pouch on the ground and wiped the tears from his face. For a while, he just stared at the dirt of the path, finding patterns in the lay of the stones, the colors of the earth, feeling as if a tremendous weight rested on his shoulders, bearing them down.

Until he heard something beside him. He glanced to his side and saw his pouch was moving. It was moving because there was a nose in it. A reddish-brown furry nose. Two deep brown eyes gazed up at him.

The dog backed away. Ken'ishi's last rice cake was in its mouth.

The sobs in the breath changed to laughter. Laughter like sweet relief from endless pain. He laughed so hard he fell onto his back holding his belly. Fresh tears streamed down his cheeks, but they were tears of a different sort. After all of his troubles, all of the injustices done to him, all of his hunger and privation, his last bit of food was stolen by a dog! He laughed all the harder.

When the laughter died, he sat up again, and the dog was still there, watching him. The leaf-wrapped rice cake was still in its mouth. Its muscles were poised to run.

Ken'ishi spoke in the animal tongue he learned as a child. "You can have the rice cake. Don't worry, I won't harm you."

The dog jumped in surprise. Animals were always so surprised when they discovered that Ken'ishi could speak to them. Some were so surprised they just ran away. Then the dog placed the rice cake on the ground at its feet so that it could speak clearly.

The dog spoke slowly. "Thought you were sleeping. Didn't move for a long time. How can you speak?" The dog's eyes glinted with intelligence. Its ribs were visible under its rusty red fur.

"Because I learned. Same as you. You can eat the rice cake. I don't mind."

"Why? So angry before."

"You were watching me?"

"For a while."

"Well, I'm not angry now."

"Why? Stole your food."

Ken'ishi smiled and lay back on the ground, resting his head on his arms. "I never have any food. I'm used to it. You look hungry."

"Hungry, yes." With that, the dog gulped down the rice cake, leafy covering and all. "Don't like man food, but eat it sometimes."

Ken'ishi did not look at the dog, just gazed up through the leafy canopy at the hot blue sky. "I imagine you like red meat, warm and bloody and still on the bone."

"Yes, rabbits are best."

The dog's feet padded nearer.

"You like rabbits?"

"Yes, but not raw. Cooked."

"Too bad. Cooking spoils flavor. Makes it taste like chicken."

Ken'ishi looked over as the dog lay down beside him. It was then he noticed the dark, wet, rusty red stain on its hindquarters, and the stump of wood protruding from the fur. "You're wounded."

"Stole food. Caught."

Ken'ishi sat up. "I can try to take it out."

The dog whimpered. The arrow had been gnawed off, leaving only a couple of fingerbreadths to grasp. The wood was wet with half-crusted blood. It would be difficult if the arrowhead were deep. But he knew what to do.

"Hold still," he said.

He leaned down with his head and clamped onto the wood with his teeth. He could taste the wood and blood, but he didn't care. The hard wood crunched between his teeth, and he knew he had a good grip, then he placed his hands on the dog's hindquarters. The dog whined again. Ken'ishi pulled with his teeth and pushed with his hands. The dog yelped and howled and leaped away, but in so doing finished drawing the arrowhead from its flesh. The animal stumbled and fell. Blood welled from the puncture wound, spreading a fresh stain in the already matted fur.

Ken'ishi spat out the stump of arrow and stood up. The dog was not moving. Its mouth was open, tongue lolling in the dirt. He picked it up and began to carry it. He had to find water to wash the wound or it might still die. The animal was surprisingly light, and its bones poked against the skin. It was starving even more than him.

He carried the dog for perhaps an hour, sighing with relief as he came upon a stream gurgling with fresh, clear water. He cleaned the wound and set the dog on a comfortable-looking grassy spot while he bathed, drank his fill, and replenished his water bottle. He felt the kami of the stream smiling at him, and he luxuriated naked in the water's cool touch, a blessed respite from the summer heat and his worries.

The air cooled with the coming of evening. The three of them found the pond just as Tetta described it, in a beautiful, secluded glade. Slanting sunbeams filtered through the leaves to dapple on the water. The pond was perhaps eighty paces across at its widest point, tapering at one end, with much of its bank draped in trees and undergrowth. He had no idea how deep it might be. Most of the waterline was choked with reeds, but as he bulled through the patches of dense growth, he found short stretches where the reeds had been flattened or removed for fishing. In these areas, he found footprints, bits of string, and even a broken fishing pole. Akao disappeared, to perform his own meticulous search. The pond was flanked along one side by a steep rock face that stretched up through the boughs out of sight. As they searched the banks of the pond, Ken'ishi felt the endless weight of the hill above looming over him, an eternal presence in this secluded spot. Water trickled down the rock face, leaving interwoven tracks of many colors, surrounded by patches of deep green lichen. The water was deep and murky in the middle, so Ken'ishi could not see far into its depths.

They searched the banks for an hour, but found no trace of Tetta. They searched the path between the pond and the village for spilled blood or any signs of a struggle, but found nothing. Eventually the gathering darkness forced them to give up.

They returned to the village as the sun was beginning to set. They found Norikage waiting for them at the constabulary. As Ken'ishi entered the office, Norikage said, "I made several inquiries around the village. No one has seen Tetta today."

Ken'ishi said, "Let's go and talk to Chiba. Perhaps he had something to do with this."

"Of course, but he would deny it," Norikage said.

"Then we will interrogate him until he confesses."

"Let us not be overzealous. Chiba and his brothers have friends among the other fishermen. We should not turn the town against us. The people of Aoka respect you, Ken'ishi, but never forget that you are an outsider. We are both outsiders. They will turn on us before they turn on one of their own unless our claims cannot be disputed. Do not confuse respect for friendship."

"They must obey."

"That is true, but we are two and they are many. Remember our position. We cannot turn to the government for assistance if they turn on us. We must keep order. When there is no doubt, then we will act."

Ken'ishi sighed, feeling helpless and worried about Tetta. Kiosé stood just behind him, and he could tell from her face that she was even more worried than he was. Despite the fact that Tetta owned her, he treated her better than most women in her position could expect, and he protected her from Chiba. Tetta had a son who would inherit the inn if Tetta were dead, but Gonta was young and inexperienced, and he sometimes ridiculed her without mercy. Ken'ishi knew that she feared what would happen to her if Tetta were gone, even more so now with the impending revelation of her condition.

Norikage said, "I have an idea. We will not arrest Chiba, but he is a stupid boy and does not like pressure. If he believes we suspect him in Tetta's disappearance, he may inadvertently provide us with what we seek."

Ken'ishi smiled grimly. "You're a devious man, Norikage."

"Remember where I come from."

Ken'ishi said, "Kiosé, remain here in Norikage's office. Do not open the door for anyone but us."

She bowed. "Understood."

"Now, Ken'ishi," Norikage said as he began to lead Ken'ishi away from the office, "Let me do all the talking. You merely have to stand and look threatening. Make sure he can see your sword."

Darkness had fallen by the time they found Chiba at the docks, securing his fishing boat for the night. The moment he saw them, he stood rod straight and glanced about for a means of easy escape. Ken'ishi and Norikage walked down the dock toward him. If Chiba were going to run, he would have to leap into the water first.

Chiba demanded, "What do you want?"

Ken'ishi caught Norikage's glance warning him to be silent. Norikage answered, "Your cooperation, Chiba."

The young man glanced back and forth between them. He was about Ken'ishi's age, but the fisherman's hard life had already darkened his skin, worked deep lines into his face, and left thick calluses on his hands. Ken'ishi sized him up. Chiba was strong and well muscled. His features were broad and blunt, like his father's, with thick lips and an outthrust jaw, close-set eyes, and thick, brine-encrusted hair hanging in ragged strands around his face. Ken'ishi noted that he wore a sheathed knife tied to his waist, perhaps the same boning knife Yoba had used to kill Masahige. Ken'ishi's fists and teeth clenched. His blood thundered in his ears. How badly he wanted to punish this miscreant for beating Kiosé! Silently he entreated the kami to coax Chiba into giving him an excuse.

"What kind of cooperation, honored constables?" Chiba's words dripped with disdain.

Ken'ishi clamped his will down upon the rage surging in his belly. He took a long deep breath, focusing his will.

Norikage said, "We only wish to ask you a few simple questions, Chiba. Have you seen Tetta today?"

Ken'ishi noted the flash of panic in Chiba's eyes. The young fisherman knew why they were here.

"I have not seen Tetta today."

"When did you see him last?" Norikage said.

"A few days ago. I saw him in the street. He stayed away from me."

"And why is that?"

"You know why! Because of his whore!"

"What of her? We know where *she* is. Tetta is the one who is missing. His family is worried about him."

"Why are you asking me these questions?"

"We are asking everyone questions. We only want to find out where Tetta might have gone. His family is concerned."

Even through the haze of his own anger, Ken'ishi noted the skill with which Norikage used his voice to alternatively wheedle and demand answers.

Norikage said, "Why are you so nervous, Chiba? Surely you do not think we suspect you had something to do with Tetta's disappearance."

Chiba's jaw clenched so ferociously that the muscles of his cheeks flexed. He said nothing.

"Very well. If you say you have not seen him, then you have not seen him. Let's go, Ken'ishi." Norikage bowed slightly, turned, and flashed a coaxing glance at Ken'ishi.

Ken'ishi took a step toward Chiba, and the fisherman took a wary step back. He thrust the hilt of his sword forward. "Chiba, if anything has happened to Tetta, I will kill you. If anything happens to Kiosé, I will kill you. Do you understand?"

Chiba's face blanched as white as a fish's belly.

"Do you understand!" he roared.

Chiba flinched, but hatred smoldered like hidden embers behind the fear in his eyes. "Yes, constable! I understand." His words were subservient, but his bearing was not.

Ken'ishi leaped forward, grabbed Chiba by the collar, and struck him across the cheek with the back of his fist. *Do you understand!*

Chiba reeled from the force of Ken'ishi's blow, and his knees buckled. The defiance drained out of him like water from a punctured bladder. His voice was quiet and respectful, quivering with fear. "Yes, constable. Understood."

"Come, Ken'ishi. There are more people we must speak to." Norikage's voice was bright and cheery, belying the tension of the moment.

Ken'ishi released the fisherman's collar and backed away several steps, then he turned to follow Norikage.

When they were out of Chiba's earshot, Norikage said, "That went well. He is frightened. Frightened men make mistakes. We shall soon see the truth, I think."

Ken'ishi grunted in agreement, but he was not so sure.

"Now," said Norikage, "I think we need to speak to Tetta's son. Gonta may be able to tell us when Tetta was last at home. And there is something else. He is the person most likely to benefit if something happened to Tetta."

Ken'ishi glanced at him. "Are you saying Gonta might have

killed his own father?"

"That is not what I'm saying, but I do not think it is impossible. In the capital, I heard of many far more heinous acts. Perhaps Gonta helped his father into an early grave so that he could take over the inn."

Ken'ishi thought about that. A son killing his own father was one of the most heinous acts he could imagine. For a moment he considered how things would change if Tetta were dead. Tetta's family would suffer a grievous loss. Kiosé's welfare would suffer, too, and Gonta might force her to cease her relations with Ken'ishi. And Ken'ishi would lose one of his most influential allies in Aoka village, the innkeeper.

When they arrived at the inn, they found Gonta hard at work preparing the noon meal. There were no travelers staying in the inn, but some of the villagers occasionally went to the inn to eat or have a cup of tea or sake. There were no customers today, but when they entered, Ken'ishi saw several small baskets of food and gifts placed on tables in the main room, an outpouring of concern from many of the villagers.

When Gonta saw them enter, he hurried toward them. His brow glistened with sweat from his work. He was long and lean, much like his father, with the same forehead and bulbous skull, but with less of the joviality that Tetta put to such good use in his inn. He was a young man, in his early twenties, and had not yet found a wife. Gonta said, "Thank you very much for coming to visit, honorable constables. Have you any news about my father's whereabouts?"

Norikage said, "I am sorry, Gonta. We have learned nothing yet. In fact, that is why we are here. Perhaps you can help us."

Ken'ishi did not believe that Gonta had anything to do with Tetta's disappearance, but Norikage had a devious mind and was crafty enough to consider uncomfortable possibilities. Therefore, Ken'ishi would pay close attention to Gonta's reactions to Norikage's questions.

"Of course, sirs! I am happy to do anything." Gonta appeared surprised and hopeful that he could help find his father.

"When did you last see him?" Norikage asked.

"Yesterday morning, he told me he was going fishing. There is a pond where he likes to fish not far from the village. I often went there with him when I was a boy."

"But you did not go with him this time?"

"No. I seldom go with him anymore. There is too much work here for both of us to be absent."

"Did anyone go with him?"

"No, he always goes alone. He says that he goes fishing to be alone."

"But no one has seen him since yesterday? Are you sure that he went fishing there?"

"He always goes fishing there." Gonta grew more fearful. "Perhaps something happened to him along the way! Robbers!"

Norikage said, "Or perhaps he did not go fishing. Perhaps he went to Hakozaki."

Gonta shook his head. "I don't think so. He would have told us if he was going to Hakozaki."

"Very well," Norikage said. His voice sounded as if he had asked enough questions for now.

Gonta said, "Um, honorable constables, there is something else. Two days ago, I saw a tanuki go under the inn."

"A tanuki?" Norikage said.

"Yes. It saw me, and then it crawled under the inn. It was in broad daylight! Isn't that strange? Perhaps it is a bad omen." Ken'ishi imagined a naughty tanuki digging a burrow under Tetta's inn, and its low-slung, furry body, with the playful-looking black mask over its eyes. Tanuki were well known for their mischievous natures, and they could change into the shape of anything, much like foxes.

"Yes, that is strange."

"I was worried that the tanuki might harm the family, or the inn, or cause some other sort of trouble, and I told Father so, but he wasn't worried. I'm afraid my father may have been tricked somehow by the tanuki."

Norikage rubbed his chin.

Gonta continued. "Or maybe what I saw was a fox that shaped itself into a tanuki so that we would blame the tanuki and not the foxes!"

"Foxes and tanuki usually don't like each other, but that seems a bit unlikely," Norikage said skeptically.

"Perhaps," Gonta conceded, "but it is possible that my father was tricked and lured into the forest, isn't it?"

A chill trickled up Ken'ishi's spine.

"Yes, I suppose it is. Well then, thank you, Gonta, for all your help. Rest assured we will find your father," Norikage said.

With that, Ken'ishi and Norikage left the inn and went to talk outside. When they were out of earshot, Ken'ishi said, "Gonta had nothing to do with what has happened to Tetta."

Norikage nodded. "You are right, Ken'ishi. That was evident, unless Gonta is an accomplished liar. It looks like the pond is going to be the place we need to investigate. What is it? What are you thinking?"

Ken'ishi said, "I am thinking about Tetta being lured into the forest by a fox. I know what it's like to be fooled by a beautiful creature like a fox."

Norikage nodded. "The scars on your spirit are still raw, I see."

Ken'ishi said nothing, but continued to imagine a beautiful woman, a fox in disguise, leading a mesmerized Tetta into the forest to work some trickery on him.

"Well, anything is possible, isn't it! We must keep an open mind, yes?"

Ken'ishi nodded, wondering what would come of all this.

A white swan swimming . . .
Parting with her unmoved breast
Cherry-petaled pond

—*Roka*

Lady Kazuko sat on her favorite balcony, overlooking Lord Tsu-netomo's cherry orchard. The air would soon grow hot with the approach of summer, but the days were still pleasant with cool, fresh breezes, and lush new greenery. The afternoon breeze was warm, smelling of new life and fresh wonder. She sighed as she remembered the Cherry Blossom Festival here at the castle several days ago. It had been boisterous and joyous and . . . dreadful. How things changed in only one year. She looked back at the way she had been only such a short time ago and saw only a naïve, innocent fool. She had been nothing more than a tool to cement an alliance for her family, and she had served her purpose. Last year, she had been a child. This year, she was . . . what? The barren wife of an aging lord? A wife who had cuckolded her future husband on the day of their betrothal?

A woman who had loved so passionately, so briefly, so brightly, that she had become blind to the rest of the world?

The beauty of the cherry blossoms, like the exquisite thrust of a dagger, so delicate, so ephemeral, should have given her feelings of wonder and happiness, but all she could think of were the events of last year, and the exultation and the devastation. She feared she would never be able to enjoy cherry blossom time again, and part of her was angered by that, as if she had lost something precious that could never be regained.

Most days, she was fine. She went about her duties, directing the business of her husband's house, having tea with Hatsumi or Lady Yukino, practicing calligraphy and painting. She wanted to continue her training with the naginata, but for some reason Yasutoki had forbidden it at first. He said that martial weapons practice was unbecoming the lady of the house. This angered her, and she went to her husband, who intervened on her behalf. She sometimes found that the physical exertion of practice left her with spirits uplifted. Lord Tsunetomo would give her anything if she asked for it. That was a great deal of power she possessed over him, and she tried not to abuse it. She could have acted like a petulant, greedy child, but she chose not to. Sometimes she felt that Lord Tsunetomo was her only ally.

Hatsumi's behavior had changed in the last year. In the old days, she had been a pleasant and kind-spirited companion; these days, she was usually sullen and mean-spirited. Kazuko wondered if sometimes her own black moods had contributed to Hatsumi's behavior.

Soon after her arrival, Kazuko had been introduced to her new sister-in-law, Lady Yukino, Tsunemori's wife. Lady Yukino was pleasant and matronly, in her early forties, more than twice Kazuko's age. Kazuko sometimes enjoyed playing a game of Go with Lady Yukino, but this made Hatsumi angry for some reason. Perhaps because it was apparent that Lady Yukino did not like Hatsumi and treated her like a servant, rather than Kazuko's friend. For this reason, Kazuko did not go out of her way to spend time with Lady Yukino, but she could hardly refuse when she was invited.

Lady Yukino enjoyed talking about her son, her pride and joy. He was a young samurai in Lord Tsunetomo's service. Did Lady Yukino have aspirations that her son would become Lord Tsunetomo's heir, if Kazuko failed to produce a son? If Lord Tsunetomo died without an heir, Tsunemori would be in a position to seize his lands. This sometimes made Kazuko wary of Lady Yukino's motives, but she had never discerned anything underhanded in her manner or her company.

Yes, some days were passable. But on others, her world was a swirling typhoon of guilt and shame and misery. Some nights she still could not sleep for the sadness that consumed her. Sometimes, she had the same terrible dream, a dream that she longed to live, a dream she wished never to end. But it always did. Sometimes she wished she would die and leave her mortal body behind and slip into the dream world, never to return, never to be reborn. It was the only paradise she could imagine. But her sleep was so disrupted that she never felt rested. She would grow tired at the wrong times, as if her spirit forever wanted to return to that dream.

The breeze caressed her face, and she imagined that it was *his* touch, listened to the breeze's susurration as it slid over the castle's stone walls, rustling the leaves of the trees. Children played somewhere, their laughter echoing among the castle walls like the breath of ghosts. She wished for children again. If she could only produce an heir, her husband would be happy with her. He consulted every astrologer he could find, he prayed daily for a son and requested that she do the same, all to no avail. These days she saw the disappointment in his eyes when he looked at her, even though he tried to mask it. There had been times where his virility flagged, or perhaps his interest in her, or perhaps his hope of ever conceiving a son, and he did not come to her bed for many days. During those times, she was both relieved and disappointed. The closeness of his body, the brief stab of pleasure she experienced at their coupling, helped to stave off the perpetual loneliness, the endless longing for someone else.

She knew that she had indeed come to love her husband. He was a good man, a wise leader, and a brave warrior. But her feelings for her husband were different than when she was with. . . . She could not explain the differences, but there were many different types of love. She wanted to please her husband, and she enjoyed his company. But she still thought of the hard, rippling body she had seen practicing in the early dawn light and the handsome features, and those eyes filled with a bewildering mixture of kindness and ferocity.

She imagined herself walking through the garden again in some far-future day when she could be happy. *A day when she could sit in the cherry orchard on a warm spring day having a picnic, surrounded by her many children, handsome sons and beautiful daughters, all laughing and frolicking under the breathtaking canopy of cherry blossoms. She hears the sound of a flute playing nearby, somewhere behind her, so close she can almost touch it. A sound she has heard so many times in her dreams, with its lovely, lilting tones, breathy and subtle. She can feel the presence of her husband so close behind her, sensed but unseen. All she has to do to touch him, to feel his warmth, is to reach behind her. But she does not. Some part of her remembers that Tsunetomo does not play the flute, but she pushes that thought away as she always does, trying to immerse herself in the sound, the warmth, the beauty, the happiness of this moment, to stay here forever, frozen in time. Somehow, she knows that if she touches him, this timeless instant will end. Some part of her knows why, but she clings to the moment, and she feels warmth and joy and happiness and boundless contentment. So wonderful, this respite from . . . something. She cannot not remember, so she lets herself forget, lets herself float on the sounds of the flute and children. But the desire to touch the man behind her, the man she loves, is strong, made more acute by the knowledge that she cannot. Maybe this time it will be different. Maybe she can reach back and lay her cold, porcelain hand upon his warm flesh and he will remain, and this moment of happiness would not shatter like a falling teacup. A sharp end to the happiness, like the sudden slash of a naginata and a gout of black blood. She tries to ignore her desire, to prolong the feeling, but the desire grows, and along with it, the longing that maybe this time will be different. The desire grows until the concentration, the will required to resist, is too strong, threatening to destroy the happiness all by itself. Finally, she succumbs and reaches back to lay her hand upon her husband's leg. She turns to look at him, smiling, and he turns to look at her, lowering his flute. She stares into his eyes, and just like all the other times, the knowledge that it is all wrong, all but a dream, out of reach, destroys the dream like a hammer hitting a pottery jar.*

She awoke back on her husband's balcony, her eyes puffy from weeping in her sleep, her spirit smothered in the same familiar ache.

A sudden, sharp cry snatched her mercifully from her timeless despair and into the moment. Someone was crying, howling in pain. She rubbed her eyes and shook herself. Had she been sleeping? Kazuko stood and ran toward the sound of the crying. There were other voices raised, loud, as if in protest. She followed the noise to Hatsumi's chambers.

A servant girl lay on the floor there, the fragile young girl called Moé. She was sprawled on her belly, with her back arched in agony, tears streaming down her cheeks, with long, bloody slashes torn in the back of her robe. Hatsumi stood over her, flailing at her with a long, thin bamboo cane. Several other servants surrounded them, looking as if they wanted to stop the beating, but terrified of intervening.

"Whore!" Hatsumi shrilled. "Whore! Whore! Whore!" The strokes of her cane fell in unison with her words. At each blow, Moé convulsed in anguish, growing weaker with each strike.

"Hatsumi!" Kazuko cried.

No response. The cane rose and fell again.

"Hatsumi!"

No response, save for the hiss of the cane as it sliced through the air.

Kazuko darted across the room and seized Hatsumi by the wrist, halting her in mid-stroke. "Hatsumi! Stop this at once!"

Hatsumi stopped instantly, a lightning quick succession of emotions in her eyes. Rage, surprise, recognition, remorse, despair, fresh anger.

"Kazuko! I. . . ."

"What is the meaning of this?" Kazuko demanded.

Moé curled up into a ball on the tatami floor, sobbing, gasping, choking in pain.

Hatsumi's mouth worked as if she was trying to speak. Kazuko tried to read her eyes, but the changes in emotion passed too quickly for her to recognize, as if she was in the midst of some terrible inner struggle.

"What is the meaning of this!" Kazuko repeated. Hatsumi was still frozen in a mixture of horror and anger. Kazuko turned to the servants and pointed at Moé. "Take her out of here. Take care of her. All of you."

The servants hastened to comply, lifting the weeping girl by the arms and carrying her out of the room. Her sobbing receded.

Kazuko grasped the bamboo cane and wrenched it out of Hatsumi's quivering grip.

"I don't know what came over me!" Hatsumi cried. The look

in her eyes told Kazuko that she was on the verge of weeping. The anger fell away from Hatsumi's face like a shattered mask, and she sank to her knees, her eyes glistening with tears.

"What were you doing!" Kazuko cried. "That was so cruel! How could you be so cruel! What could she have done to warrant such treatment?"

Hatsumi stammered, "I . . . I. . . ." Then her resolve seemed to harden. "She is a whore!"

"How can you say that?"

Hatsumi's voice grew harder with each word. "Yesterday I saw her come out of. . . ."

"Where?"

"Yasutoki's personal chambers."

"And what of it? She is a servant. And what of Yasutoki? Wait." The realization struck her then, and a sliver of dread tore into her. "Are you and Yasutoki lovers?" Normally she would have been happy to hear that Hatsumi had found a lover, but not this way, not with Yasutoki. The man was evil, and his interest in Hatsumi could not be genuine. He was a man with motives within mysteries. What kind of game was he playing?

Hatsumi's eyes flashed with defiance as she nodded. "Last week he professed his undying love for me."

"Do you love him?" Kazuko asked, dreading the answer.

Hatsumi paused. "I don't know. It's so exciting that he says he loves me! And he has a powerful position." Then her voice grew venomous again. "But that little slut trying to take him away from me. . . ."

"Hatsumi," Kazuko gently interrupted her, keeping her voice soft and even, "how do you know she was in his bed? She could have been there for any number of reasons."

"It was the look on her face! And she knew that I knew!"

"But she is so young—"

"And so ripe for the plucking! She seduced him—"

"Hatsumi, she has no such designs on anyone, much less Yasutoki. She is little more than a child."

"And what about Yasutoki? Is he not desirable? Why would she not want him for herself?"

Kazuko stiffened. The wrath and suspicion in Hatsumi's voice almost rocked her back on her heels.

"Hatsumi," Kazuko said, trying to use her voice to soothe Hatsumi's emotions, "you are distraught. Do not fear, I will take care of you. That's a bit of a change, isn't it?" She gave a feeble smile. She wanted to say that even if Moé had been in Yasutoki's bed, the liaison had been all Yasutoki's doing. But she could not suggest that without making things worse.

Hatsumi's posture softened.

Kazuko hugged her shoulders. "Even if Moé deserved to be punished, the deed is done now, yes? There is no need to punish her further. We must not be cruel to the servants or they will hate us. They serve us well, and they are beneath us, thus they deserve our kindness. Yes?"

Hatsumi's eyes began to tear and she nodded, sniffling.

"Good. Besides, you have certainly filled her with fear. You will not punish her anymore?"

Hatsumi sniffled again and shook her head.

"Good. Please come with me outside. The fresh air will help calm you." She helped Hatsumi to her feet and led her out to the balcony. "I will call for some tea. That will make you feel better, too, won't it?"

"Please don't go to so much trouble. . . ."

"No trouble at all. Just wait here." Kazuko sat Hatsumi down on a soft cushion, then went back inside and rang a small gong that she used to call her servants. A middle-aged servant woman named Yuki answered her summons. Yuki was as pale as fresh linen as she knelt and bowed to the floor. Kazuko requested a pot of tea.

Yuki said, "Of course, milady. Anything for you." She stood up to leave.

"Um, just a moment. How is the girl, Moé?"

Yuki stiffened almost imperceptibly. "She will be fine, milady. In time."

"Hatsumi feels terrible about what happened. It will not happen again."

Even in Yuki's respectfully downcast eyes, Kazuko could see the hard glitter of hatred. "As you say, milady."

"Can you tell me what happened?"

Yuki paused, thinking, as if choosing her words with great care. "I do not know, milady."

"What does Moé say?"

Yuki spoke carefully. "She says that she took Master Yasutoki his fresh laundry, and Mistress Hatsumi saw her coming out of his chambers and grew very angry. Hatsumi summoned Moé here, and started beating her without explanation."

"So Moé has no idea why Hatsumi beat her?"

Then she grew cautious. "Milady, you are a fair and kind mistress. All the servants love you. May I speak?"

Kazuko felt herself stiffen. These were bold words for a house servant. "You may speak."

"Hatsumi hates Moé. Sometimes Moé is a bit clumsy and spilled some of Hatsumi's tea once. Hatsumi threw the scalding water in her face. The poor girl could have been blinded."

Kazuko's lacquer of calm cracked. She could not imagine Hatsumi being so cruel. "That cannot be."

"I am sorry, milady. I tended Moé's burns myself."

Kazuko clenched her hands in her lap, trying to restrain her racing emotions. "When did this happen?"

"In the first month after your arrival, milady."

"Thank you, Yuki. That is all."

Yuki bowed again and departed, leaving Kazuko alone with

fresh dread. What had gotten into Hatsumi? Had she been possessed by a fox or some evil spirit? Was this no longer the real Hatsumi? Had the real woman been replaced by a tengu or other such shapeshifting creature? Any number of possible explanations raced through her mind, none of them pleasant, but her thoughts kept returning to the encounter with Hakamadare. Had the oni's evil somehow taken root inside her? Had the horror she had experienced shattered her spirit? So many thoughts, all of them unpleasant, but at least they gave her respite from her own private pain. She would have to watch Hatsumi closely.

"If a warrior is not unattached to life and death, he will be of no use whatsoever . . . With such non-attachment, one can accomplish any feat."

—*Hagakure*

Yasutoki sipped his tea in the dark, listening to the silence of the night. Darkness had fallen hours ago, and most of the castle was now fast asleep. The only people likely to be awake were guards. He darkened his room so that anyone passing by his chambers would think him to be sleeping as well. The cold moon shone down through the slats in the shutter, painting faint bars of silver on the tatami. The moon was high and aloof, little more than a sliver in the cloud-patched sky. This was Yasutoki's favorite time, the deep dark of a cold night. He sometimes felt that it most closely mirrored his soul. There were no voices, not of night creatures nor of men, to disturb the silence. Only the moaning whisper of the wind. He savored the mournful sound, like the pain of the whole world given voice. One had but to listen. There were men who could not accept the world's pain and ugliness, men who tried to fight against the misery and the injustice. The men who fought against it were fools, doomed to perpetual failure. All a man could do was to seek to carve a place for himself, to suffer less misery by inflicting it upon others if need be. The shadows of his room were pitch-black, much like the dark corners of his spirit, he imagined. The darkness held mystery, and mystery was power. Men feared the unknown, and controlling the shadows granted power over men. The power of shadow was subtle, sometimes so ephemeral that it could not be predicted, but it was power, power that Yasutoki had been trained to harness from the time he was a child.

His affinity for shadow was a potent weapon, but so was information. And information was something he gathered in great abundance. In spite of Tsunemori's recalcitrance, there was little that happened in Lord Tsunetomo's castle to which Yasutoki was not privy. He occasionally amused himself with testing bits of gossip to see how they spread and how the details changed in the telling. The news of what Hatsumi had done to the servant girl, Moé, had spread through the house like wildfire. This was something he had not foreseen. The last thing he wanted now was a confrontation with Hatsumi. Perhaps she was a bit too volatile to use as a pawn, at least until he determined a way to turn her volatility to his advantage. Making love to her had been a chore. She had been stiff and unresponsive, like bedding a dead fish. After months of his careful advances, she had consented to lie with him, and he could tell from her reactions that she was almost hysterical with fear until he was finished. But she had been possessive ever since. He was finding it difficult to take advantage of some of the servant girls he favored without offending her. And then poor, unfortunate Moé, in the wrong place at the wrong time, taking the brunt of Hatsumi's newborn jealousy, and undeservedly so. No matter. Moé was a just a lowly, cross-eyed servant girl. Perhaps if she became a bit more womanly, he might decide to partake of her charms.

It was time.

He stood and shed his voluminous robes, revealing his tight-fitting, black undergarments. He picked up a small black box made of hammered copper. The handle was warm to the touch, even through his black gloves. He slipped the black mask over his face and moved like a true shadow to the door of his chambers. The hallway outside was pitch dark. He moved with complete surety through the empty blackness, having long ago memorized the exact dimensions of every room and hallway in the castle. As he passed the shoji screens of various chambers, faintly backlit by the glow of coals or moonlight, faint snores whuffled through them. The air held the faint smell of charcoal smoke from the heating braziers. His slippered feet made no sound as they moved across the polished wooden floors. He did not expect to see any guards until he had nearly reached his destination. Nevertheless, no lord ever lived as long as Tsunetomo by being careless. There were guards at the entrance to the castle, and at the stairs to the upper floors, where the lord, his family, and Yasutoki resided.

Yasutoki's chambers were on the floor below Lord Tsunetomo's. Tsunemori's office was on the castle's main floor, near the audience hall, the kitchens, guest rooms, and Yasutoki's office. Yasutoki had only one guard post to contend with between himself and his destination, placed at the stairs between the upper floors and the main floor. Usually that guard was asleep.

Yasutoki reached the top of the stairs. He saw the opening below, a window of yellow-orange light from the lantern. The shadow of the guard, standing just out of sight, lay across the

floor in front of the doorway. As silent as a shadow himself, Yasutoki moved down the stairs. He had long ago memorized the
points on every step where the wood would not creak under his
weight. Two steps from the bottom, he saw the guard's silhouette
against the lantern light. He leaned against the wall with his
arms crossed, his head drooping toward his chest, his measured
breathing indicating he was dozing. As the castle was not under
threat, the guard was not wearing any armor; he would be an
easy target if Yasutoki had to kill him. Slipping past him into the
corridor, Yasutoki kept his attention focused on the guard. Only
when he rounded the first corner and was out of sight did he
begin to move quickly.

In less than twenty heartbeats, he reached the door to Tsunemori's office. In two more, he was inside with the door closed
behind him. The room was pitch-black. The windows were shuttered against the winter night, but only kept out the moonlight,
not the cold. The air was frigid, but Yasutoki ignored it. He
moved across the room, found the desk with his hand, and
knelt beside it. Then he opened a small door in the black box in
his other hand, and a small puddle of faint light from the candle
within spilled out onto the desk. Yasutoki's breath seeped
through his mask in vaporous wisps. He shielded the light with
his body. No one passing by in the corridor would see any
evidence of activity within the office.

Tsunemori's desk held an inkpot and brush, a neatly arranged row of scrolls, and a sheaf of loose papers. He rifled
through the papers and scrolls until he found the list of names
for the warriors serving as Tsunetomo's retainers, an inventory
of arrows, bows, swords, spears, and other weapons, a count of
horses to mount the bushi, and an inventory of the supplies
stored to feed these warriors and their horses. There were even
estimates of how many peasants could be conscripted to fill the
ranks in an emergency. His gaze darted around the pages, count-

ing, calculating, committing it all to memory. He would remember all of it in perfect detail. When he was finished, he felt a sense of satisfaction that Tsunemori would be instrumental, in some small way, for the future victory of the Great Khan. He put everything back exactly as he had found it, then closed the small lantern door, plunging him into complete darkness.

He waited for his eyes to adjust once again before slipping back into the corridor. He crept through the castle hallways until he reached the corner where he would have to move into the guard's field of vision. Ever cautious, he peered around the corner. The man was awake now, yawning into his hand and rubbing his arms to keep warm. Yasutoki cursed silently.

He waited and listened for the sound of the guard settling down again to doze, for the sound of slow, steady breathing. But those sounds did not come. Yasutoki knew this man to be a competent warrior, an honorable man, not a sluggard. It sounded now as if he was trying to keep himself awake and warm in the cold, deep hours of the night. He was rubbing himself, moving around, complaining under his breath about the chill.

Yasutoki's patience began to wear thin. He considered killing the man, but that would create far too many complications to his simple plan.

Then he stiffened at the sound of footsteps coming from behind him. The next watch was coming. If he were discovered, all of his plans would be for naught. The footsteps were closer than they should have been. He had been too focused on this guard and had forgotten when the watch changed. A lantern floated toward him down the hallway, illuminating the pale pool of the new guard's face in the lantern light. Fortunately, Yasutoki was standing near the door to a small storage room. He slid the door open, slipped inside, and closed the door behind him. Around him in the darkness, he sensed bulky stacks of barrels, bags of rice and grain, and jars of pickled vegetables and fruit. Had the two guards heard the sound of the sliding door?

He felt his way through the pitch-blackness toward the back of the room, listening to the new guard's footsteps drawing nearer in the hallway.

The guard at the stairway called out, "Kuniaki, is that you?" His voice grew louder as if he was approaching.

The second guard answered, "Yes."

"Did you hear something?"

"A door."

"I thought that sound was you."

The two guards met in the hallway a few paces away from the room where Yasutoki was hiding. They paused for a moment, and Yasutoki could imagine them looking at each other. One of them called out, "Is someone there?"

Yasutoki positioned himself behind a stack of bags of grain and tried to meld with the darkness. The light from the second guard's lantern filtered faintly through the rice-paper door into the storage room.

The door to the storage room slid open, flooding the room with light, sharpening the shadows cast by the stored foodstuffs. Yasutoki prepared to strike if necessary, easing a shuriken into his right hand.

"Is someone here?" said the second guard. The shadows on the walls shifted as the lantern moved into the room.

"Bah! Must have been a rat."

"Do rats open doors?"

The first guard laughed. "I've seen some around here big enough to open a door!"

The second guard harrumphed. The lantern moved out into the hallway, and the door slid shut.

The first guard said, "Well, then, good night."

The second guard grumbled something, and the other man

laughed as he walked away.

Yasutoki heard the new guard assuming his post, and the first guard's footsteps receding as he returned to his barracks. With the patience of a serpent, Yasutoki waited in the darkness. If he emerged from the storeroom in the early morning, dressed as he was, it would be difficult to explain. He silently chastised himself; he should have anticipated this possibility.

An hour passed, and he slipped out of the storeroom into the hallway, just out of sight of the stairway guard. The guard's breaths were even and slow, but he was fidgeting. Yasutoki hazarded a glance. This guard was leaning against the wall, much like the first, but he shifted back and forth, fighting against the dragging pull of sleep. Another hour passed. Yasutoki could not discern whether the guard was asleep or awake.

Finally, after another hour, the guard's movement stopped, and Yasutoki seized the opportunity. He slid around the corner and across the corridor, so that he moved with his back against the wall with the opening to the stairway. All he had to do was slither against the wall and around the corner into the stairway, and his work was done. If the guard awoke and saw him, he would have to kill him swiftly and try to deal with the aftermath as best he could. The guard stirred and Yasutoki froze, trying to become the very essence of silent shadow, willing the guard to remain asleep and unaware.

The guard remained in his doze. Time froze as Yasutoki crept away slowly, a finger's breadth at a time. He did not breathe. Every step was an eternity of precise, painstaking movement. Finally, he was in the stairway, stealing up the steps.

Only when he reached his room again did he suck in a huge, gasping breath. How long had it been since he had last breathed? His legs buckled under him and he sank to the floor, shaking, quivering. The strain of his success was almost more than he could bear. His belly was a sick, swirling pit, and his whole body trembled. He had led the sedentary life of a courtier for far too long. Much of the physical strength and endurance of his youth was gone now, blunted like a blade that had not been used in decades.

He sat in the darkness for a long time. Finally his breathing slowed, his limbs ceased trembling, and he was able to reflect on the information he had gained, and on his reactions to the events of this night. He was getting too old for this kind of skulking around. Better to let younger men do that kind of work for him. Before he realized it, the castle was waking up around him, and the gray light of dawn peeked through the crack between the shutters.

"Even when the body is at rest, do not relax your concentration. When you move rapidly, keep a calm, 'cool' head. Do not let the mind be dragged along by the body or the body be dragged along by the mind."

—*Miyamoto Musashi*

For several days, Ken'ishi and Akao combed the woods and surrounding countryside looking for any sign of Tetta or his corpse. He no longer believed the innkeeper was alive, but no one ever found a body. Eventually, after four weeks of fruitless searching, Tetta's family gave up the search and declared him dead. His son, Gonta, assumed control of the inn. He also assumed control of Kiosé. But Gonta was not a bad sort, simply inexperienced and overly serious at times. Ken'ishi watched that

361

he did not mistreat Kiosé, and left it at that. Nevertheless, she continued to cook for Ken'ishi and to clean his house occasionally.

One evening, Kiosé was preparing supper for him, and as he waited, he practiced his writing. She said, "I heard something strange today."

He finished the character he was writing, put down his brush, and looked at her, waiting for her to continue.

"Yoko was carrying part of her husband's catch back to their house two nights ago, and she said she saw someone acting strangely. She said there was a person sneaking around your house, like they were trying to slip inside. She tried to see who it was, but the person noticed her and disappeared into the shadows."

"Did she say anything else? Was it a man?"

"She thought it was a man."

"Perhaps I should go speak to her tomorrow. Have you heard anything else strange lately? Since Tetta disappeared." Her status was so low in the village and her demeanor so quiet and unassuming that many people did not even notice her presence. She might have heard things she was not meant to hear.

She thought for a moment. "Well, I have heard many things, all kinds of things. . . ."

"Anything about strangers in the village?"

She thought some more. "Well, I did hear a young girl say she had seen a shadow man in the forest. His clothing made him look like the forest. He frightened her, then disappeared in the trees."

"A shadow man?"

"That's what she called him. I don't know any more about that. Her name is Aya. She is Gorobei the carpenter's niece."

"Perhaps I should speak to her, too," he mused. Where to begin? There are forces at work here yet to be revealed. More bad fortune was coming, and he feared it could not be stopped. But he would still try.

The following morning, he went to Norikage's office and told him what Kiosé had said.

Norikage rubbed his chin. "More complications. One might think this 'shadow man' could be the same one seen snooping around your house. We must find out if anyone else has seen anything unusual, however, before we can draw any conclusions."

Ken'ishi agreed, and the two of them spent the rest of the day asking people if they had seen anyone strange in the village or in the forested mountains around it. This village received few visitors. He and Norikage spoke to Aya, a girl of about eleven, and the fisherman's wife, Yoko.

Aya said that she had seen the man moving through the forest one evening near sunset. She sometimes played in the forest, even though her mother had forbidden it. She saw the man moving from tree to tree. He was wearing strange clothes, she said, clothes that made him look like a bush. When he saw her, he was surprised and jumped between two bushes. She lost sight of him then, and she ran home after that, afraid. She had not told her mother, because she would be angry with her for playing in the forest. Norikage thanked the girl for her help and then gently chastised her for disobeying her mother.

Yoko told them the strange man she had seen was dressed in dark clothes, wearing a large hat like a monk. She saw him in the narrow alley between Ken'ishi's house and the neighboring house. She stopped to look at him, but he saw her, then moved around a corner, out of sight, and disappeared.

The rest of their questioning around the village yielded nothing. No one else had seen any strangers.

Norikage and Ken'ishi sat in Norikage's office that night,

sharing a bottle of sake.

Norikage said, "So we can conclude that there is likely some stranger snooping around the village."

"Someone who may have killed Tetta."

"That is possible. But what does he want? Tetta is gone, but perhaps this stranger is still here. He sounds like a man looking for something. Or someone. Difficult to guess, isn't it?"

Ken'ishi took another drink. "Could this man be connected to Chiba and his brothers? Perhaps they hired an assassin to kill me."

"If there is a connection, it is still hidden." Norikage's brow creased. "My instincts tell me that this stranger has nothing to do with that lot. Besides, hiring an assassin requires money, and they have none of that. You have some strong instincts, Ken'ishi. What are they telling you?"

Ken'ishi thought about it for a moment. "They're telling me you're right. That disappoints me."

Norikage smiled wryly. "Yes, I know. You are merely waiting for an excuse to pounce upon Chiba and his brothers. You should not let that cloud your judgment. Something else is at work here, I think."

Ken'ishi had to admit that Norikage was correct. He had been looking for a reason to confront Chiba.

Footsteps approaching outside. His hand fell to his sword resting on the floor beside him. A woman's heavy breathing sounded like Kiosé. "Sirs, may I come in?"

"Yes, come in," Norikage said.

Kiosé came inside, shut the door behind her, and bowed hurriedly. She was breathless with excitement, and the words tumbled out of her in a rush. "Sirs, I rushed over here to tell you. There is a strange man staying in the inn! He looks like a monk, but he has a basket hat, and I saw some strange clothing under his robes."

Ken'ishi and Norikage's eyes locked.

"Strange clothing?" Norikage said.

"Yes, green clothing that looked like Aya said!"

Ken'ishi said, "I think this man needs to talk to us."

Norikage nodded. "What if he runs?"

"I'll stop him."

"What if he fights?"

"I'll defeat him."

Norikage's wry smile gave his face a strange-looking vehemence. "I'm sure you will. Kiosé, where is this man?"

"He is eating in the main room."

"Very well," Ken'ishi said. "Let us go. Kiosé, stay here where it's safe."

Ken'ishi and Norikage walked into the inn's main room. Norikage walked two paces behind the constable. He wanted to stay out of harm's way and allow Ken'ishi room to act, if necessary. Perhaps it was all a misunderstanding. Perhaps the man really was a monk. But somehow, Norikage did not think so.

Gonta bowed as they came in. He looked so much like his father, tall and thin, but with a larger portion of hair on his bulbous head and fewer merry wrinkles around his eyes. "Ah, what a pleasant surprise! Please come and sit down. I will prepare a fresh jar of sake."

Norikage said, "Thank you, Gonta."

They followed him into the empty main room. There were dishes and an empty teacup still on one of the tables.

"Ken'ishi, please wait here a moment," Norikage said. "Gonta, I would like to see your kitchen for a moment."

Gonta blinked in puzzlement, then nodded. Ken'ishi waited in the center of the room. Norikage followed Gonta into the kitchen, and behind the closed door, spoke with a low voice. "There is a man staying here? A monk?"

Gonta looked surprised. "Well, yes, there is. Why do you ask?"

"What do you know about him?"

"Nothing. He came in tonight, asked for a room, and ate his supper. He must have gone to his room now."

"Have you talked to him?"

"No, he seems like a quiet type of man."

"Which room is his?"

"Down the hall, second on the right."

"Does he have any weapons?"

"Weapons!" Gonta's eyes bulged.

"Lower your voice!" Norikage hissed.

"Forgive me! Is this man a criminal?"

"We do not know, but we plan to speak to him."

Gonta's eyes remained wide with fear.

"Do not fear, Gonta. If he is a criminal, Ken'ishi will protect us."

This seemed to ease Gonta a bit, and he nodded.

"Wait here until we have spoken to him."

Gonta nodded again, and Norikage returned to the main room, where Ken'ishi had not moved. Norikage pointed down the hallway. Ken'ishi nodded and followed him. Norikage imagined him scanning the hallway, gauging distances and calculating advantages. He glanced over his shoulder and saw Ken'ishi doing exactly that.

They stopped before the appointed door, glanced at each other, then Norikage raised his voice, "Excuse me, sir."

The shift of clothing inside and the rustle of papers. After a moment came a man's voice. "What is it?"

"May we have a word with you?"

"Of course, come in." His tone was jovial, but Norikage heard something in the man's voice that indicated he was less than comfortable with talking to them. A brittle hesitation. His previous life in the capital taught him well. He glanced at Ken'ishi and gave him a silent look that told him to be on his guard. Then he slid the door open.

The man sitting on the floor behind the table looked up at them. His head was shaven clean in the manner of a monk, and his age was indeterminate, with a face cut from severe angles and planes. His body was thin and wiry, and since he was sitting, judging his height was difficult. His clothing was simple and plain, like that of an ascetic monk. His walking staff rested on the floor behind him. Norikage noticed a flicker of recognition in his eyes as the man looked at Ken'ishi. Recognition and something else. Appraisal. On the table in front of him were a brush and ink and a sheaf of loose papers. None of the papers contained writing, but the brush was wet.

"Good evening, sir," Norikage said. "I am sorry for our rudeness in disturbing your rest. My name is Norikage, and this is Ken'ishi. We keep order in this village. We have come to warn you that strange things have been happening in the village lately."

The man's face registered no emotion. "Thank you for your concern. Hopefully I will be safe enough inside the inn."

"If I may ask, how long do you plan to stay?"

"Until tomorrow. I am an itinerant monk passing through on my way to Hakata."

"Of course. But you may wish to consider that the strange occurrences involve the owner of this inn. He disappeared not long ago, and he has never been found." Norikage sharpened his attention on the man.

The man said, "That is unfortunate." His voice sounded puzzled.

"And there have been reports of strangers skulking around the village at night, or in the forest."

"That is strange," the man said implacably. "I will be careful.

I only wish to have a peaceful night's rest and continue on my way in the morning."

Norikage did not know what else to do. "Would you care to share a jar of sake?"

"I must beg your forgiveness. Sake is bad for my stomach."

"Tea perhaps, then? We would welcome conversation with such a wise, learned man as you."

"Alas, I must decline. I am too weary from my travels to be pleasant company. I am sorry. Perhaps in the morning."

Norikage nodded. "Very well. We will leave you to your rest. Forgive our rudeness. Thank you."

"Not at all."

Norikage scrutinized him. Was that annoyance on his face? Perhaps relief?

They bowed to one another, and Norikage stepped backward through the door, sliding it closed behind him.

Back in the main room, out of earshot, Ken'ishi said, "He's lying."

"Yes," Norikage said, "he is no more a monk than I am."

"We must find out what he is up to."

"Yes, but he gives us no reason to confront him."

"I have a feeling this night is not over for him. Let us ask a favor of Gonta."

Norikage saw the crafty look in Ken'ishi's eyes, and nodded.

Norikage tried to keep his breath as shallow as possible while they waited. Ken'ishi elbowed him when he started falling asleep, but he could not help it. Waiting like this in the dark was so . . . tedious. He did not know if the "monk" would do anything out of the ordinary. Ken'ishi sat near him. Norikage could sense his alertness, listening for every smallest sound, sifting the noise of the night creatures from the sounds he sought.

How long they had been waiting, he did not know. The village had long since gone to sleep, and the gibbous moon had gone away, leaving only the porcelain spatter of the stars against the night sky. This was the deep, dark of night. The sound of the crickets and frogs outside lulled Norikage toward sleep, but he had to stay awake.

Then he heard something. The muffled thump of wood on wood. A faint metallic clinking. Again. Rhythmic like the movement of a walking staff, the butt of the staff brushing the floor, the metal rings on the other end brushing each other. Coming closer to their hiding place.

Norikage froze, holding his breath. Ken'ishi touched his arm. It was time. Ken'ishi slid the door of the inn's storeroom open and stepped into the main room. Norikage uncovered his lamp but hung back. Yellow-orange light spilled across the man carrying his walking staff, wearing his basket hat to conceal his face. The man held up a hand to shield his eyes.

Ken'ishi said, "Where are you going, Sir Monk? Trying to leave without paying your fee?"

What happened next came too fast for Norikage to react. The man threw his hat at Ken'ishi's face. Ken'ishi drew his sword and slashed the hat in twain with a single fluid motion. The length of the monk's walking staff parted as if by magic, and became a sword. The long, straight blade licked out at Ken'ishi, who caught the blade on his own, forced it toward the floor. Ken'ishi thrust at the man's belly. The man still had the rest of the walking staff, the wooden sheath of the hidden sword, in his other hand, and he used this to turn Ken'ishi's thrust to the side. He planted the butt of the staff against the tatami mats and used it to support him as he lashed a kick high at Ken'ishi's head. The man's foot slammed into Ken'ishi's cheek, and he staggered to the side, wide open to attack.

Norikage dashed his lantern at the man's face. The man flinched and batted it aside, but it gave Ken'ishi the instant he needed to recover from the blow. The lamp clattered on the wooden floor, spattering a pool of oil and fire and brightening the room with its flickering orange glow. The growing fire cast dancing shadows against the walls and ceiling as the two combatants struggled. Ken'ishi faced the man again, sword in the middle guard position, pointing at the man's throat. The ceiling was too low for a powerful downward stroke. He edged toward the front hallway, blocking that escape. The man squared against him for a moment, sword in one hand with its jangling rings at the end of the long, wooden hilt, and shortened wooden staff in the other hand.

Norikage could only stare as a strange calm passed through Ken'ishi, as quick as a ripple of water settling into a bowl. Norikage glanced at the other man. His angular features were crafty and calculating, like a poisonous snake readying himself to strike. But Ken'ishi acted first. Norikage had never known a man could move with such speed. Ken'ishi's body and blade moved as one. A clang of steel, then the soft, meaty sound of metal against flesh and bone, and the man fell backward. But Ken'ishi did not stop moving. Even as the man's body landed hard against the tatami, arms and legs splayed, Ken'ishi leaped forward and landed a hard kick against the underside of man's wrist, tearing the sword from his grip and sending it bouncing across the room.

Norikage crept closer and saw the wet, dark stain spreading underneath the man's clothing. Ken'ishi stood over him, looking down at him. The man's breathing was ragged and wet, and his lips were red with blood.

"Who are you?" Ken'ishi demanded.

The man started to laugh.

"Who are you!"

"The master," the man gasped, "was right about you!" Then he laughed again.

"What?" Ken'ishi stepped back.

Norikage said, "Did you kill Tetta?"

The man's laughter trailed off into a death rattle.

For a long moment, the two of them just stared at the dead man. Then Gonta burst into the room. *"Fire!"* he cried. *"Fire!"*

Oil from Norikage's spilled lamp was still burning in the hallway, licking dangerously near the rice-paper door of the closest guest room. But the fight had lasted only moments, and fire had not yet gained purchase in the tatami or the wall. Gonta snatched a blanket from the storeroom and smothered the fire. Before they were left in darkness, Norikage lit another lamp in the smoke-thick air.

With the fire put out, Ken'ishi stood staring down at the dead man. "Did you hear what he said?"

Norikage answered, "Yes, I did."

"What does that mean?"

"It means someone knows you. Someone is looking for you."

"Who?"

"The father of your . . . woman perhaps? Or her husband?"

Ken'ishi's brow furrowed like carven granite. He sheathed his sword.

Norikage knelt and searched through the corpse's clothes, avoiding the thick, wet stain across the man's torso. He found a wooden charm box, shook it, and heard something sliding within. Inside he found a folded piece of paper. He took the paper, opened it and held it toward the lamp so that he could read.

He read it to himself, then looked at Ken'ishi, who stood waiting expectantly. "Ken'ishi, someone is indeed looking for you. Someone powerful enough, wealthy enough, to hire a man like this to find you."

"What does it say?"

"It says, 'Master, I have found the ronin you seek. He has

made himself a constable in Aoka village, along the northeastern side of Hakata Bay. I await your instructions. Signed, Yellow Tiger.' " Ken'ishi's mind raced behind his eyes. For a while neither of them spoke.

Then Gonta's voice broke the silence. "Did this man kill my father?"

Norikage's mind seized upon a sudden inspiration. "Yes, Gonta, I believe he did. He has been snooping around the village for some time, and I believe your father discovered him and was killed because of it."

He met Ken'ishi's silent gaze. *Why did you lie to him?*

Gonta sighed, but Norikage sensed a strange relief pass through him. Gonta said, "Such a horrible business, but I'm glad it's over now. It's over." He wiped at his eyes. "Father has been avenged."

Norikage caught Ken'ishi's glance. Now he understood. This Yellow Tiger would be blamed for Tetta's death, so that life in the village could return to normal, and the villagers could be at ease again.

"Gonta," Norikage said, "there is one other thing."

Gonta looked at him, wiping his eyes again. "This note, you must forget about it. You must forget everything that you heard here tonight, save that we dispatched your father's murderer. *No one* in the village must know of anything else! Do you understand?" He kept his voice even and calm, but firm as basalt and with a hint of underlying threat.

Gonta blinked once, then nodded. "As you say, Norikage-sama."

Then several other villagers came running into the inn carrying buckets of water. Their eyes were wide and fearful. "Where is the fire?" said one.

"Be at ease, everyone," Norikage said. "The danger is over. Ken'ishi has slain Tetta's murderer." He watched the parade of emotions pass through their faces, surprise, horror, relief, curiosity. "Ken'ishi and I are weary now. We must rest. If you will excuse us."

Then he led Ken'ishi outside and back to his office. Kiosé still waited there, and the relief and joy on her face when they returned were palpable. She had not slept. Norikage said, "Do not fear, my dear. All is well."

"I'm so happy to hear it!" she breathed. "I was so worried!"

"You may go home now."

She bowed and departed, but he could sense her disappointment. She wanted to stay, but discussions like these were not meant for a woman's ears.

"Ken'ishi," Norikage began, "I know you are troubled by what happened here tonight. I'm wondering who this man was, and who is looking for you."

Ken'ishi nodded, his brow thick.

"I can do nothing to reassure you, unfortunately, other than to tell you that after tonight, the villagers will be even more vigilant about strangers in town. Rest assured that if any other strangers come through, we will hear about it. Everyone will be watching."

Ken'ishi nodded again, saying nothing.

"And you understand why I lied to Gonta about this man?"

Another nod. The man was so damnably taciturn sometimes!

"It was for the good of everyone in the village."

"I hope there are no more disappearances. This man had nothing to do with Tetta's disappearance. Another disappearance will make us look very, very foolish, after what you said about Tetta's killer."

Norikage was taken aback. He had not yet reached that thought, but it was true. Another disappearance would be bad indeed.

"It is missing the point to think that the martial art is solely in cutting a man down. It is not in cutting people down; it is in killing evil. It is the stratagem of killing the evil of one man and giving life to ten thousand."

—*Yagyu Munenori*

"Sir, are you all right?" The little boy's voice was as clear and sweet as a temple bell. He stood there beside the street, bits of sticky, fermented beans clinging to his plump, pink cheeks. His hands clutched an empty wooden bowl and a pair of small chopsticks. He looked up with big, brown eyes, brimming with childlike fearlessness. His thin black hair formed a shock tied on top of his head.

Taro stopped and peered at the boy from under the edge of his large basket hat. The child's head barely came to his waist. Taro said, "I am fine." The hoarseness of his voice surprised him. He hadn't spoken to another human being for some time. "Why do you ask?"

The boy drew back a step. "Well, because you were walking funny."

A smile tugged at the corner of Taro's mouth for the first time in weeks. "How was I walking?"

The boy imitated a peculiar shambling, meandering gait, and Taro's smile widened. "Like this. Are you sick? My grandpa walks that way sometimes when he drinks too much sake. Only he's all hunched over like this." The boy put down his bowl, then bent over at the waist and pretended to walk with a cane.

"So I walk like an old man, eh?" Taro said.

"Uh-huh! Are you sick? Grandpa is always sick too."

"No, I'm not sick. I've never felt better."

"Why is your hand all wrapped up like that?"

"You ask a lot of questions."

"Why is it all wrapped up like that?"

"Because, I burned it. It's ugly now."

"Really? Can I see it? Show me!"

"No. I . . . don't want to frighten you."

"I won't be scared! I'm strong and brave! My mother always says so."

Taro looked up and down the street. Hakozaki was a busy port town, but this neighborhood was quiet this afternoon. All the men were working the wharfs, and the women were going about their household duties. A few children were playing with a cloth ball down the street. "Then come over here." He walked over into the space between two houses, out of sight, and motioned the boy to come closer. The boy followed him without hesitation.

He knelt and took off his basket hat.

The boy said, "Do you drink sake too? Grandpa's eyes look like that when he drinks sake. All red and stuff."

"I drink sake sometimes, but not today."

"And why is your hair falling out?"

"You ask a lot of questions. Do you want to see my hand or not?"

"Yes! Show me! Show me!"

"You are a special boy. I don't show this to *anyone!*"

The boy's eyes lit up. "Really?" He grinned, exposing the wide gaps between his brand new front teeth.

"Yes, really. What is your name?"

"I'm Shota."

"My name is . . . Taro."

"Are you a ronin? You look like a ronin."

"No!" He realized that his voice had come out as a snarl. The boy stepped back again and almost ran away. Taro softened his voice, mellowed his tone. "No, I'm not a ronin. I'm a constable, and I'm looking for a ronin."

"Why did you talk that way? That was scary."

"I'm sorry. My voice is rough sometimes."

"Show me your hand!"

"Very well." Taro unwrapped the linen wrappings around his right hand, revealing the disfigured member that now served him so well.

Shota's eyes grew wide when he saw the strange reddish flesh and the long, yellowed nails. His voice was a mixture of wonder and fear. "Scary! It's the color of the oni statue guarding the temple."

"Yes, that's why I don't show it to people. But you're special. You won't run away."

"No, I won't run away. I'm strong and brave."

Taro looked at his hand with fresh eyes. Every time he

exposed it, he felt a strange sense of wonder, as if it was not his own. His hand felt the same as it always had. Almost. The day he fought with the ronin, he had passed out from the bleeding. When he had regained consciousness, he was lying in a pool of his own blood, and his neatly severed right hand lay beside him. He remembered little, except for picking up his hand and feeling a sudden urge to hold the arm to the severed stump. A sudden slithering sensation, like worms in his skin, snakes in his muscles, spines in his bones. He was so surprised that he would have dropped the dead limb, except that it was attached once again by writhing shreds of flesh. He remembered losing consciousness again, and when he woke up, the arm had reattached itself completely. It took several more days before his fingers would work properly again, but he was whole again and able to pursue his vengeance against the ronin who maimed him and left him for dead. Over time, the flesh had changed color, as if he had dipped it in a vat of dye the color of clotting blood.

Since that day, not an hour passed that he did not burn for vengeance. Images of the horrible tortures he would inflict upon his prey filled his dreams. Painstaking dismemberment, burning, flaying, tearing, flensing, breaking, puncturing. The shivers of glee grew stronger with each more depraved thought.

But his thoughts were right and just. The ronin deserved it all. What was the ronin's name? He couldn't remember anymore, but he didn't need to. He did not need to ask people if they had seen the ronin or knew where he was. Taro already *knew* how to find him. When he awoke in the morning, after a night of terrible, bloody, gleeful dreams, he could smell his quarry like fresh blood on the air. As the mornings wore on, the smell of the ronin's blood became too confused with other smells, and he lost the trail, but he always picked it up again the following morning. And it was not just blood that he smelled; it was something else, something warm and metallic, like the taste of a silver coin. And it stirred memories of pain. When he thought about that smell, that taste, his heart thumped ever harder in his breast, until he was sure that everyone around him could hear the sound.

Since he left the sword school, he had made his way to the city of Hakata, then moved on to Hakozaki. He did not remember why Master Koga cast him out, but he remembered a reprimand of some kind, then leaving the school carrying his things. . . . He was too strong for the other students anyway. He always had to be careful, to hold himself back from hurting them. Well, they would not have to worry about him anymore. Master Koga could rest easy now that none of his other students would be harmed in practice again. They had all been weak.

His way seemed to point northeast along the coast. And every morning the scent strengthened, as if he was drawing nearer. Every morning, he could follow a little longer.

Then he wondered, why had he fought the ronin that day? Why had they dueled? What was the reason? The ronin had killed someone he knew? The ronin had cut him to pieces? Killed all his men and robbed him of a beautiful girl? Wait, that was not right. Parts of his memory felt like a dream. Why had he been chasing the ronin in the first place? He could not remember now, and it made him angry. Why could he not remember?

Shota reached out and touched Taro's disfigured hand. But only for a moment before he recoiled, and the smile of wonder faded from his face.

"Don't be afraid," Taro said. "It's only a hand."

Shota took a step back, and his big brown eyes brimmed with fear.

"Where is your mother, Shota?"

The boy turned and pointed across the street. "She is home,

washing laundry."

"Where is your house?"

"Over there."

"Your mother will be getting worried soon."

The boy shrugged.

"Where is your father?"

"He's working. He goes to the docks every day."

"Do you have any brothers and sisters?"

"Two sisters, but they are just *babies.*"

"Ah, so you're the big boy, eh?" As Taro spoke, he found disconcerting thoughts passing through his mind, like strangers in the street. Thoughts he did not know, thoughts that did not feel like his own. Like how it would feel to crush this boy's little skull like an eggshell, and how it would taste to drink his blood. And stranger still, part of him already knew! Part of him already knew that it would feel *good,* would taste *good.*

He realized that his crimson right hand was stroking the top of the boy's head. The boy's mouth hung open, and his eyes were wide, staring up at Taro.

Taro pulled his hand away quickly. "There is no reason to be afraid," he said quickly. "You are strong and brave."

The boy gulped, and his voice was a whisper. "Strong and brave." Then he took a step back. A tear trickled from his eye, making a streak in the dirt and fermented beans clinging to his ripe, red cheek.

Taro tasted blood on his lips. He touched his mouth with his left hand and found blood where he had bitten his lower lip. He licked the blood and a shudder went through him.

The boy took another step back, then turned and ran away toward his house.

Taro stood up languidly, like a snake coiling around a tree, and placed his basket hat upon his head. He brushed his fallen hair from his shoulders, wrapped his right hand in linen once again, adjusted his swords and his jitte. Shota disappeared into a house a few doors down the street. Taro watched him go.

Then, abruptly, he sat up. The room was dark. He had just been standing in the street, in full daylight! Now it was dark. He could feel the coolness of the night air, hear the chatter of crickets and frogs outside, the distant rustle of the surf.

He jumped to his feet, throwing the blanket aside. He was still clothed, and his weapons lay beside the sleeping mat. He looked around. This was a small room in a house, too poor and plain to be an inn. Where was he?

A moment of panic shot through him. Not again! More of his life had disappeared, and he found himself with no idea of where he was or how he had come to be there. He swore fervently. What was wrong with him?

What was that horrific smell? Death. Blood and death.

He could see clearly in the dark and looked down at his clothes. They were spattered with stiff, dark stains. He snatched up his weapons and thrust them through his sash. Then he stepped up to the thin paper door of the small room and shoved it aside.

The buzzing of flies filled the small room with the sound of death and pestilence. Shiny black specks glittered in the light of the dying fire in the central fire pit, clustering on the blood-spattered faces, crawling through the congealing blood. Five shapes, two large, three small, all lying scattered and broken around the room. And the smell was . . . delicious.

No!

Why did he think such things? That was . . . horrible!

He lunged for the front door, threw it open, and plunged down the street, running as fast as he could. The horror of what he had seen in that house paled beside the knowledge that *he* had done it, and that horror choked his throat closed until he could hardly breathe, and his breath wheezed and gurgled from his mouth.

Taro did not stop running for a long time.

Behind me the moon
Brushes shadows of pine trees
Lightly on the floor

—*Kikaku*

The days passed into weeks, and the village returned to normal after the waves of gossip created by Tetta's disappearance subsided into a period of quiet mourning. Ken'ishi sometimes heard whispers of fear as the townsfolk speculated on what could have happened to the innkeeper. A few still refused to accept the story that Yellow Tiger had killed him. It was as if people simply speculated and made up stories because those were more exciting than the truth. Perhaps it was because they never found Tetta's corpse. Perhaps it was because Norikage and Ken'ishi were outsiders. Some still speculated that Tetta might be alive somewhere. Did a hungry ghost take him? Did he fall into the sea and drown? Had a trickster fox lured him away? Perhaps he went mad and wandered away. Did someone kill him and hide his body in the forest? Perhaps the whore had killed her master.

Idle suspicion thrown at Kiosé was something Ken'ishi had not expected, and it made him angry. Norikage told him, "*That* is what I was speaking of when I told you how insular these villagers can be. Kiosé is an outsider, like you and me, and worse, she is a whore. I suspected there were some who might blame her."

But the weeks passed, and the cool, wet spring became a hot and humid summer. The air thickened, heavy and stifling. The heat did not relent, even at night. Ken'ishi often awoke in the morning soaked with sweat. Villagers toiled and complained just as they always had. Fireflies danced in the summer darkness. The sea beat against the shore with its unceasing rhythm. Monkeys chattered and screeched in the shade of the tree boughs. Frogs chirped in night-swathed bogs. The rice crop greened and grew, and the plums swelled and ripened on their branches. Kiosé began to swell also.

Throughout this time, Ken'ishi and Norikage watched Chiba and his brothers like falcons. Chiba remained defiant and reticent, but he gave them no proof or even further reason to believe he had anything to do with Tetta's disappearance.

Then one day Ken'ishi's noon meal was interrupted by a commotion outside his house, loud voices shouting his name. The day was hot and humid, his clothes clung to his back and arms, and the insects had been insistent in irritating him. As he put on his sword, he strode to the front door and slid it open. "What is it?" he demanded.

Standing outside his house were a dozen villagers, men and

women, and he noticed that most of the men were woodsmen and carpenters. Their faces held the wide-eyed, hesitant look of people expected to be protected.

One of the carpenters stepped forward, a man named Ryu. "Ken'ishi-sama, there has been another disappearance! Gorobei is missing!"

Ken'ishi's belly turned into a stone ball. Gorobei was a good man, a skilled carpenter with a kind spirit, and he had helped smooth the way for Ken'ishi's grudging acceptance into village society. For a long moment, no words would come. Finally, he swallowed the lump in his throat and said, "Does anyone know where he was last seen?"

One man said, "I saw him two days ago."

"He went to the inn two nights ago."

"He said he was going into the forest sometime soon to find a special kind of wood."

"The forest?" Ken'ishi said. "Which direction?"

The man who had spoken was another carpenter, one of Gorobei's friendly rivals. "I don't know. He was working on a very special thing, he said, and said that regular wood would not do for it."

"What was it?" Ken'ishi asked.

"I don't know."

Ken'ishi said, "Everyone, be calm. I will get to the bottom of this."

A voice from the back sneered, "That is what you said last time!"

Another voice said, "You brought us this bad fortune!"

"It all started after *you* came!"

"You have angered the spirits!"

"The kami hate you!"

Ken'ishi shoulders tensed and his jaw clenched for a moment, and his gaze flicked toward those voices, but he was unable to distinguish who had said those things. His ears began to burn. "Go home. Norikage and I will investigate, and we will find out what has happened to him." But even as he spoke the words, he felt their hollowness. "Go home." His eyes scanned the crowd and met nothing but unpleasant stares. "Go home. We will get to the bottom of this! I swear upon my honor!"

The villagers began to shuffle back to their homes. He overheard some of them speculating about the cause of the disappearances. Was it a kappa? A fox? Maybe it was a tengu playing tricks. He caught many skeptical glances as he waited for the crowd to disperse. Something terrible was happening, and only Ken'ishi could stop it. There was no one else.

He went to the constabulary and found Norikage already deep in thought. He told Norikage the news.

"I heard them out there," Norikage said. "What do you want to do?"

"Go to Gorobei's house and see if we find anything there."

"Very well. Let us go."

The house of Gorobei the carpenter was on the outer edge of the village, where he lived alone. He had no wife or living family. His skill earned him a good living in a modest house. Gorobei's workshop was redolent with the rich, earthy smells of wood and oil, mixed with the sharp tang of lacquer. Lying in the corner were several similar-looking scraps of wood. All of them looked like abandoned attempts to create a scabbard for a sword.

"Now why would he be making a scabbard?" Norikage wondered aloud.

"I don't know. You didn't ask him?"

"I did not." Norikage fingered his thin mustache. "Who would he make such a thing for? Perhaps he was making the scabbard for you. There are no other samurai in the area. I doubt that he somehow acquired a sword for himself. I know he made many bokken for you. Were you friendly with him?"

"We sometimes drank his plum wine together after he finished a commission."

"Perhaps he was making a gift for you, a new scabbard. That scabbard you have was beautiful once, but now it is a bit battered."

Ken'ishi scowled. "It is old! It was my father's scabbard."

"Of course. I meant no offense, Ken'ishi. But only the blade of a sword lasts forever. Sometimes the hilt and wrappings must be replaced. Look here! A small bag of polished stones and some mother-of-pearl. Perhaps he was going to use them for ornamentation. These discarded pieces of wood are rough. Perhaps he was unhappy with them. They would fit your blade if they were finished."

Ken'ishi nodded. "So it seems. He asked about my sword last time I saw him, asked me to show it to him. And I did."

"The forest? Is there something in the forest?"

"But there are so many villagers who come and go in the forest."

Norikage's brow furrowed, and he rubbed his chin. "It could be anything. A robber, a band of thieves, hungry ghosts, tanuki, kitsune, demons, spirits. Ah, so many dangers in the forest!"

"Something must be done. We can't wait for more people to disappear and hope for a clue. I'll go into the forest. I'll be the bait in my own trap."

"Ken'ishi! We do not know what could be out there!"

"I'll find out. This bait is not a piece of dead meat. It has teeth of its own."

The villagers were afraid to venture out of the village. The farmers should have been tending their fields and gardens, but they were afraid to leave their homes. As Ken'ishi went back to his house, he received several suspicious and hostile looks from the bolder villagers, especially Chiba and his brothers.

Akao fell in beside him as he walked. Even his usually happy face was grim. "Trouble."

"Yes."

"Something bad."

"I know. I'm going to find it."

Akao stopped and looked up into his eyes. "Are you going to fight?"

Ken'ishi stopped and looked down at him. "If I have to."

"Not a fighter."

"I know. You're a hunter. It will be dangerous."

"Ask me?"

"No, I won't ask you to help me."

"Fool. Never refuse you."

"That is why I don't ask. If something happens to me, you must look after Kiosé."

"What, and raise her pup?" Akao laughed.

Ken'ishi could not help but laugh as well. "You would be a good father," he said.

"And so will you. Coming with you."

Ken'ishi smiled. "As you wish."

When they reached his house, he packed up his bedroll, gathered some food and water, his sword and his bow, and ventured into the wooded countryside. For several hours, he and Akao moved in concentric paths around the village, searching for any evidence of any of the missing villagers, anything unusual, but they found nothing. They once came upon an area that reeked of death, but when they followed the stench, they found only the carcass of a dead deer, bloated and crawling with maggots. Ken'ishi hoped this was not an omen of things to come.

Norikage sat in his office, rubbing his hands. He thought about the disappearances, and the unknowable hostility of the forest, and felt that no good could come to Ken'ishi out there alone. His dog would help him, but if he met serious trouble. . . . But there was no one else. Norikage knew he himself would have been worse than useless if he had accompanied Ken'ishi into the forest. He could not fight, only get in Ken'ishi's way if danger appeared.

For that matter, how safe was Norikage in the village with Ken'ishi gone? Chiba and his brothers, if they were the true culprits, might take the opportunity to enact another mysterious disappearance. He noted well that they had several times walked past the office, looking toward the shuttered windows as if they could see Norikage sitting inside. He, of course, saw them through the slats, and something in their looks made him uneasy. They knew that Ken'ishi had gone into the forest. Norikage always kept a dagger secreted within his robes, but he knew that he would be pitifully inept if he tried to use it.

As the hours passed, he sometimes practiced drawing the dagger quickly, trying to strike in the same movement at some imaginary adversary, and all the while he felt foolish, even though a persistent feeling of impending dread kept building in his belly like a nest of buzzing hornets. Ken'ishi would say that Norikage's premonitions were the kami speaking to him, warning him of danger. But what could he do? He was a not a fighting man.

He spotted Kiosé coming toward his office. She was growing thicker around the middle. She looked pale and wan, and Norikage wondered if she was getting enough to eat. She glanced furtively up and down the street, and fear painted her face in broad brushstrokes. She, too, knew that Ken'ishi was absent. She was startled when he invited her in before she even reached the door.

She said, "I am sorry to bother you, Norikage-sama. I am too much trouble."

"Not at all. Come in."

"It's just that . . . I'm frightened."

He nodded. "Of course. You can stay here in my office as long as you like. These are bad days."

She bowed low, and her voice was soft and quavering. "Thank you, Norikage-sama. I am sorry to be so much trouble."

In the shadows of his office, she looked even paler. She looked ill. He said, "Are you well?"

She glanced in his direction without meeting his gaze. "I am sick much of the time. But Gonta's mother tells me that it is just the baby causing the sickness."

Norikage nodded. "I can understand your fears, with Ken'ishi being gone."

"What if something happens to him?" The tremor in her voice increased, and he could hear the almost frantic emotions behind her words. "If something happens to him, I will die, too."

"Now, there is no need for such talk."

She continued as if he had not said a word. "Something will happen to me. Chiba will kill me. But maybe that is not so bad. At least then my child would not have a life of suffering." Suddenly tears burst out of her eyes and rolled down her sunken cheeks.

Norikage felt a pang of pity for her. She was so helpless, so downtrodden. Empathy for others was not a common experience for him. He was much more accustomed to worrying about his own skin, but her plight touched even his jaded spirit.

"But even if Ken'ishi returns, what will happen to me?" she said. Her lips quivered with the fear and emotion bubbling out of her.

Why had she come to ask him these things?

"This child could belong to almost anyone. Sometimes I just

want to walk into the sea and never return. I cannot return to my family. They would not have me."

Norikage squirmed where he sat. He did not know how to deal with matters such as these. Furthermore, at this moment she reminded him of another fragile waif, a girl doomed to suffer the birth of a bastard child, the child of a careless, selfish young nobleman. But Kiosé was infinitely more unfortunate, because she had no one to care for her. Was she asking for his help? Was she plotting to run away?

She noticed his silence and glanced at him. In that instant, he saw in her eyes the reason she had come to him.

She trusted him.

Norikage's mouth fell open. He considered himself to be among the least trustworthy people in the world, but somehow she trusted him. Even Ken'ishi did not fully trust him. Ken'ishi did not know it, but his distrust in Norikage was warranted. Norikage kept unpleasant secrets, secrets that would mean both their heads if they were revealed. For a long time, Kiosé sat there across from him, waiting for him to speak.

Finally, she moved to get up. "I am sorry, Norikage-sama. I was rude for coming."

"Please wait," he said, raising his hand. "It is good that you came to me, Kiosé. You are special to me. I don't want any harm to befall you."

It was her turn to look surprised, and Norikage was inwardly amused. She said, "Norikage-sama, you are a wise man. What should I do?" The look of helpless entreaty in her eyes moved him. She truly thought he had the answer to her question, as if all of life's implacable questions had an answer.

He laughed. Stunned for a moment by his own inadequacy, he laughed. She shrank away from him, and the look in her eyes changed from entreaty to hurt.

"I'm sorry, Kiosé, please forgive me!" he said, still chuckling.

"I'm not laughing at you. I'm laughing at me."

"Wh . . . What?"

"I am the last person in the world who would know the answer to your question."

Her crestfallen look deepened, but the hurt in her eyes diminished.

"It's good not to worry," he said brightly, smiling at her. "I'm sure Ken'ishi will be fine."

"Shall I make some tea?"

"Of course," Norikage said. She got up and began to prepare the tea. As she did so, he watched the simplicity of her movements, and thought about how her situation could be improved. Norikage had enough money left to buy her contract from Gonta and set her free, but not only was he loath to part with such a sum, there were other considerations as well. While she was in Gonta's employ, she would probably have enough food to eat and a roof over her head, but she was his slave. If she was not in Gonta's employ, she would be free, but she would have no place to live and no food to eat, and she would still be a fallen woman with a bastard child. Perhaps Norikage could keep her as his mistress. He would be grateful for a woman in his house. But then, she loved Ken'ishi.

After she prepared the pot of tea and poured him a cup, he said, "I'm afraid we have much time to pass before Ken'ishi returns. Do you know how to play Go?"

She shook her head, looking uncertain.

"Then I will teach you. I have been trying to teach Ken'ishi lately, but sometimes his skull is quite dense." He flashed her a confidential smile.

She smiled back, timidly.

He looked around his office at the stacks of documents and books, rubbing his chin. "Now, where did I put that Go board?"

As the afternoon shadows grew long, Ken'ishi found himself on the path leading to the pond that he and Kiosé visited a few weeks before, where Tetta might have gone to fish. He stood on the path for a few moments, pondering. It was conceivable that Gorobei had used this path himself.

Akao stood beside him, nose to the ground. "No trail here. No humans for a while."

"We'll search again," Ken'ishi said and strode down the path.

"Night coming."

"I know." Ken'ishi glanced down. Akao's hackles stood on end. "What is it?"

Akao said nothing.

"Are you afraid?"

The dog looked up at him. "Something . . . strange."

In the failing light, the looming rock face along one side of the pond was a powerful, brooding presence. He had just enough time to make a modest camp a few paces from the water. While he did so, Akao prowled the outskirts of the pond's perimeter. Before long, a sharp bark from the far side of the pond echoed over the water. Ken'ishi moved around the pond, and as he approached the spot, his nose caught the powerful stench of death, more rotten, more foul than he had ever experienced. He covered his nose and mouth with his collar and followed the odor.

As he thrust himself between reeds taller than his head, cursing his own noise, he spotted Akao's brownish shape deep in the reeds, pointing toward the water. After he took a few more steps in the failing light, something purple and distended emerged, lying half in the water. Then he saw the human foot, twisted and swollen. He stepped nearer and clenched his teeth against the unbearable stench. The corpse lay on its stomach, knees half-curled up under it, its head submerged in the muck. Strangely, the body was naked. And even more sickening, between the narrow, purpled buttocks sticking into the air, something red, raw, wet and distended, looking as if some of his innards had been sucked out through the hole.

Ken'ishi's guts churned, and he tasted the bile rising in his throat, but he clamped his jaw shut like a band of iron. He stepped back, short of breath, allowing the reeds to hide the horror that lay among them.

Akao said, "Something strange did this. Scent is . . . wrong."

Ken'ishi could not answer. His breath came in short, painful gasps. When it began to slow, he swallowed the bitterness rising in his throat. Then he drew his sword, sliced a thick handful of reeds, and twisted them into a makeshift rope. Steeling himself, he stepped back through the rushes closer to the corpse, moved to its feet, and slipped the rope around the corpse's swollen purpled ankle, careful not to touch the lifeless flesh. He did not wish to taint his spirit with the touch of the dead. After tying the rope securely, he pulled. The corpse came out of the water with a sickening squelch and a belch of putrid air. He hauled it up onto the bank, flattening a path through the reeds. As he pulled, the corpse rolled onto its back, and he could see the man's face. Gorobei's mouth gaped in a silent death rattle, full of muck, eyes eaten to empty sockets, flesh purple and sagging.

Ken'ishi's guts heaved, and his knees buckled for a moment, but he fought it down and staggered about thirty paces away, trying to regain control of his breathing, waiting for his thrashing innards to settle. Finally, he regained control and turned back toward the corpse.

The hairs on the back of his neck rippled erect, putting him instantly on guard.

Akao faced the water, a low growl rumbling in his throat.

Ken'ishi took two steps back toward the corpse and spied movement in the reeds near its resting place. Something large squelched and rustled in the tall reeds and dashed back to where the corpse lay. Water splashed, just out of sight behind the reeds, and the tops of the plants still waved with the passing of . . . something. He parted the reeds and looked out over the pond. Ripples spread toward the water's distant sides. He looked down and saw what looked like two small footprints in the muck. He could not tell the shape of the footprints because they were already filled with water. Another chill trickled down his spine. Something had been standing here. Watching them.

"Can you scent it?" Ken'ishi asked.

"Watched us."

"Yes," Ken'ishi said. "It was watching us. . . ."

The patch of indigo sky shone through the opening in the forest canopy above the pond. The shadows among the underbrush thickened. They sat beside their small fire on the bank of the pond, cooking a small pot of rice for supper. Ken'ishi's gaze swept constantly over the surface of the water, looking for telltale ripples, anything to indicate the presence of whatever had been watching them. He kept his sword beside him and his bow strung. Three arrows jutted from the earth nearby, ready to be used at a moment's notice.

As darkness fell, Akao slunk away into the shadows. Before the dog disappeared into the forest, they exchanged looks that said, *Be careful.*

In spite of his constant vigilance, Ken'ishi listened with contentment to the awakening of the night creatures around the lake, the frogs and insects and other creatures. Evening birds voiced their mournful cries. On a high branch overlooking the water sat a lone crow, its harsh voice calling out to its comrades that all was clear.

As he watched the black silhouette of the crow preening its feathers, Ken'ishi had an idea. He called out, "Sir Crow, excuse me. Can I have a word with you?"

The crow looked at him in astonishment for a moment. Then it called back from its lofty perch. "Who speaks the ancient tongue? Who are you? What do you want?"

"I know it is late, Sir Crow. Please accept my apologies. May I ask you a question?"

"What for? I don't like humans."

Crows were perhaps the rudest of all birds, and as this one had said, they did not like humans, but Ken'ishi knew they were among the most clever and wise of all birds, and Takao, his foster father, once told him that they were the messengers of the gods.

"Would you like some rice?"

Without another word the crow leaped from its branch and glided toward where Ken'ishi sat, landing well out of reach. Ken'ishi smiled inwardly; crows were also easily bribed.

The crow cocked its head, blinking its beady black eyes. "Rice, you say? Is it ready to eat?"

"Soon."

"Then you may ask your question. But if you lie about the rice, my brothers and I will drive you from these woods."

"Very well, Sir Crow. My question is this. Is there something living in this pond?"

"What a foolish question!" The crow's eyes sparkled with silent, mischievous laughter. "Of course there are things living in this pond! Fish and turtles and frogs and insects—"

"Excuse me, Sir Crow. I should have been more specific. Is there something living in the pond that . . . that likes to feed upon human beings?"

The crow glanced at the pond, then at him, then back at the water, then smoothed its feathers. "Yes."

"What is it?"

"You said one question. Give me the rice now."

"Very well." He got up and scooped a ladle of steaming rice

from the pot onto a broad leaf. He laid the small, steaming mound at the crow's feet.

"What a strange creature you are!" the crow said. "A man who speaks the ancient tongue! Whoever heard of such a thing! It is too hot!" The crow pointed to the rice with one of its feet.

"Wave your wing to fan the rice. Sir Crow, I have one more question."

The crow seemed to sigh. "Very well. Ask."

"What kind of creature is it?"

"I do not know that, but it lives in the water."

"What does it look like?"

The crow blinked twice as if it could not understand the question. "Bigger than me, smaller than you." Then the crow gulped its portion down in three great bites.

"Thank you for your help, Sir Crow."

Without another word, the crow flapped into the air and returned to its perch high above the water.

By now, the light had all but gone, leaving Ken'ishi with only the light of his fire reflecting from the black, rippling surface of the pond. Stars flicked into view, one by one, like holes pricked in the dark patch of sky. He sat down with his back to the fire, looking over the water, weapons within easy reach. He had no idea what kind of creature might live in the water and prey upon human beings. An oni? He had never heard of oni that lived in the water. A sea dragon? This was a freshwater pond, with no connection to the sea. Perhaps the spirit of the pond itself was evil. The most powerful spirits could take physical form.

The night darkened, and the moon rose into the patch of sky, casting a trail of silver upon the surface of the pond. Ken'ishi found himself growing sleepy. It would not be wise to sleep alone beside the pond. He must remain alert, or he might disappear like the others. Even if he pretended to sleep, the danger of falling asleep would be greater. And Akao was still in the darkness somewhere, probably watching from a different vantage point. The moon rose higher, and still Ken'ishi did not move. He fought against sleep with every breath, every blink of his eyes. His eyes seemed to shut of their own volition. Several times he stood up and circled around his fire to force himself awake, but when he sat down again his body yearned for rest.

"Come, monkey-boy," said Kaa. "There is something I must teach you." His feathers ruffled in the stiff breeze that seemed to flow perpetually across the mountainside and grow stronger on sunny days. This was a sunny day in winter, and the air was cold and brittle. Snow swathed the land, weighing down upon the pine branches like a soggy, bitter-cold blanket.

The tengu set off down the slope from their mountain perch. The boy pulled his coat of straw close around him and breathed in its dusty, earthy scent. The wind was cold, but in the depths under the forest canopy, it could hardly penetrate. His sandaled feet crunched through the snow as they walked. The birds were quiet today, probably huddled against the winter chill. The boy followed his master's quick, steady stride and long legs, and he almost ran to keep up. The afternoon passed and the boy grew weary, and still they walked in silence. Curiosity burned in him, but he knew better than to ask. His master would explain when the time came.

They trekked across the faces of three mountains, into places far beyond the boy's previous explorations. They entered a valley darkening into shadow as the sun fell behind one of the nearby peaks. The air chilled even more, and still the boy wondered where they were going. He was weary, and his feet were numb with cold, the lack of feeling spreading up through his legs.

His nose caught a strange, moist smell in the air, and wisps of steam or cloud rose beyond a grove of pine trees in their path. The smell was unlike anything he had ever experienced. A bit like the smell of rotten eggs. Kaa led him along a narrow, rocky path toward the pine grove and the clouds of rising steam. As they grew nearer, the smell grew stronger. The air grew warmer as well, until they passed through the small patch of pines and stood beside a small lake of steaming water, perhaps one hundred paces across at its widest point, nestled in the crook of two mountain slopes.

The boy felt the warmth of the water on his face even while standing beside it. The water was clear and calm. Tiny ripples spread across the surface as if created from invisible undercurrents. The shapes of the rocks under the surface wavered and shifted with these otherwise unseen forces.

The boy looked at the lake with mixed feelings of wonder and unease. Then the tengu's harsh voice startled him. "You do not know how to swim. You must learn. Go into the water."

The boy turned to his master. "The water is deep!"

"Of course it is deep! That is why you must swim! You will swim across, then you will swim back."

The boy stared at the water for a few moments, unsure of what to do.

"What are you waiting for?"

The boy stepped down the rocks to the water's edge. The water was so clear he saw the rocks and pebbles sloping sharply downward. He took off his clothes as if he was preparing to bathe, folded them, and left them in a pile on a nearby rock. Except for his meager loincloth, he stood naked and shivering against the winter wind. The warm water seemed now like an inviting place, so he stepped in. He gasped as the water's heat shocked the flesh of his legs. His feet were too numb at first to feel the rocks underneath, but the heat sent a torrent of prickling ice through them. He took two steps, and the water reached his knees. Four steps more and it reached his waist. Its warmth seeped through his chilled flesh. The invisible currents caressed his skin. A few more steps, and he was immersed in hot water up to his neck.

"Now, monkey boy. Move further into the water. Move your arms like this and kick your legs." The boy watched him for a moment, then began to move into the deeper water. The water rose to his chin until he danced on his tiptoes. "Move your arms and legs, fool! You've watched how fish swim. You must do as they do!" The boy complied, moving his arms first, then lifting his feet from the rocky bottom to kick them beneath him. To his amazement, his head remained above the surface, and he felt as if he was floating, a moment of exhilaration, until he reached down with his foot and no longer felt the bottom beneath him. A jolt of panic shot through him, and he began to sink. He gulped a mouthful of foul-tasting water. He heard his master shouting at him through the water in his ears. "Relax, monkey-boy! Control yourself! If you panic like an animal, you will die!"

Something in him knew that his master was right, so he relaxed and slowed his frenzied movements. Magically, it seemed, his head rose from the water again.

"Look!" the boy cried. "I'm doing it!"

"Good! Perhaps you will not die after all!" his master shouted.

As the boy relaxed, able to revel in the sensations of buoyant warmth, small currents under the water rippled across his flesh. Moments later, he noticed that he had moved farther into deep water.

"Now, swim to the other side. Aim your body toward that pointed rock."

The boy turned his head and looked through the wisps of steam rising from the water's smooth surface. A rock jutted from the water near the edge on the opposite side. The rock stood the height of a man, with the sides near the water level painted in strange colors. He felt a burst of exhilaration and confidence as the pointed rock came closer.

When he reached the middle of the small lake, the small, underwater currents grew stronger. He felt them pulling at his feet, as if his legs were just barely slipping through the grasp of some invisible watery entity. He ceased moving toward the rock and looked down through the clear water. He could see the darkness of the rocky bottom underneath him, but he saw nothing around his legs but formless ripples.

His master called out to him, "What is it? Why have you stopped?"

"Something—!" A mouthful of water cut off his words as he was pulled under. A fresh bolt of panic shot through him, and he flailed under the water, lifting his face to the air.

His head broke the surface for a moment, and he heard his master's voice. ". . . or the lake's water spirits will. . . ."

All thoughts in his mind fell away, leaving him with a desire as clear as the steaming hot water, a desire to fight, to live. His legs and arms pumped and flailed. A gasp of crisp, cold air, then under the water again. Fighting. Kicking. Swimming. Water swirling around his knees, caressing, sliding over his thighs, tugging so gently, gently enough to pull his face under again. Then sharp pain lanced through his toes as they kicked against the stony bottom. The bottom! In an instant, he stopped fighting, gathered his legs under him, and stood up. His head and shoulders emerged, steaming in the cool air, and he stood on the lake bed, gasping for air, wiping the stinging water from his eyes. His master stood on the far side of the lake, watching him passively. The boy looked around him and saw that he stood about fifteen paces from the tall, pointed rock.

"You are alive!" his master called. "The water spirits have

found you strong enough to survive. You are a strong swim-mer!"

The boy's face flushed and a grin emerged. He had done it! He nearly collapsed with relief.

"Now you must swim back!"

The dream memory flowed away from that long-ago day and through all the days afterward when he returned to that lake and swam back and forth many times, fighting the invisible grasp of the lake's water spirits with every pass. After his first time, he had brought small offerings of rice and fish for the water spirits to thank them for sparing his life. Then in later dreams, he thought it strange that the steaming lake now had large growths of reeds, and that things were moving through the reeds, parting them with their passage. A rustle from the reeds and the quiet slosh of water jerked him awake. A chill gripped the back of his neck as he realized that he had fallen asleep. He thought he saw the tops of the nearby reeds waving rhythmi-cally, as if something had just passed through, but he could not be sure if the flickering firelight was playing tricks. He cocked his ear, listening for movement, but all he heard was the singsong chorus of the night creatures in the darkness, who seemed to giggle at his foolishness.

His fists clenched. Fool! Falling asleep like that might have cost him his life! Anger and vigilance together were sufficient to keep sleep at bay for the rest of night. When dawn came, he still sat with his back to the dying embers of his fire, watching the water.

As daylight returned, so did Akao. Ken'ishi asked, "Did you see anything?"

Akao responded with a weary huff.

When the patch of dark sky faded to grayness, swallowing the stars, Ken'ishi stretched his legs and noticed some strange indentations in a bare patch of soft earth just outside the perimeter of the reeds. A pair of strange, blunt impressions, perhaps half the size of his own feet, pressed smoothly into the moist earth, tipped by deep pits that could only have been made by long claws. Whatever left those footprints had been completely out of the water, out of the reeds, and approaching him in full view. A shiver of excitement whispered through him, and he looked at the pond again, feeling something watching him from concealment.

Then an idea came to him. He packed up his belongings and doused his fire.

"Let's go," he said.

Akao regarded him for a moment, and then followed him down the path toward the village.

One of Norikage's greatest pleasures was reading the work of the Chinese classical poet Li Houzhu. Today it helped him keep his mind off Ken'ishi's absence. Where was he? Norikage tried to focus on the graceful calligraphy and the eloquent words for the dozenth time when he heard a step outside the constabulary office. He looked out expectantly and was rewarded with a sight he had been hoping for since the previous afternoon.

"Ken'ishi!" Norikage exclaimed. "How good to see you! When you did not return last night I feared the worst." The young warrior was a bit dirty and tired-looking, but seemed otherwise well.

Ken'ishi sat down across the desk from him, his face taciturn. "I think I found something."

"Truly? Splendid! Splendid! What happened?"

"We searched the woods all day, but found nothing, so we went back to the pond where I thought Tetta might have gone fishing. When we searched the area, we found Gorobei's corpse, half in the water, hidden in the some rushes. It looked as if something had been . . . feeding on it."

"How revolting! A wolf? A demon? Did you see what it was?"

Ken'ishi shook his head. "Something that lives in the water. It was watching me. I fell asleep, and it was coming for me, but I awoke before it could reach me."

"Did you see it?"

"No. It was too fast."

"Terrible!" Norikage said, studying Ken'ishi intently. The normally stolid, dependable Ken'ishi looked as if he had seen a hungry ghost. Perhaps acting as live bait frightened him more than he expected.

"We waited there all night, but it only happened once."

"You look tired. Go home and sleep where you are safe."

Ken'ishi nodded. "I have a plan."

"We can discuss what to do after you are rested."

"Very well." With that, Ken'ishi departed.

Norikage was left stroking his chin. If only he had access to a library or a learned scholar who might be able to make sense of Ken'ishi's tale. Dealing with this problem was bound to be dangerous. Something had almost attacked him. But what *was* it?

His wandering gaze drifted out the window of his office, and he spied Kiosé carrying a large bucket full of water. She saw Ken'ishi walking back to his house, but he had not seen her. She stopped, and Norikage saw the look of forlorn adoration on her face as she watched him go. She took half a step toward him, then stopped and cast her gaze down onto the dirt. Norikage felt fresh pity for her. She knew she could never have Ken'ishi all for herself. He felt pity for the child as well, who would be born as both a bastard and a burden. Gonta had not been pleased about Kiosé's condition. He made her work harder now, to make up for the work she would not be able to do after the baby was born. As a result, she spent much less time at

Ken'ishi's house lately.

Ken'ishi entered his house without noticing her presence, and when he had gone, she sighed and continued on with her bucket.

"Poor thing," Norikage said, shaking his head.

A few hours later, Norikage sat in his house and fanned himself against the afternoon's thick, wet heat. Ken'ishi came in, looking rested and hearty, as if he had put his fear behind him. "You look much better!" Norikage said.

"We need to discuss what to do. I have a plan, but I need your help."

Norikage sat up straight, with a sudden tingle of uneasiness. "What is it?"

"The thing, the creature, whatever it is we seek, is crafty. It recognized that I could fight against it, unlike poor Gorobei and Tetta. It waited until I was asleep to approach me. Therefore, to lure it into the open, we must offer it defenseless prey. But it is fast. Fast enough to move back into the reeds after I woke up. Anything that moves that fast could be upon me before I could get my weapons out of hiding. I cannot be the bait in my own trap." Ken'ishi's gaze fixed on Norikage.

Norikage swallowed hard. "But I cannot do it! I would be helpless!"

"That's the point. But I would be hidden nearby to protect you."

"But I would be in danger!" The strength drained out of his arms. If he had been standing up, his knees might have wobbled. "I am no warrior!"

"That's why you're perfect. You're a defenseless weakling. A perfect target."

"Defenseless weakling indeed! I have little strength in physical stature, but. . . ." He tapped his forehead sharply. ". . . I am intelligent enough to avoid danger!"

Ken'ishi stayed calm in the face of Norikage's outburst. He even had a faint smirk on his lips! "You have a good head. So you should be able to see the value of my plan."

"Perhaps it is a good plan. But pick someone else to use as bait! There has to be someone else."

"Who would you suggest? Kiosé?" Ken'ishi's voice was even, dispassionate.

"Of course not!"

Ken'ishi relaxed a bit. "Then who in the village would help us?"

Norikage shifted uncomfortably. "If it's an evil spirit in the pond, could we commission a priest to purify the pond, to drive it out?"

"Is it not proper for the village administrator to be present when this threat is dealt with? It would look better on you if you were there, not cowering at home."

"Are you certain your sword can kill whatever it is? What if it is a spirit?"

"It's not a spirit. It left tracks in the mud and parted the reeds by its passing. I have slain an oni with this weapon. If it can be killed, I can kill it."

"Somehow, that does not help me feel better about this. Could I not hide with you, lay in ambush?"

Ken'ishi shook his head. "You can't sit still for long enough. Sometimes you fidget like a child. You would betray our presence. Have some courage! That's all you need! I will protect you."

Norikage began to rub his chin. "Let me think about it."

"There's no time to think about it! I have already wasted half the day sleeping. By the time we reach the pond, the day will be gone. And I must approach the pond in hiding, which takes more time. It must not know of my presence."

Norikage sighed. The young man's words had weight and sense. He had thought his plan through. "Very well. 'Have courage,' you say. Very well. I will have courage. But if you allow me to be killed, I will forever haunt you!" He said the last with a smile on his face, but it was only a mask to hide his fear. He still quailed from the thought of putting himself in harm's way. He only hoped that Ken'ishi's strength and prowess were enough when whatever was in the pond came for him.

By nightfall, their ambush was ready. Nestled in a large bush overlooking the bank of the pond, hidden from view by leaves and shadows, Ken'ishi held his bow with an arrow nocked. From his vantage point about thirty paces away, he watched Norikage sitting beside the small fire, near the spot where Ken'ishi camped the night before. Akao was not to be left out. He waited beside Ken'ishi, silent and unmoving as the statue of a guardian fox. His bright eyes scanned the darkness and his sensitive nose tasted the air.

Norikage looked toward the pond every few heartbeats, and Ken'ishi saw the tightness of controlled fear on his face, in his shoulders. As Ken'ishi predicted, Norikage could not sit still. He fidgeted with his hands, his clothes, his mustache, and Ken'ishi watched him with amusement. He hummed a tuneless melody, dug small trenches in the soft earth with a dry stick, looked nervously toward the dark water. Ken'ishi was pleased, however, that Norikage did not betray his position by looking toward his hiding place.

For hours, Ken'ishi watched him fret and fuss about the campfire, and he also watched the reeds at the water's edge. His ears were cocked for any sound of movement in the water. From time to time, the wet plop of a fish or a frog would spin Norikage about, his eyes wide, almost glowing as they searched the darkness. Ken'ishi sighed and shook his head. This was not going to work. Norikage was too worried about attack to make himself a good piece of bait. But then, finally, after a few long hours, he seemed to calm himself, and lay down beside the fire.

Akao rested his head on his paws, his pointed ears still twitching and turning at every sound.

The shadowy wall of rushes flickered with orange firelight and pitch-black shadows. The play of shadow and light tricked his eyes, always appearing to be moving, shifting.

Norikage rolled onto his side, with his back to the water, snoring softly.

But Ken'ishi's eyes were not playing tricks when a strange face parted the reeds. Two reptilian yellow eyes glowed in the firelight. He had never seen anything like this creature. Its face resembled a strange mix of both a monkey and a tortoise, smaller than a human's, with a broad, flat head. No, not a flat head, an indented head, like a bowl in its pate, with a bit of water pooled in the indentation. A crown of glistening black hair ringed the indentation. It had a wide mouth in a snout like a monkey's, two narrow slits for nostrils, and thick, muscular lips parted to reveal a mouthful of thin, needle-like teeth. Was it grinning?

It dashed into view, moving on two short legs with a quick, scuttling walk. Its body was rounded like that of a tortoise walking upright, covered in a mottled, green shell, but despite all the features of a tortoise, the creature still left the impression of a monkey as well, with its incredible quickness and its cautious, furtive movements.

Scuttling up the bank, it snatched Norikage's foot with a scaly, monkey-like paw. Norikage awoke with a startled yelp. Before Ken'ishi could even draw his bow, the creature had dragged the constable halfway to the water. Norikage squealed. Ken'ishi drew his bow and released just as the creature disappeared into the reeds with its prey. The arrow flew into the foliage and disappeared, but Ken'ishi heard it strike home, with a sound like hitting a tree. Then Norikage was jerked out of sight into the reeds, shrieking in terror. Dark, murky water splashed and sprayed. Norikage's cry silenced with a gurgle.

Ken'ishi lunged from his hiding place, leaving his weapons behind. A sword and bow would be useless in the water. He tore through the reeds into pitch-blackness. The vegetation shielded the water from the light of the fire, and the moon had not yet risen. He followed the thrashing noises and dived in, churning toward the sound. He dived under the surface, groping in the murky blackness. Suddenly a warm hand clamped onto his forearm. He grasped the wrist and hauled toward the surface, kicking feverishly. A powerful tug jerked both of them back toward the bottom. He pulled hard, feeling Norikage struggling as well, but the other man's movements were weakening. Then suddenly the pull on Norikage disappeared, and Ken'ishi dragged him up. They both gasped and choked as they broke the surface, sucking in the sweet night air.

A painful, steel-hard claw gripped Ken'ishi's foot and dragged him under, toward the bottom of the pond where it could drown him and feed upon him at its leisure. He groped for the paw holding his foot, his hand clamping around the creature's small, rock-hard arm, squeezing its thick, scaly flesh. He wrenched its grip from his foot, but the other paw clenched around his wrist. For an eternity, the two combatants blindly struggled in the blackness, tearing away grips and finding new holds, grasping, striking. Ken'ishi's chest began to burn. More than once, the feathered wooden shaft of his arrow embedded in the creature's shell brushed against him. His strength was fading, but his enemy's seemed inexhaustible. He pummeled his fist uselessly against the creature's iron-hard skull, his fingers gouging for a soft place to cause pain. Then his clawing fingers dug into the indentation on the creature's pate, gripping, squeezing. Through his fingers, he felt the creature stiffen and convulse, and suddenly he was free. For an instant, he considered pressing his advantage, but his breath was gone. After a last clenching squeeze to the ridge of the creature's indentation, he kicked back toward the surface. It seemed he would never reach blessed air again before his lungs burst. But then he exploded upon the surface, gasping for breath, thrashing for the shore. He glimpsed Norikage's silhouette standing in the shallows, dripping, wringing his hands, his wide eyes gleaming in the near darkness. Norikage's hand on his wrist dragged him toward the shore. Akao dashed back and forth behind him, barking and snarling and whining.

In moments, they were back on solid land, streaming water. Ken'ishi bent over, hands on his knees gasping for breath.

Akao jumped upon him, barking and laughing, tail thrashing like a miller's flail. "Alive!"

Ken'ishi choked out a quick reply, "Yes, I'm alive."

The dog spun once in a circle, tail wagging with such frenzy that the dog's hindquarters shook.

Norikage said, "Are you injured?"

Ken'ishi shook his head.

"It is good that you're a strong swimmer!"

Ken'ishi nodded. "I've always been a good swimmer. Do you know what that was?"

"I think it was a kappa!" Norikage said.

"Yes, a kappa! My teacher sometimes spoke of them. He said they were—"

"Excuse me, sirs," said a strange, sibilant voice.

Ken'ishi, Akao, and Norikage whirled toward the voice and stared at the creature standing just outside the reeds about ten paces away. Akao snarled and bared his teeth, but a whine tinged his voice.

It stood with its small, clawed hands clasped humbly before

it, standing as high as Norikage's chest. Ken'ishi's arrow still protruded from its back. "You have defeated me." Its voice was high-pitched, like a child's, with a disquieting hiss. "I apologize for my attack. If you would be so kind as to remove your arrow from my back, I swear I will leave this place and never trouble you again. My arms are too short, you see. . . ."

Norikage and Ken'ishi looked at each other, then at the creature. Its mottled, reptilian eyes were impossible to read.

Finally, Ken'ishi managed to speak. "Are you a kappa?" He stood and faced the creature.

"I am a kappa."

"Very well, I will pull out the arrow." He bowed low, politely.

The kappa bowed as well, spilling the water from the indentation on top of its head. When it straightened, its eyes widened, its shoulders slumped, and the corners of its mouth turned pitifully downward. "Drat," it said. It seemed deflated somehow.

Ken'ishi circled warily behind it, braced his foot against the smooth shell, grasped the arrow with both hands, and pulled. The kappa hissed in pain as the arrow came out, the tip smeared with dark red blood.

Ken'ishi backed away. "Now, keep your promise. You swore an oath to leave this place and never trouble us again. Go."

The kappa nodded forlornly, sighed, then trudged off into the darkness of the forest. They watched it until it was out of sight, lost in the shadows of the trees and undergrowth.

When it was gone, Norikage said, "What happened? I missed something."

"It was planning to attack me when I attempted to pull the arrow out. A kappa's bite is venomous."

"But it swore—"

"When I was a child, my teacher told me that kappa are polite but treacherous creatures. Its offer was a ruse meant to draw me near enough that it could bite me."

"So then why did it not bite you?"

"Because when a kappa loses the water from the indentation in its head, it loses its power. Only then was it truly defeated."

"You tricked it!"

Ken'ishi said nothing, walking toward his former hiding place to retrieve his weapons.

"Ken'ishi, I underestimated you, I think."

Ken'ishi shrugged. "Now I think the village is truly safe."

Akao's tail wagged again. He had not taken his eyes from the spot where the kappa disappeared. The dog padded toward the spot, sniffed the ground once, then looked into the forest and gave one last triumphant bark, as if to say, "And don't come back!"

Gazing at falling
Petals, a baby almost
Looks like a Buddha

—*Kubutsu*

Ken'ishi sat on a fallen log with his back against a tree, listening to the cold wind rustling the blood-red maple leaves and whispering through the forest, hearing the cries of anguish and grunts of exertion coming from the small hut a few paces away.

There had been no more disappearances in the months since he had driven the kappa away. The villagers' respect for him was renewed, if grudgingly. Strange effigies of straw and old linen that looked like strange octopi, or oni, or samurai, designed to frighten away kappa, had been hung around all the houses. The effigies must have been effective; after all, there had been no more kappa attacks since then.

This hut was old and ill kept. No one lived there. It had only one purpose, a place for women of the village to bear their children. Women gave birth in it to prevent the blood of the birth from polluting their homes. Most of the families contributed to its upkeep, but since they were poor, the hut was little more than a drafty, thatched shed on the village outskirts.

The voice of Tetta's wife, Naoko—how she had changed since Tetta's disappearance, asserting control over both Gonta and the inn with an iron will—encouraged and coaxed and praised Kiosé for her efforts, Kiosé who now gasped and strained in the throes of childbirth. Many of the village women resented allowing Kiosé to use the birthing hut because she was a whore, not even a true human being. But Ken'ishi and Norikage, and now Naoko, had been unanimous in silencing them.

They made a strange foursome, Ken'ishi thought. Akao and Norikage and Kiosé and himself. All of them were outcasts in their own ways, and at the same time, all of them had been accepted here in their own ways. Even the hatred fomented by Chiba and his brothers had subsided, sinking back into the trials and tasks of daily life. Perhaps they simply could not bring themselves to abuse a woman who was with child.

As Ken'ishi waited outside the hut, thoughts came and went, like dogs passing in the street. He noted them and let them go. It was good not to worry about things for once.

What was Kazuko doing now? Was she happy? Perhaps she too had a child by now. Did she ever think about him? What was her husband's name? He still could not remember.

Who was the spy in the guise of a monk who had come searching for him? Who was the spy's employer? Why was he searching for Ken'ishi?

What secrets was Norikage hiding? The man had a deeper, more dangerous past than he had let on. They had become friends, but Ken'ishi still did not trust him fully.

Whose child was coming into the world, inside the little hut? Was it Ken'ishi's child? Did it matter whose child it was? Kiosé would never be his wife, nor would the child ever be truly his, but he had made himself their protector. That was all that mattered. The child was being born into an existence of suffering and poverty, with little hope of escape from that fate, but perhaps Ken'ishi could ease that suffering as best he could.

How strange the scrolls of one's life, he thought. His time with Kazuko, while just a year ago, felt like a different life, as if it was someone else's existence, a different book. What other scrolls waited for him to live in the future, other lives to live before he died? The time of a warrior was usually short, so he doubted that he would live to be an old man. Who would want to be old and gray and weak, like the old beggar in the capital with no hands, slain by a callous, drunken bully? Not he, never. Better to die in his prime, strong and free. But he had things to do before then. He would make a name for himself. He would make his father, and his ancestors, proud.

Silver Crane was warm and comforting at his side, almost a companion like Akao. But even though it was as familiar to him as his own hands, he sensed that it still kept its secrets, as if waiting for the proper time to reveal them. At times, when that feeling was most acute, he wondered whether the sword belonged to him or the other way around. He had tried meditating with the sword, trying to probe the powers that it contained, but to no avail. The spirit of the blade toyed with him, shed his grasp like rain from feathers. He sometimes thought he sensed the spirit of his unknown father, speaking to him through the sword from beyond the veil of death. Or perhaps that was just his wishful imagination. Powers and secrets. Secrets and wishes. All in good time.

A new voice, a course, piercing wail, abruptly joined the women's voices in the hut. Ken'ishi smiled and rested his head against the rough bark of the tree. A new life in the world. The wail subsided. Naoko came out of the hut and stood in the doorway, framed in lamplight. The afternoon had grown dark. She waved him closer. He stood up and approached her.

Years and weariness lined her face, but her eyes sparkled with relief and happiness. "Ken'ishi-sama, it is a boy." Behind her, Ken'ishi could see bloodstained rags, and Kiosé's pale, bare feet. Sobs of relief and joy bubbled from within.

Ken'ishi smiled and bowed to Naoko. She went back inside and closed the door, and he sat on a stone near the door. He looked up at the stars appearing in the evening sky, took a deep breath, and sighed, enjoying the pleasant night.

He walked back to his house, and for the first time in more than a year, retrieved his flute. Then he walked back to the birthing hut, sat on an old tree stump nearby, and began to play. The melody seemed to take shape in the air itself, and the tune was . . . contented. The baby's voice cut like a knife through the thin walls of the hut, over Naoko and Kiosé's quiet cooing at her new child, and Kiosé's laughter of joy and exhaustion. Hearing her laugh was so rare that Ken'ishi wondered for a moment if he had ever heard it before. She sounded so happy, and that pleased him. Her happiness found its way into the tune emerging from his flute. Gone were the mournful, lonely notes he had played for Kazuko.

The sky slipped deeper into darkness. Stars emerged from their daytime slumber, and his gaze rose to meet them. His awareness of his surroundings dimmed as he floated on the music.

Then a harsh unfamiliar voice said, "You there! I'm looking

for someone."

Ken'ishi stopped playing, lowered his instrument, and regarded the man standing perhaps twenty paces away. He was tall and lithe, and wore a basket hat that concealed his face. He looked like a ronin, with his soiled, ragged clothing, two swords and something else that looked like a dagger thrust into his belt. With his music now fading on the night air, he suddenly heard the roaring, thrumming sound in his ears that was the voices of the kami speaking to him. He put down his flute and placed his hand upon his sword.

The man had approached without Ken'ishi noticing.

Ken'ishi said, "I'm the constable of this village. Tell me who you're looking for."

The man began to laugh, starting with a slow chuckle that rose in strength and volume until it reached the edge of madness. The voice was hoarse, dry, and there was no mirth in it.

Ken'ishi stood up and squared his body with the man. "Who are you?"

"I am. . . . Who I am is not important. I'm looking for a ronin. That is what's important."

Ken'ishi tensed for a moment, then let his body relax. His spirit sought the Void. This conversation was almost finished. "There are ronin everywhere."

"The ronin I'm seeking, he . . . he must face my vengeance." The man's voice was queerly halting, as if he was struggling for words. "I have followed his . . . trail to this village. I have . . . been searching for a long time."

"I think you have come to the wrong place."

"No! I know he is near! I can . . . I know he is near."

"Can you describe him?"

"He . . . he . . . he has a sword. A special sword." The man's breath became more ragged, and he seemed to be having difficulty speaking. "And he . . . he had a dog."

"Who are you?" Ken'ishi asked again.

"It's not important! Only when the ronin is dead will my vengeance be satisfied!"

"What harm has he caused you?"

"We . . . we fought. He . . . hurt me."

Ken'ishi searched his memory. Why didn't he remember his man? "Why did you fight him?"

"He . . . he killed . . . someone. Someone important."

At that moment, Ken'ishi realized the man's identity. The young deputy from Uchida village. The dagger-like weapon in his sash, the jitte. Takenaga's swords. But he had severed that boy's right hand. This man *had* a right hand.

"Tell me who you are!" Ken'ishi shouted.

"My name is Vengeance!"

At that moment, Ken'ishi's spirit settled into the Void. Words were a distraction now. And this man's identity was no longer important. Evil radiated from him like waves of heat, and Ken'ishi felt it on his face.

"You have found the ronin you seek." He drew his sword.

The man chuckled again. He reached up and removed the basket hat, tossing it aside, revealing his face.

Ken'ishi could not see clearly in the dark, but his face appeared to be streaked with dark, vertical blotches, stretching from his chin up over his forehead and across his hairless pate. The whites of his eyes seemed to glow within those dark streaks, and his gaze fixed on Ken'ishi with unwavering hatred.

The man said, "You do not know me, do you."

Ken'ishi did not reply. He raised his sword to the middle stance, holding Silver Crane before him with the point of the blade aimed at the level of his enemy's throat.

The man continued, "I am not surprised. I look different now." His voice took on a deep, rumbling timbre. "Are you so eager to fight me again that we cannot talk first?" The man laughed so harshly that the hair stood up on Ken'ishi's arms. "Why do you not speak?"

"There's nothing to say. You've come here to kill me. Why waste time with useless talk?"

"Oh, you're wrong. I didn't come here to kill you. I came here to cut you. I came here to carve off bits and pieces of you and feed them to passing dogs. I came here to maim you, and to burn you. No, not kill. You will die, yes, but I will not kill you. You will live until your soul longs for release from the agony, until your body can cling to life no longer. And when you're dead, I will splinter your bones with a hammer and scatter them to the winds."

A cold chill gripped the back of Ken'ishi's neck, and it jarred him from his readiness. The point of his sword wavered a finger's breadth.

Instantly the man leaped.

In mid-leap, the man's sword jumped into one hand, and his jitte into the other. The sword glinted like an icicle in the starlight as it whistled toward Ken'ishi's head, slicing the air with a sound only the razor-sharp edge of a sword could make.

Ken'ishi brought Silver Crane up to deflect the blow, and stepped to the side, but the sheer force of the blow knocked him off his feet and nearly tore Silver Crane from his fingers. He sprawled on the ground, and rolled to his feet just in time to avoid the slash that whished through the space his body had occupied in the dirt.

Ken'ishi no longer believed this was a man. No man could leap such a distance. And he had seen such a leap once before. At closer range now, he saw the man's face. "I do know you."

The man snarled, his teeth showing white in the night, and hatred pulsed from him like waves of heat from a sword smith's bellows. "And I know you," Taro said and leaped forward again, slashing one-handed with the katana. Ken'ishi blocked the blow, and the jitte came up the moment after their swords met, sliding onto Silver Crane's blade and twisting, wrenching. He was losing it!

In sudden desperation, he fell back and dragged his sword with him, just barely jerking it free. This . . . creature had almost taken his weapon from him! He had never imagined such a thing was possible. That jitte would be his death if he were not wary of it.

The baby wailed, and Ken'ishi saw a sliver of light spilling from the interior of the birthing hut as Naoko peeked out the door.

Taro's smile stretched into a lustful grin, stretching beyond the normal proportions of a human face. "Yes, watch, old woman. Watch him die!" He launched himself forward again in a flurry of blows that drove Ken'ishi back five steps, toward the edge of the forest. Taro's raw ferocity shattered Ken'ishi's rhythm and jarred his spirit out of the Void. He was fighting for his life, but the sound of the baby's wail reminded him that he was fighting for more than himself. He had to protect Kiosé and the baby! But to attack, he had to find his rhythm.

Taro's assault was relentless, driving forward with fearful blows and lethal slashes.

Ken'ishi needed a few moments to gather himself, but Taro pressed his awful advantage. Ken'ishi could smell Taro's infernal breath, like a putrid belch of blood and pain. He noticed the unnatural look of Taro's right hand. Somehow, it had been healed, but it was not . . . right.

With blinding speed, Taro lunged forward. The jitte swept Ken'ishi's sword to the side, and the katana slashed toward his chest. He dodged back to avoid the blow, but Taro was too fast. He felt the merest tug at his flesh, and his breastbone felt as if a hand had punched him. Strangely, there was no pain, but the strength seemed to drain from his limbs, and he fell. Hot wetness spread across his chest as he landed in the dirt. He did not need to look; he knew the cut was bad. Silver Crane was no longer in his grasp. Where was it? He couldn't breathe.

Taro stood over him, silently, primal glee in his eyes.

Pure exultation surged through every fiber of Taro's being. He had won! The sight of his long-hated nemesis, bleeding and helpless, filled him with such joy and lust as he had never imagined. A shiver of exquisite ecstasy rippled through him.

He sheathed his katana and drew his short sword, then reversed his grip and drove the point of the blade through the ronin's thigh and deep into the earth, pinning the leg to the ground. The ronin's body convulsed in pain, and he bit back a scream.

"Wait here," Taro chuckled. "I'll be back."

He turned and walked toward the small hut. The door slid closed, and a bar slid into place. He smelled something interesting inside.

"Grandmother, open the door. I'm coming in," he said, his gravelly voice as good-natured as he could make it. Someone was weeping inside, and he heard the muffled crying of the baby, and desperate whispers. He drew back his fist and punched through the wooden door. The old, thin slats exploded into splinters, and he stepped inside. A young woman clutched her newborn infant to her chest and scrambled back against the rear wall of the hut, but there was nowhere for her to go. The smell of blood in the air was thick in here, and he breathed it deep.

The old woman was sitting on her knees and turned to face him. She bowed low, pressing her forehead to the floor. Her voice was calm. "Please don't hurt them. They have done you no harm. This child has done you no harm."

Taro stepped closer to the young woman. Her shoulder

pressed against the wall, and she shielded the baby from him with her body. He knelt beside her. Her flesh was pale and glistening with sweat, and her lips quivered with delicious terror.

Taro said, "Let me see it."

"No!" she gasped.

He reached out and wrenched her body around, enough to glimpse the small pink head wrapped in a blanket. Fresh sobs of terror spilled out of her. He leaned closer and drew a deep breath. The smell confirmed it. Another surge of mirthless glee washed through him, intoxicating. A son! The ronin had a son! Another victim to glut his lust for blood and vengeance! He laughed quietly.

"Leave us alone!" the young woman screamed.

She could not go far, and in any case, he could find her now that he knew the baby's scent. He would deal with the ronin first. He stood up and gazed down at them for a moment, savoring his victory.

Then movement behind him, a low growling, and he glanced a low dark shape lunge from the doorway. Sharp teeth tore into his right heel, ripping, shredding. He grunted in surprise and pain, and slashed down with his jitte. The weapon had no cutting edge, but it was still a steel rod. The force of the blow tore the dog's teeth from the back of his leg and swept the animal away. It yelped sharply, and its claws scrabbled against the reed mats as it lunged toward the door, out of reach. It leaped outside, then turned to face him again, snarling, white teeth bared in the starlight. A challenge.

He turned and tried to follow, but his right leg nearly collapsed under him. Blood poured from the ravaged gash in his ankle, slicking the floor, and his foot would not work properly. A sudden storm of rage swallowed the joy and elation he had felt moments ago. Growling, he limped after the dog.

As the creature strode away toward the birthing hut, Ken'ishi grasped the hilt of the short sword with both hands and pulled, but the grinding agony of steel against bone was too much, and his vision went black. It returned but slowly, and he heard a dog snarling nearby.

He propped himself up on his elbows. Agony tore through his chest, and his clothes were soaked with blood. Not far away, Akao faced the creature that was once Taro. It walked with a bad limp now, but his eyes blazed with fury and hunger unabated.

Ken'ishi grasped the hilt of the short sword again, but this time, he did not try to draw it from his leg. The short sword had been driven through his leg almost to the hilt, pinning him to the earth. Gritting his teeth against the agony, he pulled with his hands and his leg, and the short sword inched free of the ground, until it popped loose. Ken'ishi rolled onto his side, with two hand-spans of blood-and-earth-smeared steel protruding from the back of his thigh. He cast his gaze around for Silver Crane, but it was lost in the darkness.

Then he felt its presence, like a clear, silvery voice in the gloom, the whisper of promised salvation. A few paces away, hidden in the foliage. He dragged himself across the dirt toward it, feeling his strength ebb with every movement, his blood seeping away. He spared a glance behind him. Akao snarling, barking, feinting, retreating as the creature lunged after him. The dog moved with a limp, favoring his front leg, but he was still quick, and dodged nimbly away from the creature's powerful kicks and slashes.

Akao's snarls sounded like nothing else to other human ears, but to Ken'ishi they were the vilest, most colorful insults and taunts he had ever heard.

Ken'ishi reached the edge of the forest foliage and cast about for his weapon, rustling the leaves and branches. The sound turned the creature's head toward Ken'ishi, and it took a step toward him.

Then the creature grunted in pain, looked back, and saw Akao's jaws clamped onto the wrist holding the jitte. Taro jerked away, lifting the dog's feet from the ground, but Akao did not relent. He snarled and savaged at the wrist with his teeth, refusing to release his grip. The jitte fell to the ground. Taro roared and spun his body, flinging his arm. The force and speed of the movement wrenched Akao's teeth free, and he went spinning through the air. His body crashed through the wall of the birthing hut in a shower of dust and splinters.

Ken'ishi lunged for the spot where he knew Silver Crane waited. His fingers closed around the familiar ray-skin hilt, and a pulse of warmth shot up his arm and spread through his body. The pain in his leg and chest diminished. Propping himself against a tree, he levered himself upright with his good leg.

Another pulse of warmth shot up his right arm, and his vision cleared. Another pulse, coming in rhythm with the thunder of his heart. He reached down with his left hand, gripped the hilt of the short sword piercing his leg, and pulled with all his might. The grinding pain in his leg sapped his strength, but the sword came free, fresh blood pumping from the wound. The wet blade fell to the earth, and he took Silver Crane in both hands. Another pulse of warmth, a pulse of strength, a pulse of courage. He stood taller, his legs firmer. There was still strength in him.

He was already dead; that was the samurai belief. With no fear of death, anything could be accomplished. He did not fear death, but this thing would not harm Kiosé and the baby. If he had to die to destroy this creature, to protect them, to avenge his friend, he would die.

Ken'ishi limped forward. The creature clutched his savaged left wrist, a stream of gore running under his arm and dripping from his elbow.

With each pulse like the thunder of a taiko drum, Ken'ishi's strength returned. His wounded leg could almost support his weight, even though pain shot through him with every step. He knew he must find the emptiness, the Void. There was no before, and no after, only the Now. Only the moment of the strike, the perfect strike. He attacked.

The creature drew his katana and blocked the blow in a single lightning motion. But the mirthless triumph was gone from Taro's twisted, dark-streaked face, replaced by frustration and rage.

Ken'ishi struck again, and again, and again.

Silver Crane's voice sang in his mind, as clear and pure as a temple bell, and the whispering song lent strength to his blows.

His spirit settled into the Void, and he found the timeless space between instants, and in that instant, he struck again.

The tip of Silver Crane's blade slashed down through the creature's face, from forehead to chin, slicing a deep gash between his eyes and splitting his nose and jaw.

The creature grunted and staggered back.

Ken'ishi struck again, and his blow cleft the creature from right shoulder to collarbone. The creature roared in pain, and blood sprayed on its horrid breath.

Ken'ishi struck again, cleaving the creature from left shoulder to breastbone. The creature dropped his sword and staggered back, arms wide.

Ken'ishi sliced across the creature's belly, and entrails spilled out with a gush of gore. His opponent's roar diminished to a groan, and he fell onto his back. Ken'ishi circled the body, raised his blade, and severed the head with a single stroke. The body spasmed, then lay still.

The baby was crying, and a surge of relief went through him.

Ken'ishi sheathed his weapon and ran toward the hut as quickly as his wounded leg would allow. Reaching the doorway, in the light of the lamp he saw Akao's motionless form lying amidst debris from the shattered wall. The women sat near him, picking away the splintered wood.

Limping to his friend, Ken'ishi knelt beside him. Akao's head hung limply to the side, blood trickling from his nose, tongue lolling, eyes staring. Empty. Tears burst from Ken'ishi eyes. Kiosé's face was already wet. Gathering the dog in his arms, he lifted him up. His body was limp and broken and lifeless. He carried his friend outside, eyes burning, cheeks hot with tears, and placed him on the ground and stroked his soft ear one last time.

Norikage came running up carrying a lantern, his eyes wide. "What happened? The whole village is buzzing from the noise of the fight. What—?" His gaze flicked to the headless corpse a few paces away. "Who is this?"

Ken'ishi looked up at him, and Norikage's eyes fell to Akao's lifeless form. His voice fell. "Ah, my friend, that's a terrible pity. What happened?"

"He saved us all." Ken'ishi could hardly speak.

Norikage nodded. "You're wounded."

Ken'ishi's wounds had stopped bleeding, but he could see the paleness of breastbone exposed in the gash across his chest, and his thigh burned like fire. Looking out into the darkness, he saw numerous shapes lumbering toward them from the village, bearing lanterns and improvised weapons like clubs and tools.

Then his strength left him like water from a shattered bucket, and his vision faded into blackness.

When he awoke, he was in a room filled with light and warmth. He was covered with blankets. His body ached as if a hundred clubs had beaten him, and he was soaked with sweat. He felt bandages wrapped around his chest and leg. He looked up at the ceiling of his own house. Kiosé's knees slid into his vision, and he felt a cool rag placed on his forehead.

"You're back!" she said, and happiness filled her voice. "The fever is gone!"

"How long?" he croaked.

"Three days."

His vision swam and his mouth felt like it was full of sand. "Water."

She brought a small cup of water to his lips, and he drank from it.

"Is the baby . . . ?"

"He is fine," she said, giggling, "and energetic!"

He heard the baby mewling and saw a small basket resting in the warm sunlight.

"Akao. Where is he?"

"Norikage gave him a hero's burial." She leaned over him, and her eyes glistened with tears. "He was so brave!"

Ken'ishi's eyes burned. "Where is the other man's body?"

"His body was burned and his head was mounted on an old spear near the road, as a warning to bandits." Kiosé's work-roughened hand touched his cheek tenderly. "Norikage says now that your fever has broken, you will begin to mend."

"Where . . . is my sword?"

"Over there," she said pointing. But he already knew where it was. He could feel it. His gaze followed her gesture, and he saw it leaning in the corner, with its mother-of-pearl cranes flying through a black-lacquered sky toward a silver moon on the battered old scabbard. It seemed the cranes were flying away, into the night, toward some shared secret, a secret they would reveal to him, in time. The silver on the hilt gleamed in the sunlight streaming through the open windows.

Indeed, it looked freshly polished.

On this plain of mist
Nothing but flat endlessness . . .
And red-rising sun

—Shiro

At the urging of her sister-in-law, Lady Yukino, Kazuko hosted a
dinner party during the Harvest Festival for all the nobles, high-
ranking samurai, and officials of the region. She had even invited
her father and was delighted when he arrived. She was surprised
with herself that she was so pleased to see him, considering how
he had handled her betrothal. During the visit, her father and
her husband shared much time together, as if further trying to

cement their alliance. Lord Nishimuta no Jiro was valuable to her husband because Lord Tsunetomo needed the support of smaller fiefs nearby to maintain his superior position. Lord Otomo no Tsunetomo was valuable to her father because Lord Jiro needed the protection of a powerful neighbor. And even she, in her ignorance of the ways of ever-shifting politics, knew that she formed the hub of that alliance. Her husband had been pleased when she asked his permission to host the party, and he had been just as pleased with the results. Sake, plum wine, and shochu flowed like a river, and in spite of the drunken revelry, the guests behaved themselves without fail. Fresh rice cakes and vegetables and sweets, delicacies from the sea, summer buckwheat noodles, all kept the guests pleasantly stuffed for the duration of their stay.

Even the sullen, sometimes spiteful Hatsumi appeared to enjoy herself. She smiled and giggled, and Kazuko could almost believe she was her old self again. Hatsumi traded coy, meaningful glances with Yasutoki, glances pregnant with the knowledge of shared secrets. Kazuko allowed Hatsumi to think that her affair with Yasutoki was still a secret within the palace walls, even though nothing could be further from the truth. Hatsumi seemed to need the illusion that her liaisons with Yasutoki were hidden, secret trysts. But then, part of the allure of such affairs, Kazuko knew, was their secret nature.

The party formed the beginning of Kazuko's realization that perhaps the bleeding rift in her belly had begun to heal. She had found solace in applying herself to naginata training. She discovered that it helped lift her spirits more than ever. The weight of the weapon and her growing strength with it gave her comfort. Her husband retained one of the most renowned naginata masters on Kyushu especially to teach her. Taking advantage of the man's services to train his troops, of course, was an afterthought. Her husband was nothing if not pragmatic.

Lord Tsunetomo even commissioned for her a special suit of armor. He had surprised her with it a few days after the party. It was uncommon, but not unheard of, for samurai lords to present their wives with armor. In the old days of warfare and strife, women had often been called to fight. She had been truly pleased, and her reaction had pleased her husband as well. It was as beautiful as it was functional, made in the haramaki style, with small, black lacquered steel plates, bound together by silk cords of deep red, with lovely yellow and orange accents. The yellow faded into orange and then deep red and made the armor look as if it were aflame. It was light and flexible, smaller and less bulky than o-yoroi, great armor. It was made to fit only her, and designed to be used with the naginata. When she tried it on, it was comfortable and well fitted, and it gave her a feeling of strength and deep satisfaction. For a moment she remembered the thrill she had felt after she and . . . Ken'ishi had defeated the oni. She felt invincible.

Master Higuchi beamed at her, exposing his gap-toothed gums as she entered the practice yard wearing her armor for the first time. "Good morning, my lady," he said as she bowed to him. "You look like a fierce, exquisite flame this morning."

"You flatter me, sensei," she said. But her heart swelled with pride, and her limbs vibrated with excitement.

Together they turned toward the yard's guardian shrine, knelt, and bowed their respect to the guardian kami of the practice yard and the castle. After they finished the necessary rituals, she began her practice routine.

Master Higuchi watched her with a sharp eye. "You see now why I have you practice in your armor. It changes your balance and weighs you down."

"Yes, sensei, it is more difficult than I expected," she said, her breath huffing as he lunged and stepped and twirled and struck. The naginata grew heavy sooner, and her steps were not as quick or as sure.

"But fear not, before long, the armor will become like a second skin. You will not mind the chafing. When you get used to wearing armor, you begin to feel naked without it. Nothing can hurt you when you wear it. Maybe you will want to wear your armor all the time!" Then he laughed.

"Yes, sensei," she said. In a strange moment, she wished she could put armor around her heart, so that nothing could hurt her there ever again. No more pain of remembering the look of a ronin's face and the feel of his hands on her. No more bouts of stabbing sorrow.

"Harder!" Master Higuchi scolded. "Your movements are already growing weak!"

Perhaps, with practice, she could indeed armor her heart. With that silent resolve in her mind, the strength returned to her naginata blows and the precision to her movements.

"Looked for, they cannot be seen; listened for, they cannot be heard; felt for, they cannot be touched."

—*Old Ninja Legend*

Yasutoki welcomed the earlier departure of the sun on these autumn days. He was more comfortable in the dark, in the shadows. Only after the sun had set would Kage appear. Yasutoki received Kage's message one evening at the local sake house. The message had been written in the bottom of a sake cup in ink that dissolved once the sake was poured.

"One last time. Payment due," the message said.

The man known as Kage was nothing if not ingenious.

So Yasutoki waited in the same sake house, one day and one hour later, as was their predetermined arrangement. Even though it was autumn, the air was warm and thick and heavy, with no breeze. He fanned himself aggressively, keeping his eyes open. The windows of the sake house were flung open wide, but no breeze came through them, only mosquitoes, drawn by the smell of blood. So many succulent, drunken targets, Yasutoki mused. Such easy marks. The smell of burning incense made to drive away the mosquitoes was pungent in the air. Yasutoki waved his fan at a tiny, shrill buzzing in one ear.

Despite his outward demeanor, his guts were a swirling tumult of suppressed excitement, for two reasons. One was that all of the spies he sent in search of the ronin with Silver Crane reported no success, and all of them reported on schedule, except one. That one had not reported at all. He did not employ men who missed appointed times. Something had happened to that man. Perhaps the man's disappearance was significant, perhaps it was only a quirk of fortune, but it warranted further investigation. It was a clue he could follow.

The second reason for his excitement was that this meeting with Kage should be the last. After this, Yasutoki would be able to send his information to the Great Khan. The Great Khan would be pleased. Yasutoki remembered the one and only time he had been in the presence of the Khubilai Khan. That one time had been enough for the young man called Yasutoki to recognize a true power in the world. Khubilai Khan, grandson of the Great Khan Genghis, who had conquered nearly the entire world, would be the man who could exact vengeance on those who had slaughtered Yasutoki's ancestors. Some men were drawn to power, and some men liked to accumulate power for themselves. Yasutoki was both. The empire of the Golden Horde reached to the far corners of the known world, and it was only a matter of time before his own country fell under the Golden Horde's dominion. Only the difficulty of crossing the sea had kept them at bay this long. The Mongols knew nothing about sailing the high seas. They had to rely on the recalcitrant Koryu people for that. But now, the Great Khan had set his sights on the palace of the Emperor in Kyoto, and nothing would stop him now.

Yasutoki had been little more than a boy when his father took him on a journey across the sea. Even then, his family had been scheming against the Shogunate, looking for allies abroad to help bring down the hated Minamoto and Hojo families. He and his father had traveled in the guise of simple merchants. With a wry smile, Yasutoki realized that was indeed what they had been. They were selling their homeland to the Great Khan. And the price was vengeance.

Yasutoki had seen much of these tribal barbarians during that journey. He had seen their uncouth, almost demonic customs, heard their barbarous songs, eaten their almost unbearable food, and smelled their overpowering stench. They reeked of horseshit and the dust of the steppes. But more importantly, he had seen their vast numbers, and the matchless power and speed of their armies. Samurai were tough, potent warriors, formidable swordsmen, and skilled archers, but they could not hope to stand against huge units of Mongol horsebowmen that moved with the speed and precision of a flock of birds, in perfect unison.

Samurai fought battles largely as individuals, seeking opponents of renown to face in single combat, to heap honor and glory onto their own names. The Mongols fought with their entire army acting as a single entity. This unity had driven all enemies before them like chaff in a great wind, and the same would happen to the Shogun's samurai.

Yasutoki noticed the serving woman and turned his attention to her. She was the wife of the owner of the Plum Blossom Sake House, and just as much in Yasutoki's direct, secret employ as her husband.

She stopped beside his table, bowed deeply, and said, "Yasutoki-sama, there is a message for you."

"What is it? Who sent it?"

"A man named Akihiro reserved a private room, my lord."

"Excellent. I will go immediately."

"He is not there, my lord. He said that you had something for him and that you should give it to me."

Yasutoki frowned. He suddenly felt the weight of the pouch in his sleeve. The pouch contained the last of Kage's payment.

"I am sorry if this displeases you, my lord." Her voice began to quaver.

"Where is he?"

"I do not know, my lord. But he left something in the room for you."

Yasutoki nodded. "Very well, but you will accompany me. Only after I see what he left will I give you what is his."

"As you say, my lord. I am sorry." She bowed several times. "Very sorry."

She showed him to the private room at the rear of the establishment. Inside, the satchel rested in the center of the table. He kept his movements calm and measured in spite of his desire to rush across the room and seize it. He opened the satchel and revealed another nest of precious scrolls. He opened one of them and skimmed the detailed report of the fighting strength of the Shimazu clan, a powerful samurai family in the south of Kyushu. A sigh of relief escaped him, a sigh so profound it surprised him.

He reached into his sleeve and withdrew the pouch full of coins and precious stones. He opened the pouch, extracted a small handful of coins, then retied the pouch.

He handed the coins to the innkeeper's wife. As her hand closed around them, he seized her wrist and squeezed so hard she gasped with pain. Then with his other hand, he snatched a handful of her hair and jerked her head back. She choked in surprise, her eyes bulging with fear.

His voice was cold and deadly, and he glared into her eyes. "This is to remind that you work for *me!* No one else! Do you understand?"

"Yes, my lord," she stammered. "I understand! I am sorry for your trouble!"

"Good." He released her hand, then gave her the pouch. "You can give this to the man called Akihiro."

"Yes, my lord!" He released her hair, and she bowed again several times, her eyes brimming with tears. "Thank you, my lord, thank you!"

"You may go."

"Thank you, my lord." She departed quickly, fear lending quickness to her step.

Yasutoki turned back to the table, with the satchel. He had a great deal of interesting reading to do. And quickly. His carefully laid plan was finally coming together.

So ends the Second Scroll

PERMISSIONS

ABOUT THE AUTHOR

Travis Heermann has been writing for as long as he can remember. The lonely plains of rural Nebraska were perfect for filling his head with hobbits, vampires, Cimmerians, Tharks, and Jedi, forever twisting him into his current, occasionally warped persona. In addition to being an engineer, an English teacher, and a writer, he has tested the waters as a museum attendant, a bookseller, a referee, a farmer, a construction worker, a comic-shop clerk, a pilot, a game designer, and a private English tutor.

He lived in Fukuoka, Japan, where this story takes place, for three years, during which time he wrote the bulk of this novel and absorbed as best he could the rich history and folklore of this ancient island nation. These days he writes full time and tries to find time to practice martial arts.